PRAISE FOR

THE HOUSE IS ON FIRE

"The Richmond Theater fire of 1811 was, at the time, the deadliest disaster in US history, killing seventy-two. This historical novel examines the event and its aftermath through four figures . . . The bad behavior of the powerful becomes a theme."
—THE NEW YORKER

"A propulsive, pulse-pounding read—one that grabbed hold of me and didn't let me go until the very last page. It is the kind of book you finish with a sigh, and hope against hope there is a sequel coming."
—KATHLEEN GRISSOM,
New York Times **bestselling author of**
The Kitchen House **and** *Glory Over Everything*

"Powerful . . . Beanland enlivens the smart and suspenseful narrative with fully developed protagonists that illuminate the community's response to mass catastrophe. Readers will relish this."
—PUBLISHERS WEEKLY
(starred review)

"*The House Is on Fire* captures the disastrous night hour by hour, reminiscent of watching a true-crime drama on TV. . . . Fast-moving, character-driven, and action-packed, *The House Is on Fire* is simply a thrill to read."
—BOOKPAGE

"Powerful . . . Beanland enlivens the smart and suspenseful narrative with fully developed protagonists that illuminate the community's response to mass catastrophe. Readers will relish this." —*Publishers Weekly* (starred review)

"Fans of historical fiction will find themselves enraptured by Beanland's take on the true story of the Richmond Theater fire in 1811. *The House Is on Fire* is an all-consuming exploration of redemption and perseverance in the face of tragedy." —E News

"Rachel Beanland, once again, has proven herself to be a remarkable storyteller." —De'Shawn Charles Winslow, author of *In West Mills*

"Propulsive . . . Full of historical detail and full-blooded characters." —*Shelf Awareness*

"*The House Is on Fire* captures the disastrous night hour by hour, reminiscent of watching a true-crime drama on TV. . . . Fast-moving, character-driven, and action-packed, *The House Is on Fire* is simply a thrill to read." —*BookPage*

"A spellbinding story of early America in all its complexity and contradiction." —Kevin Powers, author of National Book Award finalist *The Yellow Birds*

"A riveting story that places the reader at the very heart of a devastating, true-life tragedy. Beanland has clearly done her research, and the effect is both heart-wrenching and eye-opening." —Fiona Davis, *New York Times* bestselling author of *The Magnolia Palace*

"I could not turn the pages fast enough! The novel holds up a timeless mirror to the racial disparity revealed by unexpected loss—and the means through which we must all come together to rebuild. Brava!" —Afia Atakora, author of *Conjure Women*

"As the writer of a nonfiction book about the Richmond Theater fire, I recognized the faces and places Beanland brings to life and marveled at her impressive research and attention to historical detail. . . . At turns heartbreaking and hopeful." —Meredith Henne Baker, author of *The Richmond Theater Fire: Early America's First Great Disaster*

THE HOUSE IS ON FIRE

❧ | ❧

RACHEL BEANLAND

SIMON & SCHUSTER PAPERBACKS
New York   London   Toronto   Sydney   New Delhi

An Imprint of Simon & Schuster, LLC
1230 Avenue of the Americas
New York, NY 10020

First Simon & Schuster trade paperback edition April 2024

SIMON & SCHUSTER and colophon are registered trademarks of Simon & Schuster, LLC

Simon & Schuster: Celebrating 100 Years of Publishing in 2024

For information about special discounts for bulk purchases, please contact Simon & Schuster Special Sales at 1-866-506-1949 or business@simonandschuster.com.

The Simon & Schuster Speakers Bureau can bring authors to your live event. For more information or to book an event, contact the Simon & Schuster Speakers Bureau at 1-866-248-3049 or visit our website at www.simonspeakers.com.

Interior design by Lewelin Polanco

Manufactured in the United States of America

1 3 5 7 9 10 8 6 4 2

Library of Congress Cataloging-in-Publication Data is available.

ISBN 978-1-9821-8614-2
ISBN 978-1-9821-8615-9 (pbk)
ISBN 978-1-9821-8616-6 (ebook)

For Kevin

All the world's a stage,
And all the men and women
Merely players
They have their exits
And their entrances
And one man in his time
Plays many parts.

—William Shakespeare,
As You Like It (1599)

This novel is inspired by the true story of the 1811 Richmond Theater fire. While it is a fictional account of events, the four characters you will meet in these pages are based on the lives of real people who were affected by the disaster. To honor their stories, I have relied on the historical record whenever possible, using my imagination to fill in the holes and to pick up where the record leaves off.

It should be noted that in early nineteenth-century America, many spellings had not yet become standardized. When referring to geographic landmarks, such as Rockett's Landing and the Potomac River, I have chosen to use modern-day spellings for the sake of consistency.

THURSDAY

❦ I ❦

DECEMBER 26, 1811

❦ | SALLY | ❦

Sally Campbell's shoes are fashionable but extremely flimsy. She ordered them from Curtis Fairchild's specifically for Richmond's winter season, but now she feels like a fool for thinking she could get away with wearing them on the half-mile walk from her brother-in-law's house to the theater.

The shoes, which are made of silk and lined with linen, are as pretty as they come, but they are no match for the terrain. It's been so cold that the earth is frozen solid, which means that every bulge and divot beneath Sally's feet feels like a knife blade through the shoes' thin leather soles. "It's possible I would have been no worse off barefoot," she says to her sister-in-law Margaret when they reach the corner of H and Seventh Streets.

A fierce wind whips at the women's faces, and they lean into each other, drawing the collars of their coats tight around their necks while they wait for Archie to catch up. "We need you, dear," Margaret calls to her husband as he lumbers toward them.

Archie, amiable as ever, seems pleased to be needed.

"Be a gentleman and walk in front of us," says Margaret. Then she winks at Sally and says in a voice loud enough for Archie to hear, "We'll let him block the wind."

Archie gives them an exaggerated bow and touches the brim of his hat, but when he rounds the corner, he has to hold on to it with both hands. The wind comes from the east and spills down Richmond's main thoroughfare, taking the last of the leaves on the trees with it. Margaret and Sally fall into formation behind Archie, tucking their chins to their chests.

As they pass the capitol, Sally can hear the church bells from a few blocks away chime seven o'clock. The capitol is an imposing Palladian structure, and its plaster of Paris facade shines under a canopy of stars. In the pastures that surround the building, Sally tries to make out the shapes of grazing cows. She can hear their irate grunts, carried in the wind, and knows that, in weather such as this, they are huddled close together, too.

"Just another block or two," says Margaret, who married into the Campbell family just a few years after Sally did and has, over the past half dozen or so years, become not just a sister to Sally but a dear friend.

Margaret is such a dear friend, that she has not uttered a single complaint about venturing out in this weather. Sally knows she'd have preferred to remain at home, in front of a warm fire, but since Sally gave her hosts the tickets to tonight's performance as a gift, Margaret is doing an admirable job pretending there is nowhere else she'd rather be.

The truth, of course, is that the tickets were as much a gift to Sally as anyone else. She loves the theater—the extravagant props, the audacious costumes, the monologues that move her to tears. Back when Robert used to bring her to Richmond, they'd gone to the theater every chance they got, but in the three years since his death, she's had little reason to come to the capital at all, much less to see a play.

The theater sits at the intersection of H and Fourteenth Streets, catty-corner to the capitol and on the crest of Shockoe Hill. It is an impressive building, with a commanding view of the wharf. Beyond the wharf is the James River, which curls around Church Hill, winding its way past Rockett's Landing and all the way to Jamestown.

The old theater, which was barely more than an oversized barn, burned to the ground the year before Robert and Sally were married, and for several years the Charleston-based Placide & Green and other touring acting troupes had to perform in the old market building, local taverns, or not at all. Sally and Robert saw *André* at The Swan and *The Taming of the Shrew* at City Tavern, and while it was nearly impossible to hear the actors' lines over the din of the crowd, Sally thought the taverns-turned-theaters weren't all bad. She liked the buzzy feeling she got when she drank down a pint of cider too fast and began reciting Shakespeare in Robert's ear; on the nights she took his earlobe between her teeth and he called her his wee drunkard in his thick Scottish accent, they rarely made it through three acts.

The new theater has some nice upgrades: a real stage—with wings large enough to store even the most extravagant props and set pieces, an oversized pit, and a proper ticket booth. There is a separate gallery for slaves and free Blacks and plenty of box seats on the second and third floors for those who can afford them. The building is sided with brick, but it's clear the theater's managers cut corners on the finishings. They planked the lobby but left the rest of the dirt floors exposed; the boxes are sparsely furnished with a smattering of uncomfortable chairs and benches; the windows are so drafty they have to be boarded up during the winter months; and some nights, in this new space, the pitch of the crowd gets so loud Sally would almost swear the acoustics were better at The Swan.

When Sally, Margaret, and Archie near the theater, they find a large crowd gathered outside the building's double doors, waiting to get to the ticket booth inside. The exterior of the building is plastered with playbills announcing the evening's performance:

Last week of Performance this Season. Mr. Placide's Benefit. Will certainly take place on Thursday next, When will be presented, an entire New PLAY, translated from the French of Didurot, by a Gentleman of this City, Called THE FATHER; or FAMILY FEUDS.

"Isn't Diderot spelled with an *e*?" Sally asks, but Margaret isn't paying attention.

"Pardon us, excuse me. We've already got tickets, we're just trying to get inside." Margaret removes the tickets from her reticule and waves them in the air, as if they alone can part the sea of people that stand between the Campbells and the building's warm interior.

Inside the lobby, a Negro man wearing a short-skirted waistcoat inspects their tickets and directs the three of them down a narrow passage to an even skinnier staircase, which is crowded with people, everyone making their way to their seats on the second and third floors. As they file up the stairs, Sally pays attention to the other women's footwear. Most of them have worn shoes every bit as silly as hers.

"So, who's this mysterious 'gentleman of the city' who's translating Diderot?" Sally asks Margaret when they reach the first landing.

"I assume it's Louis Hue Girardin. He runs the Hallerian Academy. On D Street."

Sally doesn't know much of anything about Richmond's private academies, having spent her formative years in the country. "Is that the funny building that's shaped like an octagon?"

"That's the one," says Margaret before looking over her shoulder for her husband. "Archie, what was the story with Girardin? In France?"

"He was a viscount. A real royalist." Archie is already winded, and Sally strains to hear him. "Was about to be guillotined, by the sound of things."

"So, he fled to America?" she asks.

"Twenty years ago now," says Margaret. "Very dramatic escape."

"No wonder he likes Diderot," says Sally.

When they reach the second floor, Margaret looks at their tickets, but Sally stops her and points up at the ceiling. "Our box is on the third floor." Sally glances backward at her brother-in-law, who is bent at the waist, trying to catch his breath. "Sorry, Archie," she says.

On the following flight of stairs, the crowd thins some, although the echo of people's footsteps, combined with the buzz of so many conversations happening at once, still makes it hard for Sally to hear what Margaret is saying. "Girardin used to teach at William and Mary, but he's been here for at least a decade. Married one of the Charlottesville Coles. Polly. She's the middle daughter, I think. Anyway, I doubt Williamsburg agreed with her. How could it?" Margaret lowers her voice and Sally leans in. "Eliza Carrington was telling me she thinks the school Girardin's running barely keeps a roof over their heads, which is too bad because, from all accounts, he is quite brilliant."

"I would guess so," says Sally. "Diderot isn't easy."

Sally's own education was devoid of Diderot or Rousseau or any of their contemporaries. Her father, for all his intellect, had not been a particularly learned man. He was an excellent orator and statesman, but his arguments didn't come from what he read in books so much as what he read on people's faces. He'd practiced law without much of a legal education, then served in the House of Burgesses before the Revolution. There had been two terms as governor and a stint in the Virginia House of Delegates, and while his political life had given him plenty of wisdom to impart to his children, he was much more likely to be found rolling around on the floor with them than teaching them anything useful.

Sally's brothers' education had been outsourced. Private tutors instructed the boys in Latin and Greek, history and geography, until they were ready to attend Hampden-Sydney College, where none of them had proved to be especially fine students. Sally and her sisters were instructed by their mother, Dorothea, who read little besides *The Art of Cookery*, but had managed that singular and spectacular feat of catching a husband equal to her in wealth and rank, which—in her opinion—made her eminently qualified to educate her daughters. Dorothea taught her girls to read and write, produce neat stitch-work, and paint periwinkles and pansies that didn't drip down the paper-thin edges of porcelain teacups. She hired a neighbor to give the girls lessons on the pianoforte and a dancing instructor who came all the way from Lynch-burg to teach all the children how to dance a proper minuet.

It was Robert who had plugged the holes in Sally's education. The first time he'd ridden out to Red Hill, to introduce himself to her father and to make a pitch for the new company store he was running in Marysville, he'd spent several minutes inspecting her father's small library. The bookshelves contained legal treatises and law dictionaries, but few novels and almost no poetry or plays. Sally had been reading on the settee in the parlor when he arrived, and she stayed put when her father went looking for his ledger.

"Have you read these?" Robert asked, running his hands along the eight leather-bound volumes of Samuel Richardson's *Clarissa*.

"All of them," said Sally, watching him from across the room. "Twice."

Robert looked up at her, amused. "*Pamela*, too?"

"Don't be confused," said Sally. "I much prefer novels that don't rele-gate women to housewifery. But they're few and far between. And given our geography, I'm not in a good position to be choosy."

Robert looked out the window, in the direction of the carefully manicured boxwoods, which bordered a path that led across the yard, past the slave cabins, and down to the tobacco fields. Beyond the fields, the Roanoke River wound its way across Virginia's Southside and all the way to the North Carolina coast. "I suppose it probably is quite difficult to get books out here," he said.

Sally studied him. She guessed he was ten years older than her, although at seventeen, she was a very bad judge. His hair was still dark, but his skin betrayed either age, hard use, or both.

When he abandoned the window and turned to face her, his eyes gleamed. "So, if not dutiful wives, what kind of heroines do you prefer?"

She revealed the book she had tucked into her skirt when he entered the room, and he moved a little closer, squinting at the stamped foil on the cover.

"*Charlotte Temple*?"

"Susanna Rowson's very clever, I think."

"I think so, too, but if you don't like dutiful housewives, you can do better than reading about poor Charlotte's downfall."

"You've read it?"

"Aye."

"Most of the men I know won't touch a novel, let alone one written by a woman."

"Why not?"

"They say they're a corrupting influence."

"Corrupting to whom?" said Robert, a hint of a smirk at the corner of his mouth.

Sally had been disappointed when her father returned and their conversation was cut short. But then, less than a fortnight later, Robert returned to Red Hill with a special-ordered horse saddle for her father and a copy of Rowson's play *Slaves in Algiers* for her.

"It's not a novel," said Robert, "but it's clear she's got something to say."

After that, there had been a steady stream of books. On each of Robert's visits, after he finished his business with Sally's father, he came to find her. And, for her part, Sally made herself easy to find.

Sally's father grew ill the winter she turned nineteen. As spring turned to summer and his condition worsened, the stream of visitors to Red Hill slowed to a trickle. Still, Robert continued to ride out to the property, eventually giving up even the pretense that he had business with her father.

On one visit, he brought Sally his brother Tom's poetry collection, *The Pleasures of Hope*, which had just been published in Edinburgh to some acclaim. She read the poems several times over and eventually realized that she had stopped paying attention to the language—which was lovely—and had instead started to mine the book for details about Robert's childhood in Glasgow.

There was one line that she hadn't been able to put out of her mind, and she asked Robert about it on his next visit, when he found her under a honey locust tree, near the herb garden. "There's this part about 'the brother of his childhood,' who 'seems restored a while in every pleasing dream.' Is he writing about someone in particular?"

Robert inspected his hands. "Aye. About our brother Jamie. He drowned in the Clyde when he was thirteen."

"I'm sorry."

"My brother Archie and I were already in Berbice. But Tom was six, and he was the one who found him. First his clothes, and then his body, a little further down the river."

Sally had also lost brothers, and on days when she was being honest with herself, she could acknowledge that her father's condition was worsening and that, soon, she would lose him, too. She felt a sudden urge to wrap her arms around Robert, to tell him that she knew something of the "hopeless tears" his brother described.

But all she said was "It's a beautiful poem."

It hadn't occurred to Sally, before she met Robert, that marriage might be anything other than a series of duties, performed over a procession of years, but when they married, she had been pleasantly surprised to find she'd been wrong. In Marysville, where Robert had rented a house for them, there was plenty of work to fill her days, but there were also long, dark nights when she curled against her husband's chest, listening to the soft thud of his heart as he read to her by the glow of a lamp. It wasn't a bad way to be introduced to the French philosophers, all things considered.

There is a logjam in the third-floor lobby, where everyone has stopped to examine their tickets and confirm their box numbers. "We're this way," says Margaret, plowing her way across the lobby and down one of the long, narrow hallways that wraps around the building. Sally follows close behind.

"Pardon me," she says as she turns sideways to let a wide-hipped woman, coming from the opposite direction, pass. Behind her, the hallway is empty.

"We've lost Archie," Sally calls to Margaret as she hurries to catch up.

Margaret waves a hand over her shoulder. "I'm sure he got stuck talking to someone. He'll find us."

Archie is a factor and shareholder with Buchanan, Hopkirk & Co., one of Glasgow's oldest and largest tobacco houses. The company has fourteen stores in Virginia, where planters can bring their gold leaf tobacco to sell, and in return, buy a fine assortment of imported goods against their ever-expanding lines of credit. Robert ran the store in Marysville, but his older brother's role is far larger. Not only does Archie oversee all the company's storekeepers, but its warehouses, too. With ships from Glasgow arriving all the time—either via the Potomac, the Rappahannock, or the James—it is advantageous for the company to maintain warehouses up and down the state's fall line, which means Archie regularly travels between Richmond and Petersburg, Fredericksburg and Falmouth. Sally knows Margaret grows weary of it, and that she is especially grateful for the winter months, when all of his clients come to him.

Richmond in the winter is a perennial party. The General Assembly meets from early December through late January, its one hundred and ninety-five delegates and twenty-four senators presenting and voting on a year's worth of legislation during the brief window of time when it is too cold to plant so much as a radish in the ground. Virginia's planters travel to the capital with their families, staying in taverns and boardinghouses—if they don't have property in town—or with family and friends who can host them. During the day, the men convene at the capitol and the women shop or call on friends who live too far afield to visit during the remaining ten months of the year. At night, there are card parties and balls and—of course—plays.

"Here we are," says Margaret. "Box six." She pulls aside a thick velvet curtain to reveal a box already crowded with more than a dozen people, all of whom look far less interested in the impending performance than in each other.

"Well, if it isn't Sally Henry," says a voice that comes from a dark corner of the box, where several men are congregated.

Sally can feel the muscles between her shoulder blades tighten. She took Robert's name a dozen years ago now, as a girl of nineteen, but plenty of men still refuse to think of her as anyone other than Patrick Henry's daughter.

She turns to find Tom Marshall smiling at her.

"Mr. Marshall," says Sally, offering him her hand and a shallow grin.

Tom is a congenial man, whom Sally knew best when they were children and their fathers regularly sat on the same side of the courtroom together. When the Henrys lived at Salisbury, the families saw each other with some regularity.

"Still as gorgeous as a Greek goddess."

"Don't lie to me." Sally is a becoming woman, although she believes that, at thirty-one years old, she's lost the privilege of being called gorgeous. Her hair, which has always been dark, still falls past her shoulders in loose waves, but now there is a single streak of gray that is hard to hide when she rolls the curls that frame her face. Her eyes are a dull gray—not blue like her sister Dolly's—and while Sally was proud of her pale complexion as a girl, Robert's finances were never so secure that she could afford to stay out of the sun. In the nine years she was married, her skin turned a golden brown.

"Margaret, you know Tom Marshall?" Sally asks, almost certain that she does.

"We met at the races. Was it last year or the year before?"

Tom takes Margaret's hand, then asks after Archie. Before Margaret can explain that he is on his way, Tom cuts her off. "Do you both know my cousin, Edward Colston?" Margaret does, Sally does not. "And then, this fine fellow is my good friend Alexander Scott."

Sally does not know that she would have described Mr. Scott, who wears an oversized cravat and leans on a sword cane, as a fine fellow. He is probably no older than Robert was when he died, but he carries himself like an old man. Whereas Robert was sturdy, with cheeks the color of cherries, Mr. Scott is pale and so thin he looks ready to blow over in a strong breeze. He wears a beard, which obscures his mouth completely, and his shoulders are so stooped she is tempted to treat him like one of Margaret's children and tell him to stand up straight. All that being said, he has nice eyes, which counts for something.

"Are you any relation to Richard Scott?" Margaret asks. "The delegate from Fairfax County?"

Mr. Scott shakes his head no. "I know him. I think he's here tonight, in fact. But I can't say I'm related to him."

"Mr. Scott is himself serving in the Assembly. He's in his first term," says Tom.

Margaret gives her new acquaintance an appraising look, as if she hadn't quite seen him before. "House or Senate?"

"House."

Mr. Scott seems unwilling or unable to supply further information on the subject, so Margaret asks, "For which county?"

"Fauquier."

This might have been the right time for Mr. Scott to offer the women some cursory details about his life, or to ask them something about theirs. Instead, he fumbles with the watch fob that hangs from his waistcoat and checks the time. Margaret is not one to be easily put off, so she makes a show of looking around the box. "And is your wife with you this evening?"

Sally presses the toe of her shoe on Margaret's foot. Her rule, when she accepted Margaret's invitation to come to Richmond for the season, was that there would be no matchmaking.

"I'm here alone," says Mr. Scott.

The answer is evasive, and Sally knows Margaret won't like it, so she tries to steer the conversation into safer waters. "Do you like Diderot?"

Mr. Scott blinks at Sally. "Not particularly." She waits for him to continue, to argue that Diderot was an atheist or even that his plots are flimsy. But he doesn't justify his position.

Margaret can't let him off the hook. "Is there perhaps another playwright you find more appealing?"

"I'm not much for plays," he says and looks relieved when Archie announces his arrival in the box with a booming "What have I missed?"

There are more pleasantries and the puffing up of chests, the display of plumage. Sally removes her coat and, noting that the men have taken all the straight-backed chairs, secures an empty bench that has been pushed up against the box's railing. She pulls it out and takes a seat, placing her jacket and a small handbag beside her.

Over the next few minutes, Sally watches the theater fill.

The pit, two stories below, is a sea of people who never stop moving. Tickets to the pit are cheap, and the seats are few and far apart, so most people abandon them altogether, choosing to spend the duration of the performance on their feet, mingling with their neighbors. At the front of the pit sits the orchestra, its members tuning their instruments to the hum of the crowd.

Sally can't get a good look at the colored gallery, not from where she sits, but she can see into the boxes on the opposite side of the theater. She's searching for people she knows. None of her brothers and sisters, with the exception of Fayette, spend much time in Richmond, but her cousins—particularly on her mother's side—do. Lots of the girls she grew up going to parties with in Lynchburg and Farmville have married well enough to spend Christmas in the capital.

Margaret joins Sally and whispers in her ear, "That Mr. Scott's quite the Don Quixote." Then she gives Sally's shoulder an affectionate bump, and Sally puts her head in her hands and lets out a low laugh that could easily be mistaken for a growl.

"What do I keep telling you?"

"I know, I know," says Margaret. "You're not ready."

"And when and if I am," Sally says, tossing a quick glance behind her, "please, God, not him."

Margaret lets out a loud sigh.

"But I do appreciate it," says Sally, trying to be serious.

"I just want to know that you're going to be all right. You can't live with your mother forever."

"Can't I?" Sally says, and both women allow themselves an earnest laugh.

It was universally acknowledged, among Sally's friends and family, that she had been right to let go of the Marysville house. She stayed on there for more than a year after Robert died, but without the store, she had no income; it soon became obvious that the rent would deplete what little she'd inherited.

Sally thought about returning to Red Hill, but by then her mother had remarried and gone to live at her new husband's home in Buckingham County. The Red Hill property, which Dorothea would have been entitled to keep until her death, had she not remarried, went instead to Sally's youngest brothers, who were ill-equipped to manage a henhouse, much less an entire estate.

When push came to shove, Sally had stored her furniture and household goods at Red Hill and sent her personal effects to her mother's. Then she'd packed a trunk and gone visiting. Her friends and relations were always happy to have her and she worked hard to be useful and to never overstay her welcome. Still, over the last two years, she'd grown weary of the constant travel and longed to settle down.

"My mother's got a piece of property, Seven Islands, that my father intended for one of us girls."

"Where is it?"

"Halifax County. Just across the river from Red Hill."

"Wouldn't you be lonely, out there all by yourself?"

Sally doesn't have a good answer to that question. Maybe Margaret doesn't realize that she always feels lonely, even when she is surrounded by people, even on a night like tonight. Especially on a night like tonight. "I'd have Lettie and Judith. And Andy."

"Sally Campbell," says Margaret, as if she is scolding one of her children. "Your slaves do not count."

Behind them, Tom Marshall says something that puts the rest of the men in stitches.

Sally lowers her voice. "What choice do I have, Margaret?" It took her stepfather the better part of a year to unravel Robert's finances and to convince a judge that, with no heirs, Sally deserved more than the dower's share of her husband's estate. He won her the household furniture, the livestock, Robert's meager savings, and the couple's slaves, which didn't feel like much of a victory considering Sally had been the one to bring them to the marriage in the first place.

Margaret presses her lips together and casts her eyes about the theater, as if she is looking for a good distraction. She points at the box directly across from theirs. "That's the governor and his wife."

"The man with the big stock buckle?" Sally doesn't recognize him, but then again, she hasn't been to Richmond since he took office. "He's handsome."

"Oh, I don't know—you don't think his forehead's a little high?"

Sally cocks an eyebrow in her sister-in-law's direction. "Getting quite particular in your old age?" Archie, who is in his early fifties, is short and stout with a receding hairline and three chins where there was once only one. Sally thought Archie attractive when they first met, more than a decade ago, but the last few years have not been kind to him. She can only assume that Margaret, who is twenty years younger than him and quite comely, has noticed.

A small boy sits between the governor and his wife. "They have just the one child?" she asks Margaret.

"God, no. Seven or eight, I think. But they're all his from his first marriage."

Sally and Robert had wanted children. Sally, in fact, had been desperate for them. But each month, her courses had come like clockwork.

Her older sisters promised that if she swallowed three spoonfuls of honey each night, right before bed, she'd be pregnant in no time. But a year passed, and nothing happened. Soon, Sally was poring over Buchan's *Domestic Medicine* and Culpeper's *Complete Herbal and English Physician* and writing away to apothecaries in Philadelphia and even London for the herbs and extracts they prescribed. Over the next several years, she consumed dozens of tonics and teas, before eventually submitting to her physician, who prescribed bloodletting and blistering. The day she came home with a mercury douche, Robert finally intervened. "Perhaps it is enough for us to love each other, just as we are."

He had been right, of course. Loving Robert was more than enough, and those last years before he died, when she abandoned all of the treatments and forced herself to embrace the life she had, as opposed to the life she wanted, were some of their happiest together.

Still, sometimes when Sally sees a family, like the one in front of her, she is filled with an anguish so intense it threatens to overwhelm her. She watches the governor ruffle the boy's hair, sees the governor's wife smile at the pair contentedly, and it is all she can do to remind herself that a child—even Robert's child—would not have made his loss any easier to bear.

❧❖ | CECILY | ❖❧

M aria Price scolds Cecily as they hurry toward the theater. "I told you I wanted to leave at half past seven. How hard is it to be in the foyer at the appointed time?"

Cecily is struck by the way she can hear Maria's mother's voice in the sixteen-year-old girl. Maria has always been a good mimic, even when she and Cecily were young, but in recent years, it has gotten harder to tell what is an act and what is real. The phrase "I told you," the short, decisive sentences, the way her voice dips when she asks a question she already knows the answer to—all of it makes Cecily cringe.

She touches her forehead, just below her headscarf, and feels for the knot she knows is forming underneath the skin. "I told you," Cecily says, sure to place every bit as much emphasis on those three little words, "that Master Elliott wanted me to iron a shirt."

"You should have said you were busy," Maria says, her mouth a stubborn line across her face. Maria may be naive about a great many things, but she knows there is no telling her eldest brother that he can't have what he wants.

Maria's father, Elliott Price Sr., owns a flour mill at the top of the falls, and Cecily's parents have worked it since before she was born—her father, Cecil, hauling sacks of grain and barrels of flour and her mother, Della, sifting the bran and the middlings. Most of the slaves the Prices own are sent to the mill as soon as they are old enough to operate the sack hoist or clean the bolting cloths, but Cecily was spared the backbreaking work on account of her light skin. Instead, she was sent to work in the main house, where she helped with the sewing, and eventually became Maria's lady's maid. Cecily took to the work fine, probably liked it better than she'd have liked mill work, but what she has never taken to is that feeling she gets, up at the house, that she is easy prey.

Maria's brother, Elliott, is five years older than Cecily and eight years older than Maria. When he was young, Della used to call him spoiled, which was true enough. The Prices gave him whatever he wanted because to do anything different was to risk ruining what might otherwise have been a perfectly fine day. As a child, Elliott cried easily, was quick to disrupt a game of marbles or scotch-hopper, and had the habit of running to his mother with all kinds of complaints, both real and imagined. But there was more to him than all that childish business. He didn't seem to register other people's feelings, couldn't see other people's sorrow or hurt. Once, when Cecily's younger brother, Moses, had fallen from the old white oak in the yard, Elliott had laughed to see the boy's arm swinging from his elbow like the rope swing at Shockoe Creek.

Elliott has always treated Cecily's body like an extension of his own. She was four or five years old, just a wisp of a thing in a cotton dress, when he first dragged her into the smokehouse. Among the ham hocks and pork shoulders, he prodded her with his fingers, said he wanted to know if her chum was brown, too. She was eight when he revealed the appendage that rose like a misshapen thumb from his britches, but another year passed before he figured out what to do with it.

Once, when Cecily was maybe seven or eight years old, she had tried to fight back. Elliott had dragged her into the smokehouse and she had given him a hard shove, then raced to the door, thinking she had a chance at making it out into the yard. But he was quicker than she was, and when he caught her, he pulled her back inside. Cecily grabbed hold of the doorjamb, crying for help, and Elliott must have panicked, because the next thing she knew, he'd slammed the door shut on her fingers. The pain was so bad that, for a few moments, it was as if the whole world went white. Cecily couldn't cry. Couldn't even breathe. When she finally opened her eyes, she discovered the tip of her middle finger was as crooked as a sickle. "Try that again," Elliott warned her, "and I'll break the other nine."

Those were the darkest years, when she hadn't learned to stop wishing for her mother to save her, or for Maria to report Elliott to their parents. Cecily didn't bleed for the first time until she was twelve, and on the day she asked her mother for some rags, Della looked at her funny, then brewed her a cup of cotton-root tea, laid down on the bed in the corner of their cabin, and wept.

With age, Elliott grew bolder, until he eventually took Cecily when and where he wanted her—in the smokehouse but also in the carriage house and even the main house. The household bustled, but Elliott had little fear of being walked in on. In some cases, Cecily wondered if the risk contributed to his pleasure.

Twice, her mother's cotton root failed her.

The first time, she was fourteen, and it was her mother, who still washed her rags, who noticed right away. Della made her drink a concoction of gunpowder and sweet milk that the healer, old Mrs. Cowley, who claimed to be a descendant of the Chickahominy Indians, promised would unfix her quick. Almost immediately, Cecily suffered a terrible cramping in her stomach. She was up half the night vomiting, but the following day, she passed a clot of blood as big as her thumbnail.

The second baby, whom she'd parted with this past September, was harder to coax from her belly. The cotton root, which she chewed in large wads now, had stopped her menses, so she didn't notice the little life growing inside her until her stomach grew taut as a newly stretched drum. This time the shot didn't dislodge the child from its hiding place, so it continued to grow until Cecily could get back over to Mrs. Cowley's. The old woman put her hands on Cecily's stomach, as if she were measuring a length of ribbon, and instructed Cecily to drink a mixture of black haw and redshank roots, then to chase it with the juice of dog fennel root, which she poured into a small glass jar. When this was done, Cecily was to swallow a teaspoon of turpentine each morning for nine days. "Do that and he'll let go," Mrs. Cowley promised.

The turpentine smelled like pine trees, and Cecily worried that the poison, which burned going down, was eating her from the inside out. But the old woman's prediction came to pass. On the sixth day, Cecily felt the familiar cramping in her stomach, except this time it was accompanied by a searing pain that radiated up her back. She suffered through the early hours of labor silently, and even tried to stay busy, letting out the hems of some of Maria's dresses. But by the early afternoon, Cecily couldn't thread a needle, much less make it do its work. All she wanted to do was push.

It was an unlucky day for any baby to be born. The newspaper had predicted a solar eclipse, which Maria had impatiently explained meant that—for a few brief moments—the moon would block out the sun. When the family went out into the yard to stare at the ever-darkening sky, Cecily vanished as quickly as the afternoon light. She found a quiet thicket of St. John's wort behind her parents' cabin, and right there—among the dead flower heads—she gave birth to Elliott's son. No bigger than a turnip, but with arms and legs and eyes. When Cecily peered at the creature lying in the dirt, her body shook with rage. The baby's skin looked so translucent she wasn't sure if his heart was on the inside of his body or the outside. Hers, for certain, had flown her chest entirely.

In early November, when Elliott's parents announced their son was engaged to marry Lavinia Price, a first cousin from Winchester, Cecily thought she'd finally been delivered. Elliott's father set about building the couple a house on a piece of property in Church Hill, and Cecily counted down the days until their wedding, which was set for the first of the year. While Cecily wasn't in the habit of feeling pity for white people, she felt something akin to it for Elliott's unsuspecting bride, who was no older than Maria and would soon learn that the whole of her husband's spicket could be made to fit down her throat.

The wedding was a week away, but this evening, when Elliott had cornered Cecily in the cellar, he had not come off as a particularly eager bridegroom.

"Do you know what I just got?" he hissed in her ear.

Cecily didn't say a word. Wouldn't give him the satisfaction. So, he grabbed her by the headscarf and banged her head against the wall. "I said, 'Do you know what I just got?'"

Her temple throbbed. "What?" she finally whispered.

He let out a short laugh. "You."

Cecily didn't understand, not entirely, not yet. But somewhere, in the center of her chest, a light dimmed.

"You're coming to the new house, with Lavinia and me. Daddy says you'll be a wedding gift."

She closed her eyes, but when she did, she still saw the unraveling of her days. She would not survive a year in Elliott Price's household, much less a lifetime.

Cecily's words came out flat. "You'll have a wife."

"Yes," said Elliott, his breath hot on her neck, "but will she grind my corn the way you do?"

Upstairs, Cecily could hear Maria calling for her.

"Your sister's waiting on me," she told Elliott.

"She can wait a little longer," he said as he reached for her.

The floor began to spin, but then someone opened the door to the cellar. "Cecily, are you down there?" came Maria's shrill voice.

Cecily knew not to say anything. Instead, Elliott answered for her, his voice as cool as the dirt floor beneath their feet. "She isn't here. Said she was meeting you in the yard."

Maria didn't respond. Not right away. One of the risers groaned, but then there was nothing. Cecily could picture Maria, at the top of the stairs, trying to decide what to do. Finally, she said, "Well, if you see her, tell her I'm waiting." The door to the cellar creaked on its hinges. "And that I don't want to have to search this house from top to bottom looking for her."

The door slammed, and they listened to Maria's footsteps on the floorboards overhead. Elliott loosened his hold on Cecily, and when she whispered, "I should go," he didn't argue, just pushed her away, like he'd come up with the idea himself.

A few minutes later, Cecily found Maria in the yard. She was stomping her feet to stay warm, and all Cecily could do was wrap her shawl tight around her shoulders and brace for the torrent she knew was coming. "I swear, Cecily, it's like you couldn't be on time for something if you tried."

Now, as they near the theater, Cecily sees Maria's friend Louisa waiting outside with a gaggle of girls Cecily recognizes but cannot name. All of them wear short brocaded jackets, the color of jewels, over their pale gowns, which make them look like a bunch of ruby-throated hummingbirds, what with all that color up around their necks. When the girls see Maria cross the street, they wave to her, and she turns to Cecily and hands her a ticket to the gallery. "Meet me out here after the pantomime. I want to stay for the second show."

Cecily turns the ticket over in her hand. She can't read the words that are printed on the small scrap of blue paper, but she knows that the ticket cost twenty-five cents, as much as a spool of cotton thread or a quart of burning oil. She'd a whole lot rather Maria had given her the money, and—if she didn't want to walk back and forth to the theater alone—allowed Cecily to come pick her up at the end of the night.

"Right *here*," says Maria, pointing to the ground beneath her feet, as if Cecily has not understood her instructions. She skips toward her friends, and Cecily watches as the circle of girls swallows her up. The group moves through the doors of the theater, but just before they disappear into the small lobby, Maria turns and calls to her. "Cecily," she says, her voice a cheerful bell in front of her friends, "it'll be the new year before you know it."

Cecily tries to smile, but her eyes remain dull. Maria knows everything, but Cecily doubts she knows about Elliott's plan to take Cecily with him to his new home.

A Negro man wearing a thin jacket and fingerless gloves stands just inside the gallery door, out of the wind, and waves Cecily inside. When she thrusts her ticket at him, he barely inspects it, just directs her up an enclosed staircase that leads to the second-floor gallery, which freedmen and slaves share with the city's drunks and prostitutes.

Cecily might have tried to look for someone she knows, but the gallery is packed and the show is about to start. She sees an empty seat, which she realizes—too late—is vacant because of its proximity to the most heavily made-up whore she's ever encountered.

"Were you holding this seat?" she asks meekly after she's already sat down. The woman smells heavily of vanilla and cloves, and Cecily begins to hope the answer is yes.

"Please," she says, gesturing for Cecily to remain where she is. "I'm Augustine Saunders."

It's unusual for a white woman to introduce herself like that, and Cecily doesn't know quite what to make of it. "Cecily Patterson," she says quickly, then reaches up, self-consciously, to touch the goose egg on her forehead.

She hates Elliott. That he is big enough to overpower her and persistent enough to refuse to let her go. That he can mark her, so that even when she is not with him, she still squirms beneath his weight. Cecily's mother has taught her not to expect much from the world, but the one thing she counted on was that Elliott Price would eventually leave his parents' house. Now she realizes how naive she's been to assume he wouldn't take her with him, wouldn't pull the same tricks he relied on as a small boy—crying and kicking and cajoling—until he gets his way.

"Do you know anything about *The Father*?" asks her seatmate, and Cecily looks up at her in surprise.

"Who's that?" she says.

"The play."

It didn't occur to Cecily to ask Maria what they were seeing.

An attendant extinguishes the wall sconces in the gallery, and as the theater's lights dim, Cecily can feel herself begin to disappear. She is in the theater and then she is back in the cellar, she is a little girl in the smokehouse and a tiny seed in her mother's womb. She is all of these things and she is nothing at all, and by the time the curtain lifts, her face is wet with tears.

❧ | GILBERT | ❧

By the time Gilbert Hunt leaves the prayer meeting at the Baptist meetinghouse, it is nine o'clock. In another hour, it will be too late to be out—even with a pass—but Gilbert is unwilling to go to bed without at least attempting to lay eyes on his wife.

Gilbert makes his way two blocks up H Street and past the theater, which shines like a jewel box against the night sky. The bull's-eye window at the front glows yellow, and when he is almost directly in front of the theater, the doors swing open and the light from the lobby briefly floods the street. Gilbert dreams of being able to take Sara to the theater, like the freed couples he sees strolling through Madison Ward on Saturday nights. But the two of them are a long way off from being able to spend good money on tickets, let alone get permission to go anywhere at the same time.

When Gilbert arrives at the Mayo-Preston place, he makes straight for the kitchen house, where Sara sleeps in the loft, alongside several other women. On summer evenings, when the door to the kitchen sits open from morning till night, Gilbert whistles to Sara when he gets close, a little signal to meet him in the garden. On winter nights, they sometimes slip off to the greenhouse, but in this wind, there's no chance Gilbert's whistle will get Sara's attention.

He raps on the door, then puts his ear to it and listens for the sound of footsteps. Finally, he hears the latch lift, and the door opens wide enough for him to slip inside without letting in a blast of cold air.

"You're late," Sara whispers in a tone that tells him she's not really mad, just disappointed.

He pulls her soft head of hair to his chest and comes close to cooing at her. "I was worried you'd be asleep."

She lifts her head up off his chest and tilts her face toward his. He is over six feet tall—a colossus was what he was called the last time he was sold—and Sara is barely five feet. He lowers his head and finds her lips waiting for him. They are soft and warm and searching.

The hard part about kissing Sara is figuring out how to stop. But after a minute, Sara puts her hand to his mouth. "Not a one of them is asleep up there."

"Well, everyone best get to bed," Gilbert says, raising his voice two notches so that Sylvie and Maddie and Lecretia can hear him where they lay.

"You hush, Gillie," says Sara.

From the loft comes the wheezing laugh of Miss Maddie. "No one up here wants to hear you thumping on that poor woman."

"No one?" Gilbert asks. He loves getting Maddie, who is old enough to be his mama, worked up into a knot.

Maddie ignores him. "Honey," she calls to Sara, "you feed him some of that leftover hash. It's in the Dutch oven."

"Yes, ma'am," says Sara as she takes Gilbert's hand and leads him toward the fireplace. Maddie has already covered the coals with ash, but Sara stokes them until they shine orange again. Then she sets the pot on top of them.

Sara looks good moving around the kitchen, and Gilbert tells her so. "One day, I'm gonna get you a kitchen of your own." She raises her eyebrows up into the middle of her forehead, like he is telling her a joke she's heard before.

"You got big plans," she says sort of quiet.

"They're *our* plans now."

Gilbert grew up on the banks of the Pamunkey River, in King William County. His mother was owned by the proprietor of a tavern in Piping Tree, and by the time Gilbert and his sister reached her waist, they were cleaning the meeting rooms and running meals between the kitchen and the taproom. All of them had assumed Gilbert would eventually grow up to mix flip and punch behind the bar and that his sister might follow in their mother's footsteps and clean the guest rooms, but those plans went nowhere. The summer his sister turned sixteen, she was sent to the capital to be sold, and when the proprietor's daughter married a carriage maker in Richmond a few years after that, fifteen-year-old Gilbert was made a part of her dowry.

In Richmond, Gilbert learned the carriage-making business. He was good with a hammer, and by the time he grew into his body, he'd attracted the attention of a local blacksmith named Peter Goode, who bought him for near double the going rate because he knew Gilbert would be a natural at the forge.

Good Pete, as Gilbert had taken to calling him, was a decent man, and after he had Gilbert all trained up, he left him well enough alone. Gilbert ran the shop, and provided he got Good Pete's customers taken care of in a timely manner, he was allowed to hire himself out on Sundays. Any extra money Gilbert earned, he kept in an old tobacco pouch, dreaming of the day he'd turn the pouch inside out and buy his own freedom.

Falling in love with Sara had complicated his plans because it meant Gilbert had to put away enough money to purchase the two of them, instead of just himself. They had done the math a hundred different times, but in the end they decided that the best course of action was to buy Sara's freedom first. That way, God willing, any children they had would be born free.

Gilbert had initially figured Elizabeth Mayo might let Sara go for two hundred dollars, less if she was feeling generous and recalled all the good turns Sara had done her over the years. But now that Elizabeth had taken a new husband, all her property—including Sara—technically belonged to General John Preston, and it was unclear what sort of negotiator he'd prove to be.

Whatever General Preston decided to charge for Sara was going to be a pittance compared to what Gilbert would need to buy his own way out of the smithy. At one point, he had calculated he'd need three hundred fifty dollars to purchase his freedom, but that was before Good Pete had up and died.

Good Pete wasn't much older than Gilbert, and he was strong as an ox, but in late July of this past year he'd come down with a fever, and by August he was in the ground. His wife had no sons, so after he died, she sold the business piecemeal. The building went to Francis Longbottom, the wagon and a pair of Cleveland bays went to John Ingalls, and everything else—including Gilbert—went to Cameron Kemp, who ran a smithy of his own on Locust Alley, down near the wharf.

Good Pete had never been a fan of Kemp's operation, and he taught Gilbert how to spot the Scotsman's work—the rough edges, the crooked lines, the seams that didn't hold—from a mile away. "It's utter shite," Good Pete used to say, "but I'm perfectly happy to make a living fixing his mistakes."

What Gilbert learned from Good Pete was that something magical happened at the anvil, and a blacksmith either knew what to do with it or he didn't. A hot iron rod was nothing but raw potential—it might become a trammel to hold a pot full of food over a fire, a sickle to help a farmer with the harvest, or a tire to get a cart to market—but Gilbert never tried to force it to be something it didn't want to be. Good Pete taught him to listen to the metal as he manipulated it and to loosen his grip on his hammer; it was clear from looking at Kemp's workmanship that those were two lessons the man had never learned.

Working for Kemp was hard, there was no doubt about that. The hours were long, the rations meager, and the conditions worse than anything Gilbert had ever experienced. But the sleeping arrangements were what just about did him in. All of the men—white indentured servants and enslaved Negroes—slept in the same loft above the smithy. The room had two rows of beds in it—no privacy for more than a dozen men.

At Good Pete's, Gilbert had had a small room off the back of the shop all to himself. He used to complain about the room to Sara. It was too hot in the summer and too cold in the winter, but now he realizes what a luxury it was, for that room was where he came to know her as his wife.

When Gilbert had described his new accommodations to Sara, back in September, after the sale had gone through, he'd watched her face fall. But she recovered fast, and then she took his head in her hands and said, "I'm still your wife, even if I can't share your bed." He knew it was true, but what was also true was that when Sara was in his bed, within arm's reach, he felt like a free man.

Now Gilbert sits at the pine table in the center of the kitchen house, watching his wife spoon the hash onto a plate. She sets it in front of him and hands him a fork, but he puts the fork down and takes her hand instead. "It ain't always gonna be like this," he whispers. He's surprised by the way the words catch in his throat on their way out.

❊ | JACK | ❊

Jack Gibson waits for his cue. As soon as the commodore delivers his last line and exits stage right, Jack is to run, quick as he can, and prepare the set for the play's final scene.

When the theater company's artistic director, Alexander Placide, pulled everyone together earlier this month to announce that the company would stage Louis Hue Girardin's translation of *The Father*, the actors had groaned. Shakespeare, Goldsmith, and even Sheridan were crowd-pleasers, but according to the troupe's old-timers, Diderot was nowhere near as popular. "The French can't hold a candle to the Brits," shouted one of the actors, William Anderson, as Mr. Placide prepared to distribute parts.

Placide is French and smart enough to know when he's being lampooned. "Mr. Anderson," he said in his thickly accented English, "if you have such an affinity for the British, you're more than welcome to return to that fair isle. Please give King George my regards." That got a good chuckle out of everyone, and most of the actors accepted their parts without further complaint.

"Placide is brilliant," Anderson explained to Jack later. "Diderot's plays are no good, nothing compared to his essays, but it's Girardin and not Diderot who will pack the house. People love supporting a local talent."

Anderson is right about everyone in Richmond loving Professor Girardin. Jack, for his part, adores him. Girardin runs the Hallerian Academy, which Jack attended until two years ago, when his father got sick. Jack's mother had died in childbirth, so after his father was gone, Jack went to live with his uncle Douglas, who wasn't the least bit interested in raising a child, much less paying his school fees. Thankfully, Girardin continued to loan Jack books and periodicals and to invite him for supper, and last winter, when things got bad at his uncle's place, Girardin had offered him a bed in a cottage at the rear of his property. "Just until you can find a more suitable position," he said as he showed him where to shovel the coal he'd need for his stove.

The arrangement lasted the better part of a year, until October, when one of Placide & Green's stagehands quit, and Girardin convinced the theater's manager, John Green, to interview Jack for the position. Jack had always dreamed of a career on the stage, and here was a chance to get his foot in the door with one of the best theater companies in the country. In the interview, he tried to convey his unbridled enthusiasm for the role, but his audience with Green was disturbingly brief: Green wanted to know if Jack could carry a quarter barrel and tie a bowline knot. Then he asked if Jack had a problem with heights, and when Jack said no, Green told him he was hired.

The job pays two dollars a week and comes with room and board at the Washington Tavern, which is where most of the unmarried actors stay when the company is in town for the season. But the best part of the whole arrangement—by far—is that Jack gets to read all the plays he wants. Three nights ago, while the company got oiled in the Washington Tavern's back room, Jack snuck a copy of *The Father* upstairs and read every word of it by the light of the moon. As soon as he was finished, he read his favorite scenes again.

At fourteen, Jack is hardly a literary critic, but he thinks this Mr. Diderot tells a nice story. The main character is a kindly father named Monsieur d'Orbesson, who spends much of the play trying to decide whether to grant his son permission to marry a girl of no means. The way Jack figures it, d'Orbesson loves his children dearly, and his only flaw, aside from trusting his no-good brother-in-law, is that he thinks he knows better than his children what will make them happy.

From his position in the wings, Jack is able to peek out at the audience. He's struck by how crowded the theater is. The gallery is practically bowing under the weight of so many bodies, and the boxes are packed. Even the pit seems particularly rowdy.

"My baubles are turning to icicles," says Thomas Caulfield, who is stuffing his hair under a rather ridiculous pompadour of a wig. "Can we not get so much as one stove back here?"

All the actors ever do is complain. To Mr. Placide, they complain about their parts and the price of their costumes. To Mr. Green, it's their pay. To Jack, they complain whenever he fails to put a prop or costume piece away, or if—in putting the item away—he makes it harder to find. To anyone who will listen, they complain that the managers have moved all the available stoves into the auditorium to keep the audience from freezing to death—at the expense of the actors backstage.

Jack tries never to complain. He has worked any number of odd jobs since he quit school, and this one is by far his favorite. He likes all the hub-bub backstage and the easy way the actors rib each other—like they are part of a big family—and he is convinced that if he works hard and shows he can learn, the company will take him back to Charleston at the end of the season.

"Kid," says Anderson, nodding his head in the direction of the stage, "you missed your cue."

Jack springs to attention and sprints onto the stage, repositions a hand-ful of chairs and removes a small table. When the set looks approximately as it did during rehearsals, he scuttles offstage again.

"Watch it," says Billy Twaits when Jack skids into him. Twaits, who is tall and broad enough to make an intimidating commodore, isn't someone Jack wants to upset. "Sorry, sir," he says quickly, ducking behind one of the stage flaps, where he hopes he won't draw any attention. He takes his offi-cial orders from the theater's managers, but it is hard not to do the actors' bidding, too. And if he is sent off on some errand right now, he'll miss seeing the grand reconciliation between d'Orbesson and his three children.

In the final scene, d'Orbesson banishes the commodore from his home, then gathers his children around him. "I will do everything that I can for the happiness of all of you," he says as he gives them his benediction. Jack is impressed with Mr. Green's performance—he really does come off sound-ing like a devoted father—and, for a moment, Jack misses his own father so much, it hurts.

The play ends, and a loud round of applause swells from the audience. The senior stagehand, Clive Allen, lowers the drop curtain, and while he and Jack and a few other members of the crew ready the stage for the pan-tomime, they can hear Tommy West's baritone, accompanied by a plucky fiddle, on the other side of the curtain.

The audience expects the company's musical interludes to be raunchy, but West has outdone himself this time. The song's lyrics are so crude that, at one point, Jack laughs out loud. Placide, standing nearby, shoots him a stern look, and Jack claps his hands over his mouth.

"Perry!" says Anderson when the carpenter walks past, carrying a faux stained-glass window. "Did you get a chance to look at the chandelier?"

"Briefly," says Perry, who isn't a machinist, but is the closest thing to it. "It looked all right to me."

"It's the pulley," Anderson says. "Goes up fine, but when I tried to bring it down, it just rode in a circle."

"What were you doing bringing it down?" says Clive, who never likes the actors trying to do his job for him.

"Excuse me for lending a hand," says Anderson, and stalks off.

Placide, who is playing the Baptist in the pantomime and has been fussing with the belt of his costume, overhears the discussion. "Is that pulley giving you issues again?" he says, and while Clive fills him in on the situation, Perry hurries off to install the window.

"Doesn't matter how gently I release the rope," says Clive, "it pops right off the wheel."

The chandelier's pulley hasn't given Jack any problems, and if he were a more established member of the company, he might say so. The backdrops actually give Jack the most grief. Each backdrop—and the theater company owns nearly three dozen of them—is fifteen feet high and nearly twice as long. They're made from bolts of hemp, which are stitched together and painted on at least one side, if not both. There is a bucolic village, a medieval city, a farmyard, and a seascape, not to mention a forest and a castle interior, which Jack remembers that he needs to cue up for the pantomime.

The bottom of each backdrop is secured to a heavy, round batten, and it falls to Jack and Clive to raise and lower the unwieldy buggers using another system of pulleys installed in the rafters. Provided Jack can get Clive to count off and ease the ropes at a steady pace, it is possible to use the pulleys effectively. But if anything goes wrong, or if Clive can't be dug up, Jack must scramble up into the carpenter's gallery to release the backdrop manually. Whenever he does this, the bottom of the backdrop hits the stage floor with a loud crash that shakes the stage boards and startles the crew.

From Jack's perch in the carpenter's gallery, among cut-out clouds and stars, a sun, and three moons, he can hear Mr. Placide's daughter, Lydia, take the stage for the sailor's hornpipe. Lydia is only a couple years older than Jack, but she is a good four inches taller than him, with a smile that never leaves her face and breasts that bounce up and down when she taps her feet to the fiddle music. She runs around with Green's daughter, Nancy, and Jack is too scared to talk to her most all of the time, but he loves to watch her dance. Even now, with Lydia on the other side of the curtain, he can feel the pounding of her hard shoes on the stage floor, and the vibrations make him heartsick. As the song reaches its crescendo, Lydia's feet begin to fly, and the audience's applause is thunderous.

"Oy, Jack," says Clive from the bottom of the ladder that leads to the carpenter's gallery, "help me out down here."

Once the pantomime is underway, Jack doesn't stop running. There are backdrops to be swapped out, set pieces to move, props to place. And, as usual, none of the actors can do anything for themselves. Caulfield thinks he's meant to be carrying a sword, but there was no mention of one during rehearsals; West has misplaced the shoe polish he'll use to blacken his face for his role as the old servant; and Mrs. Green, who will soon take the stage as the bleeding nun, can't find the bladder of pig's blood Jack specifically set aside for her. "Have you looked in the back?" he asks, but he doesn't wait for an answer. It will be quicker to find it himself.

The bladder is sitting in a pail near the stage door, and when Jack takes it to her, he watches—enthralled—as she cuts a tiny hole in the thin membrane with her teeth. It takes only the slightest pressure for the viscous liquid to stream onto her white frock, and the effect is so gruesome, Jack begins to feel a little light-headed.

"How do I look?" she asks when the job is done, and it's all Jack can do to nod his head and say, "Bloody marvelous." That gets a laugh out of her.

The next thing Jack knows, the curtain has lifted, the carriage breaks down in the forest, and Raymond—played by Hopkins Robertson—stumbles out. The banditti—led by Placide—are waiting to pounce, and Jack watches him use a stage whisper to quiet his men. He really is a marvel, Placide. Perhaps the most compelling villain Jack's ever encountered. Better than Claudius and Iago and Richard III combined.

"Jack," comes a voice behind him. He turns to find Green gesturing at the stage. "Were you born under a threepenny planet?"

"What?" says Jack, glancing wildly around the stage. He's not sure what he's done wrong, but Green isn't easily angered, so he must have done something.

"Why in the confounded hell is there a lit chandelier in the middle of the forest?"

Jack's eyes drift upward, and sure enough, there the chandelier is, glowing in the dark. They'd needed it in the first three scenes, but Jack was supposed to extinguish it before Raymond set off on his ride through the forest. "I'm so sorry," he says. "I forgot."

"You forgot?"

Jack nods.

"You are allowed to forget any number of things. But when six hundred people are staring at a chandelier in the middle of a forbidden forest, I expect to hear more than 'I forgot.'"

"It won't happen again?"

"Get it out of there."

"I can't put it out right now," says Jack, desperate to appease Green, but unsure how to do so without mucking up the whole scene. "I'd need to lower it onto the stage floor, and I can't very well do that while the scene's underway."

"Then raise it."

"What?"

Mrs. Green has come over to see if she can convince her husband to lower his voice, but it's hard to take her seriously when she's dressed in that ghoulish nun's getup.

"Raise the chandelier," says Green without so much as acknowledging his wife.

"But the candles are lit," says Jack. "It could catch the backdrops on fire."

Green looks up into the flyspace. "They're a good six feet away. Just let it sit up there, out of sight, until this scene is through. Then you can deal with it."

Jack hates arguing with Green, but he doesn't know what else to do, particularly when he remembers the broken pulley. "It may not be so easy to get back down. There's a broken pulley, and Anderson says—"

"Is Anderson running this company? Or am I?"

Jack looks at Mrs. Green, silently begging her to intervene.

"John, the scene's almost over. Don't you think, at this point, it'd be better to—"

He cuts her off, and pokes Jack in the chest. "I said, raise the chandelier."

Jack nods, once, and darts off in the direction of the rigging, where he frees the chandelier's rope from its anchor and watches as the prop glides straight up into the air. When the chandelier arrives in the flyspace, Jack anchors the rope back into place, then hurries to find Clive so he can explain the situation.

By the time Jack locates Clive, Robertson has been captured and brought to the castle, where he's introduced to Margaretta—played by Placide's wife, Caroline—and provided accommodations that he will soon regret accepting. Jack tells Clive about the chandelier, but he doesn't seem concerned. "We'll get to it," he says. "Soon as this act is over."

Jack watches from the wings as Mrs. Green prepares to make her entrance as the bleeding nun and close out the first act. She squares her shoulders and takes two deep breaths, and when she moves onto the boards, he could almost swear she is floating.

God, what Jack wouldn't give to have a thimbleful of her confidence. He's begun to dream of auditioning for a role in one of the company's many performances; if it were the right part and he were smart about it, he could still keep up with his duties backstage. But what always stops him from even asking about it is the fear that he won't be any good, that when he gets out onstage, in front of all those people, they'll be able to see right through him.

Mrs. Green arrives at center stage and faces the audience. Everyone in the theater lets out a collective gasp, and by the time the curtain closes a few minutes later, she has stolen the show. The sound of the audience's applause is deafening.

Jack is still shaking his head in a kind of bemused wonderment, when he looks across the stage and sees Roy in the wings, tugging at the same rope Jack only recently tied off.

"Oy," says Jack as he takes off running across the stage. "What are you doing?"

"Twaits told me to get it down," he says. "The candles are still lit."

"Stop!"

Roy doesn't stop, and Jack watches the chandelier begin to list.

"Didn't Perry tell you?" Jack shouts, but he doesn't have time to explain. The harder Roy tugs on the rope, the wider the chandelier swings.

Jack is terrified the flames will come too close to the backdrops and set them alight. "I'll climb up there. I bet I can reach it. Just stop what you're doing!" He makes for the ladder and is up in the carpenter's gallery when he sees that, in fact, Roy has not stopped pulling at the rope. Instead, he's been joined by Perry, who is putting his whole body into making the rope move.

Jack climbs out onto the nearest rafter, shimmying over the heads of the two carpenters. Splinters of wood slice into the meat of his hands. When he is as close to the chandelier as he can get, he takes a deep breath and tries to blow the candles out, but the chandelier is too far away for the flames to even flicker. So, he licks the pads of his thumb and forefinger and stretches his hand into the air, as far as it will go. The chandelier is just out of his reach, but the way the thing is spinning, it's like a pendulum; Jack just has to be patient and eventually it will arrive in his hand.

He wants to try to get Roy's and Perry's attention, wants to tell them that he has the situation under control, but the second act is underway. Perry begins to jostle the rope, a different kind of movement that Jack immediately realizes is no good. "Stop!" he yells down to him, not caring who hears him, but it is too late—the chandelier has tipped sideways and Jack watches in horror as it kisses the edge of the nearest backdrop.

What happens next is all sound and light. Jack inches backward, along the rafter and away from the flame, as fast as he can. By the time he has made it back to the carpenter's gallery, Perry is up there, waving at the backdrop and shouting instructions at Jack. "Help me cut this down!"

Perry has a knife, but Jack has none, and he watches as the carpenter saws at one rope and then another. The fire licks its way to the top of the backdrop and threatens to touch the ceiling, which is nothing but timber and sap.

"Do something, kid!" says Perry, a tangle of ropes in his hands, but Jack can't move, can't think of a single thing to do. He barely knows how to make himself useful when everything is going right.

Below him, onstage, Robertson looks up into the flyspace, his eyes widening into orbs. The man's bottom lip trembles, as if he is trying to make words but can't force them past his lips. Finally, he pulls his eyes away from Jack and Perry and the flames that rage behind them, turns to the audience, and flaps his arms. "The house," he yells, finding his voice at last. "The house is on fire!"

❊ | SALLY | ❊

At first, *no one knows what* to make of the actor's announcement. A fire in the house? From where she sits, Sally can see no evidence of a blaze. She turns to Margaret, whose face doesn't betray even the mildest concern. "Is he serious?" Sally asks.

"Certainly not," says Margaret before she turns around in her seat to get Archie's attention. He and Tom Marshall have recently gone to get a drink, and now they stand idly talking in the box's entryway, having never returned to their seats. Archie doesn't even look up when Margaret calls for him by name.

Sally isn't familiar with the pantomime. Perhaps there is indeed a fire in the second act, but something about the way the actor has stuttered his lines doesn't feel scripted. Below, the people in the pit have stopped talking, which never happens, and in the boxes across from them, Sally watches as a few people get to their feet and move into the corridors. The governor leans forward in his chair, studying the stage, and Sally notes that the boy who has been sitting between him and his wife is gone.

The actor who is playing the old servant tries to reassure the audience. "Don't be alarmed!" He looks offstage, into the wings, where even the audience can hear a commotion. "There's nothing to worry about!" Some of the people in the boxes return to their seats, and the pit grows loud with murmurs. The actor who plays Raymond stands rooted to the spot where he delivered his last line, and in the dim light of the theater, Sally can see a fine dusting of gold land on his hair and shoulders. He holds out a hand, as if he is catching falling snow, and seems confused by what he finds there.

"I think we should leave," says Sally, standing to go. Outside their box, on the other side of the curtain, she can hear footsteps and imagines the corridor is growing crowded. She touches Margaret's shoulder. "Something's wrong."

Sally picks up her jacket, but her reticule is missing. As she bends to look for it under her seat, she hears Tom Marshall soothe the other ladies in the box. There is a girl from Fredericksburg, wearing a magnificent garnet brooch, and two sisters whom he must know from Fairfax, and he tells all of them to remain where they are. "Let's let this confusion die down a bit first."

"Miss Campbell," says Mr. Scott, and Sally turns to find the disagreeable man holding her reticule in his hand. "It must have been kicked under my chair."

She takes the small bag and thanks him. In the box next to them, a woman screams. The man playing the old servant, who has so recently issued them reassurances, darts toward the rear of the stage and begins to tear down set pieces, for no apparent reason. "What's happening?" she asks Mr. Scott, although he clearly knows as little as she does.

Across the theater, the boxes opposite them have begun to empty. The governor and his wife are gone. Archie puts down his drink so he can use both hands to pull aside the curtain and direct their party into the corridor. But the narrow hallway is already packed with people, and there is nowhere to go.

In the pit, people have begun to move toward the exit in large numbers, but from above, it is easy to see the obstacle in their path. The double doors that lead to the lobby are shut tight, and as more people push and shove to get out of the pit, it becomes impossible for those closest to the doors to open them. Cries of "Move back!" come from the front of the crowd, but nobody is listening.

The actor who is playing Raymond leaps from the stage to the pit floor and yells up at the women in the second- and third-floor boxes. "Jump into my arms—I can lead you to the stage door!" For a brief second, he makes eye contact with Sally, and she tries to read his face. Is he really so panicked that he thinks jumping a distance of thirty or more feet is preferable to taking the stairs?

Margaret must be thinking the same thing. "Is he in his right mind? We'd kill ourselves jumping that far."

"Margaret, look," says Sally, pointing at the stage. The backdrop has begun to glow, as if lit from behind. She can see the silhouettes of two men and then a third run across the stage. Below, the actor continues to hold out his arms to the women in the box seats, but when no one makes a move to jump, he bats his hands at them and takes off in the opposite direction of the crowd.

Sally thinks she smells smoke, and her heart races. "We have to go," she says as she threads her arm through Margaret's and makes for the corridor. Mr. Scott stands between them and the exit, but when he realizes they are behind him, he moves aside and gestures for them to go first.

There is nothing to do but nudge their way into the crowd of people pushing down the dark corridor and toward the stairs. "Archie!" calls Margaret, reaching out a hand for her husband. "Come, now." He obliges, despite the fact that several women remain in the box.

"Pardon us, if you don't mind," says Sally to the people who shove past their box. No one makes eye contact with her, and none of the men will pause long enough to let her into the corridor. "So much for chivalry," she says aloud to anyone who will hear her.

Finally, a petite woman with a beaver muff stops long enough for Sally to drag Margaret and Archie into the fray. Sally goes to thank her, but before she can get so much as a word out, she feels a crush of people behind her, and the woman disappears from view.

In front of her, a man with suffocating body odor says to one of his friends, "This is rather intimate," but the joke falls flat.

Everyone's pace slows, until they are at a complete standstill. Sally stands on her tiptoes, trying to see what the cause of the slowdown is.

"It's so dark," says Margaret. "Is there anything to see?"

The sconces give off only a dim light, and all Sally can see is the backs of people's heads.

"I think I see Tom," she says, but she immediately convinces herself she must be wrong. He and his cousin are at the far end of the corridor, which doesn't make any sense considering he left the box only moments before her.

Eventually, the air grows hazy with smoke. "Open the windows!" cry the voices of people at the back of the corridor. Ahead of Sally, the man with the bad sense of humor asks his friend for his sword cane. He unscrews the handle and pulls the blade from the cane shaft, then jimmies it under the first of a half-dozen boards that cover the window nearest them. The first board pops off easily, and the man passes it to Sally, who isn't sure what to do with it. Nails stick out of the board in all directions, and if she lets it clatter to the floor, one of the nails is sure to skewer a woman in the foot.

The crowd begins to move forward again, and the man with the blade has no choice but to abandon his project. "Hand me the knife," says Sally, who now finds herself in front of the window. The man laughs, but Sally shoots him a look, and he passes the blade to her.

"Take this," she says, handing the board she'd been holding to Margaret. She passes her purse and jacket over Margaret's head to Archie.

It takes Sally a moment to figure out how to work the knife under the boards, and even then she can't get a good purchase. One of the boards eventually wiggles loose, and she slides her fingers beneath it, then yanks at it with all her might.

"Help me," she says to Margaret, who grabs hold of the board and pulls, too.

The board comes free in the women's hands, and Sally lets out a small scream, surprised at their own strength.

"Use the board to break the window," shouts a man behind her, and she looks at the board in her hands with a start. It hadn't occurred to her that it, too, could be a tool.

She needs a little room to wind up her arm. "Can you move back?" she asks Margaret, but there is nowhere for her to go. "Maybe crouch?"

Margaret does as she is told, and Sally swings the board over her sister-in-law's head and into the glass, which produces a piercing sound as it shatters. The fresh night air that rushes into the corridor feels so good it makes Sally almost light-headed.

Through the hole she's helped create, Sally can see a crowd of onlookers on the green. Some point at the theater, some cover their mouths with their hands, but every single face is turned upward, toward the building's roofline. She won't allow herself to imagine what it is they see.

The crowd behind them surges forward, and Margaret screams for help. Archie has been pushed on top of her, and Sally lets the knife and the board clatter to the floor in an effort to pull Margaret to her feet. "Stop, everyone, stop!" yells Sally. "Let her get up!"

When Margaret is standing again, Sally squeezes her sister-in-law tight.

"Are we to be killed by our own acquaintances?" says Margaret, who sounds close to tears.

In the bustle, someone had stepped on the heel of one of Sally's shoes, but there is no way to stop and pop it back into place. Sally has always envied the men their sturdy boots, but never more than now.

"I'm sorry about your knife," Sally says to the man in front of her, but if he has heard her, he doesn't acknowledge the apology.

They pass the entrance to one of the other boxes, and through the open doorway they can see the theater proper. The front of the pit, closest to the stage, is already engulfed in flames, which rise as high as the third-floor boxes, but haven't yet devoured them. Behind Margaret, Archie begins to cough, and the cough turns into a prayer. "Dear God," he mutters. "Oh, my dear God. My dear God. My dear God."

"This is very bad," says Margaret, and—as if on cue—a wave of thick smoke rolls into the corridor, blanketing them in near darkness. Around them, more people begin to cough and choke. Sally's eyes burn, and she squeezes them shut. How will they possibly make it down two flights of stairs if they can't see where they are going?

Ahead of them, the crowd charges forward, and a woman's scream is followed by a man's much louder and more terrified "Clara!"

The surge is so strong that Sally is lifted off the ground and carried a dozen feet or maybe more. When she is set down again, she is in the third-floor lobby, but she's lost both her shoes and her sister-in-law.

"Margaret!" she shrieks. "Margaret!"

"Sally!" says Archie, who sounds close enough to reach out and touch. Sally feels for him and when her fingers land upon the flesh of his face and then the brocade of her own jacket, which he's wrapped around his head, she seizes his arm.

"Where's Margaret?" she asks.

"I don't know," he says, moving in the direction of the stairs with everyone else. "We lost her."

Sally tugs at his arm. "Well, let's go find her."

Archie shakes Sally off. "I'm sure she's close by."

Sally's body stiffens, and she sputters, trying to think of what to say. "Archie, she might need our help!"

"She might also be ahead of us." His voice has grown more distant. The stairs creak under the weight of so many people, and she knows he is among them.

"She's not, though!" says Sally. Margaret wouldn't have left either of them behind. She turns and tries to push against the tide of people, who have grown desperate to reach the stairs. It is impossible to make any forward progress. Her only hope is to move toward the perimeter of the room and work her way back down the corridor against the wall.

"Margaret!" she screams. "Margaret!" Her throat burns and she hacks up phlegm so thick it feels like treacle in her mouth. She wishes she had thought to ask Archie for her jacket back. It might have helped protect her from the noxious fumes.

"You're going the wrong way," say several people as she pushes past them, but she ignores them.

"Margaret!"

Her foot brushes against the thin tissue of a silk dress and then the pliant body of a woman. She leans on the wall for support and uses her free hand to reach down and touch the woman's chest, neck, and face. It isn't Margaret, thank God.

As she tries to stand, Sally's fingers brush the soft fur of a beaver skin muff, and she realizes, with a start, that the woman at her feet is likely the very same woman who allowed them out of the box just a few moments ago.

"I'm sorry," she stutters to no one in particular, before screaming Margaret's name again.

Sally begins to crawl down the hallway. She realizes the air is a good deal clearer the closer she gets to the floorboards, so she inches forward on her forearms.

Around her, more people collapse, and Sally prays that, wherever Margaret is, she'll be able to hear her own name and respond to it. "Margaret!"

"Sally," comes a weak voice. "I'm here."

Sally's stomach flips. Her throat is so tight she can barely speak. "Keep talking to me, Margaret," she begs.

"My head," she says as Sally moves in the direction of the sound. "I feel so dizzy. I can't stand."

When Sally reaches her friend, she doesn't waste a second expressing her gratitude or even checking to make sure she is all right. She simply pulls Margaret to her feet and, in one fluid motion, moves her toward the bank of windows that run the length of the corridor's exterior wall. Above them, the ceiling glows.

"The stairs," says Margaret as she coughs into her hand. "They're that way."

Sally thinks of the crowded stairway and Archie's desperation to save his own skin. If they follow him now, they'll never make it out alive. "We can't go that way," says Sally, trying to contain the panic that threatens to blot out her reason. "We've got to get air."

They move toward the effervescent light of the windows. Several have been pried open, and each is crowded with people taking gulps of fresh air and trying to work up the courage to jump.

Behind them, they hear a deafening crash that shakes the entire building and causes hot embers to fall from the ceiling. Sally covers her head with her hands.

"What was that?" Margaret cries, but Sally can't say.

A man pushes past them, leaps over a half-dozen women who are clamoring to get up onto the nearest windowsill. With one hand on the window casement, he turns to them and says, "The staircase just fell through to the first floor." Then he jumps out into the night.

❧ | CECILY | ❧

*C*ecily *is one of the first* people to make it out of the gallery, on account of being one of the last people in, and now she watches as men and women come stumbling down the gallery's narrow staircase and out into the world they very nearly left behind.

She recognizes some of them from the Baptist meetinghouse, which Cecily's family attends when the weather is good. Others she knows from the mill or the market, but now hardly seems like the right time to say hello. Old Man Sully, who is in church every Sunday, regardless of the weather, raises his hands to the heavens and utters a "Praise be" when he touches solid ground, but Cecily isn't so sure God had much to do with their quick escape. She moves to the back of the crowd, and keeps one eye peeled for Augustine Saunders, who was behind her on the stairs and shouldn't be hard to miss.

All of them congregate together, a few dozen feet from the gallery door, and they stare up at the building's roofline, where the fire licks the dry timber. Cecily has seen other buildings in Richmond burn, but she doesn't think she's ever seen one this big go this fast.

Out of nowhere, the body of a young white man lands beside them with a sickening thud. He doesn't move, and above him, in a window on the third floor, more men prepare to jump.

"Somebody ought to do something," says an old woman near Cecily. "They gonna kill him dead, landing on top of him." And yet, nobody moves.

"Move back," shouts someone at the front of the crowd, and the group breaks up as more bodies begin to fall from the sky like a hard hail. The theater green is chaos, people running in all directions, and for the first time Cecily thinks of Maria. A wave of guilt washes over her. How has she not considered the girl until now? She rushes toward H Street, where she prays she'll find her waiting in front of the theater, just as they planned.

From the street, Cecily can see straight through the theater's entrance and past the lobby—shrouded in smoke—to the pit, which is setting loose the last of its occupants. The doors to the pit were, at some point, pulled off their hinges and slung onto the floor of the lobby, and now people scramble over them in their attempt to make it out of the building.

Cecily studies the faces of the women who, having successfully fled the building, collapse on the lawn in front of H Street. Some of them cry out for help, but many say nothing at all, just hack and spit into the grass, gasping for breath. All of them are covered in a fine layer of white dust, and Cecily realizes she might not recognize Maria if she saw her. As she studies the women's faces, she tries to look for Maria's hooked nose and cleft chin—features that no amount of soot can obscure—but it is impossible to see much in the dark.

It occurs to Cecily that she never even asked Maria where her seats were. It seems it's the folks on the second and third floors who are having the hardest time getting out, and while Cecily would like to tell herself that Maria and her friends bought the cheap seats in the pit, she suspects that's not the case.

Cecily decides to circle the theater. As she rounds the side of the building, a member of the fire brigade carrying a pail of water yells at her to move out of the way. She jumps backward, then wonders at the man's urgency. Half the water has already sloshed over the top of the pail on its long journey up Shockoe Hill. Behind him, a line of volunteers—passing pails back and forth—stretch down H Street and out of sight. They could run Shockoe Creek dry, and still it wouldn't be enough.

More Richmonders have begun to pour onto the green, and they shout for the people they love. A man with no coat, wearing a fancy stock buckle, dashes past her, screaming the name George at the top of his lungs. "Has anyone seen a little boy? About this high?" he asks a group of nearby onlookers, but he barely waits for them to shake their heads no before taking off again. Cecily had probably seen half a dozen little boys since her escape, but how is she to know any of them are his?

She picks her way slowly around the building, making a point to stay far away from the windows, which teem with panicked men and women fighting to get out. Remarkably, she watches one man jump from a second-floor window, a distance of at least fifteen feet, and land on his feet. He gives a little yip and runs off into the crowd.

People have begun to drag the bodies of victims into small piles, and Cecily forces herself to stop at each one, to look at the face of every woman she comes upon. Many of them are young, around Maria's age. Some wear fine dresses and expensive jewelry, others only a torn shift. All of them wear expressions that, to Cecily, seem frozen in fear, and it is in their faces that she comes to fully understand the horror that is unfolding in front of her.

❧ | GILBERT | ❧

The wind is loud in the trees, but Gilbert thinks he hears a woman's voice, screaming out in the yard. "You hear something?" he asks Sara.

"Go stand over there," Sara says, pointing to the far corner of the room, where he can remain out of sight.

When Sara opens the door, Elizabeth Preston flies inside, screaming and yelling as if she is on a mission to wake the dead. "Get up, Sara! Somebody! All of you!"

"What's the matter, Missus Elizabeth?" says Sara in a voice Gilbert knows she works hard to control. Maddie and the others peek their heads out over the edge of the loft. Sylvie has already started getting dressed.

"Fire," says Elizabeth, breathing hard. "There's a fire!"

Gilbert moves out of the shadows and into the glow of the lamp. "At the house?"

If Elizabeth is surprised to see him, she doesn't say a word, just shakes her head so hard her body sways. Sara reaches for her arm to hold her steady. "The theater," whispers Elizabeth, squeezing her eyes shut.

"Who's at the theater?" Gilbert asks Sara, too scared to answer the question for himself. The way his wife's face has folded in on itself, he already knows.

Sara pulls her lips tight together, like she is trying not to cry. "Gillie, it's Louisa who's there."

Elizabeth nods and sinks to the kitchen's dirt floor, a sob near tearing her in half. Sara looks at him then. "Do something. Please."

The next thing Gilbert knows, he is running. Through the Prestons' yard and out into their private alley. Down Twelfth Street and through the Public Square. The streets are crowded with people—Black and white—and, for once, Gilbert doesn't worry about being stopped and having his pass inspected.

He doesn't have much use for white people, hasn't met many decent ones in his life. There was Good Pete, who Gilbert only came to appreciate after his death, and Louisa, who Sara has taught him to love, one day at a time.

Louisa is as silly now as all the other little white girls running around Richmond, but when Gilbert started seeing Sara, Louisa was twelve or thirteen and as earnest as they come. Gilbert used to complain that he couldn't ever get Sara alone because, wherever they got off to, there Louisa was, wanting to read Sara something or tell her a story or get her help untangling the threads of her embroidery. Before he knew better than to open his mouth, he used to tell Sara, "You ain't got to be a mother to that little girl," and she would tell him to hush. "That child's been through plenty. She can look for a mother wherever she wants."

The inky sky glows gold. The bells toll, and in the side streets and alleys that Gilbert passes, he hears the shouts of the town criers mingle with the voices of Madison Ward residents, who run from house to house with the news. Women who had already turned in for the night answer the door in their shifts, and Gilbert sees more than one man dash out onto the street wearing nothing but a long shirt and an overcoat.

As Gilbert turns onto H Street, the wind pummels him. He tucks his chin and pumps his arms, willing himself to go faster, but he cannot maintain a sprint. By the time he nears the theater, the street has grown crowded with people, and as the blazing building comes into view, his pace slows.

The fire is worse than he imagined. Worse than anything he's seen before. It is clear there will be no saving the structure. The city's only fire engine sits parked in front of the theater, but the cart—with its hand-operated pump and short leather hose—can do nothing other than serve as a meeting place for volunteers to congregate. Gilbert asks several of the volunteers if they have seen Louisa Mayo, but he's met only with looks of sad confusion. Taking a deep breath, he covers his nose and mouth with his arm and runs headfirst into the theater's lobby, calling her name.

Gilbert can see that the pit is empty, but when he turns down the narrow hallway that leads to the stairs, he stops in his tracks. The stairs are gone, or rather, they are buried under a vast pile of rubble. When he looks up at the ceiling, where the stairs once were, he can see clear to the third floor. Among the debris are bodies, most of them women and all of them firmly trapped, impossible to budge. Gilbert tries to look for any clue that Louisa is among the dead, but his lungs soon begin to burn, and he tells himself that she is not there. Cannot be there.

Outside again, he gulps the clean air and circles the building. The windows on the theater's second and third floors are crowded with people, who have likely discovered by now that the stairs are not passable. Is Louisa among them?

The jump from the second floor is manageable, but the jump from the third floor is anything but. Those windows have to be at least thirty-five feet in the air. If any of the folks on the third floor are to have a real chance, they need a softer place to land.

Gilbert thinks of the fiddler Sy Gilliat, who lives just down the street from the theater green. Perhaps he can convince Sy to part with his mattress. Gilbert takes off running, and within moments, is beating on Sy's front door.

No one answers, so he tries the door handle. The door doesn't budge. "Open the door, Sy!" he shouts. "It's me, Gilbert!"

Inside he can hear someone moving around.

"I don't have much time. The theater's on fire!"

The door opens to reveal the familiar face of Sy Gilliat, who doesn't seem in the least bit surprised—or particularly worked up—by the news.

"Can I borrow your mattress?"

He cranes his head. "Hell no!"

"You don't even know what I need it for."

Sy crosses his arms, like there is nothing Gilbert can say that will convince him to part with it.

"Sy," says Gilbert as calm as he can, "folks are jumping out of third-floor windows."

"Black folks? Because from what I could see, it looked like Black folks got out just fine."

"You mean you was already down there?" Gilbert asks, disgusted that a man who makes a good living playing white people's parties can't summon enough sympathy for them to stick around and make himself useful.

"You think they're coming to save you when you burn up?" Sy asks.

"It ain't about that," says Gilbert, who knows they don't have time for a debate.

"What's it about, then?"

Gilbert needs something quick. "Doesn't the Lord say we got to do unto others like we—"

Sy just shakes his head, like he can't believe the words coming out of Gilbert's mouth. "*My* Lord says to get your own damned mattress." Then he shuts the door in Gilbert's face.

❦ | JACK | ❦

By the time Jack and Perry flee the carpenter's gallery, the fire is raging out of control.

"Get out!" yells Green over the roar of the flames.

Everyone knows to exit via the stage door, and within a minute or maybe less, Jack has flung his arms over his head and is following Perry past the prop table and the drop curtain and out into the cold December night.

No one in the troupe runs very far. They gather a few dozen feet from the stage door and stare up at the back of the building in a kind of shocked awe.

"The cashbox!" says Placide, and he sprints toward the building.

"You're crazy!" Anderson shouts after him as they watch Placide slip back into the theater through the stage door. "No amount of money's worth dying for."

The performance that evening was for Placide's benefit, which means he keeps the proceeds after everyone else is paid out. Since it was a sold-out show, there is likely five hundred dollars in the cashbox, more if no one in the box office skimmed anything off the top. Five hundred dollars isn't worth dying for, but it sure is a lot of money.

For several long moments, the troupe watches the stage door. The box office manager delivered the money to Placide during the intermission, but what Placide did with it after that is anyone's guess. Jack counts the seconds that pass in his head. Ten, then twenty. When he gets to thirty, he looks over at Lydia, and realizes she has begun to cry.

"Should someone go in after him?" asks Mrs. Placide, who has never seemed especially fond of her husband, but apparently does not wish him dead, either.

None of the men move.

Charles Young, who is a devout Catholic, begins to pray.

"Come on, Alex," says Anderson under his breath, and, as if summoned,

Placide bursts through the stage entrance seconds later, carrying a small metal box under one arm.

For a brief moment, there is much rejoicing. Placide is alive, and he has saved the night's earnings! But it doesn't take long for everyone to realize that the money is the least of their worries.

The green is complete bedlam. People have begun to pour out of the front lobby and around the side of the building, where they look up at the fire's progress in quiet reverence. "It's so much worse than I thought," Jack overhears one woman say to another.

"Is everyone here?" Green asks. "We all made it out?" The players cast their eyes around the group wildly, as if they can't quite believe the answer is yes.

"Robertson's not here," says Anderson.

"I saw him in the pit," says West. "He was trying to convince the ladies in the boxes to jump."

"Where's Nancy?" asks Lydia.

A flash of terror moves across Green's face before he remembers his daughter is fine. "She's back at Mrs. Barrett's. I told her to stay home."

Everyone looks confused.

"She wasn't in the production," Green explains, "and we'd oversold the show. We needed every free seat we could get."

Mrs. Green takes one long look at her husband, like she doesn't quite believe him, and sets off running in the direction of the boardinghouse, where Placide, Green, and Young rent rooms for themselves and their families. She is still wearing the bright white nun's habit splattered in pig's blood, and Jack overhears one of the actors say he wouldn't want to bump into her in a dark alley, which gets a few uncomfortable laughs.

"Christ, they're jumping," says West as they watch a man plummet to the ground from a third-floor window.

"I don't understand," says Jack, his voice cracking. "Can't they just file down the stairs?"

West says quietly, "There's not enough time."

"What do you mean?"

"Look at how fast the fire's spreading along the roof."

Jack is having a hard time taking it all in. The roof, the windows, the people running this way and that.

A few feet away, Placide stands with his hands on his knees, trying to catch his breath. "Are you all right?" West asks him.

"What in the hell happened in there?" Placide demands, and everyone begins to talk at once.

"Someone hoisted a lit chandelier up into the flyspace," says Perry.

"Goddamnit," says Placide. "Who's responsible?"

Everyone looks at Jack, who practically shouts, "I hoisted it up there, but it was on Green's orders." Then he stares straight at Green, who won't meet his eye, or anybody else's. "Tell them."

"Tell them what?" asks Placide.

Green coughs into his hand, and Jack waits for him to recover himself. Surely he will answer Placide's question directly, admit what happened. But when Green continues to hack and wheeze, Jack grows anxious.

Placide looks at Green. "What's the kid talking about?"

Green allows himself to be consumed by a coughing fit that leaves him bent at the waist.

"Christ, man," says Placide, pounding Green's back. "Breathe."

❦ | GILBERT | ❦

After *Sy Gilliat shuts the door* in Gilbert's face, he blinks twice, then turns and beats a path around the side of the house. All he needs is something—anything—he can use to catch those falling souls. He spies a long ladder, which will be unwieldy to carry but may be tall enough to reach a second-floor window. He grabs it and takes off running once more.

Back at the green, things have only gotten worse. The glass in the bull's-eye window at the front of the theater is gone, and the flames that shoot out of the opening remind Gilbert of the tip of a hot iron, white from the forge. He runs around to the east side of the building and stops in his tracks when a girl who's caught fire shoots out a third-floor window like a comet. She lands in the grass with a thump. A man rushes to cover her with his coat, extinguishing the flames, and Gilbert waits, frozen, for the coat to be pulled back from the girl's face. When it is finally removed, Gilbert feels sick at the sight of the girl's charred hair and burnt flesh, but also relieved. She's not Louisa.

Splinters of wood begin to rain down on Gilbert, and when he looks up, he sees that someone is kicking open a second-floor window. A moment later, Dr. McCaw's head appears through the opening. Gilbert watches as the doctor, who is a giant, straddles the windowsill, then reaches behind him to help a young woman up and over the sill. Once the woman has her legs in front of her, McCaw holds both her hands in his and lowers her as far as he can without toppling out the window himself. It is a slow ordeal, and Gilbert can see a crowd of people behind McCaw, begging to be let out.

"Here!" Gilbert shouts as he races to lean the ladder against the building, beneath the window where the woman now dangles. He scrambles to the top of the ladder, which doesn't reach the window—not by a long shot—but does put him close enough to touch the woman's dainty shoes. "That as far as you can go?" he yells to the doctor.

McCaw answers, his voice strained, "Not an inch further."

Gilbert tucks the toes of his own shoes around the ladder's rails, trying his best to anchor himself in place. He wishes he'd thought to ask someone to hold the bottom of the ladder steady, but he doesn't see anyone close enough to ask. "Drop her," he shouts to McCaw, still unsure how in the hell he is going to catch a woman who is coming at him feetfirst.

When McCaw lets go, the woman lands neatly in Gilbert's waiting arms, but her weight is off balance, and before he can get his arms around her midsection, she's already sent them both teetering backward. Gilbert feels the ladder shift beneath him and wants to grab for the rungs, but can't, his arms full of cotton and silk. The night air rushes past him, and then he is flat on his back, staring up at the window where McCaw still sits, perched like an oversized crow.

Gilbert's breath has been knocked out of him, but after the woman scrambles off of him, he finds that his legs and arms work fine. The woman helps him to his feet, and when he asks her if she is all right, she touches her own face and hands, as if she needs evidence that the answer is yes.

"No more ladder," he calls up to McCaw. Better to be on the ground, where his feet can find good purchase, and if he is thrown off balance, he won't be at risk of breaking his own neck. "Hold 'em like they're babies, and I'll catch them."

McCaw steps back inside the building and helps a young girl up and over the sill. "You mean like this?" he asks, one arm under the girl's knees and the other wrapped around her shoulders.

"Yes, sir," shouts Gilbert. "Rump first."

Gilbert holds his arms out wide and bends his legs at the knees, ready to move fast in any direction if the girl doesn't fall in a straight line. He can't afford to take his eyes off her for a second, can't spare the time it will take to wipe the sweat from his brow. He tells himself that catching her isn't much different from playing a game of cup and ball.

"Ready?" McCaw yells.

"Go!" says Gilbert, then he watches the girl trace a neat path between McCaw's outstretched arms and his own. When she lands in his arms, he staggers under her weight, but manages to plant his feet on the ground and remain standing. After he tips her onto her feet, the girl stutters a thank-you, but Gilbert just waves her away. A moment later, he thinks better of it, and catches her attention. "Miss, you know a girl named Louisa Mayo?"

"Yes," she says.

"She up there?"

"I saw her on the way in. But not—"

McCaw's "Ready?" interrupts them, and Gilbert looks up at the window to find another woman in the doctor's arms.

From below, the woman's backside looks a great deal wider than the previous two women's, and when she lands in Gilbert's arms, she nearly flattens him. Gilbert hates doing it, but he sees no choice other than to shout up to McCaw, "Save the heavy girls for last. Or you'll knock me out of this race before it's begun."

McCaw nods and says something to a middle-aged woman with a fat face. She looks crestfallen, but then she moves out of view and a slim girl takes her place.

The doctor and Gilbert work in this manner for several more minutes, and all the while the fire rages. Gilbert catches three women, then four, then five. Eventually he loses count, just knows that his arms have begun to shake, the same way they do when he's been at the forge for too many hours in a row. It is hard not to wonder when and how this work will end.

"I've got to get out of here," says McCaw finally. "The fire's at my back."

"You want me to try to catch you?" Gilbert shouts, certain McCaw won't take him up on the offer. The doctor is as big as Gilbert is. Over six feet tall, with arms as thick as tree limbs.

"Catch my sister. If you can," is all Gilbert gets for an answer. The woman with the fat face is back at the window, and this time McCaw gets her up and onto the sill. Gilbert studies the old gal as McCaw does his best to maneuver her into his arms. She is a big one, almost as tall as her brother, and Gilbert begins to realize, studying her, that all he is really going to be able to do is break her fall.

McCaw doesn't even shout "Ready?" like he's done with each of the other women. He just gets his sister as many inches away from the building as he can manage and lets her go—trusting Gilbert to figure out the rest.

And he does.

When the time comes, Gilbert steps into the shadow she casts and braces for what is coming.

❧ | CECILY | ❧

C ecily is nearing the stage door at the back of the building, no sign of Maria anywhere, when she comes upon a group of actors who are still in costume. The man who played the Baptist stands next to a second man, who played Monsieur d'Orbesson, and between them is a third man—his face still wet with shoe polish—who played the old servant.

A half-dozen yards away stands a young boy, visibly upset, with dark hair and a thin face, and she wonders if he might be the missing son of the man with the stock buckle. She skirts the group and moves toward him. "Are you George?" she asks, but he doesn't answer. She waves her hands at him, but it isn't until she is right up on him that she gets his attention. "George?"

"Huh?" he says, as if he is only just seeing her.

"There's a man looking for a boy named George. I thought you might be him."

For a moment, the child looks almost disappointed. "No, I'm Jack." He wears a shirt and waistcoat but no jacket, and he shivers uncontrollably.

"Are you with them?" she says, tilting her head in the direction of the actors.

He seems unsure of the answer, but finally whispers, "Yes."

"Were you in the play?" She doesn't think she remembers seeing him onstage.

He shakes his head no, quickly, like he doesn't want her to get the wrong idea. "I'm a stagehand. I—"

A woman in a bloody nun's habit darts past them, and they watch as she hurls herself at Monsieur d'Orbesson. "She's not at the house! You said she'd be at the house!"

Cecily sees Jack stand up a little straighter.

The man looks confused, and when he doesn't say anything, the woman shoves him—hard—in the chest. "She's not anywhere!"

Cecily can't make out the man's response from where they stand, but the woman's voice, which is loud as a bell, rings in their ears. "You bloody idiot! She's in there!"

"Who's she talking about?" Cecily asks Jack.

The boy says only, "Nancy."

The woman continues shouting, until finally Jack turns back to Cecily. "Nancy's their daughter."

Cecily clicks her tongue in sympathy.

"That woman's Frances Green. And the fellow she's screaming at is her husband, John. He's one of the managers of the theater company."

Now John Green's voice booms. "Woman, I told her to stay home!"

"Was she there, do you think? In the theater?" Cecily asks Jack, but he seems incapable of answering the question.

"I saw her, John," says one of the actors, a big burly fellow with thick eyebrows, who has just arrived in the circle. "At the beginning of the night. She was on her way upstairs, with a bunch of girls."

Frances Green stands perfectly still, as if her feet have sprouted roots. Not once does she look at her husband, or he at her.

"And none of you have seen her since?" John Green asks, turning to what remains of the theater company. "Not on the way out? Not out here?"

No one says anything, but their silence tells the Greens everything they need to know.

Cecily expects Frances Green to weep or swoon, but she doesn't do any such thing. She just stands there, staring at her feet. When she finally moves her eyes to her husband's face, her expression is such a mixture of remorse and disgust that Cecily sucks in her own breath just witnessing it.

Frances Green turns and stumbles toward the front of the theater, and John Green chases after her. When they are both gone, all the actors begin to talk at once, and Jack lets out a pitiful sob.

He is a twig of a thing, all elbows and knees, with shoulder blades that protrude from his back like wings. Once he starts to bawl, those shoulders of his shake so hard, Cecily is tempted to wrap her arms around him. But, of course, she doesn't dare.

"Is this real?" he whispers.

"What?"

"The fire, Nancy, you here talking to me."

Cecily looks at the theater, then back at the boy. "You think it might be a dream?"

"A nightmare."

As if on cue, a portion of the roof closest to the stage caves into the building with a deafening crack. The sound is so loud, Cecily flings herself backward and covers her head with her hands. When she lifts her head again, she finds that the actors have scattered and the boy is gone.

SALLY

*L*adies," *says Sally to the women* at one of the open windows. "You don't
have much time." The faces of several of them are tear-streaked, and
one woman is missing a large chunk of her hair. Their dresses are in shreds.

Margaret recognizes one of the women. "Helena, where's your husband? And your sons?"

"I don't know," says the woman, who rocks back and forth on her heels.

"You can do this," says Margaret, extending her hand to the old woman.
"Here, I'll help you up."

"Help my daughter first," says another woman, who holds a small girl
of maybe four or five years to her chest. The roof above their heads groans.

"Can't you put her out yourself?" Sally asks.

"I can't do it," the woman cries. "I'm afraid I'll kill her."

Sally looks from one woman to another, then down at the little girl.
She closes her eyes and takes a shallow breath through her nose. "Fine," she
says. "Give her to me."

"No!" the woman screams, burying her nose in the little girl's neck.

"Do you want her out the window or not?"

The mother only sobs in response. Sally tries easing the little girl out of
the woman's arms, but the woman holds her daughter tight. Margaret steps
in and begins to open the woman's fingers, one by one. "Remember, dear,
when they're little, their bones are made of butter."

Sally is losing her patience. "Give her to me now, or I won't do it!"

The woman hands the little girl over, and as Sally lifts her over the sill,
she whispers in her ear, "It's going to be all right." Then she shouts at the
crowd gathered beneath the window. "Somebody catch this one!" She tries
not to think about what she is doing, about the long way down or the bodies that lay scattered in the frozen grass. A man steps forward and shouts
something up at her, but she can't hear what. Without giving herself time
to think, she releases the child into the wind.

She doesn't want to watch the child's landing, but she can't look away. At the sight of the little girl safe in the man's arms, she lets out a gasp.

"He caught her!" screams Margaret, who has peeked over the sill. "Oh my God, he caught her!"

Sally's legs shake. She has had quite enough of being the hero and barks at the rest of the women, "Let the child's mother out first, and then all the rest of you had better jump. I'm not going to stand here and push you out one by one. Do you understand?"

She makes to move away from the window, and Margaret tugs at her dress, or what is left of it. "Where are you going?"

Up and down the narrow hallway, women flock to the open windows. "If we wait until they're all out," says Sally, "we'll be dead."

Margaret touches her own neck.

"There's another window back here. Several of them. They're just boarded up."

Sally runs her hand along the wall, moving slowly toward the back of the house. Within a dozen feet, she hits another casement window, covered with the same familiar planks of wood. She starts to pull at the boards with her fingers, but they don't budge. "Margaret," she calls, "see if you can find a cane or a piece of wood on the floor, anything I might wedge between these boards."

"I've got a cane!" says Margaret, letting out a loud cough. "Oh! Sal! It's Mr. Scott's. He's here."

"Here?" asks Sally as she tries to work the first board free with her own two hands. "Is he dead?"

Margaret hands her the cane and returns to Mr. Scott. "I think I feel a life pulse. But it's very faint."

Sally has to focus, but the work is slow, and she is beginning to feel dizzy again. She looks over at the open window closest to them. Most of the women who were there a few minutes ago are gone. One lies on the floor, unconscious, and another continues to hover at the sill.

The ceiling is a sheet of flames, and red-hot debris threatens to bombard them.

"Where's Mr. Scott?" Sally asks Margaret. "We have to get out of here. Now."

Margaret moves through the dark to the slump of a man's body, and Sally follows her. "Here," says Margaret.

"What are we going to do with him?" Margaret asks.

"Let's get him out the window. After that, we can't control what happens to him."

Sally grabs him under his arms, and Margaret takes hold of his legs, and together they drag him as far as the open window. He is heavier than Sally anticipated, and they'll need an extra set of hands to get him over the sill.

A woman with a birthmark the size of a quail's egg hovers at the window, and when Sally asks her if she's going to jump, she shakes her head, a vehement no. "You should," says Sally.

The woman's face is streaked with tears. "My sister's dead. Down there."

Sally looks out the window at the theater green. The grass is littered with bodies. She returns her gaze to the woman, who can't be older than twenty-five. "I'm very sorry for your loss. But if you choose to stay, you'll die in here."

The woman blinks in acknowledgment, but she does not make a move to climb out the window.

"While you decide," says Sally, "will you help us get this man over the ledge?"

The woman nods and takes hold of Mr. Scott's belt, and together the three of them hoist him off the floor.

"Feet first, ladies," Margaret reminds them as she edges toward the window, then places his feet on the sill. He still wears his waistcoat and it snags on the splinters of wood and pieces of broken glass. Sally can't waste time with any of it; the roof above their heads is going to go at any second. She gives him a good shove and watches him disappear.

"Does the woman on the floor have a life pulse?" she asks the woman with the birthmark who refuses to jump.

"I don't know," she stutters, then crouches down beside her to check for one. "I don't think so."

"All right. In that case, you're next," Sally says to her sister-in-law.

Around them, hot embers fall like rain. Margaret flinches. "What about you?"

"You have five children," Sally says, looking her friend straight in the eye. "I have none."

Margaret doesn't argue. She squeezes Sally's arm, then uses it for support as she climbs up onto the windowsill. Once her feet are on the ledge, she turns to her friend. "Robert would be proud of you, Sal," she says, then she steps into the thin December air.

Sally didn't watch Mr. Scott plummet to the ground, but she does watch Margaret jump. The skirt of her dress billows up above her head, then her legs buckle when she hits the ground. Sally can't afford to wait long enough to see if she moves.

She turns to face the only woman who remains. The roar of the fire over their heads is so loud she has to yell to be heard. "If you don't jump now, I will."

"I can't."

A large piece of red-hot timber crashes down on the body of the woman that lies beside them, and Sally decides she's done enough pleading and cajoling.

She climbs up onto the windowsill and looks out at the green. The ground is such a long way down. She is afraid of landing on Margaret or Mr. Scott or any one of the number of people who lie below, so she clutches the sill and lowers her body against the side of the building. The brick facade scrapes the soft underside of her arms as she hangs there in the hallowed space between life and death. Finally, there is nothing else to do but let go.

❧ ❘ GILBERT ❘ ❧

When Gilbert comes to, *Dr. McCaw's* sister is screaming and pointing at the window, or more precisely, at a spot a few feet beneath the window, where McCaw dangles headfirst, a dozen feet above the growing crowd. Gilbert squeezes his eyes shut and then opens them again, trying to figure out what he is really looking at. McCaw's coat is on fire, and all Gilbert can assume is that he must have jumped from the window in a hurry. One of his gaiters looks like it's been caught on a piece of metal that protrudes from the building's brick exterior, and now he squirms like a fish on a hook, trying to free himself. Gilbert sits up as fast as he dares, no time to check for his own injuries, and grabs the ladder, which he repositions against the building. In the time it takes for him to climb the rungs, the fire has spread across McCaw's back, but there is nothing to be done—no way of putting it out—until Gilbert has got the man to the ground.

Gilbert feels his pockets for his folding knife, and when he has it in hand, he opens the knife with his teeth and brings the blade down on the soft leather that covers McCaw's boot. He slides the blade back and forth, once and then twice, cutting a deep enough gash in the gaiter to release it from the metal obtrusion. McCaw is free and then he is falling and then he is perfectly still on the ground below. Gilbert scrambles back down the ladder, leaping the last four rungs. McCaw's sister is hysterical and the crowd that has gathered around the ladder murmurs furiously, but no one rushes to the doctor's aid, so Gilbert removes his own coat and throws it across the doctor's broad back, until the last of the flames are extinguished. The man lies there, smoking like a ham, in the wet grass.

Gilbert inspects McCaw's injuries. One of his legs is all torn up, and until his blackened coat can be removed, there will be no way to gauge the severity of his burns. The doctor's breaths come in short, rapid blasts, which Gilbert watches collect in the night air. When Gilbert bends close to McCaw's face, he hears him whisper, "Will nobody save me?"

"What do you think I'm doing, Mister Doctor?"

Gilbert gets no reply.

"Should we move him?" asks McCaw's sister, but her teeth are chattering so hard in her head, she can hardly get out the whole question.

Gilbert is tempted to tell her she is on her own, that his one job was to find Louisa Mayo and bring her home and that he's wasted too many precious minutes already. But then it occurs to him that maybe Louisa is alive, on the other side of the green, because some man like Gilbert is working to save the lives of people he doesn't know. "I'm going to lift him," he finally says.

Gilbert knows the Baptist meetinghouse best, and after he's stood McCaw up and folded his body across his back, he staggers off in the direction of the clapboard building. Pastor Courtney locked the church up tight after the evening's prayer meeting, but Gilbert can only assume that the good man threw the doors wide open when he realized the apocalypse had finally arrived.

❋ | CECILY | ❋

Cecily *has yet to find Maria,* and if she can't find her soon, she'll be forced to return to the Price place and wake the girl's parents. She dreads the thought.

Maybe, Cecily tells herself, Maria will have beaten her there. If she is like the other girls and women Cecily has seen running around the green, Maria will arrive at the house coatless and maybe even shoeless, her dress filthy and torn to pieces. Cecily pictures Mrs. Price meeting her on the porch and ushering her inside the house. The lady of the house will wake Rosie and Constance; she'll order Rosie to stoke the fire and boil water for a bath, and when Maria is all cleaned up and in a freshly laundered shift, Constance will tuck a bed warmer between her sheets.

The commotion will likely reach Cecily's own parents in the quarters, and Cecily hopes they won't assume the worst when they see that Maria has arrived home alone. If Della approaches the main house and asks after her daughter, Maria won't even know to tell her that everyone from the gallery made it out just fine.

This fantasy has captured Cecily's attention so completely that she nearly runs right into Maria's father and brother as they make their way around the theater. Both of them are too busy screaming Maria's name to have noticed her, and as soon as Cecily hears Elliott's voice, she takes several steps backward, without even realizing what she's done.

She moves toward a group of dull-eyed men who are watching the theater burn like it is a hearth fire that needs to be tended to before they can go safely to bed. With them as a buffer, she can spy on Elliott and his father without fear of being seen.

Elliott's voice grows more panicked, and his father runs between the same piles of bodies Cecily has so recently checked. She should step forward, tell him not to bother, but something stops her.

If the Prices are here searching for Maria, then that means word of the fire has reached the house, but Maria hasn't.

This doesn't make sense to Cecily. She knows that dozens—if not hundreds—of people will die inside the theater tonight, but she cannot envision Maria being one of them. The girl is tough as nails and has always looked out for herself. If she didn't manage to make it out of the theater, then who did?

Elliott begins screaming Cecily's name, and she freezes and waits for him to make his way over to her. But he doesn't come. He just keeps circling the burning building, calling for her again and again, same as he was calling for Maria a moment ago. Cecily feels sick, but then it occurs to her that Elliott Price thinks she is dead, too.

Her mind works quickly, trying to tell herself a story she can understand. Plenty of people have died escaping the fire, but others never made it out at all. The theater is a fireball, as bright as the burning sun, and anyone still inside will be ash by morning.

Cecily walks to the edge of the green and tucks herself up against the side of an outbuilding. She takes several deep breaths, trying to work out what the world will look like if Elliott and his father return home with the news that they've been unable to find Maria *or* Cecily. Will the Prices really believe Cecily is dead? If they do, that means there will be no slave catcher, no advertisements in the paper, no reward money for her return. She can go anywhere, she tells herself, if no one is chasing her.

Cecily can still see Elliott, but she can no longer hear his voice over the roar of the flames. What might it be like to go the rest of her days with no sight or sound of him? To know she can put him behind her like a bad dream? It is almost too much to contemplate.

She tries to recall who, if anyone, has seen her since she escaped the theater. The boy, Jack. But she never told him her name. She *did* introduce herself to Augustine Saunders in the theater, and she is sure the woman was behind her on the stairs as they exited the galley. But will this Augustine woman really argue if she learns Cecily is among the dead? What could she possibly have to gain?

Cecily considers her family. If she goes through with this, she will leave Richmond and never return, never see her mother or her father or her brother or her sisters again. It's hard to even think about all she will lose. The stories her mother tells late at night when they are all under their quilts, staring up at the ceiling. The wood shavings she finds in her father's hair when he is carving one of his animals—a fox or a beaver or, once, a bluebird—out of river birch. The way her brother, Moses, throws rocks at the river, believing that one day he will make it clear across the mighty James. And the soft napes of her sweet sisters' necks, which beg for kisses and also big, wet raspberries that make them squeal with delight. For this to work, there can be no real goodbyes and certainly no happy reunion on this side of the great divide.

Cecily pulls her shawl tight and stares up at the copper sky. The problem with getting an idea as big as leaving is that there is no folding it up and putting it away. If Cecily returns to the Price place now, she'll live the rest of her days knowing she missed her one chance at a different life.

Flakes of ash float through the air. The larger pieces glow orange around their edges, and Cecily traps one in her hands. She waits for the hot sizzle of her own flesh, but when she opens her cupped palms, the spark has already been extinguished. Is Cecily holding a tiny piece of the theater's roof? One of the backdrops? A young girl's coat? Maybe she is holding the girl herself.

Cecily brings her hand to her mouth. She lodges the ash on the soft meat in the middle of her tongue and allows it to melt there like snow. By the time it has disappeared, so has she.

FRIDAY

❧❦ | ❧❦

DECEMBER 27, 1811

❧❧ | SALLY | ❧❧

If *Sally lost consciousness after her* jump from the theater's third-floor window, she did so only for the briefest of moments. She comes to, on her back, and slowly raises her arms to the night sky. She can't see stars, but she can see her fingers, which she flexes once and then twice. They work just as they are supposed to, and she uses them to feel her face.

Her skin is taut and cool to the touch. She moves her hands to her collarbone, then her shoulders, and is tempted to keep going, inspecting each and every part of her body with the same thoroughness and appreciation, except that when she looks up at the burning building, she sees a woman throw her legs over the windowsill from which Sally so recently hung.

Sally tries to shout for her to wait, but the sound comes out garbled. She springs to her feet, eager to be out of the woman's way should her body take the same precipitous path to earth. She is no sooner standing than the woman hits the ground beside her with a terrifying smack.

She isn't the same young woman Sally tried to coax from the window, but Sally is about to go to her when she spies Margaret sitting just a few feet away. Margaret's eyes are unfocused and her mouth is open, and something about the way she pats the tatters of her skirt down around her ankles gives Sally an uneasy feeling. She hurries toward her and, when she arrives at her side, falls down on the ground beside her.

"Oh, Margaret. We did it," she says as she throws her arms around her friend. In the dark hell of that narrow upstairs hallway, she'd had a hard time imagining both of them making it out of the theater alive. Yet here they are. It is almost too much to take in.

"Can you walk?" she asks, but Margaret, usually so accommodating, doesn't utter a word. Her breath comes in short rapid bursts, which crystallize in the frigid night air. Sally rubs her friend's back and tries to calm her. "You're all right. Everything's all right now."

Margaret's body shudders, and her mouth yawns open, but no sound issues forth. Sally watches as a long string of drool falls from Margaret's lips and onto the bodice of her dress. It is as if she is trying to scream.

"Margaret?" says Sally, her own throat so sore it hurts to speak. "Please. Just breathe. All right?" She tries to model a good deep breath, but when she expels the air in her own chest, she begins to cough. Even her insides feel scorched.

Margaret's breathing eventually becomes more measured, but her hand never stops working the hem of her skirt. Sally knows they can't afford to sit like this all night, so finally she stays Margaret's hand and says quietly, "Let me see."

As soon as she lifts Margaret's skirt, she understands the severity of the situation. Her friend's shin bone has snapped in half. There is blood—lots of it—but the worst part is seeing the bright white bone, which has pierced the skin and glints in the firelight.

Margaret takes one look at her leg and vomits into her lap; the smell is enough to make Sally want to do the same. She jumps to her feet and tries to make a plan. Margaret needs a doctor immediately, but first they need to get out of the cold—somewhere where Sally can assess the extent of her injuries and figure out how to get her real help.

Two men—one young and one old—stand nearby, watching the building burn, and Sally flags them over. "Can you help me get her somewhere warm?"

They seem willing to be put to good use, until they kneel down beside Margaret and get a whiff of what is hiding in the folds of her dress. Sally can only see the expression of the young man facing her, but he looks as if he is about to gag. "How far did you say?" he asks.

She is annoyed, but knows she needs to bite her tongue. She also knows that, at this rate, they'll never agree to haul her all the way home. "Somewhere close by?"

"Breathe through your mouth," the older man suggests, and it is all Sally can do not to search for a loose rock to throw at his head.

"Careful with her legs. The left one's broken," says Sally, but even with the warning, Margaret cries out in pain when the men lift her up and into the air.

"Should we take her to the Baptist meetinghouse?" asks the young man, but the older man shakes his head. "Let's try Mary Cowley's. It's closer."

"Who's Mary Cowley?" Sally asks as she trails behind them, wishing very much for her shoes, which have, by now, most likely turned to cinder. The ground is uneven, and in the dark, she can't see where she is putting her feet.

"Native woman," says the old man. "Married Jared Cowley. But she's a widow now. Lives just over there, on the other side of the green."

The young man scoffs. "If she's Native, so am I."

"None of my business what she is," says the old man, addressing Sally directly. "She's as close to a physician as you're likely to get, and I feel certain she'll take your friend in."

The men make their way toward a two-story clapboard house with a steep roof and a generous front porch. The house sits east of the green, and it is as if Mary Cowley is expecting them. She flings her door open wide and beckons the group through the entryway and into the parlor, which is a large and generously appointed room that reminds Sally of her parents' parlor at Red Hill. The settee is already occupied, as is the floor closest to the hearth, so the men—upon Mrs. Cowley's instruction—lay Margaret down under the window, between a wingback chair and a small drop-leaf table that has been pushed against the wall. By the time Sally turns to thank both men for their assistance, they are halfway to the front door.

"Selfish bastards," she whispers under her breath, then, in a voice loud enough for Mrs. Cowley to hear, she tries to make light of their quick departure. "I suppose they decided they'd get out of here before I asked them for something else."

"That may be true," says Mrs. Cowley, who does not look Native so much as otherworldly in the dim light of her lamp. "But in this house you may ask for anything you like."

The woman is a godsend. After making their introductions, she tucks a pillow underneath Margaret's head and scurries off. When she returns, she is carrying a quilt, which she hands to Sally. "Something to cover her with. I'm sorry I can't offer her a bed. They're all full."

Sally is so grateful to the woman, she thinks she might cry. "No, thank you. This is enough."

"Are you sisters?"

"Sisters-in-law. She's married to my late husband's brother."

"What's her trouble?"

Sally doesn't know if she is asking because she is curious or because she intends to offer aid, but she hopes it is the latter. "A broken leg, for certain. And I'm not sure what else," she says as she unfolds the quilt. "She's been sick. You really don't mind if I use this?"

"It can be washed. But do you want to try to get that dress off her?"

"She's not very cooperative," says Sally hesitantly as she eyes Margaret, who has begun to shiver uncontrollably.

Mrs. Cowley bats the air with her hands, as if Margaret's disposition is of little concern to her. She pulls a pair of shears from her apron pocket and hands them to Sally. "We'll just cut it off. I've got an extra shift upstairs."

"You're so kind."

Mrs. Cowley disappears again. By the time she returns, Sally has snipped away what remains of Margaret's skirt and is carefully working the tip of the scissors between her stays and the soft flesh of her stomach. When she is done, she tucks an arm behind Margaret's shoulders and pleads with her to sit up.

Margaret is delirious or close to it, but she does as she is told. Mrs. Cowley rolls the neck of the shift over her head, and as they work her arms into the sleeves she says "Now, isn't this better?" in the same tone she'd use to address a small child. Margaret doesn't respond. When the shift is on, Sally lowers her friend's head back onto the pillow, and Mrs. Cowley pulls what remains of her dress out from under her. "I don't see any reason to save this," says the old woman. "Do you?"

Before Sally can say anything, they are interrupted by a pounding at the door. Mrs. Cowley goes to answer it and Sally can hear two men demand to know whether a sixteen-year-old girl named Maria Price has been brought in. Mrs. Cowley must not know the answer to the question—so many people have been coming and going—so she invites them in to see for themselves.

In all the tumult, Margaret murmurs something, and Sally has to lean in close to hear her better. "What did you say?"

"Mr. Scott," she says a second time, and Sally's breathing stalls. "Did he survive the fall?"

Sally stutters something, then rises and makes her way across the parlor, slipping past the knot of people in Mrs. Cowley's entryway. When she is outside, she sprints toward the theater, which is now completely encased in flames.

The Baptist meetinghouse is mayhem when Gilbert approaches, McCaw slung over his back.

A large crowd has gathered in front of the building, everyone apparently believing—as Gilbert does—that a house of God is the most obvious place to go during a time such as this.

A few people have pulled carts up in front of the building and are loading the injured into wagon beds. Others have brought their horses and are convincing the maimed to heave themselves into the saddles. One man deposits a woman with an ugly gash on her forehead into a wheelbarrow. But most people come and go on foot.

Pastor Courtney tries to make order of the chaos. "If you are injured and need assistance, come inside. If you are looking for someone, you may enter briefly, but please try to stay to the side aisles and clear out as soon as you've confirmed that the person you're looking for is not here."

Alister Murdoch, who sings in the choir on Sundays, is standing beside the pastor with a sheaf of papers in his hand. "How do you spell that?" he asks a man with a big beard as he presses the nub of a pencil down on the page.

"T-a-b-i-t-h—"

"Pastor Courtney," Gilbert calls from underneath the weight of McCaw. "Where can I set this man down?"

The pastor takes one look at McCaw and says, "Not him, too."

McCaw is a big man, and Gilbert doesn't have enough breath left in his body to respond with anything other than a grunt.

"Any pew you can find, Mr. Hunt." Pastor Courtney turns to McCaw's sister. "Mrs. Johnston, you all right?"

Phyllis McCaw Johnston is one of those women who will be more than all right until the day she drops dead. Her clothing is fine, she wears at least a pound of gold around her throat, and it does not look like she's done an ounce of work in her life. But when Gilbert arrives at the church doors and says "You mind getting those for me?" she does as she is told.

Gilbert stumbles through the doorway and into the church's dark interior. The pastor has lit all the lamps he has, plus the altar candles and even the leftover lanterns from last summer's camp meetings. Still, Gilbert can barely see the pulpit.

From the pews, Gilbert hears the moans of the injured, and he lurches forward, looking for one that is not in use. Now he sees why the pastor has told people to avoid the center aisle; a line of bodies runs down the middle of it. Gilbert is tempted to stop and look for Louisa's slight build, the rise of her rib cage, but he is staggering under the weight of his charge, so he steps over the bodies instead.

"The pews are so narrow," says Mrs. Johnston as Gilbert comes to an empty one. "Surely, he'd be more comfortable over there on the floor."

Gilbert looks behind him at the dead. "Don't look too comfortable to me."

Pew or no pew, Gilbert doesn't know how he is supposed to lay McCaw down. The man's back is so badly burned, he can't press it up against anything. And he fell on his face, so there's no telling what is broken or bruised, aside from the left thigh, which is clearly in need of attention.

"Maybe we see about getting a cart?" says Mrs. Johnston. "Try to transport him home?"

"Maybe," wheezes Gilbert, who isn't fond of the way McCaw's sister bandies around the word *we*. She doesn't own him, and he doubts that Cameron Kemp would be so charitable as to knowingly lend him out to the McCaws, even in a crisis. "But wherever he goes next, I got to put him down now."

Gilbert squats beside the pew, then unlocks McCaw's arms from his neck and begins to roll the good doctor onto the long seat.

"Careful with him!" says Mrs. Johnston.

He wants to shout, *What do you think I'm doing?* Instead, he just lowers McCaw down onto the pew and winces as the doctor lets out a sharp cry. "Dr. McCaw, you done good," he soothes as he rips at McCaw's torn pant leg, exposing a thigh, which has been cut to ribbons.

Mrs. Johnston reaches for her brother then, which is when Gilbert notices the two dark circles spreading across the bodice of her dress. She must have seen him noticing because she immediately tries to cover her chest with her arms. "I've got a new baby. I should have been home by now."

"You don't need to explain yourself," says Gilbert, quick as he can. But in truth, her explanation *does* make him feel a tad more generous toward her. That baby came dangerously close to losing both his mama and his next meal.

He thinks about trying to find a jacket or shawl he can give her, but he's barely had time to look around the sanctuary when he is clapped on the back by Angus Graham, who runs The Bell Tavern. "Hunt, I saw it with my own eyes. Wouldn't have believed it if I hadn't."

Gilbert glances at Mrs. Johnston, who looks every bit as confused as he is. "Beg your pardon?"

"The way you snapped all those ladies out of the air. Like you was a bullfrog catching flies. Never seen anything like it."

There is something deeply discomforting about being praised like this, the dead and dying all around them, and Gilbert looks for the quickest way out of the conversation. "Dr. McCaw should get the credit. He sat up in that window, long past the point where most men would have jumped."

Mrs. Johnston nods appreciatively. "And he's paying the price, too."

Mr. Graham looks over at the pew. "I see that. You have my sympathy," he says to Mrs. Johnston, but he won't be deterred. "Hunt—I know what I saw. And what I saw was miraculous."

Gilbert needs the conversation to end. For Mrs. Johnston's sake, and for his own, too. "Thank you, Mr. Graham," he says and watches the innkeeper make for the door.

When he is gone, Gilbert tries to apologize to Mrs. Johnston for taking up so much of the man's attention. If he has learned anything in his life, it is that no good can come from showing up a white man, and certainly not a white man as well-connected as Dr. McCaw. "I don't know what he was going on about. Any man would have done the same thing."

She tilts her head a little. "I'm not so sure about that."

Cecily *is one block away from* the theater green and then she is two, but it's when she can no longer hear the lick of the flames or the shouts of the crowd that she begins to feel truly afraid.

The back roads of Court End are quieter than she expected them to be, and it is the quiet that makes her uncomfortable. She jumps every time she hears a door slam or a dog bark. The creak of a dray, drawn by a pair of horses, sends her diving for the tree line, but she is not so quick when a man in a dress coat bolts past her on foot. All she can do then is hold her breath and hope his business is not with her.

Already she is second-guessing her decision to run. If she is caught, she will be dragged back to the Price place in chains. When Master Price discovers that she intended to fake her own death, he'll take her straight to the whipping post that sits in the center of the yard. He has made use of it only a handful of times in Cecily's recollection, but each left an indelible impression on her.

What Cecily hates the most about the whippings is the way Master Price calls everyone up from the quarters and makes them watch. She imagines her parents, Moses, and even her little sisters being forced to stand by as he fillets the flesh on her back, and before she realizes it, she has started to heave.

If the whipping were the worst of it, that'd be one thing. But Cecily's got Elliott to worry about, too. He looked half-crazed as he circled the theater, screaming her name, and she knows he'll be waiting to exact his own special kind of revenge once the dust has settled.

The worst punishment of all—far worse than whatever Master Price and Elliott can mete out—will be seeing the looks on her parents' faces when they learn that Cecily let them believe she was dead. Her mother knows how miserable Elliott has made her and for how long, so maybe— just maybe—she'll understand. But her father, Cecil, who has been deliberately shielded from Elliott's misconduct, will be doubly hurt when he realizes the what and why of her disappearance.

Is it too late to reverse course? Surely not. All Cecily needs to do is return to the green and find Elliott and his father. When they ask her where she's been, she can make up some excuse about how she was looking for Maria at the homes of some of Maria's friends. They'll believe her. Why wouldn't they, when she's standing right there in front of them, begging to be taken home?

Home is such a tantalizing prospect, particularly now. Her family lives down in the quarters, in a one-room cabin set up on blocks. A fireplace stretches the length of one wall, and in the winter they've got to keep the fire going all night to combat the cold that seeps in through the floor. The room is sparsely furnished; there's a small table and a couple of straight-backed chairs, a stool, a cradle, and a bed that her papa made for her mama when Master Price allowed him the use of some scrap lumber and a cord of rope. All the children sleep on a pallet on the floor—a knot of arms and legs that Cecily complained about right up until the moment Mrs. Price offered her a bed in the sewing room down the hall from Maria's room.

That pallet is home. But home is also the cellar and the smokehouse and all the other dark places she cannot escape, even in her dreams. Home is the thicket of St. John's wort, where the bones of her baby rest in a shallow grave. And soon, home will be Elliott and Lavinia's house, on the other side of town, where she is unlikely to be allowed to see her parents or her siblings from one year to the next.

She touches the bump on her forehead. Even all these hours later, it still throbs.

No, she decides. She cannot turn herself over to Elliott and his father.

It is that hazy hour between people's first and second sleeps, when it wouldn't be unusual—on an ordinary night—to see a candle or even a lamp burning in a window. But tonight, the houses Cecily passes are lit up like stars. Smoke pours from the chimneys, and the houses' curtains have been thrown open so that their occupants can better watch the street.

When a man shouts at Cecily from his stoop, asking what news she has of the fire, she thinks she is done for, and it is all she can do to say "It's bad" as casually as she can. She worries he won't be satisfied with that answer, so she volunteers a little extra information—tells him how the roof caved in. She says it like she's just gossiping, like she could stand there all night shooting the breeze, but the trick is her feet never actually stop moving, and when she has passed the house, she picks up her pace.

At the rate she is going, Cecily will be at the edge of town in a matter of minutes. But she has no plan as to what she'll do then. She doesn't actually know where she's going, doesn't understand the first thing about how to get from here to anywhere. She has only ever been allowed to walk to church and the shops on E Street. Sometimes, Mrs. Price sends her to the mill with a message or a midday meal for Master Price, and then, of course, there are the nights Maria—desperate for a chaperone—drags her out to the theater or a dance. With such limited knowledge, Cecily can barely imagine what lies on the other side of Prior's Gardens, much less the other side of the Potomac.

The wind whips through Cecily's thin dress, and she hugs her shawl tight around her shoulders. All night she's been so scared that she has barely felt the cold. But now it gnaws at her face and hands and feet.

The fire presented Cecily with an opportunity, but now she needs a real plan. Immediately, she needs a place to hide, somewhere warm where she can rest. Eventually, she'll need food, and if she is to travel north at this time of year, warm clothes and a good pair of boots. But what she needs, more than anything, is a person she can trust. And there is—unfortunately—nobody Cecily trusts like her own mother.

❋ | SALLY | ❋

As *Sally hastens toward the theater* to see what became of Mr. Scott, she reminds herself that she doesn't owe him anything. He was barely civil when they met in the box before the show, and if he is dead, there is nothing for it.

She thinks that, if anything, it's the shoving him out the window that makes her feel at least partially responsible for his welfare, but as she crosses the green, she reminds herself that he would most certainly have died if she and Margaret had left him in that third-floor hallway.

Sally returns to the spot where she presumes Mr. Scott landed and spies his crumpled form right away. His head rests in the lap of a young girl, who wears a blank gaze. It is an indecent sort of posture—on both their parts—but it isn't until Sally sees that the girl's neck has snapped and that Mr. Scott's head is, in fact, resting on her posterior that she lets out a small yelp. She squeezes her eyes shut, then opens them again, refusing to look in the direction of the girl's frozen face. Instead, she focuses on Mr. Scott, whom she also assumes is dead. His eyes are closed, his skin unnaturally pale. Even when she gets close, she can't detect the rise and fall of his chest.

She speaks to him in as loud a voice as she can manage. "Mr. Scott? Can you hear me?"

Miraculously, he mumbles something, as if he is a drunk slowly coming to.

"Can you stand?" she asks, reaching for one of his arms. When she grabs it, in a bid to encourage him to get up, he screams in pain.

The building has started to fall in on itself. Sally looks up at the windows on the second and third floors, which were so recently crowded with people fighting for air. Now they are empty, engulfed in flames. "You can't stay here."

She tries Mr. Scott's other arm, and he allows her to pull him to his feet. "Do you think you can walk?" she asks, and he doesn't say no.

He is more substantial than she assumed him to be when they first met, and when he leans on her, she sways under his weight. She places a hand on his back, but immediately retracts it when she realizes his shirt is soaked with blood. Sally thinks about stopping, trying to find the source of the bleeding. But she wonders what good it will do. It isn't as if she can stitch him back together in the middle of the green. No, she decides, it is better to keep him upright and moving, so she replaces her hand and leads him, ever so slowly, in the direction of Mrs. Cowley's.

By the time they arrive at the house, Sally's shoulders ache, and she cannot feel her feet. She pushes open Mrs. Cowley's front door without knocking, and calls to her as she helps Mr. Scott up the steps and over the threshold. "Do you have room for one more?"

Mrs. Cowley meets her in the entryway with a lamp. "He's bleeding?"

"It's his back. I think."

Since Sally left, the parlor has filled with people. "We'll just put him here in the hall," says Mrs. Cowley as she kicks a thick braided rug out of the way. "Lay him down near the stairs, and he won't be in the way of the door."

Mr. Scott is all too willing to return to recumbency, but Sally forces him to remain seated so she and Mrs. Cowley can peel off his jacket and waistcoat and eventually his shirt. The watch piece, which Sally remembers him studying so intently in the box, falls from his pocket, clinks against the floor, and springs open. She stoops to pick it up and is surprised to find that it is not a watch at all but a *fausse montre*. Where a watch face should be, there is instead a miniature of an attractive woman with dark hair and mirthful eyes. Opposite the miniature, under a plate of glass, is a lock of hair, which has been artfully arranged to form the letters *FS*. The piece is exquisite, and not knowing what else to do with it, Sally tucks it into her own pocket for safekeeping.

Once Mr. Scott is disrobed, it is easier for Sally to assess his injuries. "It's his lower back," she tells Mrs. Cowley as she inspects the wound. "A big gash. Maybe five or six inches." All she can figure is that he was cut when she and Margaret heaved him up and over the windowsill.

Mrs. Cowley hands Sally the lamp, then goes to fetch a wet rag with which to clean the wound. Once she can clearly see the gash, she inserts her fingers beneath the folds of his skin and offers an official diagnosis. "Whatever it was that snagged him very narrowly missed his kidney."

Sally doesn't know what a kidney does, but she assumes it's important. "That's good?"

"Very," says Mrs. Cowley as she begins to prod Mr. Scott's arm and eventually his shoulder. "His shoulder's dislocated. Not broken. Which is another lucky set of circumstances."

She gives him a dose of laudanum, and the next thing Sally knows, the old woman has grabbed Mr. Scott's wrist and extended his arm straight out in front of him. Mr. Scott screams in pain, but Mrs. Cowley is quick, and by the time Mr. Scott has opened his bleary eyes to get a good look at his assailant, Mrs. Cowley has given the arm a mighty wrench back into the socket, where it belongs.

Sally is speechless. Most of the physicians she's encountered aren't half so skilled as the woman who sits before her. "Where did you learn to do that?" she asks as she watches Mrs. Cowley inspect the burns on Mr. Scott's face.

"My mother was a healer."

The way she says healer, and not medicine woman, makes Sally sit up and take notice. It is the same word Lettie and Judith and Andy use for Mariah, who mixes cures for the other slaves at Red Hill.

Mrs. Cowley returns Mr. Scott's arm to his chest, then calls for someone named Birdie, who turns out to be a dark-skinned girl of nine or ten years old. "Will you get us something to bind this with?" she asks her, then follows the request up with a "Please."

Birdie runs off, and when she returns, she is carrying a silk scarf that looks far too dear to ruin. "This is all I could find," she says.

"It's fine," says Mrs. Cowley, then directs Birdie and Sally to ease the scarf around Mr. Scott's torso. As they prepare to tie it off, Mrs. Cowley tells them to wait. She disappears into the back of the house, returning with a bottle of brandy. Carefully, she pours the amber liquid onto the wound. "This will hold him for a little while, until we can get him seen to."

After the scarf is tied tight, Sally's thoughts return to Margaret. "Do you know how to set a bone?" she asks Mrs. Cowley.

The old woman sighs. "You're talking about Mrs. Campbell's leg?"

Sally nods.

"You don't want me to set that bone."

"I don't?"

Mrs. Cowley shakes her head regretfully. "She needs that leg cut off at the knee."

"Pardon?" says Sally, certain she's heard her wrong.

"It's the way the bone splintered," explains Mrs. Cowley. "When that happens, the leg's much more likely to become infected."

"*How* much more likely?"

Mrs. Cowley squints. "In at least half the cases I see, the leg becomes gangrenous anyway."

Sally tries to comprehend what she is being told. "Would it not make sense to try to set the bone first? Then amputate if it gets infected?"

"By then it will be too late."

Sally puts her head between her legs. That Margaret might die of a broken bone, after being spared a fiery end, is too much to contemplate.

Mrs. Cowley pats her on the shoulder.

Sally looks up at her. "Would it be you? Who operated?"

She purses her lips, as though she doesn't like what she's got to say. "She needs a surgeon."

"Where do I find one?"

"I've got a neighbor out looking for one now."

"How long will that take?" she asks.

"On a night like tonight, could be hours."

"What do we do until then?" Sally's voice wobbles ever so slightly in her throat.

Mrs. Cowley takes a nip from the bottle of brandy and hands it to her, uncorked. "The very best we can."

3※| JACK |※€

The actors trickle into the Washington Tavern's back room over the course of a couple of hours. The room boasts a large stone fireplace and a smattering of tables and chairs, but by the time Jack arrives, at a little after one o'clock in the morning, most of the tables are full. He finds Lydia seated against the wall in the far corner of the room and sits down next to her.

"Have you heard anything more about Nancy?" he asks.

"No," she whispers. Her eyes are red and puffy. If she were his, he might put an arm around her, whisper some comfort into her ear, but all he can do is hug his knees to his chest.

The room is eerily quiet. Roy lies on the floor a few feet away from them, staring up at the ceiling, and Perry is perched on a window seat, slowly opening and closing his folding knife, so that the click of the blade is the only sound any of them hear.

When Anderson arrives, he finds a seat at a table in the center of the room and motions for Jack to join him. Jack doesn't want to give up his spot next to Lydia, but he is too afraid to argue.

"Is everyone here?" asks Placide, who is pacing back and forth in front of the fireplace.

"Robertson's not," says Perry.

"Where is he?"

Twaits clears his throat. "I think he's still helping."

"Helping?"

"Burke said he exited through the pit. Got stuck helping people out a first-floor window."

"Huh," says Placide, as if he's never considered the fact that Robertson— or any of them, really—might have an altruistic bent. "Do we have everyone else? With the exception of the Greens, of course."

People look around, and no one offers up any other names, so Placide asks Anderson to shut the door. "All right," he says when Anderson returns to his seat. "Now that we're all in a room together, I want someone to explain what happened."

Young is eager to contribute to the conversation, but all he can tell Placide is that the fire started in the flyspace, which is the same thing everyone else is saying.

"Anderson," says Placide. "Get out a piece of paper."

Anderson does as he is told.

"I want a list of everyone who was backstage when the fire started."

The words have barely rolled off his tongue when Perry's hand shoots up in the air. "I was."

"Me too," says Roy.

"I was, too," Clive says. "And Jack."

"Are you getting all this?" Placide asks Anderson.

"You don't need a list," Jack says impatiently. "I can just tell you what happened."

The room goes quiet.

Placide's lips are as thin as thread, but he says, "Go on."

Jack is so relieved to have everyone's attention that he rushes to get out all the details. The forest, the chandelier, Green's insistence that he raise the lamp. The whole story comes out in one long torrent. When he is through, he looks around the room, and everyone's eyes have gone wide with surprise.

"So," says Placide slowly, "what you're saying is that, if you hadn't forgotten to lower the chandelier, none of this would have happened?"

That's true, although Jack doesn't like the implication that this is all his fault. He hurries to clarify. "If Green had allowed the chandelier to stay where it was, once we realized my mistake, we'd also have been fine."

Placide does not look convinced.

"Jack's right to suggest that there were several contributing factors," says Perry, who has always been a decent sort. "I should have replaced that pulley as soon as Clive told me there was something wrong with it."

"I told you about it weeks ago," says Clive.

"I said I should have replaced it," says Perry. "What do you want me to do about it now?"

"Roy's the one who wouldn't leave the rope alone," Jack says.

"No one told me what was going on with it," says Roy, never taking his eyes off the ceiling.

"That's not true," says Perry. "I told you."

"You did not!" Roy says defensively.

"Enough," says Placide as he rubs at his temples.

Everyone waits for him to say something.

"Who here knew the pulley was busted?"

Around the room, hands go up in the air. Young's, Burke's, even Lydia's.

Placide counts aloud. "Thirteen, fourteen, fifteen, sixteen, seventeen—including me. That's more than half of us."

He allows them to ruminate on this information.

"There is going to be an inquest," Placide says solemnly. "And I don't think I need to remind you that there are few people held in lower esteem than actors."

The men and women in the room quietly acknowledge that this is true.

"If we go to the public with this story," says Placide, "I see no reason to believe we will not be immediately dispatched to the gallows."

The gallows are for criminals. Jack waits for an actor to argue this point with Placide, but when nobody does, he feels like he has no choice but to speak up. "We didn't intend for any of this to happen. Shouldn't we admit it was a horrible mistake and apologize?"

Placide laughs, then addresses the room. "Mr. Gibson wants to apologize."

"Come on, Jack," Anderson says in a quiet voice. "Everyone in the balconies is dead."

Placide and Anderson and the rest of the actors keep talking, but Jack can't hear a word. All he can hear is that phrase, *Everyone in the balconies is dead*, reverberating in his head like a gong. If he is, at least in part, responsible for the fire's outbreak, and everyone in the balconies is dead, then it stands to reason that he is responsible for the deaths of everyone in the balconies. Is that a hundred, maybe two hundred people? "That can't be," he says finally, but no one is listening to him.

"So, are we in agreement?" Placide says, recapturing Jack's attention. "That we don't breathe a word about the pulley to anyone outside this room?"

"I say we also keep this business about Green to ourselves," Anderson adds. "The poor man's going through enough."

Anderson is a giant bootlicker, and Jack wonders how he's failed to see it before now.

"Here, here," says Twaits, and several of the men beat on the tables to demonstrate their support of Placide's proposal.

Jack doesn't know what to make of any of them anymore. "What will you have us tell people? That I raised the lamp of my own volition?"

Placide cuts in. "Certainly not."

"So, what shall I say?"

"Something more plausible."

It takes Jack a second to realize what Placide is telling him. "You want me to lie? You want all of us to lie?"

"It's not lying, Jack," says Anderson, his voice as smooth as churned butter.

"He's perfectly right," Placide says. "In our business, we call it acting."

❧❦ | **GILBERT** | ❦❧

*G**ilbert is gone five minutes, maybe ten—**long enough to take one turn around the sanctuary and make sure Louisa isn't there. He wanders outside, where he yanks a picket from the fence that surrounds the church and snaps it in two, then returns to McCaw's pew to find Phyllis Johnston deep in conversation with a man he doesn't recognize.

"Oh, you're back," she says softly when he holds up the two pieces of fencing. "This is my husband, Richard Johnston." To her husband, she says, "This is Gilbert Hunt."

Mr. Johnston doesn't acknowledge Gilbert. All of his attention is on McCaw. "His back's a mess," he says to Mrs. Johnston. "What the hell happened to him?"

Mrs. Johnston seems tongue-tied, so Gilbert offers a short retelling of the evening's events. "He was sitting up in one of the second-floor windows, until the bitter end. Must have saved a dozen women."

If Mr. Johnston heard what Gilbert said, he doesn't let on. "James," he shouts into McCaw's ear. "Can you hear me?"

"It wasn't just him," says Mrs. Johnston. "Mr. Hunt risked life and limb, too. Trying to catch me and Mary Watkins and Catherine Kilbourne and the rest of the women James evacuated. He plucked us right out of the air, like we weighed next to nothing."

"Is that so?" says Mr. Johnston, who doesn't seem inclined to give his wife's claims much credence.

But Mrs. Johnston won't quit. "He's a hero."

Mr. Johnston eyes the pieces of wood in Gilbert's hands. "What are those?"

"Pieces of fencing. I thought we could use them to stabilize his leg," he says, and hands them over.

Mr. Johnston inspects the thin boards. "What am I supposed to tie them with?"

Gilbert knows better than to tell a man of his station what to do, but he allows his eyes to settle on Mr. Johnston's cravat, which is as fancy a one as he's seen. Must be at least five yards of linen holding that thing together.

"Fine," says Mr. Johnston loudly as he begins to pull at the fabric that swaddles his neck.

When the cravat is undone, Mrs. Johnston steps aside, and Gilbert helps her husband wrap McCaw's leg. The doctor moans anytime he is moved, but eventually the job is done.

"Do you need help getting him home?" Gilbert asks against his better judgment. He has no desire to see McCaw home, especially if it means spending another minute working alongside Mr. Johnston. But he doesn't know how to excuse himself without at least offering.

Mr. Johnston shakes his head. "I sent our man for a cart."

"I see," says Gilbert, relieved. "In that case, I think I'll take my leave."

Mr. Johnston doesn't seem to care whether he stays or goes, but Mrs. Johnston, who still clutches at the front of her thin dress, looks anxious. "You don't want to stay? Until the cart arrives?"

"I've got someone I'm trying to locate. Before the night gets too far gone."

He can tell Mrs. Johnston wants to be helpful. "Anyone I'd know?"

"Louisa Mayo?"

Mrs. Johnston bobs her head up and down like a parrot. "Yes, yes, of course. A dear girl. Don't tell me Louisa was in the theater."

"I think she was."

"Does her mother know?"

"Her mother's who alerted me to the situation."

Mrs. Johnston gives him a sad look that he isn't quite sure how to interpret.

He hasn't asked for her permission to go, but for some reason, he finds himself waiting to be released.

"Give her my regards."

He touches McCaw's shoulder, tries to say goodbye, but the doctor doesn't stir. It feels strange to leave him like this. The two men made an odd team, but they did more good together in a few minutes' time than Gilbert has otherwise done in his entire life.

"I'm down at Kemp's smithy, on Locust Alley, if you want to send word about his condition. I'd appreciate it."

She nods, and he turns to go, picking his way back up the aisle and trying hard not to look into the frozen faces of the dead. When he is nearly at the door of the church, he hears Mrs. Johnston call his name, and he turns to find her hurrying toward him.

"Yes, ma'am?"

"Mr. Hunt, thank you. Truly. I won't soon forget this. And neither will the rest of those women and their families, if I have anything to do with it."

❧| CECILY |❧

ecily hides in the trees behind her parents' cabin, listening to the
sounds of the quarters.

Six cabins sit up alongside the woods in two neat rows, doors facing
each other to form a short street. The arrangement is nice on summer evenings, when people stay up late, trading stories, but if there's one thing it is
not good for, it's slipping home undetected.

Cecily can tell that everyone in the quarters is all stirred up. Constance
and Millie, who sleep in the main house, must have passed what facts they
know about the fire along to Woody, who works in the stables, because he's
down in the street, telling everybody about how Maria and Cecily haven't
come home and Master Price and Elliott are off looking for them. Among
the people who have gathered, Cecily can make out the voices of Constance's husband, Gregory, and Millie's daughter, Justice, and even Rosie,
who usually sleeps in the kitchen house but has come down to the quarters
to see who knows what. What Cecily can't hear is her parents' voices, and
she wonders if they've already been called up to the house.

She presses her ear to the slats of her family's cabin and listens for either
of them, but all she hears is her brother, Moses, telling one of their sisters to
quiet down and go to sleep.

Cecily wishes she could be in multiple places at once, wants to be inside that cabin, tucking the girls into bed, and also up at the main house,
where the Prices have no doubt given Della and Cecil the bad news. What
she wouldn't give to be able to whisper the truth in their ears, to save them
from believing—even for an instant—that what the Prices say is true.

But it has to happen this way. She has to wait until her parents return
to the cabin, until the children are asleep and the neighbors have taken
themselves to bed. Then and only then can she reveal herself.

Nobody has much in the way of information, but the gathering on the
street grows, until eventually just about everyone Cecily knows is standing

there, stamping their feet and blowing into their hands and trying to piece together what happened. Gregory says he heard the fire started backstage. Rosie says she heard from Old Man Sully, over at the Rutherford place, that most of the folks in the gallery made it out all right. "I don't need to remind any of y'all," says Constance, "that Maria's the type to send a servant into a burning building for so much as a lost button." This gets so many *mmmmhmmm*s from the crowd that Cecily feels a twinge of sympathy for Maria. She's bad, but she's not *that* bad.

It is strange to hear these people Cecily has known her whole life try to make sense of her death. *Such a pretty girl*, someone says. Then *Cecily had it real hard*, as if being burned up might be preferable to what they all know she's been putting up with. No one says anything unkind, but something about all the theorizing and prophesizing leaves Cecily with a lump in her throat. Like she is already gone.

Cecily sits in the trees for a long time, waiting for the talk to peter out and for everyone to get back inside their cabins and put themselves to bed. Eventually, Rosie returns to the kitchen house, promising to sleep with one ear open and to report back if she hears anything. The rest of the women shoo their men inside, and Cecily listens to the groan of their rope beds as they sink into troubled sleep.

❋ | SALLY | ❋

"*Anyone with burns needs to begin* treatment at once," says Mrs. Cowley to Sally and a few other women who have assembled in the parlor.

She hands out squares of linen, which she's instructed Birdie to cut from an old tablecloth. Behind her sits a stack of mismatched bowls. She holds up a large lancet. "If the skin has begun to blister, puncture it first." To illustrate, she pierces a large blister on a woman's face, and Sally nearly faints.

"Use the linen cloth to press the water out. Like so. Then pour the vinegar over the burn. If you can soak the wound in a bowl of vinegar, that's even better."

Sally eyes the jug of vinegar Birdie clutches in her arms. "What do we do when we run out?"

A woman whose daughter has suffered a bad burn on her backside says, "My mother always swore by spirits of turpentine for burns."

Mrs. Cowley shakes her head. "Turpentine won't do anything for the inflammation," she says. "I've got a little more vinegar in the kitchen. Then we'll—"

"We need help!" a man yells from upstairs.

Mrs. Cowley rolls her eyes, then says under her breath, "That family has been nothing but a problem since the moment they arrived."

"I'll see what's the matter," Sally offers, then sticks her head out into the hallway. "Sir?"

On the landing is the younger of the two men who came looking for Maria Price. By some blessed miracle, they found the girl—alive—in an upstairs bedroom, and since then they've been up and down the stairs at least a half-dozen times, asking for one thing or another.

"What's the matter?" she asks the man, from the bottom of the stairs.

"She's vomiting," he says frantically.

Sally grabs a spittoon and follows him upstairs, where Maria rests in one of two small beds in the back bedroom. The other bed is occupied by a young girl with such severe burns, she is unrecognizable. Mrs. Cowley says she is unlikely to live until morning.

The room smells of vomit and charred flesh, and Sally is desperate to open a window, but she can't bring herself to do it, not with how cold it is outside.

Instead, she places the spittoon under Maria's chin and whips off her bedsheet, which is covered in sick. "Take this downstairs to the kitchen," she says to the man, who seems startled to have been ordered to do anything, "and fetch me some water and rags."

Once he is gone, she examines Maria. Her skin is coated in a fine layer of white dust, and Sally wonders what the man, whom she presumes is her husband, has been doing upstairs this whole time, if not cleaning her up.

"I need to lie down," says the girl. Her request echoes off the bottom of the spittoon.

"You don't feel too sick for that?"

"It's the sitting that's making me sick," she whispers, so Sally quickly removes the spittoon and helps lower her head back onto the pillow behind her.

"Is that better?"

"Much."

The girl has a nasty goose egg that sits high on her forehead, and Sally leans in to get a better look. Already, it has turned the color of nutmeg.

When the man returns with the supplies, Sally dips a rag into the bowl of water and begins to wipe down Maria's face, revealing a pronounced cleft chin. "Your wife needs to be bathed."

"He's my blother," Maria says, and Sally tries to recall whether her words had sounded slurred before.

"She's trying to say I'm her brother," says the man.

"I see," says Sally, although this new information does nothing to excuse the fact that the girl is still covered in soot.

"I'm Elliott Price, but please call me Elliott."

She gives him her name but does not offer to let him call her Sally.

While she works, she appraises him. He does, in fact, bear a strong resemblance to his sister. Both of them are tall, with square jaws and long necks, dark hair and nut-brown eyes, but on Elliott those features look regal, whereas on Maria they look a little horsey. He has to be at least five years younger than Sally, but if she had met him at a ball when she was eighteen, he'd have turned her head. Now he just makes her feel old.

She rewets the rag and asks, "The other man who was with you? Is he your father?"

"Yes, he went home to fetch my mother. And a carriage. But I'm not sure how we're going to get Maria home if she can't so much as sit up without being sick."

"Mrs. Cowley says that with blows to the head the senses can become disordered." She holds three fingers in front of Maria's face. "How many fingers am I holding up, dear?"

"Four."

"She's also complaining of a ringing in her ears," he volunteers.

"I wouldn't move her," says Sally. "Not now."

This is clearly not the advice Elliott wants to hear. "She needs a doctor."

"We've summoned one," says Sally. "But in the meantime, you have Mrs. Cowley, who's very knowledgeable."

"Right," says Elliott, who seems doubtful of her credentials but also smart enough to realize that he has perhaps pushed too far. "Thank you."

Sally washes Maria's face, neck, and shoulders. Like Margaret, her dress has already been cut from her body, so when Sally unties her shift to wash around her collar, Elliott turns away from the bed and walks over to the window.

"Cecily?" says Maria, her words now as clear as a bell.

Sally looks at Elliott, who has done an about-face. "Who's Cecily?"

"Nobody," he says.

Maria is clearly agitated. "Where's Cecily?" She is trying to sit up again.

Sally squeezes the girl's hand, trying to soothe her. "It's just us, Maria. You've been through a terrible ordeal."

"Cecily is one of our Negroes," explains Elliott.

Sally narrows her eyes at him. "Not *nobody*, then?"

Elliott shakes his head slowly. Almost apologetically. "She was Maria's chaperone. Last night."

"I see," says Sally. "So, she was at the theater?"

His face darkens. "Up in the gallery."

"And you don't think she made it out?"

"I . . ."

Sally waits.

"I suspect not," he says, and there's something about the way his voice shakes, getting the words out, that makes her feel a stab of sympathy for him.

Maria calls for the girl again, and this time Sally knows just what to say. "Cecily's not here right now, Maria. What would you have me tell her?"

Maria balls up her fists so tight, Sally can see the whites of her knuckles even in the lamplight. "Tell her to come back."

❧ | JACK | ❧

W hat we need," says Placide, who is once again pacing back and forth in front of the fireplace in the tavern's back room, "is another explanation for how the fire might have started."

"Who has ideas?" says Anderson, and a few men raise their hands.

Caulfield goes first. "What if one of the stoves in the front of the house caught fire?"

"Like it tipped over?"

"Or maybe just sparked."

Placide thinks for a moment. "That's an option."

"Could be one of the sconces, too," says Twaits. "All it'd take is some woman standing too close to the wall. Her hair catches, and poof."

Placide claps his hands together, like they're getting somewhere, but Anderson scowls and says, "Those excuses won't work."

"Why not?" asks Placide.

"Everyone knows the fire started in the back of the house. Behind the drop curtain."

The room gets louder, all of the men talking over each other, and it's like Jack doesn't recognize any of them. He knows they're actors and that they lie for a living, but this is real life. Surely, it'd be better to play dumb than to go out with information that's blatantly false?

Jack looks for Lydia, who is still sitting against the wall, where he left her. When her eyes meet his, she whispers, "I'm sorry."

"Anderson's right," says West in a loud-enough voice to silence the room. "When Robertson made the announcement, no one in the front of the house could even tell there was something wrong."

Jack is surprised West is willing to contribute to this charade. Rising stars like Anderson are always looking to get in the managers' good graces because they want the choicest parts and to one day be made managers themselves. But it's obvious West, who's a terrible actor, gave up on getting into Placide's and Green's good graces a long time ago.

"Well," says Placide, "in that case, let's think through what might have happened backstage."

"I have an idea," says Young. "Though it might be a stretch."

Placide stops pacing.

Young bites his lip, as if he's trying to decide whether to keep the idea in his head where it belongs.

"Go on," says Placide.

"Well, Richmond's always having slave revolts."

Jack does not like where this is going.

"Richmond had *one* slave revolt," says West. "More than a decade ago."

Young doesn't back down. "It was a fairly large one, though, wasn't it?"

Placide glances at West. "Let him finish."

"Suppose there were a bunch of Negroes running around out back with torches. If they set the building's exterior on fire, it'd be the people backstage who caught wind of it, long before the audience did."

"You're absolutely right," says Placide. "That's brilliant."

Like most boys in Richmond, Jack grew up on stories of Gabriel Prosser's rebellion. Supposedly, Prosser rallied a thousand men to rise up against the city's white elite, but the plan was found out, and within weeks, Prosser and at least two dozen of his friends and allies had been killed.

Jack hesitates to say anything, but none of the actors know the city the way he does. "The last time someone said the words 'slave revolt' in Richmond, a lot of innocent men died."

"*Innocent* men?" asks Placide with a hint of amusement on his face.

"Yes," says Jack as confidently as he can, but his voice cracks in the middle of that one tiny word.

"Like who?"

Jack wishes he'd paid more attention to the details of the case. All he knows, for sure, is that his father believed the trials were a big sham. "I don't know names, but ..."

His voice trails off, and it's clear he's lost Placide's attention.

"Mr. Young," says Placide, "I think you're onto something. What we need to do is get out ahead of the story. Plant the seed that we were attacked."

"By a band of rebellious slaves?" says Perry, like he can't quite believe where this is going.

"Exactly," says Placide. "We'll write to the paper. Give our account of events. Before people have a chance to come to their own conclusions."

Jack looks at Anderson, who is nodding along agreeably. Sometimes he reminds Jack of an oversized lapdog.

"It's good thinking," says Twaits.

Even West doesn't argue, and when Jack looks over at Lydia, she won't meet his eyes.

Jack reminds himself that Placide and the others aren't keeping him here against his will. They can't force him to go along with this. He'll leave. Go to the authorities, or maybe to Girardin. What a relief it would be to lay all of this at his professor's feet, to admit his mistakes and ask what he should do next.

At the academy, Girardin used to make Jack and his friends read the Greek philosophers. Plato, Socrates, Aristotle. Jack's Greek was never very good, but he remembers a bit of Aristotle, who was so concerned with the virtue of man. *Virtue means doing the right thing, in relation to the right person, at the right time, to the right extent, in the right manner, and for the right purpose.*

He thinks about that now as he looks around the room, taking in the faces of the men and women he's spent the last two and a half months getting to know. They are gifted actors who are transforming the American stage, and who might—if given enough time—have come to recognize his own talents, but they are not virtuous.

"Do any of you know anyone who volunteers with the slave patrol?" Placide asks in a booming voice that brings Jack back to his senses. "If we get the patrollers riled up, that might be all it takes."

"Wait," says Jack. "We're going to go to the slave patrol?"

"Do you have a problem with that?"

Jack's uncle volunteers with the patrol, and Jack saw enough—when he was living with him—to know that the group does more harm than good. "They're a bunch of ruffians."

"Yes, but they're not going after us," Placide reminds him.

Jack doesn't think too hard about what he's doing; he just pushes his chair back from the table and leaps to his feet. "I can't go along with this," he says, in a voice that manages to come out too high and too loud, all at the same time.

Everyone's surprised, and he uses that to his advantage, darting across the room and out the door that leads to the taproom before any of the actors can give chase. Behind him, he hears Placide yelling for Anderson to bring him back, but by then Jack has exploded out of the tavern and into the dark night.

❈ | **GILBERT** | ❈

Maddie *is alone in the kitchen* house, kneading dough, when Gilbert lets himself in.

"Is it a little early for all of that?" he says as he closes the door behind him.

Maddie presses her knuckles deep down into the dough. "Friday still bread day, last time I checked."

"I was hoping you'd all be in your beds. That I'd wake you with my knocking, and you'd tell me Louisa showed up hours ago."

Maddie frowns and pounds the dough with her fists. Gilbert can hear her knuckles crack. "I was hoping you'd tell me you just finished delivering her into her mama's arms."

"I couldn't find her." He can scarcely get the words out. Certainly can't look Maddie in the eye doing it. A fine layer of flour covers the table where Maddie works, and Gilbert runs a finger through it, tracing the beginnings of his own name. "It was a mess over there. People being carted off in all directions."

"She wasn't nowhere?"

Gilbert shakes his head no. "How's Sara holding up?"

"You know how she loves that child. But what choice she got other than to put her feelings aside?"

"She over at the main house?"

"And will be till kingdom come," says Maddie as she puts the ball of dough in a bowl and covers it with a damp cloth.

"Missus Elizabeth in bad shape?"

"The worst I've ever seen her."

"Worse than after Mr. Mayo died?"

"And the little boy, too," she says as she measures water and flour into a clean bowl, then reaches for the salt.

Gilbert didn't know Sara when Louisa's father and brother died, but she had told him how, after those two deaths, which came one right after the other, Elizabeth changed. She stopped going places, stopped seeing people, stopped even coming downstairs for meals. Most important of all, she stopped mothering Louisa, and it fell to Sara to love the poor child twice as hard.

Half the time, when Gilbert came 'round to visit Sara in the evenings, Louisa was still in the kitchen house, practicing her French or copying words out of her blue-backed speller. He got in the habit of greeting her with a *Bonjour* and a *Parlez-vous français?*, which she had told him on one of his early visits meant *Do you speak French?* While Maddie fixed him a plate, Louisa would ask after the smithy, want to know if what Sara said about him pulling out people's teeth with a special key was true. "Only when business is slow," he'd say with a sly smile that she didn't know quite what to do with.

Louisa was a good egg, but Gilbert was careful around her. He knew she didn't like sharing Sara with him; her mouth twisted up like a corkscrew if his hand so much as fell on the curve of Sara's waist. Once, when he'd pulled Sara onto his lap, drunk with wanting her, he'd looked up to see Louisa staring at him like he had horns growing out of the top of his head. Sara was their prized possession, and Gilbert realized quickly that if he didn't want to jeopardize his visits, he was going to need to make real nice with Sara's four-and-a-half-foot-tall keeper.

He made it his mission to win Louisa over, just as surely as he'd won over Sara. He started bringing her little gifts—a rosette he made out of scraps of leather, a flute he fashioned out of a piece of river cane. Once, when Sara scolded Louisa for always losing her hair ribbons, he showed up with a pretty hook he'd hammered out of a scrap of copper, a hole stamped in the top. "I figure it'd be just the right size for hanging ribbons," he said with a wink.

Before too long Louisa was asking Gilbert his opinion on the length of her skirts and telling him long, winding stories about her school friends. He tried to follow along, but all those white girl names sounded the same, and they were each as mean as the next. "Which one's Maria again?" he'd ask for the third time, and Sara would thump him in the back of the head, which made Louisa laugh.

When Gilbert knew he had Louisa on his side was the day he asked her about a book she was reading, and instead of just reciting the title and getting back to it, she slid the book across the table and said, "You want to give it a try?" He had looked at Sara then, trying to ask her what he was supposed to do with an offer like that, but all she did was shrug her shoulders.

Louisa taught Gilbert how to read in fits and starts over the winter of 1808. She was thirteen years old, which must have made him about twenty-eight, give or take. At first, she used whatever she had on hand, a copy of *Tristram Shandy* or Benjamin Franklin's autobiography, and just pointed out the small words that were easy for him to wrap his tongue around. But eventually she went looking for her old primer and started at the beginning.

A   In *Adam's* Fall
     We Sinned all.
B   Thy Life to Mend
     This *Book* Attend.
C   *Christ* crucify'd
     For sinners dy'd.
D   A *Dog* will bite
     A Thief at night.
E   An *Eagle's* flight
     Is out of sight.
F   The Idle *Fool*
     Is whipt at School.

Gilbert was no fool. He was a good student, always aware that each lesson with Louisa could be his last. There wasn't a law against Black folks reading, and plenty of people could, but ever since Gabriel Prosser had been tried and hanged, learning like the kind Louisa was offering Gilbert had gotten harder to come by. Word was Gabriel Prosser could read and write; that he'd managed to plot a slave rebellion—without hardly ever leaving Brookfield—was a testament to the power of the pen.

Once Gilbert knew his letters, the whole world cracked open. There were words everywhere he looked. Advertisements for spices and ready-made pants and runaway slaves practically shouted at him as he walked down E Street; old playbills stared up at him from mud puddles; even his own pass, which Pete Goode wrote out for him annually and which Gilbert took care to keep in a leather sleeve, transformed before his eyes. *Let my servant man, Gilbert Hunt, pass and repass without hinderance or molestation, until the thirty-first day of December.* Gilbert realized, turning the piece of paper over in his hand, that there was nothing magic about the words that kept him out of the clutches of the slave patrol. They were just words like any other, but what the white man counted on was men like Gilbert not knowing any of them.

In church, Pastor Courtney was in the habit of printing his most hair-raising sermons in these fancy little pamphlets that the white folks in the congregation took on their way out the door. Gilbert had never dared take one, but now he kept a stack of them under his mattress, and he marveled at the fact that he could relive the good man's fire and fury any time he felt like it. Once he got good at reading big, long sentences, he removed eleven shillings from his pouch and bought himself a Bible at Thomas Ritchie's bookshop. He felt guilty spending money that had been earmarked for the purchase of his own freedom, but he told himself that being able to talk to God was also going to help him get where he was going. When he opened that Bible to the back page and wrote his name in it, and then later added Sara's alongside it, he didn't know if he'd ever felt more proud.

Gilbert tries to think of something to say that will ease the pinched expression on Maddie's face. "Maybe Missus Elizabeth stronger than we think. Now that she's married to the general."

Maddie arches her eyebrows real high and gives him a long *mmmm-hmmm*.

"Where he at?" Gilbert asks Maddie.

"Home now. But Sylvie had to go dig him out of some grog shop."

"I was surprised I didn't see him at the green. Figured Missus Elizabeth would have sent for him first thing."

"He was so drunk, he'd have been liable to fall in the fire hisself."

Gilbert just shakes his head. There is no accounting for white folks.

"Go on home," she says in as firm a voice as she can muster. "Sara ain't coming back down here tonight."

"I want to help her."

"You get thrown in the birdcage, and it won't help her one bit."

Gilbert looks out the window, squinting at the dark sky. "There's still a little more night. I'll wait."

Maddie reaches across the table and pats his hand. "You're a good man, Gilbert Hunt. The Lord's gonna reward you in the next life, if not in this one."

❧ | CECILY | ❧

The night is half done before Cecily hears the soft fall of her mother's footsteps approaching the cabin. Moses is still awake, and the moment Della is inside, Cecily can hear him pepper her with questions. "Where's Cecily?" and then, "Papa ain't with you?"

Della hushes him, then says, "Missus Price gave him permission to go looking for her. They sure to be back soon."

Cecily can't bear to think of her papa arriving at the theater green and taking his first look at that building. When he sees the fire and how big it burns, he will know there is no hope. Will he shout her name anyway? Race around the building, the way Elliott did? She can't picture it. Neither of her parents are the type to perform their grief for a bunch of strangers.

Cecily hears Moses ask about Maria, but Della is done answering questions. Through the cabin's thin walls, she hears her mother tell him to sleep, then she sits down heavy on the bed.

Moses can't stop himself. "They ain't dead, are they?"

Cecily stands with her ear pressed against the cabin wall, straining to hear her mother's reply. But Della has begun to cry, and her words come out garbled.

All Cecily wants to do is hurry around the side of the cabin and up the steps, throw open the door, and shout: *Here I am! I'm fine! See?* But she tells herself to be patient. Della won't sleep tonight, but Moses likely will, and Cecily wants him in dreamland before she tiptoes over to her mother's side of the bed. Her brother is thirteen this year, and he considers himself a man, but Cecily can't see burdening him with a secret this big. It will be better for him to think her dead than for him to be interrogated by Elliott or Master Price and for either of them to find his answers wanting.

When enough time has passed and Cecily is sure Moses is asleep, she tiptoes around to the side of the house. For a while, she sits watching the doors of the other cabins, until she is convinced everything really does look shut up tight. Then she takes a deep breath, climbs the steps to her parents' cabin, pushes the door open, and slips inside.

"Cecily?" her mother says in a sharp whisper. "Is that you?"

"Shhh," Cecily says. She moves like lightning to the side of her mother's bed and touches her finger to her lips.

"Mama, listen to me," she says in the quietest voice she can manage. "I gotta talk to you, but we can't do it here. Nobody can know I'm back."

Della pulls her head back to get a better look at Cecily. Like she is trying to figure out if it's her daughter's spirit visiting her house or the real thing. "What you mean?" she says slowly.

"Quiet," Cecily whispers, then moves toward the door. "Come with me."

When Cecily glances over at the pallet in front of the fire, she is relieved to find Moses asleep, the little girls curled up around him like cats.

A jacket hangs on a peg by the door. It used to belong to Master Price, and when it became too threadbare, he gave it to Cecily's papa, who eventually passed it on to Moses. Cecily doesn't even ask if she can take it. She is so desperate to get warm she discards her shawl and wraps herself in the soft, quilted flannel, which smells like her mother's cooking fire and the rosemary and thyme she hangs from the beams to dry.

Cecily cracks the door open, and when she is sure the path is clear, she leads her mother down the steps, around the side of the cabin, and through the woods. They walk in silence for several minutes, guided by the light of the moon, until they get close enough to the river that Cecily can be sure anything they say will be drowned out by the sound of the water rushing by.

"The fire's bad, Mama," Cecily starts. "The place was packed, and the flames spread quick."

"I'm just glad you're—"

"Don't get glad yet. Hold on." Cecily takes a deep breath. "Lots of folks is dead. A hundred. Maybe more. Some of the people dead from jumping out the windows, trying to get away from the flames. Other people burned up inside, no hope of getting anywhere."

Della clasps her hand to her mouth and closes her eyes, and Cecily is certain she is praying. Praying for all those souls, yes. But also thanking God that her daughter's body and soul are still one and the same thing.

"Mama?"

Della opens her eyes. The whites of them shine in the dark.

"What I got is a unique opportunity."

Her mother starts shaking her head.

"Hear me out," says Cecily. "The building will be gone by morning, all them bodies with it. No one's going to be able to identify any of them."

"What are you saying, child?"

Cecily takes a deep breath. "I'm saying if everyone thinks I'm dead, I might finally be able to be free."

❊❘ SALLY ❘❊

I n the middle of the night, there is a knock on Mrs. Cowley's front door,
and Sally opens it to find an older gentleman standing on the front
porch. He has a wiry frame, his coat hangs on a pair of stooped shoulders,
and while he may have been clean-shaven a day ago, the whiskers on his face
now bear a long shadow.

"Mrs. Cowley sent for a surgeon," he says by way of an introduction,
and Sally nearly screams in delight. "My name is Dr. Foushee."

"Please, come in," she says and ushers him inside. "A neighbor was out
twice, trying to track someone down, and he came back empty-handed
both times."

"It's hard to find anybody," he acknowledges. "I know of at least two
physicians who were injured in the fire or are missing."

"I'm so sorry to hear that," says Sally as she shuts the door behind him.

"Is Mrs. Cowley in?"

"She just stepped out." What Sally doesn't tell him, because it's not her
place, is that there's been a steady stream of colored families at Mrs. Cowley's back door, and that when a woman, whose husband worked as an attendant at the theater, showed up screaming about burns up and down his
body, Mrs. Cowley had gathered a few supplies and taken off running.

The doctor takes one look at Mr. Scott, who lies at the foot of the stairs.
Immediately, he hands Sally his leather valise and begins to unbutton his
coat. "Is this the patient?"

"No," says Sally, but Mr. Scott's condition has so thoroughly captured
the doctor's attention that there is no pulling him away.

"This is the new delegate from Fauquier County," he says as he inspects
Mr. Scott's burns.

Why his office should matter at a time like this, Sally has no idea.
"And?"

"I met him at a party the other night," says the doctor, who wastes no

time unwrapping Mr. Scott's makeshift dressing. "Looks just like his father."

Sally wonders if his father might be someone she could call on for help.
"Is he alive?" she asks.

"The patient?"

"No," says Sally. "His father."

Dr. Foushee shakes his head. "James Scott has been dead for years. He
fought in the Revolution and died shortly thereafter."

Sally wonders if her father knew him. It's likely he did. She turns the
fausse montre over in her pocket. "Do you know if Mr. Scott is married?"

"I'm sorry. I don't," he says as he inspects the wound.

She watches the doctor carefully, curious if he'll conduct an examination half as thorough as Mrs. Cowley's. He doesn't seem inclined.

"Mrs. Cowley says he's lucky his kidneys are intact," says Sally, but she
can't get the doctor to commit to much.

"Is that so?"

"She seems very knowledgeable."

"I find no fault with her cures," Dr. Foushee says, "but she must be careful not to overstep."

"How so?"

"I think you know what I mean."

"I don't," she says indignantly, although she wonders if it has anything
to do with what those men who carried Margaret to Mrs. Cowley's were
saying about her not being Native.

Dr. Foushee's knees crack when he goes to stand. "Mrs. Cowley can
stitch this up. I'll leave her some catgut if she doesn't have any."

Sally acknowledges that they could probably use some.

"And as for the burns, keep bathing them in vinegar. In another few
hours, make a poultice of bread and milk, with a little sweet oil or butter
to hold the mixture together. Lay the poultice on the sore for maybe six or
eight hours, and then at that point, switch to chalk."

"Chalk?"

"If you don't have any, the apothecary should. It'll help dry everything
out."

She leads him into the parlor, where people are sprawled from one side of the room to the other. He begins to count the victims. "Four, five, six, seven. Is there anyone else?"

"Three more upstairs," she says, but she is already guiding him to the spot where Margaret lies beneath the parlor window. "This is the woman Mrs. Cowley wanted you to see after. She's my sister-in-law."

As soon as his eyes come to rest on Margaret's face, which is unduly pale and glistening with sweat, he sucks his teeth. "Not Mrs. Campbell."

"You know her?"

"A bit. I know her husband quite well," he says as he kneels down beside her. "Did he make it out?"

It's a simple question, but Sally doesn't know how to answer it. One minute she was trying to convince Archie to turn back and look for Margaret, the next the stairs collapsed. She has a hard time believing he made it out, but explaining the circumstances of his probable demise feels a little like speaking ill of the dead, so finally she just says, "I don't know."

Dr. Foushee kneels down beside Margaret, and Sally crouches next to him. "Margaret," she says in a loud voice, "Dr. Foushee is here, and he's going to examine you." She gets no response.

When the doctor lifts the quilt that covers Margaret's legs, he scowls.

"She jumped out of a third-floor window," Sally offers.

He inspects the raw bone.

"It's bad?" asks Sally, already knowing the answer is yes.

"It's a severe break."

"Mrs. Cowley says the leg needs to be amputated? To reduce the risk of infection."

"That's an option."

Sally cocks her head to get a better look at him. "Are you suggesting there's another one?"

"We can always set the bone and hope for the best."

"Why would we do that?" Sally demands. "If the risk of infection is much higher?"

"Well," says Dr. Foushee slowly. "She is a mother."

"What does that have to do with anything?"

"Mr. Campbell will have to consider how she is to look after so many young children if she becomes a cripple."

Sally is outraged that Margaret's ability to chase after a toddler should be the measure of her life's worth. "How is she to look after all those children if she's dead?"

Dr. Foushee places a hand on Sally's shoulder. "These are exceedingly trying times."

She cannot bear his condescension, and when he stands to go, she says as assertively as she knows how, "I believe I speak for her when I say I want the leg amputated."

He nods, but it's like he's not hearing her. Finally, he says, "We'll see."

"What do you mean? Aren't you here, right now, to perform the surgery?"

He shakes his head no. "I need a few hours to fetch more supplies. And an extra man."

"Is that not too long to wait?"

"It's all I can do," he says.

"What do we do until then?"

"I'd start by trying to locate Mr. Campbell."

"Why?"

"Well, he is her husband," says Dr. Foushee. "And, assuming he is alive, it is up to him—and not you—to decide if she keeps the leg."

❧ | JACK | ❧

J
ack is almost to Professor Girardin's when Anderson overtakes him.
He's been closing in on him for the last several blocks, shouting at Jack
to slow down, but it's not until they are in front of the house that Anderson
finally grabs him by the collar and pulls him to the ground.

Jack lies there in the freezing muck, staring up at the still-orange sky,
and wondering if he's about to be murdered. That's usually how it goes in
the theater. Pick a play. Whenever one of the characters knows too much,
he gets expended.

Anderson looms over him. "Christ, Gibson," he says, trying to catch
his breath.

Jack squeezes his eyes shut tight. "Please don't kill me," he whispers.

"Who said anything about killing you?" says Anderson as he grabs Jack
by the hand. "Get up."

When they have both recovered themselves, Anderson says, "Placide
would greatly prefer you not report us, but he's not really the murderous
sort."

A feeling of utter relief washes over Jack. "He's not?"

Anderson laughs. "No."

For a few moments, they both stand there, staring at Professor Girardin's house. The windows are aglow.

"Is this where you were headed?" Anderson asks.

Jack nods. "It's Girardin's place. I stayed with him for a while, before I
got the job with Placide and Green."

At their Thursday rehearsal, Girardin had told Jack that he didn't plan
to stay for the pantomime, and it reassures Jack to know that his friend was
home long before the fire broke out.

"Are you going inside?" Anderson asks.

"I was planning to."

"To tell him what happened?"

"I've got to tell somebody," says Jack.

"You think he won't tell you to cover your tracks? To do what Placide says?"

"He's a good man."

"He's a realist."

"You barely know him."

"I know he could have stayed in France and died alongside all his royalist friends. But he snuck out of the country, first chance he got."

Jack has never thought of Girardin's escape in that light. To him, it always seemed heroic. Giving up home and country for his beliefs. "That's not true," he says with a firm shake of his head.

"Just walk with me a minute," says Anderson. "You don't have to go back to the tavern, but I'm going to freeze to death out here without a coat."

Jack hesitates.

"Oh, come on. You're not making a deal with the devil. You're just walking."

Jack glances back at Girardin's house, then allows himself to be led away.

"Do you know why the Globe burned?" Anderson asks when they are on H Street and closing in on the theater green.

"You mean in London?"

"Right."

Jack lets out an exhausted sigh. "I have no idea."

"I'll tell you. The actors shot a bloody cannon into a thatched roof in the middle of a performance of *Henry VIII*."

Jack doesn't know what he was expecting Anderson to say, but it wasn't that.

"Ask me who did it."

Jack acquiesces. "Who?"

"No idea," says Anderson, and he slaps Jack on the back. "It happened two hundred years ago."

"Very funny."

"I'm not trying to be."

When they approach the green, they both stop to stare at the fire, which is greatly diminished but still hot enough to warm their faces and hands from a couple dozen yards away.

"The thing is, there's plenty I *can* tell you about that fire at the Globe," says Anderson. "I can tell you it took a year to rebuild the theater and that doing so nearly bankrupted the King's Men. I can tell you the whole business ruined Shakespeare's health and signaled the beginning of the end of his career."

"Really?"

Anderson nods, and they begin moving again, in the direction of the tavern.

"There's been a lot written about that fire over the years. But no one's ever identified the man who lit the fuse."

Jack looks at him. "Am I the man who lit the fuse in this scenario? Or is it Green?"

"Theaters catch fire, Jack. You can't put all those pyrotechnics under one roof without occasionally running into problems."

"This," Jack says, waving his arms in the direction of the theater green, "feels like a fairly big problem."

"I'll give you that. But what I'm trying to say is that Placide's not out to get anyone."

"Except the city's Negroes?"

"I'd argue he's not even out to get them," says Anderson.

Jack rolls his eyes. "Come on."

"He's just trying to create a diversion."

"Once people start thinking it was slaves who set this fire, there's going to be blood in the streets," says Jack.

"Well, that would most certainly be a diversion, wouldn't it?"

"Are you serious?"

"Of course not," says Anderson. "But can you just trust that Placide knows what he's doing?"

Jack doesn't know that he can.

"He's looking out for us. He is. And you, of all people, could use someone to look out for you."

"What's that supposed to mean?"

"Just that you're in a different position than most of us," says Anderson. "You don't come from a family of actors."

Jack acknowledges that this is a shortcoming. "You were raised in the theater?"

Anderson nods. "Same goes for Twaits and, of course, West. Young, Green, even Caulfield. Acting can be a dreadfully difficult profession to break into, if you don't know the right people."

"And Placide's the right people?"

"A letter of introduction from Placide can get you a position at the Old American Company, the Southwark, even the new Theater Royal in New York."

Jack would be thrilled to work anywhere half so grand. And if he should be allowed to act, he'd scarcely know what to make of himself.

"But that's provided you don't want to come back to Charleston with us."

"Is that even an option anymore?"

"Of course it is. We'll get through this. And, if you make good decisions, there will be plenty of opportunities for a boy like you."

"Really?"

"Placide is considering staging *Twelfth Night* in the spring. You'd make a convincing Feste."

"You think so?"

"Could be your big break."

They have arrived in front of the tavern, but Jack is still not sure he can follow Anderson inside.

"Just do what he says," says Anderson. "And who knows? Maybe two hundred years from now, some git will be talking about how they've got no bloody clue who started the Richmond Theater fire."

GILBERT

Gilbert *lets himself into the smithy* just after daybreak and is surprised to find that the shop is empty, save for Marcus, who sits at the table by the fireplace, his head cradled in his arms. "You sleeping?" Gilbert asks.

"Not anymore," Marcus says, pointing one eyeball in Gilbert's direction.

"Where is everybody?"

"Some of them upstairs, trying to get some shut-eye. Some still out."

"What about Kemp?" Gilbert says quietly, in case he's in the loft, or getting ready to walk through the front door.

Marcus raises his head up into his hands and presses on his eye sockets with his palms. "I don't think he's been back all night."

"He patrolling?"

"Assume so," says Marcus. "Though it seems to me that, if he's bent on serving his community, it might have been better to head on over to the green and see what he could do."

Kemp is one of about seventy men who ride with the night watch, also known as the slave patrol. It's an all-volunteer force that's supposed to police gambling, prostitution, and the like, but all any of them ever do is harass Richmond's Negro population. Gilbert can remember when rich white men—slave owners, all of them—made a point of riding with the patrol at least once or twice a month. But over the years, the makeup of the group's membership has changed. Now the volunteers are low whites, who do plenty of their own gambling and prostituting, and barely have the money to buy a slave, much less maintain one.

Kemp, of course, is the exception. In addition to Gilbert, he owns Marcus and Ibrahim, who do odd jobs in the shop, and a girl named Fannie, who keeps his house.

Most of the men who work at Kemp's smithy are not enslaved. There's Ned, who worked as a whitesmith's apprentice in Yorkshire before signing an indenture to come to the United States. Now he does all Kemp's cutlery work in exchange for room and board. There's Nick, who completed an apprenticeship with Kemp many years ago, but made such a lousy journeyman, traveling the backcountry, that he had no prayer of hanging out his own shingle. Then there are a slew of apprentices—many more than Kemp should ever have agreed to take on. It's easy to think of these boys, some of whom are barely fourteen, as free labor, but a good blacksmith puts far more into an apprentice than he ever gets out of him. Apprentices require careful tutelage and constant supervision, and Kemp's apprentices receive neither, but are expected to contribute to the shop's output all the same.

One night, when Gilbert was up late talking to Marcus and Ibrahim, he asked if they had ever aspired to learn the trade. Ibrahim started to chuckle to himself, and when Gilbert asked what was so funny, Marcus answered for him. "What makes you think we haven't?"

Gilbert didn't understand, and when he said so, the men explained that Marcus had grown up working for a blacksmith on a plantation in Nottoway and that Ibrahim was the son of an ironworking family in the kingdom of Jolof, in West Africa, where blacksmiths were revered for their ability to control the earth's elements.

"So, why does Kemp have you sorting nails?" Gilbert asked, dumbfounded. "He really don't know you got training?"

"He never asked," said Marcus, and Ibrahim just shook his head and laughed at the upside-down world where a know-nothing man like Kemp got to be the one in charge.

Gilbert can't blame Marcus and Ibrahim for wanting to keep their talents to themselves. It's the same way he feels about letting Kemp know he can read and write. He sees no advantage to telling him, aside from the fact that it makes him feel a little crazy sometimes, pretending not to be able to recognize the words in front of his face.

He slipped up once recently, but—thankfully—Marcus was the only one to notice. An old man had come to pick up a cook pan his wife had dropped off, and when Gilbert turned to the shelf where they kept small finished jobs, there were three pans, all of which looked roughly the same.

He asked if the man recognized his wife's, but of course he did not, so without thinking, Gilbert took hold of a paper tag that hung from one of the handles and read aloud, "Mrs. Fisher?"

"That's the one," said the man, and it was only after he was gone that Marcus gave him an appraising stare.

"What?"

"I didn't say nothing," said Marcus, throwing his hands in the air.

Ever since that day, a camaraderie has existed between the two men, and Gilbert leans into the intimacy whenever he can.

"You go over to the theater?" Gilbert asks Marcus now.

Marcus nods. "I was at the cockfight at—"

The door to the smithy swings open, and they both know who it is without having to look up.

"Morning, Master Kemp," says Gilbert, who deeply regrets not getting the fire in his forge going the moment he arrived.

Kemp hangs his coat and hat on a hook by the door. He is an unattractive man under the best of circumstances, but this morning he looks like he's been rode hard and put up wet. His face, which is mostly jowl, is unshaven, and there are dark circles under his eyes. He keeps what little hair he has tied up in a neat knot at the back of his thick neck, but this morning the ribbon is gone, and his gray hair hangs down around his shoulders in slick cords.

"Where the hell is everyone?" Kemp asks as soon as he takes a good look around the shop.

"Ibrahim's out in the yard," says Marcus. "A few of the men are asleep upstairs. And Ed and Jeffery told me they needed to go check on their families."

"Are you the boss now?"

"No, sir," says Marcus. "Just trying to help."

"What would help is if everyone were at their stations," says Kemp. "It's not a goddamned holiday."

While Kemp tramps up to the loft to rouse anyone who was bold enough to have gone to bed, Gilbert puts on his apron and refills the coal bucket. His whole body aches, but he can't afford for Kemp to see him slowing down.

By the time Kemp herds everyone downstairs, he is spitting mad. "Laziest bunch of no-good good-for-nothings I ever saw," he says as the last of them slip aprons over their heads and try to look alive.

Kemp makes a big show of lighting Gilbert's forge, like Gilbert's not standing right there.

He uses the slice to turn over the coals, then moves back around to the bellows to give the leather bag a squeeze. Gilbert can tell, just listening to the wheeze of the instrument, that Kemp hasn't gotten enough air into the chamber. All the coals are going to do is smoke.

Kemp puts down the slice and picks up a fire hook, then points it at Gilbert. "Where the hell you been?"

It doesn't pay to lie to him. The most Gilbert dares to offer is a half-truth. "This morning, sir? I been right here."

Kemp stabs the air with the fire hook. "Don't pretend you didn't just walk in this door an hour ago."

Gilbert glances at Marcus, who gave him no indication that Kemp had already been by the shop. Marcus shrugs his shoulders apologetically. Maybe he didn't know.

"I went and helped at the theater," says Gilbert.

"That fire burned out hours ago," Kemp says, still brandishing the fire hook.

Gilbert is glad to have his forge between them. "It did, but then I went over to Elizabeth Preston's place to see about her daughter." It pains him to add, "Louisa Mayo, she among the missing."

Kemp's face screws up so tight it looks like a walnut, and Gilbert braces for what he knows is coming. "You work for Elizabeth Preston? Or you work for me?"

Gilbert hates to admit he works for Kemp. The man is so angry—all the time—and even though it's only been a few months since the sale went through, Gilbert is already sick and tired of tiptoeing around him. Finally, he swallows and says, "I work for you, sir."

❧✻ ❘ CECILY ❘ ✻❧

Cecily and her mother stand in a dark tangle of trees, by the river, letting the loud rush of water coming down over the falls cover up their voices.

Cecily tries to explain what she needs, but Della is not listening. She keeps shaking her head and saying that there is no way she is going to help a daughter of hers do something this dangerous. "You know what will happen to you if you get caught?"

"I know, I do."

"I'm not even talking about the beatings. If they think you at risk of running, they'll sell you south."

"It ain't going to come to that."

Della runs her hands up and down her arms, like she's all of a sudden started feeling the cold through her thin shawl. "You don't think nobody saw you?"

Cecily thinks about Augustine Saunders and that boy with the bony shoulders. John? No, Jack. If she tells Della about either of them, it'll just give her one more thing to worry about. "Even if somebody saw me," Cecily says, "there's no saying I didn't run back inside. I could have been trying to find Maria."

"That poor child."

Cecily can't keep herself from asking, "You know what happened to her?"

"Rosie says Master Price and Elliott found her over at Mrs. Cowley's."

Cecily hadn't thought to check with Mrs. Cowley, although she might have guessed that someone with her expertise would be in high demand at a time such as this.

"So, Maria's alive?"

"Last I heard."

"I looked everywhere," Cecily starts to say, but even as those three little words escape her lips, she knows they aren't true. She didn't try very hard to find Maria. It could be because Maria's always been so difficult, but Cecily is beginning to wonder if, in some deep-down part of herself, she always knew she'd run if and when she got the chance.

"You really think there was a hundred people killed?" Della asks.

Cecily nods. "There won't be a soul in Richmond who hasn't lost someone."

"But I didn't lose you," Della reminds her pleadingly.

Cecily reaches for her mother's hand. "I can't stay, Mama. Not with Elliott the way he is. He told me Master Price gave him permission to take me with him to his new place. I'm to be a wedding present."

Della wasn't counting on that, Cecily can tell. "When'd he say that?"

"Earlier this evening."

"God damn him," she whispers. "He knows better than that."

"Elliott?"

"No, his daddy."

A rumor has long circulated in the quarters, about how it's Master Price who's really Cecily's father. Cecily has never dared bring it up to her mother. How could she, knowing how much it would hurt her? Instead, she has looked for clues: the tawny color of her skin; the way Master Price's gaze comes to rest on her, like she is a rare curiosity, when he thinks no one is looking; the fact that Mrs. Price is forever short with her, no matter how nicely she does up Maria's hair or tends to her frocks.

It is clear Della holds some pull over Master Price. When rations run short or a child needs medicine, she can often disappear up to the main house and get what the family needs. She returns with a bag of rice or a bottle of camphor, and Cecily's father goes quiet for a few days, but then Della will say, "What would you have me do?" and eventually he comes around.

Cecily would believe the rumors but for two reasons. The first is that her father adores her. And the second is that her mother has never been able to put a stop to the ugly business with Elliott, and Cecily knows she must have tried.

Somewhere above their heads an owl coos.

"Master Price ain't never going to look out for me, Mama," says Cecily. "Not the way you want him to." It is the closest she can come to acknowledging what has long gone unsaid between them.

Cecily watches her mother's face and thinks she detects the softening of her features, an openness that was not there before. "Where would you even run?" she finally asks.

All Cecily knows to say is "north."

"North?" Della repeats, with a shake of her head. "That ain't a plan."

"I didn't say it was."

"Running is serious business."

"I know, Mama. That's why I need your help," Cecily pleads.

Della is stewing on something, and finally she takes a deep breath and nods, once.

"So, you'll help me?" For the first time in a long time, Cecily feels hopeful. Her mother is the most capable woman she knows, and if she turns her attention to spiriting her eldest daughter out of Richmond, Cecily feels sure she'll succeed.

In the distance a dog barks, and they both jump. Cecily knows the animal isn't coming for her, but she can't steady her racing heart. "What do I do now?"

"We got to get you hid."

It will be light soon, and Cecily can't think of anywhere on the Price property that is safe enough for her to go.

"There's that old boathouse, down on the Fulcher property," says Della. "Go on in there and find somewhere to hide, and I'll be there when I can."

"How long, you think?"

"I don't know," says Della. "A day. Maybe two. Just get some sleep and don't come out till I say."

"Mama," says Cecily, wanting to tell her something true, "I'm scared."

Della nods quiet and slow, then she gives her daughter a sad smile. "I'd be more scared if you wasn't."

❧ | SALLY | ❧

y the time Sally arrives in front of Archie and Margaret's house, it's almost morning and she is delirious with exhaustion. Even the latch on the gate, which is a simple enough mechanism, seems impossible to open, and she tugs at it once and then twice before gaining entrance to the yard.

The creak of the gate's hinges attracts the attention of Archie's dogs, mongrels both of them, who alert the household, or what is left of it, that there is a visitor. By the time Sally has taken a half-dozen steps into the yard, the Campbells' gardener, Joe, has started hollering, "Miss Sally's here! Everybody! Miss Sally's alive!"

Sally gives him a sad grin. It has been a long time since anyone was this excited to see her coming. But her face freezes when, behind Joe, she sees Archie hurry around the side of the house.

God almighty. It is like seeing a ghost. She knows she should be relieved to find him in one piece, but all she can ask is "What are you doing here?"

"My dear girl," he says as he pushes past Joe and closes the distance between them. He is breathing hard. "You're alive. I can scarcely believe it."

"No, Archie, seriously. How did you—"

She can't get anything else out. Her brother-in-law has caught her up in his arms and is squeezing her so tight that her feet lose contact with the ground.

"I thought you were dead," he says, and because Mrs. Cowley loaned her a pair of boots, which pinch her heels, she allows Archie to lift her off the ground and rock her back and forth, until she feels his chest heave with sobs.

"Put me down, Archie."

It's all so infuriating. How can it be that he has barely a scratch on him, when across town Margaret is fighting for her life?

"Now," she says.

He does as he is told, then grips her hands and presses them to his face as he cries, "Oh, my poor Margaret."

It is tempting to let him carry on like this, but she doesn't have the stamina. She eases her hands out of his grip. "Archie, Margaret is alive."

His breath catches in his throat and he sputters, "What?"

"I found her. In the passageway."

"But the stairs."

"We jumped."

The color drains from his face, and his lower lip trembles. "I circled the building. Twice, three times. I checked all the windows. You weren't there."

"I don't know what to tell you," says Sally, who has to remind herself not to apologize for her own survival.

"And she's," Archie hesitates to ask, "all right?"

"She has a badly broken leg, which will require surgery."

"Surgery?"

Archie knows, as well as anyone, that surgery is a dangerous enterprise, but she fills him in on everything Mrs. Cowley and Dr. Foushee have told her. "Dr. Foushee will return to Mrs. Cowley's in a couple of hours, and he needs to know what we want to do." If Archie notices her use of the word *we*, he doesn't let on.

Archie closes his eyes and shakes his head, as if he can't believe he is having this conversation. "What does Margaret say?"

"She's in no condition to say much of anything."

If what Mrs. Cowley said about the risk of infection is true, then amputating the leg is the only logical choice. But Sally worries Archie won't see it that way.

"I feel sure she'd want me to try to keep the leg," he says, confirming her worst fears.

"But at what cost?"

Archie doesn't answer the question, just plows ahead. "I doubt she wants to be a cripple for the rest of her life."

"Given the alternatives—"

"She'll be immobile."

Sally knows Margaret will struggle mightily in the months and years to come—that, in fact, some aspects of her life will always be a struggle from here on out. But Margaret is the woman who came to Marysville after

Robert's death and spoon-fed Sally bone broth, until she could convince her to get out of bed and eventually to dress for dinner. When Sally told her she didn't see the point in living if Robert was dead, Margaret took her chin in her hands and said, as sternly as she could, "You listen to me, Sally Campbell. There is always a reason to live."

"Margaret isn't like most people," she says. "I know she'll make the best of things. That she'll find a way to cope."

A bell tolls, and Archie turns toward the noise.

"Archie, listen to me. I watched her jump out of that window. She didn't have to do it. Many women—women who knew that jumping was their only salvation—didn't. But Margaret is strong and bold and brave, and she jumped out of that window because she wanted to live."

"I can't believe this," he says, more to himself than to her, and she backs off. It's not the right time to push him. So, she turns to Joe and says, "Will you gather all the vinegar we've got, and any alcohol, too? Ask Effie if she can put her hands on some bolts of linen." She tries to think of anything else Mrs. Cowley might need. Extra quilts, spare shifts, another set of shears. "If there's any laudanum, pack that, too."

Joe promises he'll see what he can find, and makes toward the house, where Margaret's children must be beginning to stir. Through a window, she can see Joe's wife, Effie, pacing the parlor with Archie and Margaret's youngest boy, Robert, on her hip. Sally still remembers the words Margaret used when she wrote to her, mere months after Robert's death, to announce the child's arrival. *We have decided to name him Robert, after his uncle, and hope he will grow up to possess half of Robert's goodness and light.*

"Where does Mrs. Cowley live?" Archie asks as Sally turns to follow Joe into the house, and it occurs to her that if she tells him, he will take off running before she has a chance to so much as change her boots, let alone clean herself up and eat something.

"I'll take you."

"I want to go now," he says sharply. "Tell me where she lives."

Sally can't risk Archie and Dr. Foushee powwowing without her. "Give me a half hour."

"I won't. Not when she needs me."

This is the last straw. "*Needs you?*" Sally spits. "Where were you last night, then? That's when she *actually* needed you!"

He squeezes his eyes shut and begins to shake his head. "It was so dark," he whispers. "I couldn't see."

"Yes, I know. Neither could I."

Sally has never seen her brother-in-law so agitated, and she tries to re-call the man Robert introduced her to on the eve of their wedding. He was funny and kind, and Sally loved listening to the brothers' easy banter. At the luncheon, which Sally's mother held on the lawn at Red Hill, Archie was the first to raise a glass to the happy couple. "Take care of each other," he said.

"Forgive me," he pleads now.

"It's not for me to—"

Archie is on his knees, clutching at her skirt. "Will she? Forgive me?" he asks, and the whole thing is so miserable she feels almost sorry for him.

What can Sally possibly tell him? That the question is not whether his wife will forgive him but whether she will live to one day contemplate the concept of forgiveness. "I think," says Sally slowly, "that if Margaret lives to lord your failures over your head, you should consider yourself a very lucky man indeed."

❈ | CECILY | ❈

ecily finds the boathouse easily. From the spot where she and her mother parted ways, it's just a short hike upriver, until she can no longer see the Price family's mill perched at the edge of the falls.

The structure is nestled in the curve of some silver maples that line the north bank of the James, and in the gray dawn of morning, it hides in plain sight. It is not much more than a shack, really. Just a bunch of logs with no chinking and a shingle roof that has begun to rot. The air smells foul—like mildew and bat droppings and maybe something dead—but Cecily is so relieved to be out of the wind, she scarcely notices.

When her eyes adjust to the ill-lit room, she sees that the boathouse contains a small rowboat and a few canoes, stacked one on top of the other. An assortment of oars and push poles lay in a pile on the floor, but Cecily doesn't realize they are there until she trips over them. The paddles make a sickening clatter, and she prays no one is close by to hear.

A big piece of thickly woven sailcloth lays in folds at the bottom of the rowboat, and Cecily shakes it out in a hurry, desperate to get warm. Immediately, she hears the panicked cries of a family of displaced mice. "I'm sorry," she whispers as she wraps the nubby material around her shoulders, then looks for a good spot to hide.

Her eyes settle on the stack of canoes. If she can climb into the topmost canoe and pull the sailcloth over her, no one will know she's here. But the problem is, Cecily's body has begun to work against her. Her head is pounding, and in the last several hours, the marrow in her bones has turned to ice; she shivers uncontrollably and feels clumsy with cold. When she tries to hoist herself into the boat, her feet feel too large to find a foothold and her fingers too fat to find a grip. All her strength is gone.

She scours the boathouse for something she can use as a step stool—a crate or an empty pail—but finds nothing that will work. So, she tries to pull herself up a second time and then a third, and when she finally manages to heave herself into the belly of the canoe, she is breathing so hard she thinks she will die, right there on the spot.

Cecily pulls her knees up tight against her chest and wraps the sail-cloth around herself like a cocoon. Then she waits for her shallow breaths to warm the space. For a while, her body is shaking so hard, she worries she'll cause the boats beneath her to topple. But eventually, her breathing grows steadier, and her body relaxes into a dreamless sleep.

❧ | JACK | ❧

Where is everyone?" *Anderson asks Placide* when Placide walks through the door of the tavern's back room—alone—at seven o'clock in the morning.

When Anderson convinced Jack to return to the tavern, several hours ago, they had been surprised to discover the back room empty. They checked the upstairs bedrooms, but could find none of the actors, so they plunked down in front of the fire to wait for the troupe's eventual return. The first hour or two passed quickly, both of them relieved to doze in their chairs, but Anderson had recently begun to pace, worried about where everyone had gotten off to.

Placide goes to warm himself by the fire. "The men are out, trying to dig up members of the slave patrol."

"And the women?"

"I just got them settled back at the boardinghouse."

"Any sign of Nancy?" Anderson asks.

"None," says Placide with a shake of his head.

"That's too bad."

Placide turns to Jack. "So, our friend convinced you to return to us?"

In lieu of an answer, Jack shoves his hands into the pockets of his trousers.

"As you've probably guessed by now, he's not in favor of blaming the fire on a slave revolt," says Anderson.

"Because you think it won't work?" Placide asks Jack. "Or because you are a man of principle?"

Jack doesn't know what the correct answer is, so he says, "Both?"

"What about the principle of loyalty?" Placide says. "Or, dare I say, gratitude?"

"Alex," Anderson warns.

"What? We gave him this job as a favor to Girardin. He gets a decent wage, room and board, and the opportunity to make something of himself. And what does he do? He burns the place down, then has the nerve to question the means by which we ensure our own survival."

"He's on our side," says Anderson. "I'm just registering his concerns."

"I am grateful for the job, Mr. Placide," says Jack. "Truly, I am."

"Well, then, act like it," Placide says as he pulls out an empty chair and gestures for Jack to sit.

Jack doesn't argue.

"How's your penmanship?" Placide asks.

Jack clears his throat. "Penmanship?"

Placide goes to get a piece of letter paper, an ink pot, and a pen and places the items in front of Jack. "I've been thinking, what we need is a letter."

"A letter?" says Jack.

"You were a student of Professor Girardin's. Surely you can write a decent one?"

Jack eyes the materials suspiciously.

"I'm not so good with a pen at present," Placide admits, and when he holds his hand up, Jack can detect a significant tremor.

Jack fingers the letter paper. "To whom am I writing?"

"Thomas Ritchie."

"The newspaper editor?" Jack asks.

"You know him?"

Jack doesn't, but his father did.

"You look concerned."

"It's just—"

"Just what?" Placide pushes.

What can Jack say? That he's sure Ritchie will see through this charade? That he's embarrassed for Ritchie to discover that Zeke Gibson's son is a liar? Or at least the sort of boy who associates with liars? "Nothing."

"Well, then, get to it," says Placide, gesturing at the blank page.

Jack prepares the letter paper, then dips his pen in the ink pot and writes the appropriate salutation. When he's finished, he waits for further instructions.

"Write this down," says Placide. "Last night, about seven hundred persons were in the theater, at my benefit . . ."

He does as he is told.

"Then say something about how we know the audience suffered."

Jack thinks of the scene in *The Tempest*, when Miranda recalls the ship-wreck she witnessed. *O, I have suffered with those that I saw suffer!* There is another line, he can't remember exactly how it goes, then the clincher: *O, the cry did knock against my very heart! Poor souls, they perished!* Jack knows it won't do any good to quote Shakespeare to the editor of the *Enquirer*, not at a time like this, but he tries to capture some of the Bard's frothy abundance.

"That's very nice," says Placide, reading over Jack's shoulder. "Now be sure he knows that we, too, have been laid bare."

"You want me to say something about Nancy?"

"No, no. We can't be certain about Nancy. I was thinking music, scenery, wardrobe—that sort of thing," says Placide. "Describe how everything fell prey to the flames."

Jack tries to follow Placide's instructions, but it feels a little strange referencing props and costumes at a time like this. He waits for Placide to get around to explaining the cause of the fire, and when Jack has filled three-quarters of a page with frivolous grievances, he works up the courage to ask him when they are going to get to the point.

Placide taps the page. "Now is when we make our suspicions known."

"About the slave revolt?" says Jack warily.

"Correct," Placide says.

Jack thinks of Girardin's house servant, Ivy, who used to save Jack extra pigeon pie when he first went to stay with the professor. He was a stick, having subsisted for six months on his uncle's slop, and Ivy considered it her responsibility to fatten him up. How were people like Ivy ever to have a chance if they were blamed for every act of negligence and spate of bad luck that occurred in their proximity?

"Write this down," says Placide. "This has been the work of some worse-than-vile incendiary ..."

Jack hesitates long enough that a drop of ink falls from the nib of his pen onto the waiting page.

"I'll repeat it," says Placide, and he does, but Jack isn't listening. He's thinking about the plays he loves and how, for a play to work, the hero has to want something—usually very badly. Maybe he wants love or to return home or to make something of himself. The want has got to obscure all reason, to be so primal that the hero is willing to sign a deal with the devil, or at the very least, sacrifice his own principles to get it. Is this what Jack is doing now? Going along with Placide's plan in the hopes that it secures him protection and maybe even a livelihood when this is through?

Placide waves a hand in front of Jack's face.

"Some worse-than-vile incendiary," Jack whispers, and he begins to write.

❧✳ | **GILBERT** | ✳❧

W *ord spreads quickly down Locust Alley* that all businesses are to close for the next two days.

"By order of the Common Council," says the man who stops by the smithy to tell Kemp the news. And then, because he must not think Kemp is the type to understand the symbolism of closing up shop, he adds, "Out of respect for the dead."

Kemp doesn't like it, and says as much to his visitor as he steers him out of the smithy. "What I want to know is how they think me giving up two days of income is going to change what happened in that theater?"

When the man is gone, Kemp locks the door and tells everyone to keep working, same as before. "We won't take any new orders, but there's no reason for us to get behind on the jobs we've already got."

None of the men are happy with this arrangement, and it is as if they collectively decide, without saying a word, that they will work at half speed to compensate. Gilbert makes three skillets in the time it usually takes him to make six, Marcus sweeps the same pile of metal filings halfway across the shop and back again, and even Ned, who is nothing if not conscientious, spends an inordinate amount of time polishing a pair of fish servers.

Kemp is useless on a good day, but today, it's like he's trying to win a prize for his own fecklessness. He restacks a shipment of pig iron that Ibrahim did a perfectly fine job laying up when he hauled it in off the cart the day before; he spends a half hour perusing the account book without making a single mark in it; and at one point, he wanders over to Gilbert's forge and tells him that if he didn't allow his pan handles to cup so much on the edges, he'd get a better curve on them. Gilbert wants to remind him that the cupping is what makes his handles comfortable to grip, but instead he just says, "That's good advice, sir."

When they hear a loud banging at the smithy door, everyone jumps.

They're all worried that maybe there's a penalty for working after the Common Council tells you to stop.

"Stop hammering there for a second," Kemp warns Gilbert as he unlocks the door to reveal two gentlemen without hats or coats.

"We're looking for a Mr. Cameron Kemp," says a big man with bushy eyebrows. He's accompanied by a handsome man of average build, with a thick head of hair.

"I'm him," Kemp says.

"Splendid," says the man. "I understand you're in charge of the slave patrol."

Kemp pats his own chest. "Captain of the first class of patrol."

"Good, good. I'm Billy Twaits, and this is Charles Young. We're with Placide and Green."

Kemp isn't much for the arts, so when he gives them a blank stare, Twaits has to elaborate. "The theatrical company."

Twaits waits for the words to register—eventually, they do—then he steps forward to shake Kemp's hand. "Please pardon our appearance. The fire claimed our coats."

Kemp nods slowly, like he doesn't quite know what to make of these two. "What can I do for you?"

"We're rather hoping there's something we can do for you."

"Not sure I follow."

"We have reason to suspect that the theater fire was started as part of a slave rebellion."

Gilbert sucks in his breath, and the room goes so quiet he can hear the lick of the flames in his forge.

"What proof do you have?" asks Kemp, which is a good question, but Gilbert knows that Kemp has never let proof—or the lack of it—get in his way before.

The men describe a band of a dozen or so Negro incendiaries, whom they saw near the stage door during the performance, and Kemp is so giddy he's practically hopping up and down. "This is big."

"That's what we're saying," Twaits says, and there is something about the way he eggs Kemp on that makes Gilbert immediately suspicious of both him and his friend.

The iron rod Gilbert was hammering on has gone cold and gray, so he returns to the forge and sinks it into the hot coals.

"We think it's extremely likely that many of these men are still at large," says Twaits with some urgency in his voice, and Gilbert steals a glance at Marcus. They've both got to be thinking the same thing, which is that there was no band of Negroes running around Shockoe Hill last night. Gilbert walked right past the theater on his way to Sara's, and the neighborhood was quiet as a crypt. And if Marcus was at a cockfight, he surely would have heard rumblings of a revolt.

"I'll alert the patrol," says Kemp. "And we'll ride out at once."

"We haven't horses," says Twaits. "Will you need us?"

"Only once we start making arrests. Did you get a good look at them?" Twaits nods his head vigorously.

"Anyone you could identify?"

"Certainly," Twaits says, and Gilbert looks at Marcus, wanting to know what he thinks the chances are Twaits can tell one Black man from another.

The rod glows a dull red, then turns bright red and finally orange. It's time for Gilbert to remove it from the coals, but if he does, he's got to go back to banging on it at the anvil, and he won't be able to hear anything the men say. Just a minute longer, he tells himself, as he watches the orange change to yellow.

Kemp is inexhaustible. "We'll start at the armory, then move in the direction of the penitentiary, and if that doesn't turn up anyone, we'll head out to Brook Road and take a look around." While the men exchange information, he puts on his coat and grabs his gun. "Ned," he says, "I'm leaving you in charge."

Everyone in the shop likes it when Kemp leaves Ned in charge. Ned's got a girl over in Manchester, and he doesn't think twice about shutting the smithy down early if he's sure he won't get caught. "How long you think you'll be gone?" Ned asks Kemp in as casual a tone as he can manage.

"Could be all day," says Kemp. "If anyone comes by looking to ride out with us, tell them we'll convene at the slaughterhouse at midday."

Ned promises he will.

"Oh, and Gilbert," Kemp says as he places a cap on his fat head. "No more gallivanting."

The iron rod is white between Gilbert's tongs, and he's in danger of it turning to liquid. "No, sir," he says.

The man with the good head of hair brightens. "Wait—are you Gilbert Hunt?"

Gilbert closes his eyes, prays that whatever's about to come out of this fool's mouth is suitable for Kemp's ears.

"I heard about you. Catching all those ladies. Such a feat!"

Twaits joins in. "Oh, this is him? Yes! What a hero you are. You could have been killed!"

Gilbert wants to tell them he's fixing to be killed now if they don't shut their mouths.

"You heard, I suppose?" Twaits says to Kemp. "Caught a dozen women, from a third-floor window. Like there was nothing to it."

Gilbert is afraid to look at Kemp. He clears his throat, and says, "It was the second floor" in as quiet a voice as he can manage.

"Still," says Twaits. "Bloody impressive."

If Gilbert knows Kemp—and he thinks that he does—Kemp will play along and pretend he's heard all about Gilbert's adventures. But eventually, there will be hell to pay.

"He is an impressive specimen," Kemp concurs, and it is only after he has waved the actors off, promising to be in touch, that he says another word about it.

"To think," he blasts, as the men pretend to get down to work, "that we were living with a hero among us."

Gilbert tries to explain. "Sir, you see—"

"No, *you* see," says Kemp, and Gilbert shuts his mouth.

"You cost me more than four hundred dollars at auction, and that was—what?—four months ago? Who, exactly, is going to pay my damages when you get clobbered by some old biddy?"

"Master Kemp, I was just trying to—"

"I am not finished!"

The men around him have stopped even pretending to work at this point.

"You listen and you listen good. You are *my* property, and if I wanted you plucking ladies out of the night sky, I'd have sent you up to the theater green myself."

⚜ | SALLY | ⚜

Sally *allows herself to sleep for* exactly one hour.

"You said to wake you before too long," says Effie, Robert back on her hip.

Sally would swear she still smells smoke, but slowly, she remembers the bath, the fresh dress, the feeling of Effie's hands on her head as she wove her wet hair into a thick braid.

She stands too quickly, and when she is on her feet, she wobbles. Effie grabs hold of her elbow and steadies her. "You all right?"

"Just tired."

"All of this is going to catch up with you."

"I know," says Sally, allowing her eyes to blink shut for slightly longer than necessary. "Everything's ready?"

"I gathered up all the scraps of fabric I could find. There's an extra bottle of laudanum, and I went next door to ask Mrs. Millhiser for some vinegar. Mrs. Ross, too. All she had was turpentine, but I took it anyway."

"That's perfect. Can Joe help me get it over there?"

Sally borrows an extra coat of Margaret's and uses the latrine. Back in the house, she splashes water on her face and eats the beef pallets set in front of her. They taste better than anything she's ever eaten, and she asks Effie, "Will you pack up whatever's left of this, too?"

Before they leave, Sally pats herself down and realizes she's left Mr. Scott's *fausse montre* in the kitchen house, beside the tub. "I'll be right back," she says to Effie and Joe as she hurries to retrieve it.

The trinket is where Sally left it on the windowsill, and on the walk back to the main house, she opens the case front and studies the woman's face staring back at her. The mysterious FS looks every bit as amused as she did a few hours ago, and Sally wonders how easy it will be to track her down.

When Sally can think of nothing else that needs to be done or packed or put away, she kisses Margaret's children one more time and signals to Joe that it is time to go. Effie has gathered enough supplies that she's filled two wooden crates; Joe carries them both, one balanced atop the other, in his arms. In her own arms, Sally carries the boots she borrowed from Mrs. Cowley and a small bag containing two of Margaret's shifts and a shirt of Archie's, which she intends to give to Mr. Scott. She has also packed a change of clothes for herself, since it seems unlikely she'll be able to return home for several days.

Joe walks slowly, on account of the fact that the crates make it hard to see where he's going, but Sally doesn't mind the plodding pace. If anything, she's grateful to have a reason to put off what she knows is waiting for her.

"You see Gilbert Hunt last night?" Joe asks her while she waits for him to cross Eleventh Street.

"Who is he?"

"Negro blacksmith. Works at Cameron Kemp's shop. About my age, but a lot bigger."

"It was pandemonium last night," says Sally apologetically. "I'd hardly have recognized my own mother."

"You'd remember him if you saw him," says Joe. "I was down at The Bell this morning, and it's all Angus Graham was talking about. Word is, Gilbert Hunt caught more than a dozen white ladies. Right out of the sky. Was a risky business, but not one of them had so much as a scratch on her."

Sally thinks of the women she encountered in the third-floor hallway and how difficult it was to coax them out the window. "They just jumped? Straight into his arms?"

"I heard Dr. McCaw was up in one of the windows, tossing them to him, one at a time."

They had to have been on the second floor, Sally decides. She has stood in a third-floor window, contemplating the distance between herself and the ground, and even if there were a willing volunteer waiting for her, she wouldn't have had a prayer of being caught.

She likes the idea of this McCaw fellow shepherding the women out the window to whatever uncertain futures awaited them. "By the time Margaret and I jumped," she tells Joe, "all the men on the third floor had disappeared."

"Except that one fellow you was telling me about?"

He's talking about Mr. Scott. "Yes, except him."

As they approach the wreckage of the theater, their pace slows. Sally dreads seeing the building, but she is also drawn to it.

"That's Samuel Myers's place," says Joe, nodding at the lot next to the theater, where a wood-framed house has also burned to the ground. The house sat at least a hundred feet from the theater, but the wind last night was wicked, and all it took was one spark for the whole thing to go up in flames.

Eventually, the theater, or what is left of it, comes into view. "Have you seen it yet?" Sally asks Joe.

"I was down here last night, looking for you and Missus Margaret. And again this morning."

"Of course you were. I'm sorry. I should have assumed."

"Nothing for you to be sorry about. I'm just glad you made it out, is all."

Together, they stand and stare at the smoldering ruins. The northern-most wall of the theater remains standing, but the rest of the building's brick façade has been reduced to rubble. Some of the joists are charred, but not gone.

"Looks like they finally got all those little fires put out," says Joe, and Sally just nods. Earlier this morning, when she had walked past the green on her way to Archie and Margaret's place, small fires—none of them much bigger than a cook fire—had dotted the site. People were desperate to begin combing the wreckage for clues to their loved ones' whereabouts, but all they could do was wait impatiently for the flames to extinguish themselves.

Now those same people carry rakes, spades, and shovels—anything that will allow them to sift through the hot ash. A man points to a wheel-barrow and shouts at the folks who have gathered around him, "Valuables go in here. Glasses, chains, keys, anything we might be able to give to the family. No souvenirs."

Another man interrupts him. "If you think the item will help us iden-tify someone's remains, leave it where it is until one of us can come check."

"Where do the remains go?" asks someone in the crowd.

"We're spreading sheets on the grass," says a third man, who looks like the type who is used to being put in charge of things. "Put them on the sheets."

A boy of maybe fifteen or sixteen years, in a pair of britches that are much too small for him, raises his hand. "How are we supposed to know if they're remains?"

The man with the wheelbarrow spits a stream of tobacco juice out of the side of his mouth. "Sometimes the skull's intact."

Sally shudders at how close she came to becoming a shovelful of ash on a white sheet, identifiable only by the wedding ring she wears on a thin gold chain around her neck. Robert engraved her ring, not with her initials or his but with the line *My friend, my goddess, and my guide*, which he'd borrowed from the Lady Montagu poem "A Hymn to the Moon." She tries to remember whether she ever told anyone that, but she can't be sure, all these years later, that she did. How horrible if her sad little pile of ash went unclaimed, all because no one knew about the inscription.

She turns to Joe. "I can't watch this."

They start to move in the direction of Mrs. Cowley's, but they don't get far before they hear a great outcry behind them. A man, who has tied bricks to the bottom of his shoes, is standing amid the ruins, near the foot of the stairs—or what was once the stairs. He is shouting about something, but Sally can't tell what. The crowd begins to murmur, and Sally turns to a woman, who looks as exhausted as she feels, and asks, "What is he going on about?"

"He thinks he's found the governor."

The tumult of the theater comes back to Sally in flashes. Margaret waving the tickets in front of her, Mr. Scott looking at his watch, Governor George Smith ruffling the hair of his young son.

"How's he supposed to know he's looking at the governor?" Joe asks, and without even realizing she's done it, Sally raises her hand to her neck. The stock buckle Governor Smith wore to the performance was so big, she was able to see it from the other side of the theater. She watches the man with the bricks tied to his shoes remove a handkerchief from his pocket and stoop to pick something up, and the next thing she knows, he is holding a mound of silver up above his head, where it glints in the sun.

"Is this not his?" the man shouts, but all of the onlookers are too stunned to say anything.

Sally looks for the woman, touches her sleeve. "He had a little boy with him last night."

"Aye," she says, as if she'd like to be done with the whole sad business. "The boy got out fine. His father just didn't know it."

❧❋ I GILBERT I ❋❧

O nce *Kemp is gone, the smithy* clears out fast. The men make one
excuse or another to put down their tools and go upstairs to bed,
and after Ned slips out the back door, it's just Marcus and Gilbert left alone
in the shop.

Gilbert can't go anywhere until he chokes the fire in his forge, so he
shovels the green coal to the far edges of the firebox, then uses a rake to
break up the coke at the center. He keeps turning it over until the flames
subside. What remains glows a dull red.

Marcus stays behind, pretending to organize the punches and chisels
while he waits for Gilbert to finish up. He holds up the stamp with Cameron Kemp's touchmark. "You want that over here or in the drawer with
the others?"

"How about you put that one at the bottom of a deep well?"

Marcus laughs through his nose. "That's about right."

Gilbert continues to rake the fire, then gets around to saying what
they're both thinking. "A slave revolt, huh?"

"You don't believe it, do you?"

"The gallery was packed," Gilbert says. "What kind of Negro is going
to light up a building with fifty or sixty colored folks inside?"

"Don't make a lick of sense."

"Nope."

"What I was hearing last night," says Marcus, "is that the fire started
backstage."

Gilbert shakes his head. "Who'd you hear that from?"

"Some actor. Robert Hopkins? I could have that backwards. Maybe it's
Hopkins Roberts? I can't recall. He seemed like a good sort, though. Spent
the better part of the night hauling the injured home in a gig he got from
God-knows-where."

"And he told you it started backstage?"

"Mmmmhmmm."

"He was sure?"

"Didn't act like there was a doubt about it."

"Well, then, what are his friends doing trying to make Kemp believe otherwise?"

"It's a good question," says Marcus wearily.

"You think they know what happened and mean to make us scapegoats?"

Marcus looks him straight in the eye. "You don't?"

Gilbert doesn't know how to answer that, so he just rakes the coke, looking for clinkers.

From a few feet away, clinkers look just like pieces of coal, but up close they're thick and glassy. All they are is waste—the sand and dirt and mineral deposits that don't burn, but they are not without value. People come by all the time asking for them—if they're putting in a footpath or preparing for the planting season. Most almanacs tell farmers to bury a clinker in each corner of their garden if they want their plants to grow healthy and strong.

Gilbert sees a clinker in the center of the fire, picks it up with a pair of tongs, and examines it in the light. He knows that, sometimes, he can be blind to people's failings, that he's so eager to see the good in people, he ignores their ugly centers. He thought Good Pete was a decent man because he let Gilbert hire himself out on Sundays, but now he realizes that if he'd really been as good as all that, he'd have freed Gilbert a long time ago. Same goes for Elizabeth Preston, who treats Sara like she is a beloved member of the family, but not so beloved that she is allowed to grieve for Louisa, too. It's all a game to them, and maybe it's Sy Gilliat who has the right idea—refusing to contribute so much as a mattress to their salvation.

Gilbert thinks about the two actors who stood before them. Had they deliberately lied to Kemp's face? Were they really willing to let a bunch of Negroes take the blame for what may very well have been their own mistake? Gilbert knows the answer is probably yes, but it's still hard to swallow.

He squints at the clock Kemp keeps on his writing desk. It's almost ten. "I got to go."

"Where?"

"Back to the green," says Gilbert.

"Did you hear what Kemp just told you? If he catches you . . ."

Gilbert hangs up his apron. "He ain't going to catch me. Not if he's all the way out on Brook Road."

Marcus clicks his tongue. "This still about the Mayo girl?"

Gilbert doesn't answer him directly. "Maybe I can find someone who saw her. Someone who knows something."

"Is it worth it? All so you can get her mama some answers?"

Gilbert can feel himself getting irritated. "I'm not doing it for her mama. I'm doing it for Sara. She's loved that girl since she was a baby, and I can't just sit here, twiddling my thumbs, while she's across town, waiting for news."

"But you think she's dead?"

Gilbert recalls the way Louisa used to wait patiently while he sounded out the words in her primer. She never hurried him along, never acted like she had somewhere better to be. When he read *Keeper's Travels in Search of His Master*—about a dog who is injured and trying to get home—aloud, she had sighed at the end. "I've never heard anyone do the animal voices half as well as you do," she said, and it felt like the sincerest compliment he'd ever received. If Louisa was dead, where did all that goodness go? Surely, it couldn't just disappear.

"I can't give up on her," he says to Marcus finally. "Not yet."

❄ | JACK | ❄

Once the letter is done, *Placide* asks Anderson and Jack to deliver it to Thomas Ritchie.

"Put it in his hands directly," Placide shouts after them as Anderson holds the door for Jack.

Outside, the sun is high in the sky, but the air remains frigid. Anderson is still without a coat, same as Jack, so he tucks the letter into the waistband of his trousers and crosses his arms across his chest for warmth. He looks up and down the street, which is unusually empty for a Friday, before turning to Jack. "Where are the offices again?"

"On E Street. Before you get to the wharf."

"Lead the way," he says as good-naturedly as if they are out for a stroll in Haymarket Gardens.

On the corner of Ninth and Bank Streets, a man in a nightshirt and sleeping cap stands in the intersection, shouting Bible verses at anyone who passes by. " 'And the angel took the censer, and filled it with the fire of the altar, and cast it to the earth; and there followed peals of thunder and sounds and flashes of lightning and an earthquake.' " He points at the sky and screams, "This is God's will! This fire, it is retribution for man's sin!"

"And what sin is that, other than being drunk on a street corner?" Anderson shouts back at him.

Jack knows there is some truth to what the man says. Richmonders can find their way around a gaming hall, a horse track, and a theater, but it's rare for them to find their way to church. Even the men his father associated with, who were all of them upstanding citizens, preferred to spend Sundays at the Quoit Club, where Jasper Crouch served up barbecue and plenty of rum punch.

"Can I ask you something?" Jack says when they can no longer hear the man's shouts.

"I have a feeling you're going to, even if I say no."

"What makes you so sure we'll hang for this? I mean, I know it's terrible, what happened. A sin, even. But isn't it Christians who preach forgiveness?"

Anderson sighs. "There is a long history of our kind not getting their fair due."

"Our kind?"

"Actors, players, thespians."

Jack doesn't know how he feels about being lumped in with a bunch of actors anymore.

"We used to be considered royal servants," says Anderson. "And as such, we had immunity from prosecution."

"In America?"

"No, no. This was years ago, in England. If anyone wanted to sue an actor, they had to first petition the lord chamberlain, who was an employee of the crown, and he never agreed to it."

Jack wonders what this has to do with anything.

"But then the Society for the Reformation of Manners comes along." He says the name of the society in a stuffy voice. "And they start footing the bill whenever their members want to take an actor to court."

"Why do they care?"

"Because they're a bunch of religious fatheads who can't stand to see anyone enjoying themselves."

"As bad as that fellow on the corner?"

Anderson lets out a small laugh. "Worse. They wanted the old Jacobean Act to Restrain the Abuses of Players enforced. And, as if that weren't enough, they passed an addendum to it."

Anderson might as well be reading from one of Jack's father's law books.

"First, you can't say the names of the Father, the Son, and the Holy Ghost onstage. They're all outlawed. Then, there's no sex. Eventually, they began suing playwrights whose plays don't offer sufficient 'moral instruction.'"

"They really took the fun out of everything."

Anderson gives him a wry smile. "Before long, all the biggest names in the theater—George Bright, Thomas Doggett, John Hodgson—are getting hauled into the Court of Common Pleas and being fined ten pounds for their trouble."

"So, what happened?"

"The playwrights cleaned up their scripts, the playhouses agreed to submit their scripts to the master of the revels, the actors tried their best to stick to their lines, and when there were slipups—which were inevitable—the censors learned to look the other way.

"But our days of being treated like house servants of the king were over. The reformers had vilified us; to them we were nothing more than rogues and vagabonds, intent on spreading disorder wherever we went."

"And you think that's what everyone here thinks of us, as well?"

"This new United States would like to pretend it bears no relation to Mother England," Anderson says, "but test the winds and you'll find a country growing more puritanical with every passing day."

SALLY

Mrs. *Cowley barely waits for Sally* to slide out of her coat before tossing her an apron.

"You look like a new person, dear. All cleaned up. I'd hate for you to get anything on that dress."

The dress is the least of Sally's concerns. "Dr. Foushee hasn't been back?" she asks as she cinches the apron around her waist.

Mrs. Cowley shakes her head no. "I did meet your brother-in-law, though."

Sally peeks her head into the parlor, but she doesn't see Archie anywhere. "Has he gone?"

"He was underfoot, so I sent him out to get some chalk."

Why does that not surprise Sally?

She checks on Margaret.

"Margaret, it's me," she says as she kneels beside her friend, but there is no response. She watches Margaret's shallow breaths push past cracked lips. "Has she had more laudanum?"

"I gave her some a little while ago," says Mrs. Cowley. "She was in a great deal of pain."

Sally picks up one of Margaret's hands and kisses it, then asks Mrs. Cowley what she can do to help.

"These vinegar baths will consume us all," says her hostess as she hands Sally a bowl of vinegar and a rag. "And I'm down a set of hands."

Sally gives her a questioning look.

"I finally had to send Birdie to bed."

Mrs. Cowley looks exhausted, and Sally thinks it would probably be wise for her to follow suit. "You should try to sleep, too. At least for a few hours."

"I will. If we can finish up these baths and get the poultices applied. Mrs. Stetson, down the street, has offered me a bed at her place."

"I'll take the upstairs," says Sally as she follows her out of the parlor and down the hall. There is a bloodstain on the floor, at the bottom of the stairs, and it dawns on Sally that Mr. Scott is not where she left him. "Where did he go?" she asks, her voice laced with panic.

"Who?" says Mrs. Cowley.

Sally stutters trying to say his name.

"Oh, your Mr. Scott?"

Sally is tempted to clarify. Mr. Scott is not hers. But it will take too long to explain, and she is sure Mrs. Cowley does not care—one way or the other. "Yes."

"I asked Mr. Campbell and Mr. Price to take him upstairs. The Crumps came for their mother, so I had a spare bed."

Sally feels weak-kneed with relief, and she lets out a burst of nervous laughter. "I don't know what's wrong with me," she says. "It isn't as if I even know the man."

"Pull a man from a burning building," says Mrs. Cowley, "and you'll convince yourself you do."

The two women spend the next hour slowly working their way through the house, bathing burns and applying poultices. When they get to Mr. Scott, who has been installed in the bedroom down the hall from Maria's, Mrs. Cowley shows off his new stitches, which are neat and evenly spaced.

"You did these while I was gone?"

"Took three of us to hold him down."

"I do wish he'd come to," she says, staring at his blistered neck.

"Don't count on it anytime soon," says Mrs. Cowley. "We gave him enough laudanum to kill a small child."

From downstairs comes Archie's booming baritone. "Dr. Foushee is here!"

Sally moves to the top of the stairs, where she can see both men down below, shedding their coats and hats.

"I can't tell you what a relief it is to hear that you're the one who's been seeing to my Margaret," says Archie to the doctor as Sally hurries down the stairs.

Dr. Foushee demurs, then gestures toward the parlor. "Such a mess we're all in."

Sally hopes that the doctor can convince Archie to amputate the leg, so when she reaches the bottom of the stairs, she plays along with the little routine Archie's established, even though it seems better suited for a garden party than a surgical appointment. "How do you two know each other again?"

"Through Tom, I suppose," says Archie fondly.

"Tom Marshall?" Sally asks.

"No, no. Tom Ritchie. He owns the *Enquirer*."

"He's my son-in-law," Dr. Foushee explains.

"Ah," says Sally. Her late sister's husband, Spencer Roane, is a cousin of Ritchie's, but she's not sure what good it will do to mention it.

"Tom wasn't there, was he?" Archie asks.

"No, no. Now he is, of course. Trying to conduct interviews. But he and Isabella were at a dinner party last night, thank God."

"I bet he's having a time of it," says Archie. "Are they saying anything about the cause?"

"Not yet," Dr. Foushee admits. "But he'll get to the bottom of it, you can be sure."

"Dr. Foushee," says Mrs. Cowley as she joins the party. "So good to see you."

Sally is ready to get on with things, so she gestures toward Margaret, and Dr. Foushee traces a path across the parlor to give Margaret another look.

When he lifts the quilt that covers her mangled leg, he shakes his head and says, "Let's get her into the kitchen."

Mrs. Cowley scurries ahead of them to clear a path, and Sally stands by as the two men lift her friend into the air.

"Grab my bag, will you, Mrs. Campbell?" Dr. Foushee says as he steps over a Mrs. Cousins, who lies prostrate in the middle of the room.

"You were going to bring an extra man?" says Sally.

"None to be found, I'm afraid."

By the time they enter the kitchen, Mrs. Cowley has cleared the table and wiped it down with a damp rag.

"Do you have a sheet?" Dr. Foushee asks her.

"They're all in use," she says, and the doctor shrugs and directs Archie to set Margaret down on the bare wood. Their timing is off, so when they lower her onto the tabletop, her leg jars and she lets out a cry of discomfort.

"Be careful," Sally whispers, but if they hear her, they do not pay her any mind.

Sally hands Dr. Foushee his bag, and while he roots around in it, he addresses her directly. "I trust you've discussed the patient's options with her husband."

Sally clears her throat and makes a point of looking directly at Archie. "I have. But perhaps it would be helpful if you went over everything with him again."

She listens as Dr. Foushee runs through the options, but her brother-in-law just stares at the gleaming bone, and she can tell he isn't hearing him.

"I don't think she'll be very happy without the use of her leg," says Archie to the room at large.

Dr. Foushee doesn't even try to argue, just nods agreeably and says, "So, we'll set it."

Sally has to do something. She takes Archie's hands in hers. "Brother, friend, listen to me. This decision you're making—it's potentially the choice between life and death."

Archie doesn't make eye contact with her.

"Margaret will adapt. If there is anyone who can do it, it is her."

"But to spend the rest of her life hobbling around . . ." Archie trails off, unsure of himself.

Sally tries to shake Margaret awake, to get her to weigh in on her own probable demise, but she doesn't stir.

"Mrs. Cowley," says Sally, desperation in her voice, "tell him what you told me. About how high the risk of infection is with a break like this." But all Mrs. Cowley does is quietly acknowledge that what Sally's said is true.

"You told me yourself that you wouldn't keep the leg."

The old woman stiffens. Sally is putting her in an uncomfortable position, but she doesn't know what else to do. So much is at stake.

"Isn't that right? You'd amputate if it were up to you?"

There is something that passes, unspoken, between Dr. Foushee and Mrs. Cowley, because the next thing Sally knows, Mrs. Cowley is kowtowing to the doctor. "The good doctor knows what he's doing."

Sally is not having it, and she can hear her own voice rising. "She's afraid to contradict you, Dr. Foushee. But we both know that allowing Archie to make a decision that is so clearly—"

"Mrs. Campbell," Dr. Foushee says sharply. "Mr. Campbell is within his rights to determine what is in his wife's best interests."

"What about Margaret's rights?" Sally is screaming now. "What about the fact that she jumped out of a burning building so that she'd have an actual chance? What about the fact that she told me, just last night, that she was in favor of whatever course of action might give her the best possible chance of survival?"

"Is that true?" Dr. Foushee asks.

It is a blatant lie, but she is desperate. "Yes."

The doctor speaks directly to Archie. "If we know her wishes, that changes things, doesn't it?"

"Hmmm?" says Archie, as if he's been in a trance.

"Will you allow me to amputate?"

Sally holds her breath.

Archie stares at Margaret's pale lips, her furtive brow. Then he shakes his head, as if he has reconciled himself to something unpleasant and has decided it is best to just get on with it. "No," he says finally. "She deserves to be whole."

爨 | GILBERT | 爨

I t is strange, not seeing the theater in its usual spot. Almost like a trick of the eye. Or the way, when a man is missing a button on his jacket, its absence is all Gilbert can see. The building itself has never seemed like anything special—nothing compared to the pictures of all those European amphitheaters and opera houses in Louisa's schoolbooks. But now that it is gone, Gilbert realizes how big and grand it actually was.

A great number of men are at the site, and after scanning the crowd for Kemp, Gilbert proceeds cautiously. Some men are combing the ruins, others are sifting through small piles of debris that have been placed atop large white sheets. But most of them are simply standing around, talking about who saw what when. "I was there," says a man with an exceptionally long beard, "and I tell you—there was nothing to be done."

One man, in an angora hat, has established himself at a small table, which someone took the trouble of dragging outside. He takes down the names of the injured, along with people who are believed to be among the dead, but sometimes he gets confused and Gilbert can hear him say, "No, wait, wait. Did you say survived or died?"

Another man stands watch over a wheelbarrow, and when Gilbert leans in, he sees that it is full of jewelry, pocket watches, and even a pair of wire-rimmed spectacles that have survived the blaze. Gilbert tries to decide whether Louisa might have been wearing any jewelry; she sometimes wore a thin gold chain around her neck, but he doesn't think he's seen her in it lately. He draws closer to the wheelbarrow and reaches out a hand, thinking that if he can just sift through the mess, he might see something he recognizes.

"Hands off!" says the man in charge, and Gilbert yanks back his hand, as if the metal is still hot enough to burn him.

"Sir, I was just—"

"Just what?" the man says, crossing his arms in front of his chest.

"I was just wanting to check to see if anything in that wheelbarrow belonged to my wife's mistress—Miss Louisa Mayo."

The man's expression doesn't soften, but he does uncross his arms. "Her stepfather's already been by. Just a few minutes ago. Didn't find a thing."

Gilbert wants to tell the man that General Preston barely knows Louisa, that Gilbert wouldn't need two hands to count up the hours those two have spent in the same room. Even if General Preston knew what to look for, it is unlikely he'd find it among so many other baubles. He can barely find his way out of a bottle.

He looks for the general in the crowd. Maybe if he can find him, he can convince him to circle back to the wheelbarrow and look for the necklace one more time, this time with Gilbert's help. A large group of men in fine coats stands near what used to be the theater's gallery door, and Gilbert trudges toward them.

He passes a group of young boys and one looks at him, then whispers something to the others and runs off. A few men, gathered behind them, also turn to stare. Gilbert is used to being watched by white men, but this is something different, and the feeling unsettles him.

Someone in the crowd shouts at him, and he searches for the source. There are a couple of customers he recognizes, but no general. "Gilbert Hunt!" comes the voice a second time, and a man wearing a riding coat steps forward.

Gilbert can't know what the man wants with him, so he holds his breath, waiting to find out. But then the man does the most peculiar thing. He brings his hands together and begins to clap. And the next thing Gilbert knows, the fellow beside him is clapping, and then all of the men in their fine coats are putting their hands together, too. The applause moves like a ripple through the crowd, and before Gilbert knows quite what is happening, more groups on other parts of the theater green have joined in. Men set down their shovels and rakes to put their hands together. The man who sat at the table has risen to his feet. Even the man at the wheelbarrow is clapping now. Gilbert whips his head around, trying to take in the whole green at once.

The applause is thunderous. Gilbert points at his own chest, trying to decide whether all this fuss can really be for his benefit, and the man in the riding coat nods and shouts over the noise, "You saved my sister last night."

Another man steps forward. "And my daughter."

"My wife," comes a voice from the crowd.

"My mother."

For a brief moment, Gilbert thinks of Kemp. If he didn't like Twaits and that other actor fawning all over Gilbert this morning, he's surely not going to like Gilbert getting this kind of attention. And he's bound to find out about it. But a little voice inside Gilbert's head tells him not to think of Kemp now—that this moment belongs to him and to Dr. McCaw and to all the men and women who worked to save the lives of folks in the theater.

A few yards away, the newspaper man, Thomas Ritchie, is jotting down notes in his little book. Even though Gilbert knows the paper doesn't run stories—or even the obituaries—of Black folks, he pictures Ritchie taking those notes back to the *Richmond Enquirer*'s offices and turning them into a piece that is every bit as magnificent as the way all this applause makes him feel.

The individual faces of the men and women on the green blur, and Gilbert realizes his eyes have begun to tear up. He doesn't dare dab at them in front of so many people, so he just nods his head slowly. Gilbert always tries to do the right thing, by himself and the people around him, but he doesn't know if he's ever been recognized for it, and this recognition—now, in front of so many people—leaves him feeling overwhelmed. Everybody in this city has lost somebody in that fire, and if these men can stand before him on this sad day and demonstrate their gratitude, like he is an honest-to-God citizen of this city and not just somebody's property, then maybe there is hope for him after all.

❧ | SALLY | ❧

After Dr. Foushee sets Margaret's leg, Archie makes a big show of writing down the instructions for her care, but Sally can't bear to witness the performance.

Archie means well—she knows he does—but the very idea that he's going to clean Margaret's wound, keep the leg wrapped, and watch for signs of fever is ridiculous. Ultimately, the job will fall to Mrs. Cowley and Sally, and eventually Effie, back at home.

"Are you hiding?" Mrs. Cowley asks Sally when she finds her upstairs in Mr. Scott's room.

"I can't be down there right now."

"That's understandable," she says.

Sally knows she should probably leave well enough alone, but she can't help it. So, she asks, "Do you really think Dr. Foushee and Archie were right? To keep the leg?"

"No," says Mrs. Cowley decidedly. "But nothing I said was going to change their minds."

"You don't know that," Sally argues. "You're an experienced practitioner, who—as far as I can tell—knows a great deal more than Dr. Foushee does."

"But I did not go to the University of Edinburgh." She says the word *Edinburgh* with contempt.

"Neither did half the physicians in this town. In fact, I'd wager most of them have no real training to speak of."

"But they are men. And they are white."

Sally has to admit she is right on both those counts.

"I am allowed to practice medicine because my cures work and because I treat colored patients that physicians like Dr. Foushee would prefer to pretend do not exist," says Mrs. Cowley. "But, if at any point the powers that be decide I am doing more harm than good, I can be arrested and even killed."

"But that's an old slave law. It doesn't apply to—"

Mrs. Cowley raises a sharp eyebrow in her direction.

"Oh," says Sally. Suddenly, it all makes sense. The Negroes who've been knocking on Mrs. Cowley's back door, Dr. Foushee's dismissiveness of Mrs. Cowley's cures, the men who carried Margaret to Mrs. Cowley's door but refused to stay. Mrs. Cowley's skin is the color of cream, but Sally has spent enough years on a plantation to know that a person's skin color doesn't always tell the full story. "Was your husband also—"

"An Aboriginal?"

Sally understands then that Mrs. Cowley will never speak to her plainly—not about this.

"My husband was born in Buckinghamshire."

"So, he's British?"

"Was."

"Right. I'm sorry."

"As long as he was alive, people left me alone."

"And after he died?"

"I don't have to tell you that a widow rarely enjoys the same protections as a married woman."

She does not. It is positively primitive, the way Sally has witnessed her own rights and liberties slip through her fingers in the years since Robert's death. "Some days, it feels like I don't exist at all."

Mrs. Cowley moves around the side of the bed and takes Sally's hand. "It is hard being ignored."

"Yes, I think that's it," she says, and she is surprised to feel her lower lip begin to tremble.

Mrs. Cowley opens her arms, and Sally is glad to lean into this unfamiliar woman's embrace, to press her face against Mrs. Cowley's shoulder and allow her tears to fall onto the well-worn cotton of her calico dress. Mrs. Cowley pats her back and *shhh*s her like a baby, and because it has been so long since anyone has taken care of Sally, the gesture makes her cry all the harder.

After a few minutes, her tears slow and she chokes out the words "It was like that in the theater, too."

Mrs. Cowley waits patiently for Sally to continue.

"We couldn't find Margaret, and Archie wouldn't go back for her. I think that's why the situation downstairs makes me so furious. That he should abandon her so completely, only to be able to make such an important decision about her future well-being. It's not fair."

"Very little is." Mrs. Cowley pulls back to get a good look at Sally, then she pats her cheek affectionately. From her apron pocket, she removes a piece of letter paper folded into quarters. "Here."

"What is it?" Sally asks as she unfolds the document, but the answer soon reveals itself.

Mrs. Archibald Campbell, of Richmond, broken leg
Mr. Alexander Scott, of Fauquier County, laceration, burns
Miss Maria Price, of Richmond, head injury
Mrs. Milroy Kimball, of Manchester, burns
Mrs. Charles Crump, of Hanover, burns
Mr. Norman Hargrove, of Petersburg, shortness of breath, burns
Mrs. Oliver Cousins, of Richmond, burns, sprain
Miss Winifred Harris, of Richmond, burns
Unidentified girl, burns

"Is this everyone in the house?" Sally asks.

Mrs. Cowley nods.

Sally's eyes settle on the last entry. "That poor girl in Maria's room. We still don't have any idea who she is?"

Mrs. Cowley shakes her head. "Who could recognize her?"

It's a fair question.

Sally gestures at the list. "So, what are we doing with this?"

"John Gamble stopped by while you were out. He's been asked to head up the burial committee and is trying to get a firm count on who's going in the ground."

"What a horrible job."

"I don't disagree with you," she says. "But will you deliver this to him? At the capitol?"

"Aren't I more useful here?"

Mrs. Cowley gives her a pitying look, and Sally recalls the fit she just threw downstairs. "I thought it might be good for you to get out."

❧ | JACK | ❧

The Enquirer's *offices are housed in* a clapboard building that sits close to the street. On one side of the building there is a small bookshop, where Jack used to buy his schoolbooks when his father was alive, and on the other side is the print shop, where Ritchie and his staff produce the *Enquirer*, along with a reliable farmer's almanac and half the books and pamphlets that circulate the city.

Anderson lets out a low whistle as they enter the print shop. "Quite the operation," he says.

In the middle of the shop sit two printing presses—an old wooden number that looks like it was built before the Revolution, and a newer one on an iron frame. Two men—one white and one Black—work in tandem at the new machine; the white man beats the plate with a pair of ink balls and the Black man positions the paper and pulls the lever. They work in perfect rhythm, and every few seconds, the Black man removes a finished sheet from the press and hangs it on a large drying rack, which runs the length of the back wall. Near the window there is a cabinet stacked with type cases, and in the far corner of the room sits a giant pile of rags, waiting—Jack can only assume—to be sent to the paper mill and turned into slurry.

"Sorry to bother you," Anderson says. "But is Mr. Ritchie here?"

The white man looks annoyed to have been interrupted, but he nods in the direction of a small door at the back of the shop.

Anderson is at the door of the office in several long strides, and Jack follows close behind him. A quick rap, and Mr. Ritchie says, "Come in."

The newspaper editor is a thin man, older than Anderson, but not nearly so old as Placide. He has a square jaw, thin lips, and a hawkish nose, and he sits at a small desk positioned directly in front of a wood-burning fireplace that doesn't look like it's been swept once all winter. The desk is piled high with papers, and a settee is pushed against one wall. When Anderson addresses him, the editor doesn't look up, just holds out a hand and continues to scratch his pen across the page, until he comes to a full stop. "This is a very bad time."

"Yes, I know," says Anderson. "We're with Placide and Green. Alexander Placide asked us to deliver a letter to you."

Ritchie deposits his pen in an inkhorn and gives Anderson his full attention. "Oh?"

Anderson pulls the letter from his waistband. "I believe he hopes you'll publish it."

"Do I get the privilege of reading it first? Or am I to publish it sight unseen?" says Ritchie, and Anderson steps forward to give it to him.

Jack holds his breath as he watches Ritchie's eyes move across the page. At one point, they grow wide, and Jack can only assume he's gotten to the part about the vile incendiaries.

"You both work for Placide and Green?" Ritchie asks, and Anderson answers affirmatively, but Ritchie is looking directly at Jack.

"I'm a stagehand."

"From Charleston?"

Jack shakes his head no. "Richmond."

Ritchie gives him a questioning stare. "What's your name?"

"Jack Gibson."

"Are you Zeke Gibson's son?"

Hearing his father's name spoken aloud always turns Jack's insides to mush, but there's something particularly painful about hearing his name invoked now, when he would so heartily disapprove of what Jack's doing. Jack gives Ritchie a strangled "Yes, sir."

Ritchie says only "Hmmm." Then he waves the letter at both of them. "Have you read this?"

Jack knows not to admit to writing it, but he can't see the harm in claiming to have read it. He nods.

"I've been at the site since midnight, and I've interviewed at least two dozen people," says Ritchie, tapping a small notebook that lays open on the desk, on top of some papers. "And in all of those interviews, not a single person has referenced—what does he call them?"

"Vile incendiaries," Jack offers, and Anderson shoots him a look.

"He means Negroes, I presume?" says Ritchie.

Anderson says yes, and Jack says no at exactly the same time.

Ritchie asks, "Which is it?"

"Negroes," says Anderson. "Most certainly."

Ritchie looks at Jack, and asks, "Why did you say they weren't?"

Jack goes to speak, but Anderson cuts him off. "Jack just got confused by the question. He's not terribly quick."

Ritchie eyes Jack over his spectacles. "A shame. His father was quite sharp."

Jack's cheeks burn.

"This is a big claim Mr. Placide is making. Does he have the evidence to support it?" Ritchie asks, and Jack defers to Anderson, who clearly wants to do all the talking.

"Mountains of it."

"It would have been nice if he'd included it here," says Ritchie, reading through the letter once more.

"I think he tried," says Jack, who is unable to think of the last lines of the letter without cringing.

"An attempted box office break-in, back in October, hardly qualifies as proof that someone wanted to burn down the building."

Ritchie isn't wrong, but Jack doesn't dare admit it with Anderson standing just a few feet away.

"What kind of proof do you need?" Anderson asks. "We can get it."

Ritchie lets out a low laugh. He looks every bit as exhausted as Jack feels. "Tell me, Mr. Gibson. Do *you* think I should publish this letter?"

Jack looks at Anderson, who nods at him.

"Do you need permission to speak freely?" Ritchie asks.

"No, sir," says Jack. "I just, well, I can't really say . . ."

Ritchie leans forward. "It's funny. Several of the people I spoke with seem convinced the fire started backstage. They said it was an actor who first made the announcement." He flips the pages of his notebook, looking for the exact quote, but he needn't have bothered. Robertson's words will be with Jack forever. "'The house is on fire.' Did I get that right, Mr. Gibson?"

Jack whispers, "That sounds right."

Anderson is quick to explain. "We did make the announcement. But that's just because the fire started out back, and to our knowledge, we were the first to notice it."

"Out back?"

"Near the stage door," says Anderson.

"It's a brick building," says Ritchie. "How did these incendiaries of yours manage to get the thing to catch?"

Anderson is drowning, Jack can tell, so he tries to throw him a rope. "I'd left a few hay bales near the door. We needed them during the second half of the pantomime, and there was nowhere to store them inside."

Ritchie glances at Anderson. "Is that true?"

Anderson gives them both an enthusiastic nod.

Jack expects to feel terrible, lying about something this important, and there's a part of him that does. But there's another part of him that feels elated to have come through with a logical explanation that Ritchie appears to be buying.

"How do you know the hay bales are what caught?" asks Ritchie.

"Thomas Caulfield saw the whole thing," says Anderson.

Jack is always a little awestruck when the actors improvise their lines. One actor inadvertently goes off script, and the others have to adapt, until they've eventually guided him back to the lines he knows by heart. If you've got the script memorized—and Jack always does—it's a terrifying couple of minutes, watching the actors move further and further away from the words on the page and wondering if the audience will notice the mistake. But what Jack has learned is that, if the actors deliver their improvised lines with confidence, nobody ever notices.

"Mr. Caulfield will corroborate this?" Ritchie asks Anderson.

"Certainly."

Ritchie sits very still in his chair, like he's trying to take in everything he's just heard. Finally, he says, "I'll need to interview Mr. Caulfield before I can run with a story this inflammatory."

Anderson nods in agreement.

Ritchie refolds the letter, slides it between the pages of his notebook, and pulls out his pocket watch to check the time. "Tomorrow's paper goes to press in two hours."

❦ | SALLY | ❦

S*ally stands at the bottom of* the capitol steps, clutching Mrs. Cowley's list in her hand.

The capitol looks as if it belongs in ancient Rome. All columns and pediment, with a portico large enough to accommodate a country dance. A replica of Maison Carrée in Nîmes, her father told her, when he brought her to Richmond for the dedication. She was eight.

Sally makes her way up the steps, and a man on his way out holds the door for her. She is usually only at the capitol on Sundays, when Archie and Margaret drag her to church services in the Hall of Delegates. It is a peculiar place to worship, but the Presbyterians are without a church, and the Episcopalians are too lazy to walk all the way to Henrico Parish Church in their good shoes. For several years, two ministers—a Presbyterian and an Episcopalian—have traded off giving the Sunday sermon, every other week, from the Assembly floor. The joke is that no one in Richmond knows when to pull out the *Book of Common Prayer*, but Sally is not so religious that she minds the mix-ups that inevitably occur. In fact, she is strangely charmed by them.

On Sunday mornings, the rotunda echoes with the click of men's sword canes on the marble floor and the gossip of women who have waited to share the week's most tantalizing secrets with one another. When everyone talks at once, their voices fill the cavernous space, and it is hard to believe that anyone can hear the voice of God.

This afternoon, the rotunda is largely empty. When Sally comes face-to-face with Jean-Antoine Houdon's sculpture of George Washington, she stops for a moment to consider the man her father loved so dearly. She has always liked the sculpture. His double chin, the wrinkled uniform, the fact that Houdon intentionally left a button off the general's jacket. Washington is depicted, not as the god that many would make him, but as a man who, like everyone else, had faults.

On the far side of the rotunda, some men lean over a table, which has been pulled in front of the doors to the Hall of Delegates. Two chairs sit empty and in a third sits a middle-aged woman, who wears a nun's habit streaked in blood. She looks familiar, but it takes several seconds for Sally to realize that she is the actress who brought the crowd to their feet.

"Excuse me," says Sally to the men at the table. Her words echo. "I was just wondering if anyone knows where I might find—"

"Shhhh," the men say in unison. One of them whispers, "They're in session."

"What? Now?" she asks. She can't imagine what business the Assembly has that can't wait a few days, then she remembers the stock buckle that was pulled out of the ruins. "Is it about the governor?"

"No," says a man in a crooked hat, before asking—too quickly—"What do you know about the governor?"

"Just that he's dead."

"We haven't confirmed that yet," says a third man, who looks familiar.

"Do I know you?" Sally asks.

He looks at her for the first time. "William Marshall. How can I help you?"

"Are you Tom's uncle?"

"Tom Marshall? Yes, you know him?"

"I'm Sally Campbell." As soon as the words are out of her mouth, she thinks better of her decision to use her married name. If there is ever a time to trade on the name Henry, it is now. "Sally Henry Campbell."

Marshall blinks wildly. "Oh, my dear, you're Pat's daughter? Delightful."

"I was with Tom last night. At the theater," she says, afraid to ask the obvious question. "Did he make it out?"

William Marshall nods his head vigorously. "Yes, yes. He's no worse for wear. Thank God."

"And his cousin, too?"

"Mr. Colston? Not a scratch on him, you'll be relieved to hear."

What Sally feels at this news isn't relief, but resentment. How should those two men—like Archie—have fared so well when the women around them came out so poorly? None of it makes any sense. "That's . . . good news," she manages to finally say.

"I'll tell him you asked after him."

She waits for him to remark on her own survival, but she can tell she is losing his attention. "I have a list. Of people being treated at the Cowley residence. I was told I should bring it to John Gamble."

"Oh, yes. He's not here now, but I can take it."

Sally hands him the piece of paper, and watches as Marshall scans the names. "Rodney," he says to one of the other men. "Alexander Scott was there."

"Dead?" Rodney asks when he looks up from his paperwork.

"Injured." Marshall hands the list to Rodney, who studies it carefully, then sets it down on top of a pile of other lists—some written on letter paper, but others scratched onto playbills and broadsides and the back of old receipts.

"Do you know him?" Sally asks.

Marshall nods. "He's a delegate. From Fauquier County."

"Yes, I know that. But I mean, has anyone come looking for him?"

"Not since I've been here," says the man in the crooked hat. "But people have been coming and going all day. Everyone's trying to track somebody down."

"Do you know anything about his family?" says Sally.

"Whose family?" asks Rodney.

It is all Sally can do to keep the frustration out of her voice. "Alexander Scott's. Does he have a wife? Someone I could write?"

Rodney squints at the ceiling. "That I don't know."

"You know who might?" Marshall says, looking pleased with himself. "Tom."

"Right," says Sally, who feels suddenly exhausted. She forces herself to ask, "Do you know if Tom's staying at his parents' house?"

"Yes, there was talk of a hunting party, but that's all been canceled now. I should think he'll stay in town for a little while, now that his father needs the help."

"The chief justice needs help?" Sally could swear Tom told her his father had stayed home last night. Or maybe he'd said his parents had gone to a dinner party. Either way, she didn't think Chief Justice Marshall had been anywhere near the theater. At least, she prayed he hadn't. "He wasn't there, was he?"

"Oh, no, he's fine. It's not official yet, but he's agreed to head up the monument committee."

Sally exhales, then allows herself to ask, "Monument for what?"

"The fire victims, of course."

The woman in the chair begins to weep.

Sally doesn't doubt that a monument will eventually be called for, but it seems premature to begin fundraising for it now. She thinks of the girl in the bed beside Maria Price. Burns on more than half of her body. "Shouldn't we get everyone buried first? I mean, before we memorialize them?"

Marshall nods. "There's a committee for that, too."

"The burial? I heard."

"We're going to bury everyone together. There's just no way around it."

"When?"

"Tomorrow, if the weather holds."

Sally is all for a quick burial, but she doesn't see how John Gamble will get all the victims identified by tomorrow morning, much less in the ground. Some of them, like the girl in Mrs. Cowley's upstairs bedroom, might not even be dead by then.

There is a commotion behind them, and everyone, including the woman in the nun's habit, turns to watch the doors of the Hall of Delegates swing open. Dozens of men stream past them, clapping each other on the back and talking over each other like they've just left a cockfight and not an emergency legislative session. "What in the world were they doing in there?" Sally asks Marshall, but her audience with him has ended.

"Passing a resolution," says the woman in the habit. "But a lot of good it will do my Nancy."

Sally turns to look at her. "What's the resolution for?"

"How did they put it? I think they called it an expression of their sorrow at the loss of the governor, and 'other worthy and meritorious citizens.' "

Not one of the men in the crowd looks half as sorrowful as the woman sitting before her, which makes her wonder how a resolution written by women might have read.

❈ | CECILY | ❈

The sound of the boathouse door opening wakes Cecily with a start.

She has no idea how long she's been sleeping, just that it is daylight and she can feel the warm rays of the afternoon sun on the sailcloth that envelops her.

The only person who knows Cecily is here is her mother, and if it is her, Cecily feels sure she will announce herself right away.

She holds her breath.

Nothing.

The door closes, and still Della has not said a word.

At first, this silence confuses Cecily, but after several long seconds pass, she begins to panic. Something isn't right.

"Cecily?" comes a small voice. Cecily closes her eyes, thinks she might die right there where she lies. It's her little brother.

She sits up quickly in the canoe. "Moses," she says, "what are you doing here?"

Her brother scrambles backward, trips over the push poles in the middle of the floor, and lands on his rear.

"Shhh," says Cecily as she frees herself from her canvas cocoon and climbs out of the canoe. "You trying to let everyone this side of the river know I'm hiding in here?"

She helps him to his feet.

Moses looks at her in disbelief. "You're alive?"

"How'd you know?"

"I didn't. I mean, I thought I did. But Mama said I was dreaming."

"You saw me in the cabin last night?"

He nods. "I know I wasn't meant to."

So much for the hours she'd spent standing there in the cold, behind her parents' cabin, waiting on her brother and sisters to fall asleep. "You haven't told nobody, have you?"

He shakes his head. "Just Mama."

"What'd she say?"

"That she didn't need me giving her any extra grief at a time like this."

It sounds like something Della would say, especially if she was trying to put him off the track. "So, she didn't tell you to come?"

Moses laughs. "No way. She'd kill me dead if she knew I was here."

"Speaking of people who are fixing to kill you," says Cecily, "what's the overseer going to have to say about you not showing up at the mill?"

"It's closed today, on account of the fire. Overseer's wife is still missing, and the Prices are all the way over on the other side of town, seeing about Maria."

If the overseer's wife was at the theater last night, Cecily never saw her. And she's a hard one to miss, on account of the fact she's got a birthmark the size of a quail's egg that sits smack-dab in the middle of her forehead.

"So, if Mama didn't send you, how'd you know where I was?"

"I followed you," he says, like it's the most obvious thing in the world. "Last night, after you came for Mama."

"Jesus, Moses," says Cecily. "You're going to get me killed."

"No one saw me. I swear."

"What about now? You walking down here in broad daylight. You don't think that's going to raise anyone's suspicions?"

Moses holds up a pail and points to a rod he's got leaning against the wall. "I told everybody I was going fishing, so if they see me down here, it won't be no big surprise."

Moses has got all the answers, and it scares her a little—how sure he is of himself. He doesn't understand that the Prices and the people they employ aren't the only ones who can turn on him. That for the right bribe, any one of the folks in the quarters might be convinced to give him up.

"You can't be coming down here," she says.

He retrieves a small bundle, wrapped in a kerchief, from inside the pail. "If you don't want me coming down here, then I guess I'll take this ham hock home with me."

Cecily's stomach growls, and she snatches the bundle out of her brother's hand. When she folds back the cloth, she finds not only the piece of pork but a heel of bread and a rind of cheese. "Moses, where'd you get all this?"

"I ain't telling."

If this were any other day, she might hit him upside the head and tell him to stop taking stupid risks. But she's too hungry to argue.

She eats all the pork, but saves a little of the bread and cheese, in case her mother doesn't show back up again anytime soon.

"I brought you this, too," Moses says as he peels off an old sweater that belonged to one of the Price boys and hands it to her. "It'll be snug, but I thought you might be cold."

"I already took your jacket," she says as she sinks her fingers into the thick wool.

Moses shrugs. "I'll find something else."

"Moses," says Cecily slowly. "What I'm doing is dangerous. For me and for anyone who helps me."

"Who said anything about helping you?" His smile is lopsided, too many big teeth in a too-small mouth.

"It's not funny."

"I didn't say it was."

"I'm going to run. Just as soon as me and Mama figure out the details. But none of this works if anyone gets so much as an inkling that I'm alive."

"I can help."

"You trying to put Mama in an early grave?"

"She doesn't have to know."

"If you get caught down here, what our mama knows is going to be the least of it."

❧ | GILBERT | ❧

Gilbert figures that if Louisa was badly injured, she might have been taken to a nearby home for treatment. So, he starts knocking on doors, beginning with the houses that face the green and working outward.

Most places, he turns up nothing promising. But at Mrs. Cowley's, she leads him into an upstairs bedroom where there is a young girl who has been burned beyond recognition. As soon as he approaches the bed and sees the extent of the girl's injuries, he wants to look away. The face is ruined, poor child, so he looks at the parts of her body the fire didn't destroy—her wrists, her forearms, the curve of one of her shoulders. Louisa's wrists are skinny—Sara always said she had bird bones—and this girl's wrists have some meat on them. "It ain't her," he says to Mrs. Cowley, and they move out of the room quietly so as not to wake the girl sleeping in the other bed.

Mrs. Cowley gives him a few other homes to check, places where she knows folks have taken in the injured. "It's awful, isn't it?" she says as he prepares to go.

"Sure is."

Once Gilbert works his way through the houses that sit in the immediate vicinity of the theater, he moves farther afield. It wouldn't make sense to carry anyone down Shockoe Hill and across the creek, so he sticks to Court End, and eventually moves west through Madison Ward.

He is nearly to Court's Addition when he rounds a corner and spies Kemp and three of his men on horseback.

Quick as he can manage, he draws himself up alongside a shed, holds his breath, and waits for them to pass.

But they don't pass. They're interrogating someone, over by the barn, across the way. A couple of someones he realizes, once he gets bold enough to poke his head around the corner.

Gilbert can't hear what they're saying, but it's clear as day what's going on. The men lined up against the barn have skin as dark as Gilbert's, which is all anyone needs to get stopped by the patrol.

Gilbert's too far away to get a good look at the men, but one of them reminds him of his sister's husband, Cecil, who is thin as a reed, with a long neck that bends like a blue heron's.

Gilbert skirts the shed, trying to see if he can get himself a better view, but it's no good. He looks around. A dozen feet away is a woodpile, and if he can make it over there, he should be able to get a decent look at what's going on.

It's risky to run for it. But Kemp and his men aren't looking his way. Gilbert counts to three in his head, then starts to move—fast, but not so fast as to make a sound.

He was right. From the woodpile, Gilbert can see straight across the street, and his stomach drops when he realizes that the reed of a man is indeed Cecil. Kemp is in Cecil's face, and he's yelling loud enough that his words carry. "You mean to tell me that you were given free rein to search, but no pass to explain what the hell you're doing?"

Cecil speaks softly and whatever he says to Kemp doesn't make its way all the way to Gilbert's ears. Who's Cecil searching for, he wonders, and why? "What I think," says Kemp, "is that the three of you were part of the plot to burn down the theater."

The man next to Cecil begins to weep, but it's like Cecil's face is carved from stone.

Kemp gives an order to one of the other men on the patrol, who gets down from his horse and shackles all three men. "Take them in," says Kemp. "We'll keep pushing out, toward the slaughterhouse."

Gilbert watches as Cecil is led away, then waits for Kemp and the rest of the patrol to head off in the other direction. Once the road is clear, he darts across it and takes off through the woods to the Price place.

By the time he arrives at the quarters, he is breathing hard, but he doesn't wait to so much as catch his breath before he bangs on the door of his sister's cabin.

It's Moses who answers. Gilbert looks past him, into the cabin's dark interior, but all he sees are the little girls playing near the hearth. "Your mama here?" he asks his nephew.

Moses shakes his head no.

"Where she at?"

He doesn't say a word, just shrugs.

"I got to find her. It's important. She at the mill?"

Again, nothing.

"Your papa's been taken in," Gilbert says finally. "And I need your mama to tell Master Price, quick as she can."

Moses looks like he's close to tears.

"What's wrong, Mo?"

The boy stutters, "Nothing."

Gilbert is starting to get concerned. "Is your mama all right?"

He nods.

"And your sister?"

No nod this time.

Gilbert remembers what Kemp was saying to Cecil before he hauled him in. "Hey, Mo, was your papa out looking for someone last night?"

It's like his nephew's afraid of saying the wrong thing. Finally, he whispers, "Cecily."

Gilbert's confused. "What was he doing looking for her?"

The boy's voice shakes. "She was with Maria Price. At the theater."

All of a sudden, Gilbert feels unsteady on his feet. "She make it out?"

Moses looks at the floor. "No, sir," he says. "She did not."

❈ | JACK | ❈

When *Jack and Anderson return to* the Washington Tavern from the *Enquirer*'s offices, they find Placide has stretched out in front of the hearth and fallen asleep. Anderson pokes him gently in the shoulder. "Do you want to hear how it went?"

His eyes pop open, and he scrambles to sit up and rub the sleep from them. "Yes, yes," he says. "Tell me everything."

Anderson pulls up a chair. "I think he's buying it. Don't you, Jack?"

Jack nods, then offers, "He wants to interview Caulfield."

"Is that good?" Placide asks Anderson.

"I think so," says Anderson. "We told him Caulfield saw a band of Negroes light a hay bale on fire. Near the stage door."

"A hay bale?"

"It was Jack's idea."

Placide seems impressed, which makes Jack feel a little squeamish.

"Where's Caulfield?" asks Anderson.

"I think he just hauled himself off to bed," Placide says.

"How did everything go with the slave patrol?"

Placide combs his fingers through his hair. "Twaits and Young met with some success. So did some of the others. The patrol's going to step things up, keep an eye out for any Negroes who look suspicious."

Jack wonders if there has ever been a Negro the slave patrol did not deem suspicious.

Anderson snaps his fingers at Jack. "Will you go wake Caulfield? Tell him we need him down here now."

Jack makes for the back stairs, but Placide instructs him to wait. "Are we sure it's a good idea to put Caulfield in front of Ritchie?"

Thomas Caulfield is known for his looks, not his intellect, and Jack can only assume Placide is nervous that he won't hold up under Ritchie's scrutiny.

"It's too late to worry about that now," says Anderson. "I was desperate, trying to think of someone who wasn't onstage when the fire broke out, and—unfortunately—his name's the first one that came to mind."

Placide doesn't say anything, just gets up, stretches, and shovels more coal into the grate. There's something about his silence that feels like an indictment. Anderson must pick up on this, too, because he's quick to offer reassurances. "We'll go over everything with Caulfield. We can prepare him for what Ritchie's likely to ask."

"He'll get it," Jack agrees. "I can help." Sometimes, in the afternoons, the actors ask Jack to run lines with them, and he's good at it because he's patient and interested and because he rarely, if ever, has anything better to do.

Placide doesn't seem convinced, but he changes the subject. "I just saw William Wirt down at the Market Hall," he says.

Anderson rolls his eyes.

"He seemed quite sure he was about to be tapped to head up the inquest committee."

Wirt is a local attorney, whose claim to fame is that he unsuccessfully prosecuted Aaron Burr for treason. The problem is that he also fancies himself a playwright and is always trying to talk his way backstage. "Your most important job," said Placide on Jack's second day, "is to make sure that man with the big chin doesn't come within twenty feet of me."

"He's going to be devastated when he hears about Nancy," says Anderson.

At the mention of Nancy, Jack's chest tightens.

"Christ," says Placide. "I forgot about that."

"Forgot about what?" says Jack. If it's Nancy Placide forgot about, Jack will have no choice but to give up on him entirely.

Placide explains, "Wirt's play. *The Path of Pleasure*. He wanted Nancy to play the lead. I think he figured she'd convince Green to stage it."

"Could she have?" Jack asks.

"I'm the artistic director," Placide reminds him. "So, no."

"Why were you down at the Market Hall this early in the morning?" Anderson asks.

"The Common Council called an emergency meeting."

"What for?"

"To establish the burial committee. And while they were at it, they passed an ordinance: no public shows or spectacles for four months. Seems a bit beside the point, but what do I know?"

"Does that mean no theater?" Jack asks them both.

"I'm afraid so," says Placide.

"It's not like we've got a place to perform anyway," Anderson says, and Jack can feel the weight of his accusation.

"There's The Swan," says Jack, trying his best to remain sanguine. "And the City Tavern. We could fit a small orchestra in their side room."

They both ignore him. Anderson addresses Placide. "Do you think they'll enforce it? The ordinance?"

"The penalty's stiff, so I would think so. Six dollars and sixty-six cents per hour."

Anderson lets out a loud laugh. "Very puritanical of them."

Jack doesn't dare ask what's so funny, but Placide takes pity on him. "One who understands can calculate the number of the beast."

This means nothing to Jack, but he nods along anyway. Unfortunately, Anderson is on to him. "The Book of Revelation, Jack."

"Six-six-six," says Placide.

Jack can feel his cheeks flush.

"None of it matters," says Placide. "There won't be any theater in this town for years."

"Years?" asks Jack.

"Not until there's a new playhouse," says Placide. "And not even then if we're being likened to the Antichrist."

"We can rebuild," says Anderson. "Fireproof the whole thing from top to bottom."

Jack likes that idea. He can't imagine Richmond without a theater. Some of his earliest—and fondest—memories are of sitting on his father's shoulders, at the temporary theater on D Street, and watching plays like *The Irishman in London* and *Every One Has His Fault* come to life in front of him. Jack's father—like so many intellectuals of his day—was not a religious man, and for him the theater was his church and the actors his minister. Art, his father always said, was the closest any of them were likely to get to transcendence, and that was more than all right with him.

Jack and his father were in the audience when the new theater opened, in January of 1806, and a little later that season, when the great Thomas Abthorpe Cooper traveled to Richmond from New York, for one night only, to star in *Hamlet*. "Pay attention," his father had told him. "This performance will be one for the ages." And Jack had done as he was told, never realizing, as he watched Cooper assume the role of a grieving son, that it was one he would soon be taking on himself.

"There's another meeting at the capitol this afternoon," Placide offers. "Mayor Tate's presiding."

"Are you going?" Anderson asks.

"I've got to lie down."

"Do you want me to go?"

Placide gives him a hesitant nod, as if he doesn't enjoy being so reliant on Anderson, but has realized he has little choice in the matter. "First, wake Caulfield and send him on his way."

Anderson rises, and Jack follows suit. They're almost to the back stairs when Placide stops them. "Go over his statement with him a dozen times if you have to. He's got to get it right."

號 | SALLY | 號

When Sally knocks on the door of the Marshalls' house and Tom comes bounding to answer it, she is so surprised, she can scarcely sputter a greeting.

She knows what Mr. Marshall said—that his nephew was no worse the wear—but there's something about seeing Tom in such fine form that makes her want to hit him.

"Tom," she says, adopting the names they used as children.

"Sally."

"Your uncle said I'd find you here."

"Come in, come in," he says, ushering her into the large dining room, which doubles as an entryway. It's been years since Sally visited the Marshall family's home, but the interior is much the way she remembers it. A large mahogany bookcase sits on the wall opposite the fireplace, and Sally is reminded of the time Tom was nearly skinned alive for tearing all the frontispieces out of his father's books. The chief justice had signed his name on most of them, as a matter of bookkeeping, and Tom was discovered to be making a pretty penny selling the signatures to all his classmates at Princeton.

It shouldn't surprise Sally that he's still a dandy prat.

Tom deposits her in the parlor, then waits for one of the house servants to ask if she wants something to drink. While this dance is performed, Tom stays busy sorting a stack of mail. "Father must get more correspondence than any man alive," he says casually as he tosses the pile of letters on a nearby card table. "Now, to what do I owe this pleasure?"

"Your uncle thought you might know something about Alexander Scott."

"Oh, bugger. I haven't even thought about him. Do you know if he made it out all right?"

Something tells Sally this is going to be an excruciating conversation.

"He did." She wants to add, *No thanks to you,* but instead, she says, "But with some serious injuries."

"That's no good," says Tom, but his cheerful countenance does not change.

Tom doesn't ask anything more about Mr. Scott's fate, but Sally volunteers the information anyway. "He's got some bad burns on his face and neck, and a nasty gash on his back."

"Poor man. Where is he?"

"Over at Mary Cowley's, just down the street. As you probably know, some of the residents who live near the green have opened up their homes to the injured."

"I did hear something about that." He is picking pieces of lint off the leg of his trousers, so Sally gets to the point.

"I'd like to locate Mr. Scott's next of kin."

"Oh dear. That does sound serious."

"I know he attended the performance alone, but your uncle thought you might be able to tell me more about his family. Does he have a wife at home?"

"He doesn't," Tom says.

"Oh?"

"She died several years ago. Can't remember the exact details."

Sally doesn't know why it should bother her that Mr. Scott's wife is dead, but it does. She reaches into her pocket and removes the *fausse montre.* "Is this her?"

Tom squints at the tiny portrait. "Yes, maybe? It's been a while."

"Did they have children?" Sally presses.

"I think there's a boy and two girls."

"Are they small?"

"Yes?" He obviously has no clue.

"Who's caring for them while he's in Richmond?"

"A sister. Of his? Or hers? I can't remember."

Sally keeps pushing. "If I wanted to write to her, where would I find her?"

"You know, I'm really not sure. But someone's got to be at Clermont, in any case."

"Clermont is his estate?" Sally asks.

"It was his father's. Nice piece of land, not too far from my place. The family wound up with it after his uncle was lost at sea."

"How sad," says Sally, and in an instant she is reminded of Robert's brother Jamie, who drowned in the Clyde. She had always thought that drowning would be a particularly horrific end, but that was before she witnessed so many people meet a fiery one.

"Quite."

Sally repeats the name of the estate once more, just to be sure she has it right.

"That's correct," Tom says. "If you send a letter there, someone can—at the very least—forward it on."

Sally waits to see if Tom will offer to write the letter, but he makes no move to do so.

Finally, she spells it out. "I thought this might be something you could take on?"

"Oh," says Tom, who rears back his head as if he's dodging a punch. "I would. But I must say, I scarcely know him."

"I thought you said he was your 'good friend'?"

Tom looks uncomfortable. "Did I say that?"

"In the box. I'm fairly certain of it."

"You know how it is. Everyone's a friend, if you're in the right mood."

They are all the same. Archie, Tom, Elliott Price. These men don't have a selfless bone in their bodies. "Well," says Sally with a steady gaze, "might you convince yourself you're in the right mood now?"

Tom nods, repeatedly, as if he's trying to work himself up to something. Finally, he offers a weak "Of course."

"Thank you," she says, and stands to go before he can change his mind.

He follows her to the front door, and a servant brings her coat. As Sally slides into it, she turns to face him. "Tom, I have to ask."

He looks terrified of whatever is coming.

"How did you get out of the building so fast?"

He blinks like an animal caught in a trap. "Sally," he says, his voice barely a whisper.

"Don't 'Sally' me."

He pushes his hair off his forehead. "What would you have me say?"

"The truth."

He shoves his hands in his pockets and gives her a pleading look.

"How did you do it?"

Still, he says nothing.

"I want to know."

He sighs, then looks her straight in the eye. "I pushed and shoved, like everybody else."

❧ | JACK | ❧

J ack and Anderson have gone over Caulfield's statement with him more times than they care to count when they point him in the direction of the *Enquirer*'s offices.

"You'll do splendidly," Anderson shouts after him from the tavern's front porch.

"You really think he will?" Jack asks once Caulfield is out of earshot.

Anderson sighs. "It's anybody's guess."

After Caulfield is gone, they head to the taproom with West to make a quick meal of some roast chicken and peanut soup. It's the first food Jack's eaten since before yesterday's curtain call, and it goes down so fast he barely tastes it.

They're soon joined by Twaits and Young and a few of the other actors, who are riding high off their success with the slave patrol. "You wouldn't have believed it," says Twaits. "All we had to do was say the word 'Negro' and they were on their horses, kicking up dirt."

West doesn't seem particularly impressed.

"Who did you talk to?" Anderson asks.

"Young and I went to see that cock of the company. What's his name?"

Anderson looks at Twaits blankly, but Jack knows precisely who he's talking about.

"Was just made captain of the first class of the patrol," says Twaits. "Why can't I think of it?"

"Cameron Kemp," Jack offers, and Twaits smacks his forehead.

"That's it," says Twaits, giving an involuntary shudder. "He's a hideous creature. But his face lit up like a papist's church when we told him about the slave revolt."

"Really?" Anderson says.

"The whole thing's perfect," says Twaits as he grabs a chicken bone off Anderson's plate, breaks it in half, and begins to suck out the marrow.

"Hey!" says Anderson. "That was mine."

Twaits points the bone at Anderson. "Everyone on the patrol was already so agitated that all we had to do was mention the slave revolt. Worked them right up into a proper lather."

West warns them all to keep their voices down, but the men are giddy with the promise of being let off the hook.

Jack can't understand their enthusiasm. "What makes you so confident Placide's plan will work?" he asks as he begins to stack their plates in the middle of the table.

"Placide's plans always work," says Anderson.

"Always?" says Jack.

Anderson laughs. "He's a genius."

"A genius?" says West. "That might be taking things a bit far."

"What do you know about him?" Anderson asks Jack.

Jack considers the question for a moment. "I know he's a trained dancer. And an acrobat."

"What else?"

"He grew up in France, worked in Paris, then Haiti. New York, too. Eventually, he established a dance company in Charleston, which merged with West's father's acting troupe."

"All true," says Anderson. "And yet, it doesn't come close to describing this man's talent. Placide wasn't just 'working in Paris,' he was dancing in the court of Louis XVI. In Haiti, he shared the stage with Suzanne Vaillande. Then they go and debut *The Bird Catcher* in New York, and it's—quite literally—the first ballet production our young country has ever seen."

"Did you see it?" Twaits asks Anderson.

"Did I see it?" he croons. "I was in the front row."

"No . . ."

"Yes."

Twaits rests his chin in his hand. "That had to have been something."

"I can still picture Placide's grand jeté perfectly."

"Now he's just boasting," West tells the rest of them.

"The man's brilliant," says Anderson. "So, when you ask me why I'm confident the plan will work, it's because nothing Placide's tried has ever failed."

"Well, there was that spectacle commemorating the Battle of Fort Moultrie," says West. "It wasn't very good."

"That was one performance!"

West throws his hands up. "I'm not saying he's not brilliant!" He turns to Jack. "I don't know what gave him the idea that the local militia could act."

"I once heard Louis Duport say he owes the man everything," says Anderson. "Louis *bloody* Duport."

Jack is too embarrassed to admit he doesn't know who Louis Duport is, so he just says, "Impressive."

"There isn't an actor, a dancer, or a director alive today who doesn't know who Alexander Placide is. And people will still be talking about him long after the lot of us are dead."

"Here, here!" says Twaits. Some of the men raise their glasses to Placide. Everyone begins to talk at once, and by the time a barmaid clears their plates, they're taking guesses on when the troupe will be allowed to return to Charleston.

"They haven't even established an inquest committee yet," says West, pushing up from the table. "So, you're a bunch of fools if you're even thinking about what comes next."

They all watch as West exits the taproom. "What's stuck up his ass?" Twaits asks, and there is general agreement that, indeed, West must have something large impacting his bunghole.

⚜ | GILBERT | ⚜

*G*ilbert walks back to the smithy* from the Price place in a fog. All he can think about is Cecily, and how if he had known she was at the theater, he might have focused on saving her life, instead of that of Louisa or a dozen women he doesn't even know.

Behind him, a woman calls his name. "Mr. Hunt! Oh, Mr. Hunt!"

He turns to find Phyllis Johnston hurrying down Locust Alley, waving a reticule over her head in greeting, and all he wants to do is run in the other direction. But then he remembers Dr. McCaw and the fact that he asked her to bring him word of his condition, and he forces himself to wait for her.

"I'm so relieved to have found you," she says as she picks her way around several large piles of horse manure. She is wearing a gown that looks like it was ordered for a woman of far narrower proportions, and when she arrives in front of Gilbert, she is quite out of breath.

It's cruel that he should be forced to converse with anybody right now. He searches for something to say and finally manages, "You look improved since last night."

"Thank you," she says, apparently glad for the compliment. "I've never felt more relieved to have a bath in my life."

It is a reminder of the difference in their stations. Gilbert has not had a bath since the fire, nor is he likely to have one anytime soon. Of course, he does not tell her this. Instead, he asks after Dr. McCaw.

"His condition is very grave," she says. "My brother refuses to allow anyone to remove his jacket, so it's impossible for us to determine the full extent of his burns."

Gilbert's eyes grow wide. "He cannot be convinced?"

"I think he understands that to remove it properly, a great deal of flesh will have to come off with it."

Gilbert shudders involuntarily.

"I know, it's quite gruesome," Mrs. Johnston agrees. "The leg has been properly wrapped and splinted, though, and Dr. Foushee thinks it's possible that he'll have the full use of it in time."

"That's good," says Gilbert, and prays that she will soon be through with him.

Mrs. Johnston wrings her gloved hands together, like she is working up the nerve to say something important. "Actually, I'm here to discuss something else with you," she says. "Do you have a moment?"

Gilbert is tempted to scream *Not for you!* but instead he lies through his teeth. "Master Kemp will be wanting me back to work soon."

"It's about Mr. Kemp, actually."

Curiosity gets the better of him. "Go on."

She removes a piece of paper from her handbag. "The women you saved. I've identified eleven of them. There might have been more than that, but I'm certain of these."

She shows Gilbert the list, then apologizes. "I don't know if you can read."

Gilbert won't admit to her that he can, so he asks, "What's it say?"

"It's a list. Of all of us."

Most of the women's names have check marks beside them. A couple are crossed out. One has no markings at all. "I've spent much of the day calling on them."

"And they are well?"

"Remarkably so."

"I'm glad."

"It's a testament to my brother's bravery. And yours."

Gilbert repeats what he told her last night. "We did the same thing any other man would have done."

Mrs. Johnston folds the piece of paper in half and tucks it back in her reticule. "That's where I think you are wrong. I suspect a great many men would have looked the other way. And, in fact, did."

She waits for a response, but when he doesn't give her one, she pushes forward. "We would like to do something substantial to thank you for your service."

"You already thanked me."

"I have proposed a fundraising campaign. We would like to buy your freedom."

Gilbert can't have heard her right. "My freedom?"

"It strikes us as grossly unfair that the city's most venerated hero should be enslaved."

Gilbert could have argued the unfairness of the entire institution, but he knows Mrs. Johnston is not standing in front of him trying to solve that particular injustice.

"I'm expensive," he warns. "I'm not saying that to scare you off. I just want you to know what you're getting into."

"How much?"

"I was sold to Master Kemp in August for a little over four hundred dollars."

To her credit, Mrs. Johnston doesn't blanch. "There will be eight or nine of us contributing. Provided Mr. Kemp is a reasonable man, we should be able to pool our resources and settle on a fair price."

Provided Mr. Kemp is a reasonable man. If only she knew.

Kemp isn't going to part with Gilbert, not when he just paid top dollar for him. And certainly not after the fuss this morning. Mrs. Johnston could offer Kemp twice what Gilbert's worth, and Kemp would say no on principle.

"I appreciate what you're trying to do," Gilbert says. "I really do. But might I propose an alternate arrangement?"

She seems surprised, but says, "I'm listening."

"Would you consider buying my wife, Sara?"

"Instead of you?"

"It's delicate with Kemp. But Sara is in a good position. She's owned by the Prestons, and they just lost their only daughter, who was Sara's chief responsibility."

"You would have us purchase her freedom, with no promise of your own to come?"

"If Sara's got her freedom, she can work and start saving for mine. I'm hopeful there will come a day when Master Kemp . . . softens." What he wants to say is *dies.*

Mrs. Johnston gives him a pitying smile. "All right, then, that's what we'll do."

She makes like she is about to go, but Gilbert can tell there is something else she wants to say. "I realize I am probably speaking out of turn here, but I assume you are aware that General Preston is in a great deal of debt?"

It's something he and Sara muse about—some of Mrs. Elizabeth's silver serving pieces have started to disappear—but he's not about to admit all that to Mrs. Johnston.

"I'm not trying to gossip," she says quickly. "I'm just saying that I believe it is extremely likely the general will agree to our proposition."

Gilbert thinks how nice it would be if something good could come out of this mess. "I'm glad you think so."

She promises to let him know as soon as she's got an answer from General Preston, then she gives him a small wave, turns, and hurries back up Locust Alley before he can remember to thank her.

Gilbert can't keep all the events of the day in his head—witnessing Cecil's arrest, learning of Cecily's death, and now getting this offer. Could the key to securing Sara's freedom really have been as simple as showing up at the theater and doing the right thing? It seems hard to believe, but right about now, Gilbert could stand to believe in something.

❧ | JACK | ❧

Jack has never been inside the capitol, and he is slack-jawed crossing the rotunda.

"Is that Washington?" he asks Anderson as they pass a six-foot-tall sculpture of a man so lifelike that Jack practically expects him to reach out and shake his hand.

"Who else would it be?" Anderson says, and Jack shrugs.

The Hall of Delegates is easily the fanciest room Jack's ever been in. Several dozen sleek desks, which look like they've been fashioned out of mahogany or maybe walnut, sit in neat rows that face a dais, and above their heads, a two-tiered chandelier looms.

The hall is packed with people, many of them mourners, and there's little room to move, let alone sit. Eventually, Anderson and Jack secure standing room in the back of the hall, and while they wait for the room to quiet, Anderson whispers in Jack's ear, "Watch how easy this is."

Before Jack has the chance to ask what he means, Anderson turns to their neighbor, a portly man in his sixties, and says, clear as day, "Did you hear they think it was a band of Negroes who started the fire?"

The man's eyes bulge, and he stutters a disbelieving no before turning to a skinny man next to him. "Did you hear what he said? Says it was Negroes who are to blame for all this."

The skinny man peers at Anderson. "Slaves?"

Anderson throws up his hands. "That's what I heard."

Jack's flabbergasted watching Anderson work. He's so confident. Like he's played this role—of concerned citizen—a hundred times and knows the part backward and forward.

"How many men?" asks a third man in a yellow scarf standing a few feet away.

"I heard there were at least a dozen of them. Maybe more." Anderson looks around, like he's trying to ascertain whether he is in danger of being overheard, but it's so obvious—to Jack, at least—that being overheard is exactly what he's after. "They're saying it looks like a coordinated effort."

"Who's they?" asks a fourth man with a big beard, but Anderson is saved by Mayor Tate, who calls the meeting to order.

A hush falls over the room, and the mayor begins by trying to offer words of comfort. "We have been visited by a calamity the most distressing of which society can be afflicted. It has deprived us of so many of our most valuable citizens, pervaded every family, and rendered our whole town one deep and gloomy scene of woe."

Woe hardly seems the word for it. When Jack looks around this room, at the families of the dead, what he sees is utter devastation.

Jack is surprised the mayor doesn't invoke the name of the theater company in his remarks. He doesn't even say the word *theater*. It is as if the fire is no different from an earthquake or a lightning strike—something delivered by God. Placide would be much relieved.

There is the requisite beating of chests, on the part of members of the Common Council, who feel duty bound to say something profound to their constituents, each in their own turn. Then the bereaved are invited to speak, although most of them cannot, in fact, put words to their grief. One man approaches the dais and falls to his knees, another just stands there and weeps. A woman is so distraught, she has to be carried from the room.

Jack can hardly watch the whole scene unfold, and he glances at Anderson to see if he's holding up any better. Anderson has one of those faces that doesn't give much away, but Jack finds it hard to believe anyone could listen to this and not be tempted to admit the company's role in the disaster.

Eventually, the chamber comes to the business at hand and resolves that there should be three people in each ward appointed to collect information about the deceased, and that the twenty-eighth of December—tomorrow—should be reserved for a funeral at Henrico Parish Church.

In front of Jack, a man whispers to his wife, "How are we to have her remains by then?"

Jack closes his eyes and tries to convince himself that the girl whose remains they are discussing is not their daughter. But then he has to ask himself, is it better if she is their niece? Their governess? What about their slave?

Jack tries to follow the remarks as closely as he can, but he's distracted. He keeps waiting for someone to turn around and point at him, to call him out in front of all these people. *This is the boy who forgot to put out the chandelier's candles at the appointed time. This is the boy who did not hold his ground when Green insisted he raise the lamp into the flyspace. This is the boy who was not quick enough to cut down the backdrop when he realized it had been set alight.* But no one says anything. The question of what—or who—caused the fire is barely mentioned. People are much more concerned with the details of the burial. They want to know what time it will take place, who will lead the service, and how—again—are all of the bereaved to fit inside Henrico Parish Church?

There are no good answers, but people take heart when Mayor Tate begins to announce committees. In addition to the burial committee, which the Common Council has already established, the mayor declares that he will appoint people to two other committees: a monument committee, led by Chief Justice John Marshall, and an inquest committee, headed up by— of all people—Thomas Ritchie.

Anderson rubs the bridge of his nose.

"You're not pleased?" Jack whispers.

"Wirt would have been better, as far as the company's concerned."

Jack looks for Wirt's mop of blond hair in the crowd and finds him sitting near the front of the hall, chin in hand, observing the proceedings dejectedly.

"Say what you will about that damned play of his," says Anderson. "He's still a man who favors art above all else."

Ritchie sits just a few feet away from Wirt. Some of the men in the editor's circle clap him on the back—an indication that they believe Tate has chosen wisely—but it's hard for Jack to judge. On one hand, Ritchie has indicated he will give the troupe's story, as absurd as it may be, his full consideration. On the other, he is a newspaper man, trained at separating fact from fiction.

When Tate names John Marshall's brother, William, to the inquest committee, Anderson nudges Jack in the ribs. "He's a member of the theater's board of investors. That's good news for us."

Tate gives his closing remarks, and it's clear the meeting is about to adjourn, when the man with the yellow scarf puts his fingers to his lips and lets fly a loud whistle. Tate and Ritchie and Wirt and all of the other men at the front of the room turn toward the source of the sound.

"Over here!" says the man, trying to get their attention. "What's this we're hearing about the fire being intentionally set by a bunch of slaves?"

It's like all the air has gone out of the room. There are several long seconds of silence, then a few people begin to murmur to one another, and soon the room is in an uproar. "Is that true?" more than one person shouts in the direction of the dais.

"Order! Order!" says Mayor Tate as he struggles to get the room under control.

"And what should we do? Just wait to be killed in our beds?" screams a woman near Jack who seems to be teetering on the edge of delirium.

Jack wants to know what Anderson was thinking, lighting a fuse like this. But when he turns around to ask him, his friend is gone.

It takes Jack several seconds to locate Anderson, more than a dozen feet away, near the exit. "Wait!" he calls after him, but Anderson doesn't stop. He just motions his head in the direction of the door, which Jack interprets to mean they should meet outside, in the rotunda.

"Excuse me," says Jack to the men beside him as he attempts to slide past them, but they do not so much as shift their weight.

"Do we know whose slaves are responsible?" one man shouts at Tate.

"Tom Rutherford's Negroes are never where they belong," another offers.

Soon, everyone is hurling names and accusations at the dais. Tate keeps promising that the inquest committee will do a thorough investigation, but that in the meantime no one is to take the law into their own hands. "You must trust that justice will prevail," he pleads.

"Where's justice for my Mary?" one man yells from the gallery, and another man follows suit. "My Jane was with child!"

The crowd is in an uproar now, everyone relieved to have found someone to blame for the fire and its resulting destruction, and Jack feels a paralyzing sense of guilt. What has he done, allowing this lie to take root and grow?

Jack has to get out of this room. He tries, again, to slip through the venomous crowd and out into the rotunda, but this time it is Ritchie's voice, loud as a gong, that stops him. "What do you think you're doing?"

Jack turns around slowly, sure Ritchie is about to rip into him, but when he is facing the dais, he realizes that Ritchie is addressing the room.

"How is any of this helping?" the newly nominated head of the inquest committee continues when the crowd has quieted.

Jack takes a series of small side steps, moving incrementally closer to the door.

"Who here knows anything about this slave revolt?" Ritchie asks the crowd.

"We all do," says the man with the big beard, and there is general agreement from the people around him.

"Yes, but did any of you actually witness a Negro—free or enslaved—light the theater on fire?"

A low murmur makes its way around the room like a wave, but no one says anything.

"None of you?" Ritchie asks, surprised.

The room is quiet.

"So, who is the source of the information?"

Jack knows, without needing to look up, that the men in the back of the room are searching the crowd for Anderson's broad back and loose curls. "Where's that man with the kid?" he hears one of them say, but by then Jack is out the door and skidding across the rotunda, where he finds Anderson waiting for him.

𝕊 | **SALLY** | 𝕊

S*ally is on her way back* to Mrs. Cowley's, ruminating on what Tom Marshall has just told her, when she hears someone calling her name.

She turns to find Maria Price's brother waving at her from the interior of a five-glass landau drawn by two horses.

"Mr. Price," she says as she picks her way slowly across the rutted road.

"Are you headed back to Mrs. Cowley's?" he asks through the open window.

"I am."

"Let me give you a ride."

The carriage is a beautiful contraption—all sleek lines and gracious curves—and he looks at ease in it. More comfortable than he's looked at any point since his sister's arrival at Mrs. Cowley's.

"Are you sure it's not too much trouble?" she asks. "I really can walk."

He is already out of the carriage and offering her his hand. "I insist."

When she is inside the cab and seated across from him, he places a bear-skin blanket across her lap. The press of the heavy pelt on her tired limbs feels like heaven, and after Elliott gives word to the coachman and the carriage begins to move, she thinks she might very well fall asleep, right here, with him staring at her.

"You've got to be exhausted," he says.

"I am."

"Where are you coming from?"

"The Marshall residence."

"You know the chief justice?"

"I do, but I was there to see his son, Tom. I'm trying to work out the identity of the man you and Mr. Campbell took upstairs."

"Oh, I thought you knew him."

"Well, yes, I mean, we were introduced the night of the fire. But I don't have the means of contacting his family."

"That's funny."

Sally is confused by the comment, and her face must show it.

"I just mean, I assumed you and he were attached."

Sally is startled. "Oh, no. Not at all."

"Are you attached to anyone?"

She tries to read his tone. In another lifetime, she might have interpreted it as flirtatious.

Usually, this is when Sally would tell him about Robert—that she was married, that her husband died three years ago, and that, no, they did not have children. But something stops her from offering Elliott the same tired story. Instead, she just shakes her head ever so slightly and whispers, "I am not."

"Well, good," he says. "I am very glad for it," and Sally allows herself an uncomfortable laugh.

The carriage slows as it approaches the theater green, and as much as Sally would like to look away, she can't quite manage it. The ruins appear much the same as they did this morning, only now even more people are picking through the rubble. The carriage windows have begun to fog over, and when she squints, she can almost see the building still standing—the brick facade, the *oeil-de-boeuf* window, the pair of doors that opened into the lobby.

When Elliott speaks, the spell is broken. "Mrs. Cowley tells me you jumped from a third-floor window."

"It's true."

"And you look hardly the worse for wear."

She thinks he means the statement as a compliment, but something about his tone makes her uncomfortable, particularly when so many women jumped from the same window and wound up dead or seriously injured. "A lot of people weren't so lucky," she says.

"I know, but wouldn't you say that most people got out?"

"What?" says Sally disbelievingly.

"I mean, the theater holds six hundred people, maybe more. And I'm hearing they think less than a hundred people perished."

"What is it you're saying, exactly?"

"Just that the odds are good on a person making it out in one piece."

"Are we speaking of one person in particular?" says Sally. "Because, as someone who was sitting in a third-floor box, I must say it felt like the 'odds' were not in my favor."

His face reddens, and she wonders if she's overstepped.

"It just doesn't make any sense," he says, and she can hear the pitch of his voice rising. "Everyone I'm talking to, they say their bondsmen made it out. Freedmen, too. Henry Gordon, over at the Virginia Tobacco Company, was in the gallery. He got out fine. Solomon Freeman at the armory. Hector Lucas, down at the wharf. All of them, they said they just took the stairs. Said it was like they were filing out of church on Sunday."

"Is that what you've been doing this afternoon?" she asks. "Going 'round to all of these people and asking after Cecily?"

Elliott swipes at the fogged-over window with the side of his hand. "I had to do something."

Sally doesn't know what to make of this man. A moment ago, she was ready to write him off entirely, but now she feels *almost* sorry for him. "Do you think it's possible—"

Elliott interrupts her. "If you're going to ask whether I think she went back inside to find Maria, the answer is no."

That was what Sally was going to ask, but she can admit it doesn't make much sense. By the time Cecily made it out of the gallery and around to the front of the building, the lobby would have been an inferno.

"It's not just the timing that doesn't work out," says Elliott. "It's that I've never known a slave to lay down his life for his master."

"It happens, surely," says Sally.

"Give me one instance."

Sally remembers the story Joe told her this morning. "I heard there was a slave who saved close to a dozen women last night."

"You're talking about Gilbert Hunt?"

Sally nods.

Elliott shakes his head dismissively. "He was in the right place at the right time. And there was never any real risk—not to him, anyway."

Joe had made it seem more complicated than that, but she doesn't argue.

"No," says Elliott. "What I'm talking about is a man willingly laying down his life for his master."

She thinks about her family's most devoted slaves—Critty and Beck,

Jessee and Pedro. She would have called any of them family when she was growing up. But as she grew older, she realized they had their own families, their own troubles, their own lives. Even Andy, who saw her through Robert's death and the letting go of the Marysville house, barely gave her a backward glance when she announced that he and Lettie and Judith would be going back to Red Hill to work until she could find a more permanent arrangement. She can't think of a single slave—at Red Hill or in Marysville—who would have willingly given their life for hers. And why should they?

"You're right," she says. "Of course you're right."

Elliott seems thrilled to have won her over, and smiles at her conspiratorially. "So, you see why I'm convinced she's alive."

"Alive and hiding from you?"

"Exactly."

"You think she intends to run?"

"If she hasn't already."

❧ | JACK | ❧

As soon as *Jack and Anderson* are down the capitol steps, Jack begins to stammer his annoyance.

"What were you doing back there?" he says, but Anderson either can't or won't hear him.

Anderson is a head taller than Jack, with a long gait, and he seems determined to put as much distance between himself and the capitol as possible.

"No one is chasing us," says Jack, who has to run to keep up with him. "So, can you just wait?"

Anderson crosses Tenth Street, where a throng of people stand in line outside an apothecary. He pushes through the crowd, and Jack follows suit.

"You could slow down," says Jack a little louder.

Still, Anderson ignores him.

Jack is so tired of Anderson and Placide and all of these men who think they know what's best. He may be a mere stagehand, but he'd never—not in a thousand years—have done what Anderson just did, back in the Hall of Delegates. "We can't just walk into a room full of grieving families and feed them lies," Jack shouts. "Our lies have consequences."

Anderson stops in his tracks. "Consequences?" he says as he spins around to face Jack. "You want to talk to me about consequences?"

Jack knows what he's alluding to, but at this point, he can't be made to feel any worse about his role in the fire than he already does. "Those men in the Hall of Delegates, they were seeing red," says Jack.

Anderson rolls his eyes, and starts moving again, but Jack isn't going to be ignored. He bolts ahead of him, blocking his path. "What do you think is going to happen when that crowd comes pouring out of the capitol?"

"Get out of my way," says Anderson through clenched teeth.

Jack won't stop, not now. "Those people are going to go after every Negro in this town—free or enslaved."

"And?"

"And none of them will be safe!" Jack is screaming now. "Is that what you want? For a bunch of innocent people to pay for our mistake?"

"*Your* mistake," says Anderson with a tight smile as he sidesteps Jack and begins to move in the direction of the tavern.

Jack watches him walk away and is filled with a white-hot rage. Without realizing what he's doing, he charges at Anderson and shoves him hard in the back. "Take that back!"

Anderson pitches forward, arms flailing, but he catches himself before he lands facedown in the mud. Then he rears around and glares at Jack, but Jack is so angry, he doesn't care.

"If you won't go back there and make it right, I'm going to go to Ritchie myself," Jack says. "I'll tell him everything. What I did. What Green did. And what Placide and you are doing now."

Anderson is on him in a half second, maybe less. He grabs Jack by his collar and lifts him straight off his feet. When their faces are within inches of each other, Anderson hisses, "I wouldn't do that if I were you."

Twelve hours ago, Jack might have heeded the warning. But he's sick of being told what to do by a pack of animals. "Or what? I won't be invited to Charleston? Get a letter of introduction from Placide?" he screams. "There are worse fates!"

Jack's dreamed of becoming an actor since he was a little boy, but if a career in the theater means working alongside a bunch of frauds, maybe he doesn't want anything to do with it.

Jack doesn't know what possesses him, but he clears his throat, which is still raw from the smoke he swallowed the night before, and lets a thick ball of spit fly from between his chapped lips. It lands on Anderson's face with a satisfying *thwap*, which is as big a surprise to Jack as it is to Anderson.

Anderson's eyes go big in his head. "You ungrateful bastard."

In one fluid motion, Anderson wipes his cheek with his sleeve and drags Jack off the road and into a thicket of trees. Jack knows he should apologize, and that if he does, Anderson will likely go easier on him. But something inside him has snapped, and he can't make himself say the words it would take to quell Anderson's temper.

When they are a half-dozen yards from the road, and completely hidden from view, Anderson slams Jack's body against the trunk of a hickory tree. The back of his head bounces off the trunk, which is wrapped in a thick and gnarly bark. He feels a shooting pain, and then a wooziness that creeps over him, the same way it does when he downs a tankard of ale too quickly.

Anderson grabs him by the throat and squeezes. "This has gone far enough."

Jack is surprised by the sudden tightening around his neck, the immediacy with which his throat closes. He kicks at Anderson's shins, digs his fingernails into his wrists, anything to loosen the actor's grip, but Anderson's arms are longer than Jack's and his efforts come to naught.

"I have tried to talk sense into you, but you are being frighteningly obtuse."

Jack can't respond, can't make so much as a sound.

"You may not like this idea. It may even fly in the face of your principles. But if you think I am going to let you take down an entire theater company all because you've developed a conscience, you have another think coming."

Jack's field of vision is narrowing, and Anderson's voice sounds garbled, like his head has been dunked in a bucket of water. Jack closes his eyes, wonders—briefly—if this folding in of the world around him is what his father experienced in his final moments on earth.

Just when Jack assumes he is as good as dead, Anderson releases his hold on him and allows him to crumple to the ground. Jack gasps for air, but can't spare the time it will take for his breathing to return to normal. He must crawl toward the road, get the attention of someone who can intervene, but as soon as he is on all fours, Anderson sets a foot down on the hand closest to him.

Jack studies Anderson's boot, which is heavy enough to break all of his fingers. "Please let me go," he begs.

"No more talk of going to Ritchie?"

Jack agrees.

"Wonderful," says Anderson, and he helps Jack to his feet. "I don't know about you, but what I could really use right now is a nap."

GILBERT

Kemp back?" *Gilbert asks as soon* as he walks through the door of the smithy.

"No, but you got a visitor," says Marcus.

Gilbert looks around the shop, can't see anyone waiting on him.

"It's your sister, Della."

"She still here?"

"Out back. Said she didn't want to come in."

Gilbert practically sprints around the side of the building. "Della?" he croaks, and she steps out of the shadows, nearly scaring him half to death.

"Is it true about Cecily?" he says. "I keep praying it ain't."

She holds a finger up to her lips and eyes the smithy. "Can you walk with me a little bit?"

Gilbert nods, then follows her toward the slip. When they are a few dozen feet from the shop, she looks behind her, then starts to talk real fast. "Who told you about Cecily?"

"Moses."

"What he say?"

"Just that she was at the theater and she didn't make it out."

Della looks over her shoulder before saying another word. "She did, but as far as you know, she didn't."

"What?"

"Cecily ain't dead," says Della quickly. "But she meant to be."

"You gotta slow down a minute," Gilbert says. "I'm not following."

Gilbert often has this feeling, talking to Della. Like they are two strangers, trying to understand each other. Most of the time, he blames this on the fact that Della is so much older than him and was sold away from their mother so much earlier. But he also has to remind himself that they've led very different lives as a result of their circumstances. In their early years in Richmond, while he was learning a trade and beginning to save a little money, Della was fighting for the essentials and—he suspects—fending off the elder Mr. Price at every turn.

Della looks tired, and when she speaks, slower this time, she sounds tired, too. "Cecily was up in the gallery."

"And she made it out?"

"Yes."

"Praise God."

"Don't go praising God just yet. Not until you hear what I got to say."

Gilbert studies his sister's face—her tight mouth, her narrow eyes. Whatever's coming ain't good.

"Cecily's in trouble."

"What kind of trouble?"

"Things haven't been good with her and Master Elliott for a long time."

"Your Master Elliott?"

"No," says Della sharply. "The son."

"Go on."

"He's meant to be getting married New Year's Day. But now he says he's taking Cecily with him to his new place in Church Hill."

"And she don't want to go?" It's not that Gilbert isn't sympathetic. He is. It's just that stories like this one are so common, it's hardly worth getting worked up about them.

"She can't go," says Della. "It'll kill her."

"Della," says Gilbert, "what's this got to do with the theater?"

"I ain't told anyone this. Not even her own papa. So, if you can't help, I'm trusting you to keep quiet."

Gilbert can't begin to predict what she is going to say. "You know I will."

His sister takes a deep breath. "Cecily's been hiding. Ever since she got out."

"Out of the theater?"

Della nods.

Gilbert's head is spinning. "You mean to tell me, she's been hiding since last night?"

"That's what I'm saying."

"Oh, Della."

"Don't 'Oh, Della' me. It's not the craziest thing I ever heard of."

Gilbert feels an overwhelming urge to get off his feet, but they have arrived at the canal, and he sees nowhere to sit. Just a lot of river barges, knocking against each other.

"Running's dangerous," says Della. "We all know that. But it's a hell of a lot less dangerous if no one's looking for you."

"How you so sure no one's looking for her?"

"Are you hearing what I'm telling you?" Della says. "The Prices, all the folks in the quarters, even her own father—God help him—they all think she's dead."

"So, wait. You know about Cecil?"

"Moses told me he's been taken in."

"I saw Kemp stop him," says Gilbert. "I wish I could have done something."

"I'll get to Cecil eventually, but right now it's Cecily I got to figure out."

"Della, I'll help however I can. But I don't know nothing about running."

It's true. Gilbert has never paid much attention to the stories of daring escapes and moonlit river crossings. Maybe he's naive, but he has always believed his freedom will taste sweeter if he buys it, fair and square. That he'll breathe easier, knowing no one's looking for him.

"Brother," says Della coolly. "I'm not coming to you because you know a thing about running. I'm coming to you because you know a thing about writing."

"Writing?"

"She needs a good pass," says Della without batting an eye. "The kind that will take her on out of here."

"What you gonna do when she has it? Just put her on a stagecoach?"

"It's not a terrible idea."

"God almighty. Are you serious?"

"Remember Samuel Jefferson?"

"Of course I do."

"I went to see him today."

Samuel Jefferson is a wheelwright who Gilbert used to work with at Callum Murrow's Carriage Shop. Between the two of them, they were responsible for making the wheels for all the gigs and coaches the shop produced. Samuel would construct the nave, the spokes, and the felloes out of wood, and then Gilbert would strake the wheel in iron. Gilbert wasn't smithing—not yet—but fitting all those iron plates onto the rim of the wheel gave him some sense of the ways he might one day be able to make a piece of metal move.

Samuel is a freedman, has been for close to a decade. Most men leave town once they buy their way out of bondage, but Samuel stuck around Richmond and kept working for Mr. Murrow. Said Mr. Murrow was the finest carriage maker this side of the Atlantic, and he didn't aim to work for anyone who was second-rate.

That might have been true, but there were also rumors that, sometimes, when Samuel was called upon to deliver a carriage to one of Mr. Murrow's northerly customers, he traveled a little heavy, delivered something extra when and if he could. Gilbert was always too scared to ask Samuel about it directly and assumed he wouldn't get a straight answer out of him if he did.

"Did you ask him if he could help?"

"In a way," says Della. "I didn't tell him who was needing the ride, but he could probably figure it out if he spent half a minute thinking about it."

Gilbert realizes he's been holding his breath. He releases it, then asks, "So, what'd he say?"

"That he has a northbound carriage that's almost ready for delivery, and that if I give him a couple of days, he can get her as far as Washington."

Gilbert is floored. Not just that Della thought to go to Samuel, but that she managed to confirm that the rumors are true.

"I'm impressed," he says.

"Well, don't be. He charges a hundred dollars a passenger."

Gilbert couldn't have heard that right. "What'd you say?"

She nods emphatically. "Told me, and I quote, 'I'm not risking life and limb to sit on the right hand of God.'"

Gilbert always liked Samuel, so he has a hard time believing what Della's telling him. "A hundred dollars?"

"That's what he said."

Gilbert thinks about the tobacco pouch he sewed inside his mattress, soon as he arrived at Kemp's. He's got seventy dollars in it, maybe seventy-five, but it's earmarked for purchasing Sara's freedom. Even if this business with Phyllis Johnston works out—and it seems hard to believe something so outlandish will—Gilbert would be better off putting the money toward his own eventual purchase, so that Sara and he can one day have a chance at a real life.

Still, it's hard to look at his sister standing there and not feel guilty about keeping the money to himself. "Think you can talk him down?" he asks.

She shakes her head. "Hardly matters. Cecil and me, we got nothing between us. The Prices haven't let anyone hire themselves out in years."

Della doesn't know how much money Gilbert's got saved, and he's grateful for that. But he's starting to wonder if, at the very least, he should offer to talk to Sara.

"Samuel got me thinking, though," Della says, "that maybe we do just put her on a stagecoach. Let her ride right out of town like she's one of those high yellows going back and forth to Philadelphia."

A stagecoach ticket to Philadelphia should cost no more than ten dollars. A pittance in comparison to Samuel's fee. "You think she could pull it off?" Gilbert asks.

"She good at pretending things is all right," says Della. "Been doing it since she was a wink of a girl. If she's got a pass, and no one's looking for her, I don't see why it won't work."

Gilbert doesn't disagree.

"Of course, I don't have the fare for the stagecoach, either."

He gives her a tired shake of his head. "Where's Cecily now?" he asks.

Della hesitates.

"You trust me enough to ask me for stagecoach money, but you worried about telling me where she's at?"

Della rolls her eyes at him. "At the boathouse on the Fulcher property. Upriver from the mill."

"You're hiding her that close to the Prices'?" asks Gilbert. "She's a sitting duck."

Della gets defensive. "There was no time. But if you so full of ideas, you help me get her somewhere better."

Gilbert looks at his sister. Even in the dark, he can see the fear and desperation on her face. Her voice cracks. "Gil, I'm begging you—"

"Shhh," says Gilbert as he pulls his sister to him. "You don't have to beg me for nothing. I'll write the pass, and we'll figure the rest out."

❧ | SALLY | ❧

When *Sally walks through Mrs. Cowley's* front door, around suppertime, Archie waves a newspaper at her in greeting. "Funeral's been pushed back a day."

Sally ignores him and moves to check on Margaret, who was transferred back to her sad little pallet in the parlor after Dr. Foushee set her leg. Archie was eager to get her home, but Mrs. Cowley and Sally advocated for a few more days of Mrs. Cowley's expert care, and when even Dr. Foushee came down on their side, Archie relented.

Now Archie follows Sally into the parlor and perches on a stool he scrounged up from somewhere.

"You're in the way, Archie," she says mildly, and he moves, giving her—at most—an extra six inches of space.

Sally is relieved to see that Margaret's more alert than she's been in some time. "You're looking well," she says as she bends down to kiss her friend's forehead.

"Isn't she?" says Archie, and it's all Sally can do not to ask him to leave the room. That he should be allowed to comment on Margaret's well-being is galling, but when Sally studies Margaret's face for signs of perturbation, she sees none. *She doesn't know he abandoned her*, she reminds herself as she snatches the paper from Archie.

"What is this?"

"The *Enquirer*," says Archie. "All the news of the fire is on page three."

"They couldn't have spared the front page?"

Archie shrugs. "I assume it was already typeset."

The first page of the paper is full of nothing but advertisements for imported wine, gunpowder, and cigars. Next comes the want ads for tutors and coopers and slaves for hire. Then a lengthy dispatch on the fighting in Spain, which has reached an impasse now that Napoleon is directing all his attention toward Russia. Congress is considering the request to fund the building of a canal between the Great Lakes and the Hudson River. And in mid-December, there was an earthquake in Savannah, which was felt as far away as Tennessee.

Finally, Sally finds the account of the fire under a headline that reads OVERWHELMING CALAMITY. She reads the first few sentences aloud, at a clipped pace:

> *In the whole course of our existence, we have never taken our pen under a deeper gloom than we feel at this moment. It falls to our lot to record one of the most distressing scenes which can happen in the whole circle of human affairs. The reader must excuse the incoherence of the narrative: there is scarce a dry eye in this distracted city. Weep, my fellow-citizens; for we have seen a night of woe, which scarce any eye had seen or ear hath heard, and no tongue can adequately tell.*

Something about Thomas Ritchie's prose grates on Sally's nerves. She knows he considers himself to be part of Richmond's literary elite, but "deep gloom"? "The circle of human affairs"? "Night of woe"? It is all so excessive. Like he was torn between writing a newspaper article and a novella, and settled on something in between.

"Why'd you stop reading?" asks the woman who's been stretched out on Mrs. Cowley's settee all day.

"I don't believe we've met," says Archie, and introduces himself.

Sally is ready to roll her eyes at the gesture, but the woman on the settee seems to appreciate it. "Mrs. Edwina Kimball."

"Yes, Sally," says Margaret in a quiet voice, "why did you stop?"

"I suppose I just want the facts," she says as she skims several more paragraphs, which all come up short—in Sally's opinion.

Again and again, Ritchie tries and fails to describe the scene inside the theater. He has some details right—the blocked stairway, the crowded lobbies, the governor's decision to rush back inside in search of his son. But Ritchie gets so much wrong that Sally would have known he wasn't in the building—even if his father-in-law hadn't already given him away.

"Is it true, Sally?" Margaret asks. "The governor is dead?"

She nods. "The boy is all right, though."

Margaret's eyes grow wet, and Sally wonders if she, too, is thinking about the conversation they had in the box before the lights went out. It was so easy to pull at the threads of Governor Smith's life—his wife, his children, even his hairline. She feels guilty about it now, and also a little heartsick, because it's hard to believe that Margaret and she will ever again be able to laugh about something so trivial.

She reads the rest of the article in silence.

"I thought it was a balanced account," says Archie.

"Hmmm," says Sally with a faint shake of her head. It's no wonder Archie appreciated the article. Ritchie makes no mention of his failings, or the failings of any other man in attendance. In fact, he does quite the opposite: he turns many of the men at the theater into heroes.

In a few days, the survivors' testimonials will begin to pour into the paper, and Sally feels sure they'll tell the same story.

"I take it Ritchie still refuses to publish any women?" asks Sally.

"That hardly makes him an outlier," says Archie defensively.

At the end of the article, Ritchie has reprinted an ordinance the Common Council passed, and a series of resolutions the mayor has put forth. Sally reads the most asinine of them aloud. " 'Be it resolved that the citizens of Richmond wear crepe for one month.' "

Mrs. Kimball sighs. "My mourning clothes are at our country home. I shall have to send someone to fetch them."

It is hard not to appreciate Mrs. Kimball's optimism. Not only does she believe her burns—which are substantial—will heal, but she assumes she will soon be going places where she will need black gowns and a satin-lined pelisse.

"If you were a little bigger, I'd suggest you borrow mine," says Margaret. "I suspect I will have little use for them."

"It'd be nice if the mayor spent less time worrying about our mourning clothes and more time worrying about how to get us fresh supplies," says Sally. "We ran out of anything resembling a bandage in the first twelve hours."

Archie ignores Sally and addresses Mrs. Kimball. "Do you have a frock you could dye?"

Finally, Sally comes to the list of the dead and missing.

There are maybe sixty names on the list—arranged alphabetically, by ward, and then by skin color. Unmarried women are listed by first and last name, and married women are listed under their husband's names.

Colored people are distinguished as free when the information is available.

Sally whispers the names aloud, like the words of a prayer: Adeline Bausman, Mary Clay, Margaret Copland, Lucy Gawthmey, Patsey Griffin, Arianna Hunter, Cyprian Marks, Elizabeth Stevenson.

Two women on the list share the same last name—Page—and she thinks of the young woman who refused to jump from the window, paralyzed by the knowledge that her sister was dead on the ground below.

Near the bottom of the list is the name Cecily Patterson. The newspaper identifies the Price family's servant as a woman of color, but what is more significant are the words that follow that brief description: *Supposed to have perished.*

Sally reads the rest of the names on the list. At least a half-dozen other colored people have perished, but no one else's name is accompanied by this odd phrase, this "Supposed to have." Did Elliott get to Ritchie? He didn't say anything about the *Enquirer* on the ride back to Mrs. Cowley's.

As Sally studies the list more closely, she notices something else. "It's almost all women," she says in surprise as she looks up from the paper.

"What do you mean?" says Archie.

"The dead. They're overwhelmingly women."

"That can't be."

Sally begins to count quietly to herself. When she gets to the bottom of the list, she starts again. Finally, she announces, "I count just fourteen men among the dead. And two of them are young boys."

"How many women are there?" asks Margaret.

"Fifty."

"Heavens," Mrs. Kimball says. "That many?"

"It's not a definitive list," says Archie. He points to a small note from the editor at the top of the column. "See, it says so right there."

He is right. Ritchie warns that the list will grow. But it doesn't matter if it does. The ratio of men to women is unlikely to shift.

Sally rereads the article. There's something about it she doesn't like, but it takes her another pass before she decides what it is.

Ritchie describes fathers shrieking for their children, husbands for their wives, and brothers for their sisters, but it was the other way around. It's the women who were shrieking, while the men pushed past them—and in some cases, climbed over them—to get to the door.

❋ | JACK | ❋

Anderson *has been asleep upstairs for* an hour, maybe two, when
Thomas Ritchie raps on the doorframe of the tavern's back room.

"You again," he says to Jack in lieu of a greeting.

Jack was half-asleep sitting up, and he pushes back his chair and stumbles to his feet. He's so very tired, and Ritchie is the last person he wants to see right now. "Can I help you?"

"I'm looking for Mr. Placide and Mr. Green."

"They're not here," says Jack.

"Where are they?"

Jack is terrified of saying the wrong thing. But he also doesn't want to look like he's got anything to hide. "They board at Mrs. Barrett's," he says, then offers to wake Anderson, whom he promises will be only too glad to take Ritchie to see them.

"You seem perfectly capable," says Ritchie. "Why don't you let him sleep?"

Jack wants to scream, *Because I'll be buried in a shallow grave!* Instead, he nods politely, pushes in his chair, and leads Ritchie onto the street, resolving to tell him nothing except the absolute essentials.

Mrs. Barrett's boardinghouse is a short walk from both the tavern and the theater, which is one of the reasons, Jack assumes, that Placide and Green have never looked further for accommodations. The house isn't particularly grand, but there is plenty of space—so much space, in fact, that in addition to taking in boarders, Mrs. Barrett runs a girls' school on the first floor.

While they walk, Ritchie asks Jack how long he's worked for Placide & Green, and when he learns that the company hired him two and a half months ago, he has more questions about what Jack's been doing with himself since his father died.

Jack tells him about the brief stint with his uncle and about how Professor Girardin offered him a place to stay when things got bad. At some point—maybe after explaining how Girardin got him the job—Jack wonders if he's said too much and if it might have been wiser to keep his mouth shut.

Mrs. Barrett's boardinghouse is quiet when Jack leads Ritchie through the front door and into the entryway, where Ritchie wipes his boots and stows his cane. "If you wait here," says Jack, "I'll go get him."

"Them," Ritchie says, correcting him.

It takes Jack a minute to remember he means Green, too. "Right."

He takes the stairs two at a time, but in the upstairs corridor, he comes to a quick halt. He isn't sure which rooms belong to Placide's family and which belong to Green's, and—despite Ritchie's request—he has no desire to stumble into the Greens' rooms by mistake. Not at a time like this.

He listens at the door of one room, then another, and thinks he hears the soft sobs of Lydia Placide. He knocks gently, and when the door opens to reveal Lydia's tearstained face, he sucks in his breath. Even distraught, she is stunning. "Sorry," he says, "I don't want to interrupt, but do you know which room your father is in?"

She throws the door open to reveal Placide, still in his costume, passed out on the bed behind her. "He's out cold," she says, not even bothering to lower her voice.

"With drink?" asks Jack, horrified.

She shakes her head no. "He takes something to help him sleep."

"And Mr. Green?"

"He stays in the room next door. But no one's seen him since last night."

"Christ."

"What's the matter?"

"Thomas Ritchie's downstairs. He's leading the inquest and wants to talk to someone in charge."

"Now?"

He tips his head in the direction of the bed. "Can you wake him?"

"I think so. If you can help me get him downstairs."

Lydia and he are a good team, and together they get Placide—who is heavy on his feet and having a hard time keeping his eyes open—out of bed and into the hall. It's hard for Jack to look at this man, who can barely stand on his own two feet, and see the man Anderson is, apparently, so enamored by. In this condition, Placide doesn't seem like much of a man at all.

As they make their way slowly down the stairs, Jack summarizes everything that happened at the capitol—the speeches, the committee assignments, even Anderson's rumormongering. He leaves out the bit about Anderson threatening to kill him, in case it should give Placide any ideas.

"They really believed the story about the slave revolt?" says Lydia, but before Jack can answer her, Placide does it for him, in a slightly slurred voice. "Why in the world wouldn't they?"

"Is he drunk?" Ritchie asks them after Jack and Lydia have guided Placide into the parlor and settled him on the settee.

Placide doesn't confirm or deny the accusation, so Lydia apologizes on her father's behalf. "I'm so sorry. He took a sleeping tonic a little while ago."

"I'm fine," says Placide, but he comes off sounding like a petulant child, and Jack prays he hasn't just made a huge mistake, delivering him to Ritchie in this condition.

"Where's Green?" Ritchie asks Placide.

"Indisposed."

"What's that supposed to mean?" Ritchie says, and Jack, who is perched on the arm of a chair, squirms in discomfort. Things would go so much better for Placide, Jack has to believe, if he started giving Ritchie straightforward answers.

Placide asks if anyone would like coffee, but makes no move to call for it. Ritchie will not be distracted. "I said I wanted to talk to Green, too."

Placide just nods, so Lydia finally says something. "We believe Mr. Green's daughter, Nancy, is among the dead."

Ritchie casts a quick glance at Jack, and Jack wonders if he should have divulged the information sooner. "Sorry," he says quickly. "There's been so much going on."

Ritchie gives him a small nod of understanding, then clears his throat. "Well, I'm very sorry to hear that."

Placide accepts his condolences with the sanctimony of a fool.

"I *will* need to speak to him at some point," Ritchie says. "But in the interim, please give him my condolences."

"Nancy was a talent," says Placide, whose body has pitched slightly to one side. Lydia takes a seat beside him and tries her best to prop him up.

"It goes without saying, but I shall say it anyway," says Placide. "This is a devastating loss—for all of us."

Ritchie leans back in his chair, as if he needs some distance to properly assess the room and its occupants. Placide is not lying—the fire was devastating, in every possible respect—but Jack wonders if Ritchie believes a word coming out of his mouth.

"I've been named the head of the inquest committee," says Ritchie.

"I heard."

"So, you can understand my obligation—devastating loss or not—to provide the citizens of this town with answers."

Placide doesn't argue with him, but it's clear he wants to steer the conversation. "We sent Thomas Caulfield to find you. Did you speak with him?"

"About your slave revolt theory?"

"It's more than a theory," says Placide. "Didn't he tell you what he saw?"

Jack realizes he's holding his breath. They rehearsed what Caulfield should say, how he had run back to the tavern between *The Father* and the pantomime to get a pouch of tobacco, and how when he had returned to the theater, he'd noticed a group of Negroes—men mostly—congregating near the rear of the building. *Make sure you say that several of them were carrying torches*, Anderson had reminded Caulfield several times before he'd set out.

"I spoke with him," says Ritchie.

"In that case, I assume he told you that we are convinced the fire was brought about by outside forces?" Placide asks.

"I believe the words you used in your letter were 'vile incendiaries.'"

Placide bobs his head in appreciation. "You have a good memory."

"I do," says Ritchie, and there's something about the way he says those two little words that makes Jack's stomach muscles tighten.

"Caulfield must have told you about the way they were all loitering about?"

"Yes," Ritchie agrees amiably. "But he said they were by the entrance to the gallery."

Jack's heart stops. Caulfield was most definitely meant to tell Ritchie he'd seen a band of Negroes milling about in an agitated state near the stage door.

"I asked him, 'Isn't the gallery entrance precisely where they *should* have been loitering?' And he seemed confused by the question."

Placide looks like he's been turned inside out, and he begins to sputter.

Jack's torn. On one hand, he'd like for the truth to come to light, for Ritchie to realize exactly what the company's trying to get away with. But on the other, Anderson has scared him within an inch of his life, and Jack worries that failing to save Placide, when he has the chance, will look just as bad as turning on him entirely.

Jack clears his throat, trying to get both men's attention, but they ignore him. "Excuse me," he finally says. "It was Twaits who saw them by the stage door."

All heads—including Lydia's—turn to look at him, and he burns with shame.

"So, why did you send me Caulfield?" Ritchie asks, and Placide looks at Jack with pleading eyes, begging him to come up with something that makes sense.

Jack swallows. "Anderson thought it was Caulfield who saw everything, but he got it wrong. It was Twaits."

"Twaits?" says Ritchie.

Jack nods, once.

"So, I want to make sure I am understanding you correctly," says Ritchie. "You are confirming that the theater was set on fire as part of a slave rebellion?"

Jack glances at Placide, who pretends to be insulted. "Isn't that what we've been telling you?"

"And these slaves," says Ritchie. "What were they rebelling against?"

"How should I know?" says Placide. "The ticket prices? The long lines? Tommy West's overacting?"

Jack winces at Placide's joke, though he's not wrong about West. He does his best, just never quite hits the mark.

Lydia clears her throat and says, "Should we not assume the Negro might always have reason to rebel against his condition?"

It is a principled argument, and all Jack can think about now is how much she must despise him. He's as big a liar as the rest of them.

Ritchie rubs his temples. "Mr. Placide, I will give your theory a thorough examination, but in return, here is what I need from you."

Placide offers Ritchie a slow nod, but Ritchie has given up and is speaking directly to Jack. "I need a list of all his employees, whether they were at the theater last night, and where I can find them now."

That will be easy enough to put together. "Shall I bring it to you?" Jack asks Ritchie.

"Just have it ready by tomorrow morning. I want to begin conducting interviews first thing," he says. "Is the tavern the most convenient location?"

"Most of the men stay there," says Jack.

"Then the tavern suits me fine." He puts on his hat. "I'll be there at nine o'clock. Make sure everyone's expecting me."

Placide rests his head on Lydia's shoulder, and Ritchie stands to leave. "Oh, and one more thing."

"Yes?"

He glances at Placide. "For the love of God, make sure he's sober."

❧ | GILBERT | ❧

Lecretia," *Gilbert whispers from behind the* hemlocks that grow up next to the Prestons' back porch. She has come outside to empty a dustpan, and she jumps when she hears her name.

"It's just me," he says quickly.

She cranes her neck to make him out in the dark. "Gilbert?"

"Don't say nothing. Will you just tell Sara I'm here? See if she'll meet me in our usual spot."

She shakes her head in disbelief. "You think she wants to fool around with you at a time like this?"

"Shhh," says Gilbert, although he should know by now there is no keeping Lecretia quiet. "Who you think's fooling around? I need to talk to her, is all."

Lecretia rolls her eyes.

"I'm serious, Lecretia. Tell her it's important."

Inside, General Preston is calling for someone, and Lecretia turns toward the noise. "You can go on out there, but don't hold your breath waiting." She nods at the house. "Everything is upside down in here."

"No word on Louisa?"

"Got word from the Prices that their girl Maria made it out. Bad knock on the head, but other than that, she all right."

Gilbert wonders if it's bad news for Cecily that Maria made it out alive. He can't see why it would matter. "Did Maria know anything about Louisa?"

Lecretia nods her head real slow. "They sayin' she was with her till the end."

"What do you mean?"

"What I said."

"Are you saying Louisa's dead?"

"Nothing's certain," says Lecretia, "but it's looking that way."

It feels like something thick has lodged in Gilbert's throat and he can't get it out. For the second time that day, his eyes begin to water.

Lecretia looks down at the dustpan and taps it against her skirts. "I'll let her know you waiting."

Gilbert is dying to tell Sara about Cecily, but the last thing he wants to do is give her one more reason to worry right now. "Make sure she knows it's fine if she can't make it. I just ain't sure when I'll be back. Kemp's watching me close."

Lecretia makes like she's about to go back inside the house. But then she turns and says, "I heard about what happened at the green."

With this new information about Louisa swirling around inside his head, Gilbert can barely focus on what she's saying.

"General Preston's footman, Fergus, was there. Said it was something to behold. All those white folks cheering for what you did."

How had he managed to convince himself Louisa was just going to turn up somewhere? Like she's some kind of trumpet mushroom that only appears after a hard rain?

Lecretia is still talking. "Fergus says he don't know the last time he saw a Negro, who wasn't swinging from the gallows, get the attention of a crowd like that."

"That's a nasty thing to say," says Gilbert.

"I'm just repeating what he said, is all."

"They was grateful."

"Think you'd have gotten a hand-clapping like that if you had caught a bunch of colored ladies?"

❧ | SALLY | ❧

Sally *has to ask two people* for directions to the *Enquirer*'s offices, but eventually she finds the right place. At this time of night, the bookshop is closed, but she can see a lamp on in the print shop, and she pounds on the door until someone—a man—emerges from the back of the shop.

The man's hair looks like it hasn't seen a comb since Thursday morning, and he doesn't even get the door open before he points to a sign with the store's hours. "Can you not tell we're closed?"

Sally notices that the man's fingers are stained with ink. "I'm looking for Thomas Ritchie."

"That's me," he says in an exasperated voice, and Sally is the tiniest bit surprised. She assumed he'd be a little more composed.

"I'm Sally Campbell. I want to talk to you about the fire."

Ritchie looks skeptical. "I'm meeting with someone right now."

"Sally Henry Campbell," she says, putting the required emphasis on her maiden name. "Mr. Roane is my brother-in-law."

He immediately lets her in, and she follows him through the print shop to an office in the back of the building.

She is barely inside the little room when a delighted voice booms at her from the settee. "Mrs. Campbell!"

She can barely hide her disappointment. "Mr. Wirt."

"It has been too long!"

Nothing could be further from the truth, but she agrees with him all the same.

Wirt has spent the last five years badgering Sally's family to provide their recollections of her father to him so that he might write his biography. He has argued—quite passionately—that his tome will do for Patrick Henry's legacy what John Marshall's five-volume set did for George Washington, but Sally is not convinced Wirt can write. *The Letters of the British*

Spy, while commercially successful, was difficult for her to get through, and several of his other projects have been considered flops. She has advised her siblings to remain mum, and thus far, Wirt has succeeded only in soliciting the memories of her stepfather, who, it should be noted, knew Sally's father the least well of any of them.

"I trust your wife is well?" she asks him.

"Yes, quite. She has her health, which is all any of us can wish for at present." Sally waits for him to give her the floor, but he plows into a long-winded story about how he and his wife hosted a dinner party yesterday evening, with plans for everyone to go to the theater afterward. "Through some act of divine intervention, our party ran long and we decided not to make use of our tickets. What a fine bit of luck, you'll agree?"

"Never has a man been so well-rewarded for being an easy drunk," says Ritchie, and Wirt blushes.

"So, you know each other?" Wirt asks. "You *should.*"

"She was just explaining the connection."

Wirt looks momentarily confused.

"Spencer Roane," Sally offers, and then he nods his head knowingly.

Sally directs her attention to Ritchie. "I made the acquaintance of your father-in-law this morning. He set my sister-in-law's leg."

Ritchie seems poised to speak, but Wirt beats him to the punch. "Do you mean Margaret?"

"Yes."

"That's an absolute shame."

Sally can't disagree with him there.

Wirt explains, "Sally was married to Archie Campbell's brother Robert until—" He turns to Sally. "When did Robert die?"

"Three years ago this past September." Without realizing she's even done it, she touches the ring around her neck.

Because it is impossible for Wirt to consider anyone for more than a moment or two without passing judgment on him, he says, "He was a splendid fellow."

If there is one thing Sally does not want to do, it is listen to William Wirt's reminiscences of her late husband. She addresses Ritchie. "I have read your coverage of the theater fire, and I wish to speak to you about it."

"By all means."

"Surely, you have noted that among the list of the dead, there is a high proportion of women."

"I have."

"And how do you explain it?"

"Well, I think there are likely several logical explanations . . ."

"Such as?"

Ritchie coughs into his hand. "Well, for one, the dresses."

"What about them?" asks Sally curtly.

"They're highly flammable," Wirt offers.

"No more so than a dress coat."

"It is thought that so much fabric may have impeded the ladies' escape," says Ritchie.

Sally unbuttons her coat and reaches for her own skirt. "This thing? It hardly weighs an ounce."

"Mrs. Campbell," says Ritchie. "It is good of you to assume the role of detective, but we do not, in fact, even know if the house was filled with men and women in equal numbers."

"What I heard," says Wirt, "is that the show was so popular, many of the men gave up their seats. They allowed the ladies to keep the box seats, and they went to the pit, never thinking—of course—that the pit would be far easier to escape in the event of a fire."

"Mr. Wirt," says Sally as calmly as she knows how, "I can assure you that, in box six, which is where I was seated, our party was equally divided between men and women. And not a single man volunteered to give up his seat."

She has gotten Mr. Ritchie's attention. "You were in the boxes? Last night?"

"Yes," she says.

"Christ," says Ritchie. "I'm sorry. I didn't realize."

"You mistook me for just another busybody?"

"Not at all," says Ritchie, although that's obviously exactly what he thought.

"How ever did you manage to escape?" asks Wirt, who cannot contain his enthusiasm for a good story, no matter how much it might pain the speaker to retell it.

Sally chooses the most succinct version. "I jumped out of a third-floor window."

Wirt lets out a low whistle, but she ignores him and addresses Mr. Ritchie instead. "Shall I tell you about the men who helped me escape?"

He doesn't say anything.

"I'll be brief."

"Please."

"There weren't any."

"Surely—"

"The reason there are so few men on the list is because they pushed past us—and in some cases, climbed over us—to get out."

"I can't believe—"

"Ask any of the women who survived, and they'll tell you the same thing."

"Mrs. Campbell," says Ritchie. "These claims are serious and jeopardize the good standing of many decent men. Men who have also been through a harrowing ordeal."

"I do not wish to topple any empires, only to see the record reflect my experiences and the experiences of women in my position."

"How do you suggest I do that?"

"Interview us. I dare say a few of us can even write."

F rom the other side of the boathouse door, Cecily can hear her mother whisper, "It's me."

She scrambles out of her canoe, and drags another one out of the way of the door. After Moses caught her by surprise, she decided the safest thing to do was to turn the boats into a barricade.

As soon as Della is through the door, Cecily flings her arms around her. "I thought you'd never come."

Della kisses the top of her head.

"Tell me what's going on."

"Child, I'm not sure I know where to begin," says Della as she eyes the canoe near the door and motions for Cecily to help her turn it over. They take a seat on the hull.

"First things first," says Della as she retrieves a small forcemeat patty from underneath her headscarf and hands it to Cecily. "Supper."

She takes a bite of the patty, and it's so good, she's tempted to swallow it whole. But she has to be smart and ration what she's got, so she tucks it away with the leftover bread and cheese from Moses.

"I talked to your uncle Gilbert," says Della, "and he's going to help."

"He is?"

"He says he can write you a pass, and I think he's gonna buy you a stage-coach ticket, too."

A stagecoach ticket? Cecily begins to panic. "Is that wise? What if someone recognizes me?"

"Who's going to recognize you?" asks Della. "So long as the Prices aren't in the coach?"

Maybe her mother's right.

"If you got the right pass and no one's looking for you, there's no good reason you can't take a stagecoach, just like everybody else."

It strikes Cecily as a terrifying prospect, traveling all that way with more than a dozen people who might turn on her the first time they stop to switch horses. "You sure it wouldn't be safer for me to go on foot?"

"It's at least two hundred miles to Philadelphia, and we're entering the coldest months of the year."

It will take weeks to cover that kind of ground on foot—more if she comes to a river she cannot ford. "I'll do whatever you say," she tells her mother, and Della nods, like she wouldn't have expected less.

Della's never been good at sitting still, so she starts picking up the oars and push poles that lay in the center of the room and stacking them against the wall.

"Mama, there's something I got to tell you," Cecily says as she watches her mother work.

Della leans on a push pole, like it's the only thing holding her up. "About what?"

"Moses," she says apologetically.

Della's eyes go narrow in her head.

"He knows I'm alive."

"What do you mean he knows?"

"He found me down here. Earlier today. Brought me some food."

Della closes her eyes and whispers, "Mercy."

"I'm sorry."

"How did he find you?"

"Said he followed us last night."

Her mother looks angry enough to break the push pole in two. "He asked me about you last night, when I got home. Said he thought he'd seen you, and I told him he was dreaming."

"Well, he was testing you," says Cecily.

Della looks fit to be tied. "He came down here in broad daylight?"

Cecily nods.

"Does he not have the sense God gave a goose?"

"He means well. Told me he wanted to help."

"I assume you told him it'd be a help if he didn't go leading the slave patrol right to your door?"

"I explained everything."

"Has he been back down here since?"

Cecily shakes her head no.

Cecily wonders if maybe they're both underestimating Moses. He's not a little boy anymore, and he's seen all the same ugliness they have. Not all of it, Cecily corrects herself, but enough. He knows what happens when information gets into the wrong hands, knows that the Prices can be punishing, and knows that—at the end of the day—his family is all that matters. "I think he can keep a secret."

"He shouldn't have to," Della spits back. "Especially when it's a secret that could get him killed."

"I'm so sorry, Mama," says Cecily as her eyes well with tears.

Della sighs. "I know why you had to run, but you shouldn't have come back here. It's putting too many people at risk."

Cecily wipes her eyes with the palms of her hands, then gets to her feet. "I can go."

Della motions for her to sit down. "Stay where you are. The patrol's out in force right now. They're picking up anyone they think might have had anything to do with the fire."

"The *theater* fire?"

Della nods. "They think it was a bunch of Negroes who started it."

Cecily balks. "That don't even make sense."

"Since when do white folks have to make sense?" Della's tone is sharp.

Cecily knows she did the wrong thing—getting her mother and her brother and her uncle involved—but Della's so angry, Cecily wonders if there's something else going on, something more she's not saying.

"I'll go tonight," Cecily offers. "Really, I will."

Della inhales, then says no. "Give us another day or two. If we can get you on a stagecoach, it'll be the best thing for you."

Cecily agrees to sit tight.

"And if you see your brother . . ."

"I'll send him straight home."

❄ | JACK | ❄

I*t's late at night, and Jack* sits in a corner of the tavern's taproom, making a list for Ritchie of all the players in the company.

It helps if he thinks in terms of productions—who has starred in what, when. Just last week, the company staged *Town and Country*, and Hopkins Robertson played Reuben Glenroy. Green played Hamlet the week prior, and it was Thomas Caulfield who starred in Elizabeth Poe's benefit performance, *The Wheel of Fortune*, which the company put on the boards shortly before her death.

Since starting the job, back in October, Jack has assisted with almost two dozen performances, which amount to twice as many plays. Placide & Green has produced tragedies, comedies, farces, pantomimes, operas, even a few very bad ballets, and Jack has felt lucky to witness all of it.

At a table on the other side of the room sit West and three men who look vaguely familiar. West looks unhappy, as if he'd like to get up and leave, but eventually it is the men who leave, and Jack watches as West downs the remainder of his drink and follows them toward the door. He stops in front of Jack's table.

"What are you up to?" says West, craning his neck to read Jack's scrawl.

"Trying to make a list of everyone in the company."

"Who's asking for it?"

"Thomas Ritchie."

"Ah," says West as he pulls out a chair rather abruptly and sits down beside Jack. He picks up the piece of paper and looks at it in earnest, then says, "You forgot Burke. And the Youngs."

Jack takes the list back from him and adds their names to the bottom of the page.

"And Hanner. Everyone always forgets about Hanner."

For the life of him, Jack can't picture what Hanner looks like, but he dutifully writes down his name.

"What do I do about Nancy?" asks Jack.

"I think it's safe to leave her off the list."

"You think she's really dead?"

"The Greens have looked everywhere."

When the list is finished, they both sit there, staring at it. It is an impressive group of people. More than thirty men and women who have made the theater their life's work.

"Were the men over there giving you a hard time?" Jack asks.

"No more than I deserve."

"Who were they?"

"Investors."

"What do they want with you?"

"They want me to sell the property to the city."

"The theater?" Jack asks, surprised that anyone would want the burned-out shell of a building.

"What's left of it."

"I didn't even realize you owned it."

West lets out a bitter laugh. "Why do you think Placide and Green keep me around?"

"Oh, I see," says Jack, and he finally does. West is a terrible actor, but if he owns the property the theater sits on, the managers have to make use of him.

"It was my parents who owned it." West wears a signet ring on his right hand, and he twists it absentmindedly. "They were talented. Worked at Drury Lane and Covent Garden before coming to America, and when they arrived in Virginia, they went straight to work for the Old American Company, in Williamsburg."

"The Old American?" Jack says in awe.

West nods. "They were there a few years, but the pay was terrible, so they got it in their heads that there was probably enough room in Virginia for two theater companies. Next thing you know, they'd moved to Richmond and set up shop."

"Richmond is the better for it," Jack says, although he wonders if this is true.

West reaches for Jack's pencil and turns it over in his hands. "First place they leased was Quesney's Academy, which they eventually bought. Did you ever see that place?"

Jack decides not to remind West that Quesney's burned to the ground before he was born. Instead, he just shakes his head no.

"It was on the green, same site as the current theater," he says, then catches himself. "Well, former theater, I suppose."

"I knew what you meant," says Jack.

"Quesney's was too big. It was impossible to heat. But it had a large stage, with floor traps and generous flies, and the troupe started putting on the kind of spectacles we're known for today—sea battles and cavalry charges. That type of thing."

Jack's heard more than one story about the time the company staged *The Siege of Gibraltar*, which included more than a hundred ships of various sizes, all equipped with live guns.

"Once they'd found success in Richmond, they expanded to Norfolk and then further south to Charleston. The Old American Company had the Philadelphia and New York markets cornered, but the South was open for the taking. Everywhere my father went, he built a theater, and by the time he died, West and Bignall had proper theaters in Norfolk, Charleston, Petersburg, Fredericksburg, and Alexandria."

"But not Richmond?"

"He'd always dreamed of replacing Quesney's. Even had Henry Latrobe draw up plans. Do you know who he is?"

Jack shrugs.

"It doesn't matter," says West, who seems to realize he's steered the conversation off course. "He could never manage to justify the cost. Until, of course, Quesney's caught fire and there was no other choice."

"Was that first fire anything like this one?"

"Not nearly so dramatic as all this," says West, waving a hand in the direction of the theater green. "Caught fire at the end of the season, with no one inside. But back then, nobody had insurance. Not for fire, anyway. So, after my father died and my mother took over the business, it took her years to put away enough money to rebuild."

"But she finally did it?"

"She did," says West, and Jack can hear the pride in his voice. "At first, she put up something cheap. Just a simple wooden structure—not much bigger than a milking shed. But she could barely pay the actors' wages with what she was making. So, that's when she gets the idea to get a bunch of investors to finance the construction of a fine building. Not nearly as fancy as Latrobe's design, but something that would accommodate a crowd. She goes to a dozen of the wealthiest men in town—including William Marshall—and sells them on the idea, which is that she'll retain the deed to the land, but they'll put up the money for the new building. Each year they get a share of the profits, plus box seats and some other perks—namely, the right to invite themselves to our parties and diddle the actresses."

Jack nearly falls out of his chair.

"I was kidding about that last part," says West. "Sort of."

In two and a half months of working for Placide & Green, no one—not even Anderson—has ever spoken to Jack this honestly.

"So, I have a question," he says to West. "What's the city going to do with the land? If you agree to sell?"

West sighs. "Hand it over to the burial committee."

Jack is confused. "What do they want with it?"

West gives him a look, like he's wondering if he's really got to spell this out for him. Obviously, he does. "They want to bury everyone there, Jack."

"What?" Jack says. "On the theater green?"

"In the ruins."

"But if they turn the site into a burial ground, we'll never be able to rebuild."

"An added benefit, as far as the committee is concerned."

Jack is dumbfounded. "Surely, they can't make you sell?"

"Technically, no. Not yet, anyway. My mother put down the land as collateral when she borrowed the money for the building. The deal was that, if she failed to perform the conditions of the agreement for a period of one year, she'd forfeit her rights to the property."

"And now that she's gone?"

"All the same rules apply to me."

"But you haven't failed to perform anything. There was that big subscribers' meeting just last month. Everyone got their money."

"Right," says West. "But what they're saying is they know we'll come to next year's meeting empty-handed."

"That's not true, necessarily."

"Isn't it?"

"We can rebuild."

"But the question is, why would we?"

❧ | GILBERT | ❧

Sara never shows at the greenhouse. So, eventually, Gilbert gives up and returns to the smithy.

"Not a good night to be out," Marcus says when he sees him walk through the door.

"Kemp back?"

"Yes, sir. He's upstairs looking for you."

"He check the shitter yet?"

Marcus shakes his head. "Don't think so. If you head out back now, you might be able to act like you was in there the whole time."

The outhouse is at the rear of the smithy. In the mornings, there's always a long line of men wanting to take a squat, but tonight the facilities are mercifully empty. Gilbert yanks open the door and ducks inside. For authenticity's sake, he drops his pants and takes a seat, then watches the smithy through a crack in the boards.

Gilbert can hear Kemp carrying on from all the way across the yard, but he can't make out most of what he says. He hears his name at least twice and knows it's just a matter of time before Marcus suggests Kemp check the latrine.

When Kemp finally marches across the yard and rips the door of the outhouse open, Gilbert tries to act surprised by the interruption.

"Get out here," growls Kemp.

"You need something, Master Kemp?" Gilbert makes a big show of pulling his pants up and is still cinching his belt when he feels Kemp's fist connect with his jaw.

Nothing Kemp does should take Gilbert by surprise, but that punch does. He feels like his head's come clear off his body, and the force of it sends him staggering backward.

"What's this I hear about you getting a goddamn *tribute* at the theater green?" says Kemp as he shakes out his hand and tries to flex his fingers.

It takes Gilbert a minute for his ears to stop ringing.

Kemp yanks him out of the outhouse. "You didn't think I'd hear about it?"

"It just happened," says Gilbert. "There wasn't nothing I could do to stop it."

"What were you even doing there?"

Gilbert rubs the side of his face, tries to think of something fast. "I was making a delivery."

"Don't give me that bull crap. Seth says you all cut out of here early."

Seth Fenwick is one of Kemp's newest apprentices, and clearly Ned has not gotten to him yet.

"He must have been confused," says Gilbert, and before he realizes quite what is happening, Kemp is charging him like a bull. He knocks him flat on the ground, and Gilbert just lies there, staring up at the stars, too stunned to speak. Above him, Kemp snorts and spits.

"I'm going to give you one more chance to tell me why you weren't at your forge this afternoon."

Gilbert has long known that the best lies are half-truths. They roll off the tongue a little easier, and they usually check out if someone is of a mind to start asking questions. "I got word my sister's daughter died in the fire."

This news has at least some effect on Kemp. "I didn't know you had a sister."

"Yes, sir," says Gilbert. "She a good bit older than me."

"And you say her daughter was in the gallery?"

Gilbert didn't say anything of the sort, and now that Kemp has started to ask questions, he wonders if it was a mistake to use Della as his alibi. "We think so."

For a moment, Kemp looks almost contemplative. Then he walks right up to Gilbert and feels around in his front pocket for the leather sleeve where they both know Gilbert keeps his pass.

Kemp removes the piece of paper and tosses the empty sleeve at Gilbert. The soft piece of leather lands on his chest with a quiet thwap.

Kemp holds the pass out in front of him, where Gilbert will be sure to see it. He wants Gilbert to plead with him, to beg him not to take it from him, but Gilbert is done with groveling.

"It'll be pretty hard to see that wife of yours without one of these, won't it now?"

It will and it won't. Gilbert can write a new pass any time he wants. What he can't do is convince Kemp to let up on him.

"This is for not staying put," Kemp says as he rips the pass into pieces.

Gilbert should have known that if Kemp didn't like those two actors calling him a hero, he was never going to put up with Gilbert receiving the acclamations of an entire city.

"And this," says Kemp, kicking him once and then twice in the ribs, "is for not knowing your place."

Gilbert closes his eyes, trying to picture Kemp's reaction if Phyllis Johnston had arrived on his doorstep, offering to buy his freedom. He was right to believe it would never have worked.

SATURDAY

❧ | ❧

DECEMBER 28, 1811

SALLY

Sally has slept for three, maybe four hours on the floor beside Margaret's pallet, when she is awoken by the sound of something crashing to the floor above her head.

She jumps to her feet and flies up the stairs, sure that Mr. Scott has tried to get out of bed and failed doing so.

Sally ignores the ruckus coming from the other side of Maria Price's door until she is standing at the foot of Mr. Scott's bed and has confirmed that he is sleeping peacefully.

"I don't understand," comes a man's voice from down the hall. Elliott's.

Maria's voice is quieter, less distinct, and Sally has to move out into the hall to hear it. "I told you everything," the girl whimpers.

"Tell me again."

"Elliott, what possible good is this doing?" asks their mother, who must have stayed the night.

Elliott tells his mother to be quiet. "Maria, continue. You were in Blair Hayley's arms."

His sister is crying, and Sally can't—for the life of her—figure out why Elliott is pressing her so hard. And at this time in the morning. Sally doesn't wear a timepiece, but she'd be surprised if it is yet six o'clock.

"He carried me out of the theater and onto the green."

"And then what happened?"

"There were people everywhere, and the sky was so orange."

"Keep going."

"To what end?" says their mother.

Elliott ignores her.

"This is difficult for her," Mrs. Price continues.

Elliott laughs. "For all of us, Mother."

Sally screws up her face. For *all* of us? As far as she knows, Elliott was safely ensconced at home while his sister was inside the theater, fighting for her life.

Maria forges ahead. "Mr. Hayley stopped briefly to shout something at someone, and when he spun around, I caught a glimpse of the theater, which looked like the mouth of hell."

"A little less hyperbole, perhaps?"

"You want to know what I saw, and I'm telling you that it wasn't of this world."

"All right, fine. You saw the gaping mouth of hell," says Elliott. "Now continue."

Maria is quiet for a moment, and Sally leans against the wall and takes a deep breath. Elliott can be charming when he wants to be, but any man who would talk to his sister this way is not a man she wants to know.

Finally, Maria speaks. "It was in the middle of that hellfire that I saw Cecily."

Sally slides to the floor and pulls her knees up to her chest. Is Maria really admitting to having seen her? And what will this do to Elliott, who is already completely preoccupied with her disappearance?

"What was she wearing?" he asks.

"I don't know," says Maria. "Whatever she wore to the theater, I suppose."

"And what did she do?"

"She just looked straight at me. Like she could see inside my soul."

Sally can hear a chair scrape across the floor, and imagines Elliott pushing himself out of it.

"Do you hear this, Mother?" he says. "She's alive."

"I don't think that's what your sister is saying," says Mrs. Price in a measured voice.

"It's not," says Maria. "Elliott, will you listen to me?"

"I *am* listening." Sally can hear him pacing on the other side of the door.

Maria continues. "It was a vision. A visitation. Cecily was dead, and she was waiting for me to let go of the last cord tethering me to earth."

"So, you're saying you think Cecily meant to usher you into heaven?" Elliott's voice is thick with condescension.

"I never said that."

"What, then?"

"I think she meant to drag me straight to hell."

"God damn it, Maria." Elliott has clearly had enough. Sally can hear it in the timbre of his voice. "Would you think about what you are saying for a minute?"

Sally is tempted to knock on the door and interrupt the argument, pretend she has to check on that doomed girl in the other bed, but she thinks it might be too late for that. They'll know she's been listening.

"Your sister has been through an ordeal," says Mrs. Price. "And I don't think it's helpful to—"

"To what?" Elliott interrupts her. "Demand she speak sense? Tell us something true?"

"I *am* telling you something true," Maria insists.

"Maria, hear this," says Elliott, his voice low enough that Sally has to move closer to the door to hear it. "If you saw Cecily Patterson on the theater green, there are only two explanations. Either she's alive, or you're a raving lunatic."

Before Sally knows quite what is happening, the door to Maria's room swings open, and Elliott Price is standing in front of her, teeth bared. When his eyes light on her, she thinks they might bulge out of his head.

It is obvious she's been listening at the door, but nothing can be done about it now. "Good morning, Mr. Price," she says coolly.

He places his hat on his head. "Mrs. Campbell."

❧ | JACK | ❧

Placide is at the tavern by seven o'clock in the morning, calling upstairs to the second floor, where all of the unmarried actors sleep three to a bed. Ordinarily, Jack rooms with Robertson and Burke, but last night, Anderson insisted he sleep on a pallet in his room. "In case you get any wild ideas," he said as he drifted off to sleep.

In the early hours of the morning, Jack dreamed that Anderson had led him into a theater much like theirs, only larger. When the two of them were standing at center stage, looking out into the dark and empty auditorium, Anderson pointed up at the ceiling, where hundreds of lit chandeliers hung from the rafters. There were so many candles burning that the flames looked like stars in the night sky. Jack could pick out whole constellations—Hercules and Orion and Ursa Major and Minor—and he wanted to tell Anderson how beautiful the effect was, but when he turned to say something, he realized Anderson had disappeared out the stage door, locking Jack inside the theater, alone. He didn't panic, not at first, but then the chandeliers began to spin, slowly at first and then faster and faster, until the flames looked more like comets than stars. Jack pounded on the door, screaming to be let out, but Anderson wouldn't open the door, and when it occurred to Jack that he would die, right there in the theater, he woke up, covered in sweat.

Jack hasn't been able to fall back to sleep since.

Now Placide's voice travels up the back stairs and down the narrow hallway. "All of you! I want you downstairs. At once!" He's as loud as a rooster greeting the dawn, but no one stirs, with the exception of Anderson, who kicks Jack in the ribs and says, "Get up."

"Huh?" says Jack, who has decided it's worth pretending to be asleep.

"Placide's here. Go wake everyone."

While Anderson relieves himself, Jack stumbles down the hall, knocking on doors. "Placide's here. He wants us downstairs."

"They're not listening to me," Jack reports to Anderson when he returns to the room a few minutes later.

"Cocksuckers!" Anderson yells down the hall. "If you'd like to avoid the gallows, might I suggest listening to young Master Gibson and getting your ugly arses downstairs? You don't want Placide to come up here."

Now Jack can hear the sounds of the actors' feet hitting the floor, chamber pots being dragged out from under beds, suspenders snapping into place.

Jack slips on his boots and follows Anderson downstairs, where Placide is waiting for them.

He's a different man from the one Jack saw the previous evening. Lydia has accompanied him, and when Jack goes to greet her, she whispers to him, "He got out of bed all by himself today." He smiles, not so much at what she's said but at the fact that there now exists a joke that only the two of them understand.

Anderson flags down a barmaid, who brings the men breakfast—eggs and bacon, with potatoes, and coffee to wash everything down.

The barmaid is back and forth between the back room and the kitchen, until Placide gets annoyed and asks her to give them five minutes alone. "Ritchie's arriving soon," he says when she is gone, "so we don't have much time."

Jack takes a seat next to Lydia, who is staring at an untouched cup of coffee in front of her. He doesn't know what possesses him, but he reaches for her hand, which rests in her lap, and gives it a light squeeze. She seems surprised—how could she not be?—but also maybe appreciative of the gesture. After all, she is mourning her friend. As Jack watches the color rise in her cheeks, he wonders what it must be like to be Placide's daughter. Wherever she goes, for the rest of her life, she will not want for roles—not with his last name. But will she want for a father who is honest and kind, who cares more about doing right by others than about saving his own skin? Jack's father could never have helped him establish a career on the stage, but he was an honorable man, and Jack is beginning to see that that counts for more than he ever realized.

Placide rehashes the conversation he had with Ritchie at the boardinghouse, then asks Anderson to tell everyone what happened at the capitol. All of the actors, with the possible exception of Perry and West, seem impressed that Anderson was able to seed the slave revolt story so effectively, and they begin whooping with delight when Twaits reports that the slave patrol has been out all night, arresting any Negro man—free or enslaved—who looks even vaguely suspicious. "The birdcage is brimming with them," Twaits says. "And Kemp wants me to go down there this morning to identify the men I saw out back."

Already Jack regrets offering up Twaits as a witness. The success of the slave revolt story now hinges, in large part, on his testimony, and in the same way that the role of the no-good commodore was the right fit for his talents, this one also suits him exceedingly well.

"What will they do to those men?" Jack asks him. "Once you've identified them?"

"That's up to them," says Twaits with a shrug of indifference, as if it hasn't occurred to him to care.

"Ritchie is going to want to talk to you first," Placide warns Twaits. "Get that out of the way, and then you can head down to the jail."

Twaits nods in agreement before shoving a whole hard-boiled egg into his mouth.

"Now, for the rest of you, remember—there will be no talk of chandeliers or broken pulleys or flaming backdrops," says Placide. "You didn't see anything unusual backstage, at least not until Twaits alerted us to the fire out back."

"And then what did we do?" asks Young.

"Twaits and Perry tried to put it out, but it had already spread to the roof. Young, you ran to warn the others."

Young seems to like that.

"What if he asks us about the Negroes?" says Burke.

"Just tell him that Twaits saw about a half dozen of them, and that they were angry and brandishing torches."

"Is a half dozen enough?" asks Twaits.

"Good question," says Placide. "A dozen?"

The only sound is the scratching of heads.

"Does that seem about right?" Placide asks the room.

Young yawns. "Seems good to me."

"Fine. About a dozen Negroes. With torches."

"All of them had torches?" Caulfield asks. "Or just some of them?"

Jack can't even bring himself to listen to Placide's answer.

There is no way the troupe is going to be able to keep a story like this straight. The actors have a hard enough time delivering their lines when they've walked around, for days beforehand, with scripts in front of their faces. Once Ritchie begins interviewing them, they are bound to contradict each other, to conflate events, to color in their own details. Jack can't blame them—it's who they are. None of them would have gone into the theater if they didn't—at some level—like to hear themselves talk.

Gilbert's jawbone is sore to the touch, and when he takes the stairs from the loft down to the shop on Saturday morning, he feels a sharp, stabbing pain in his side.

The Common Council's decree is still in effect—no businesses are to operate until after the burial. But Kemp's outburst the previous evening has set everyone on edge, so they are all in their places, tools in hand, at the regular time.

Gilbert has barely begun to rake the coals in his forge when he hears the sound of a horse in the alley and, a few moments later, a pounding at the door of the smithy. "Are we meant to answer it?" Ned asks the room.

"What if it's someone trying to shut us down?" says Nick.

"That'd be more than all right," Gilbert says as he limps toward the door.

The knocking continues, and when Gilbert finally gets the door unlocked, he is surprised to find himself face-to-face with Elliott Price Jr.

"Can I help you?" he asks.

Mr. Price seems agitated, and when he speaks, the words tumble out of his mouth. "Is Kemp around?"

Gilbert has run into Price, on visits to Della's, at least a half-dozen times, but he's fairly sure Price doesn't recognize him. "I'm afraid he ain't. Anything I can help you with?"

"When do you expect him in?" Price asks.

"I couldn't tell you. Master Kemp's been staying busy with the patrol ever since the fire, but I would assume he'll check in here first before he rides out this morning."

Price seems uncertain of his next move.

"Do you have a card?" Gilbert finally asks. "I can be sure he gets it."

Price eyes the shop's interior and tells Gilbert he'd rather wait, so Gilbert has no choice but to offer him a seat at the table in front of the fireplace.

The man has a hard time sitting still. "Do I know you?" he asks Gilbert at one point as he runs his hands along a rack of tongs.

Gilbert sees no advantage to telling Price he is Della's brother. "I worked at Pete Goode's before I came here. You a customer of his?"

Price sucks air through his teeth. "That's not it."

At one point, Price walks out into the alley to watch for Kemp's arrival. "What do you think he wants with him?" Marcus asks as they peer at the man through the window.

"It's anybody's guess," says Gilbert, but before they can get around to doing much guessing, Kemp gallops down Locust Alley on his horse.

"Mr. Kemp?" Gilbert hears Price say, after Kemp has dismounted. "I was talking to John Gamble, and he said to come see you. Says you're now the captain of the first class of patrol?"

Kemp stands up a little taller. "I am."

Gilbert and Marcus move closer to the window, where they can get a good look at the two men. "I need the patrol's help finding a runaway."

"Who?" says Kemp.

Gilbert's body stiffens. If Elliott Price is looking for a runaway, there's only one person it's likely to be.

"It's a house servant named Cecily Patterson."

"That your family name?" Kemp asks. "Patterson?"

"No, I'm Elliott Price. But my mother is a Patterson."

Marcus snaps at Gilbert to get his attention, then whispers, "That your niece?"

He hesitates for a moment. What choice does he have but to own the connection? If Marcus suspects he's been lying to him—or, at the very least, withholding the truth—he'll begin to believe that Price is onto something. "That's her," Gilbert confirms in a quiet voice.

Elliott follows Kemp into the shop, and Gilbert and Marcus hurry back to their respective workstations and try their hardest to look busy.

Kemp signals for Price to take a seat at the table, then he roots around in a cupboard for a bottle of whiskey and two dirty glasses. He pours each of them two fingerfuls of whiskey and downs his immediately. "So, how long's this Cecily Patterson been missing?"

"Since the night of the fire. She was at the theater, up in the gallery, and hasn't been home since."

"What makes you think she ain't dead?" Kemp asks Price, and Gilbert listens hard to what he has to say.

"My sister says she saw her that night. Out on the theater green. And that she didn't have a scratch on her."

Gilbert closes his eyes briefly, then remembers that Marcus is not far away. He can give nothing away to him or any of the other men in the shop.

Kemp starts telling Price about the slave rebellion. "Is there any chance she's tied up in that?"

Price says he doesn't think so, says that what he's interested in are the rumors that some of the slaves in the gallery may have faked their own deaths in order to run. "You hear about that?"

Kemp doesn't commit, which means he hasn't.

"Everyone's saying it wasn't hard to get out of the gallery. That if you've got a slave who's missing, there's something funny going on."

Marcus looks over at Gilbert, no doubt wondering if, indeed, something funny is going on. But Gilbert just shakes his head no.

Still, the conversation between the two men grows increasingly animated. "I wouldn't be surprised," says Price, "if we come to find out every last one of them Negroes in that theater made it out, and they're all of them halfway to Philadelphia by now."

Gilbert can tell Kemp is getting excited. He wants to know what Cecily looks like, how far she's ever traveled from Richmond, whether she knows any of the roads outside of town, and if she has kin who live in far-flung places that she might be aiming to reach.

"She's got a mother, a father, a brother, and a couple of sisters," says Price, "and I own all of them. Or, my father does."

"Any extended family?"

"None," says Price, and again Gilbert can feel Marcus's eyes on him.

Kemp keeps peppering Price with questions. He wants to know if Cecily had a pass with her and if Price has found evidence that she packed any personal effects.

"Her pass will only get her as far as the mantua maker on E Street," says Price.

"And her personal effects?"

Gilbert watches as Price pauses to contemplate the question. "I haven't looked," he says, like he's embarrassed to admit such an obvious failure. "But I will."

❊ | CECILY | ❊

By Saturday morning, *Cecily's throat feels* like it's full of sand. She eats the rest of the forcemeat patty her mother brought her, but what she needs, more than anything, is water.

Cecily can attribute her exhaustion to two nights spent sleeping in the bottom of a canoe, but she worries the dizziness she's starting to experience is a sign of a more serious problem. A little while ago, she woke from a trance, sure that Old Mrs. Cowley was in the boathouse and that she had brought her a cure that would turn her into a horsefly. "See?" she told Cecily. "Now you can make it all the way to Philadelphia."

Cecily promised her mother she wouldn't leave the boathouse for any reason, but the James River is just a few yards away, and if she can get something to drink, maybe she'll be able to stop having conversations with people who aren't there.

She gets up slowly and stands by the door. When she cracks it open, she can see straight down the narrow path that brought her here and all the way to the water. There's no one out on the river this time of morning, but she doesn't know how long that'll last. Cecily opens the door wider and listens to the sounds of the woods. She can hear the soft purrs of a ring-necked duck near the water's edge and from somewhere above her head comes the tangled call of a persnickety waterthrush. Aside from the sounds of the birds, all she hears is the river rushing past.

She takes a few tentative steps away from the boathouse and turns to glance back at the woods. They look peaceful and perfectly still, so she sprints to the riverbank and falls to her knees at the water's edge. The river water is so cold it numbs her hands, but it feels good going down her throat. She swallows one handful of water after another, and when she is satisfied, she stands and wipes her hands on her skirt. She looks up and down the riverbank, wishing she had some pot or pail she could fill and take back inside, but sees nothing that will serve as a receptacle.

It's then that Cecily hears the sound. Like the yelp of a wild turkey, but not quite as loud. She looks back up into the woods, where it wouldn't be uncommon to see a flock of hens and maybe a tom turkey foraging for food on the forest floor. But there's nothing there. The sound comes her way again, and this time she looks up into the trees, where wild turkeys like to roost at night. There, in a white oak, just behind the boathouse, sits a small brown boy. She squints to see him better. Moses.

Cecily raises her hand to her lips, trying to warn him not to shout at her, now that he's got her attention. She hurries back toward the boathouse, and when she gets around to the backside, where she can look straight up into the tree's branches, she motions for Moses to climb down.

She's so mad, she could scream. But she's got no choice other than to bite her tongue and wait for him to arrive in front of her. When he does, she puts her finger in his face and asks in a tight whisper, "What in God's name do you think you're doing?"

"I'm watching out for you," he says.

"Watching out for me?" She wants to strangle him. "How you going to watch out for me up in a tree?"

Moses holds up a spade. "If anyone comes looking for you, I'm going to strike 'em with this."

Cecily doesn't know if she wants to hug him or hit him. He's a sweet boy, even if he is likely to get her killed.

"Moses, you is sitting up in a tree, spitting distance from where I'm hiding. If they find you, don't you think they going to find me, too?"

Moses scratches the side of his face with the handle of the spade, like he hadn't thought of that. "I couldn't just do nothing."

"Doing nothing is exactly what you need to do. You got to act like the fire really got me. Do all the same things you'd do if I was dead."

"I don't know what I'd do if you was dead," he says, and the way his lips tremble getting the words out makes her immediately regret deciding to go. She's spent all this time thinking about how hard it will be to leave her mama and papa and brother and sisters behind. But maybe what she should have been thinking about was how hard her leaving was going to be on them.

"I'm sorry this is going to hurt you," she says to Moses as she pulls him close. He is still small enough that he fits in the crook of her arm, but he is starting to smell like a man. "And Mama and Papa and the girls."

"Did Mama tell you what happened to Papa?"

Cecily pulls back, looks him straight in the eye. "What?"

"He got picked up by the patrol yesterday morning while he was out looking for you."

"*Because* of me?"

Moses shakes his head. "I don't think so. He was with Big John and Terrance, and they all got taken in."

"How'd you find out?"

"Uncle Gilbert."

Cecily is stunned. She tries to picture her papa, already exhausted and afraid after a long night of looking for her, having to explain himself to some patroller. "Mama didn't say a thing to me."

"Maybe I shouldn't have, either?"

"It's fine," says Cecily. "I want to know what's happening—even if there ain't nothing I can do about it."

"I ain't sure there's anything any of us can do about it."

"Is he all right? Papa?"

"Appears to be. I ran down to the birdcage soon as I heard, and tried to talk to him. But he wouldn't say much."

"Did you tell him I'm alive?"

Moses shakes his head again. "The place was packed full. I was scared to even try."

Cecily reaches out and picks a twig out of her little brother's hair. "You're a smart boy."

Moses beams.

"I'm lucky to have you looking out for me," she says, "but you got to go home. You understand?"

"I'll do a better job hiding."

"No," Cecily says firmly. "No hiding. I want you home."

S*ally doesn't dare check on Maria* until half past eight, when Mrs. Price goes home for a few hours. Sally knocks once, but when she gets no answer, she pushes the door open. "I brought you some coffee. And a turnover."

Maria is not in her bed, and Sally spins around the small room, looking for her.

The only person she sees is that poor girl in the other bed. Yesterday evening, Mrs. Cowley instructed Sally and Birdie and the other volunteers to stop treating her burns—it was a waste of what precious vinegar they had left—and to focus on giving her heavy doses of laudanum instead. "With any luck, she'll be dead by morning," Mrs. Cowley had said, which sounded callous, but wasn't intended to be.

Sally is about to check the closet for Maria, when she hears a choked sob coming from underneath Maria's bed.

She places Maria's breakfast on top of the dresser, then walks around to the side of her bed and gets down on her hands and knees. Sure enough, Maria lies flat on the floor, staring up at the underside of her mattress and sobbing.

"Maria? Are you all right?"

She doesn't answer.

Sally presses her cheek to the floor and asks, "Is this about what happened this morning? Did Elliott upset you?"

Maria shakes her head no, but it's impossible to know whether she's answering Sally's question or having some sort of fit.

Sally is patient.

"The room," Maria says finally. "It won't stop spinning."

"Is it better under there? In the dark?"

Maria nods her head so violently Sally thinks she might do damage to herself.

"In that case, maybe I'll join you."

Sally is not as spry as she once was, but she manages to move into position beside Maria with relative ease. "I can see why you prefer it here," she says, and the two of them lie side by side in silence for several minutes, listening to the sounds of the room. There is the fire, which crackles in the small coal-burning fireplace, and also the labored breathing of the girl in the other bed.

Finally, Sally says, "I would imagine that it's difficult to lie here all day, with nothing to do but think."

Maria whimpers in agreement.

"I've been so busy, I haven't had much time for thinking. But, sometimes, when I slow down for a minute, everything that happened at the theater comes crashing down on me."

"Were you there?"

"I was," says Sally with a frown. "On the third floor."

Maria turns to look at her. "That must have been very bad."

Bad doesn't begin to describe it, but the last thing Sally wants to do is compete with a sixteen-year-old girl, and certainly not over something like this.

"I was on the second floor," says Maria. "With my friends. In a box." A tear slides across the girl's cheekbone and disappears into the folds of her neck.

"If it's too painful, you don't have to—"

Maria clears her throat. "No, I want to."

Sally doesn't push. She just waits as Maria takes a deep breath and continues.

"It was Roberta and Imogene, Louisa and me. There were others, too, but when that actor said the house was on fire, the four of us hooked arms and made for the stairs."

Sally has a feeling she knows where this story is going.

"We'd made it almost all the way to the first floor when the ceiling above our heads began to groan."

"Oh, Maria."

"I knew I didn't have much time. That if I didn't do something, I was going to die."

"So, what did you do?"

Maria runs a finger along one of the ropes that holds the bed's mattress in place. She is far away. "I let go."

"Of what?"

"Louisa's hand."

"I see," says Sally. "And she didn't make it out?"

Maria's eyes are glassy. "None of them did. There was one last surge, and I was pushed down the remaining stairs. Then I heard a loud crash, and the next thing I knew I was in the arms of a friend of my father's."

"Was that the man who brought you to Mrs. Cowley's?"

Maria nods.

"I'm so sorry, Maria," Sally whispers.

"I thought I was dead," she sobs.

"Of course you did. We all did, there for a minute."

Sally reaches for Maria's hand and squeezes it. At sixteen, she is considered a woman—old enough to marry and, if she is fortunate, bear children. But, at almost twice her age, Sally finds it preposterous that the world should see this girl as anything other than a child.

❦ | JACK | ❦

By the time Ritchie arrives at the tavern, the tables are littered with the detritus of the morning meal.

Placide isn't eating, but he has had three cups of coffee, and the cup rattles in its saucer when Ritchie slaps two folded newspapers down in front of him. "Do you want to explain this?" he asks.

Placide looks at both papers briefly. "Explain what?"

"Well, let's see. One paper is the *Enquirer*, which I publish. You will note, on page three, there is a lengthy article about the fire that does not make reference to how the fire began because—at the point at which I wrote it—the only information I'd been provided was a pack of lies."

"We didn't—"

"I'm not finished," says Ritchie, who is so angry he can barely draw breath. "The other paper is the *American Standard*, which arrived on my desk this morning via courier. It turns out the editor, Simon Skelton, was at the theater the night it burned."

"I suppose that's a lucky accident," Placide offers.

"Given what he witnessed, he'd probably argue otherwise," says Ritchie.

Jack can't figure out why Placide isn't at least pretending to be more cooperative. A little remorse would go a long way with Ritchie, but Placide doesn't seem inclined to play the part of a contrite theater manager.

Ritchie places his spectacles at the end of his nose, picks up the paper, and reads aloud. "He was informed that the scenery took fire in the back part of the house, by the raising of a chandelier; that the boy, who was ordered by some of the players to raise it, stated that if he did so, the scenery would take fire, when he was commanded, in a peremptory manner, to hoist it. The boy obeyed, and the fire was instantly communicated to the scenery."

Jack is dumbfounded. He is the boy! It's his story Ritchie's reading! Skelton doesn't know all the details—Jack's name, for instance, or the fact that it was Green and not "some of the players" who ordered him to raise the chandelier, but he's got most of the facts right. Jack looks around the room, trying to see if any of the actors are as startled by this as he is, but their expressions don't give much away.

"Does someone want to explain to me why I'm chasing down a dead-end story about a slave revolt while Simon bloody Skelton gets the exclusive on a backstage fire that, frankly, sounds a lot more plausible?"

Placide acts offended. "It's all lies, I tell you."

Jack wonders if, maybe, it was Green who tipped Skelton off. It's not impossible, now that he thinks about it. A father, distraught over his daughter's death, decides to clear his conscience.

For the most part, Jack is relieved to know that the story is out. If Ritchie realizes that there's another—more probable—version of events, he'll ask more pointed questions of the actors and work harder to poke holes in their testimonies. Of course, it also means he's more likely to come after Jack, and Jack has no idea what that will look like.

Ritchie gives Jack a hard look. "You were backstage? Isn't that what you said yesterday morning?"

Jack's throat has gone perilously dry. "I think what I said was that you should talk to Placide."

"Right," says Ritchie, and Jack can tell he's disappointed in him, that he mistakenly assumed Jack possessed the same scruples that made his father such an exceptional lawyer, father, and friend.

Ritchie returns his attention to Placide. "You realize that, even as we speak, free and enslaved Negroes from all over the city are being rounded up, questioned, and, in many cases, detained for a revolt that no one—save your own men—actually witnessed?"

If Placide has any regrets, he is in too deep to backtrack now. "We have several witnesses—"

Ritchie cuts him off. "Save it for your official statement."

Anderson has remained quiet up until now, but he must feel he owes Ritchie something. "We have never tried to mislead you."

"Is that so?" Ritchie says.

"It is."

"How nice."

Jack would give anything to be able to disappear right now.

"I should remind all of you that I am not here in my capacity as editor of the *Enquirer*, but as head of the inquest committee, which is an official arm of the Common Council."

The room is so quiet you could hear a pin drop.

Ritchie continues. "And it will be to your advantage to forget that you are actors, intent on swaying public opinion, and instead remember that you are human beings who want to provide answers to scores of grieving families."

Jack isn't so sure Placide is capable of putting his own self-interests aside, but maybe some of the others can.

"Now, where is everybody?" Ritchie asks, looking around the room at the men.

"They're right here," says Placide.

"Do you think I'm a numbskull?" Ritchie says, then turns to Jack. "Where's that list I asked for?"

Jack retrieves the piece of paper from his pocket and carefully unfolds it before handing it over.

Ritchie peruses it, then says, "Who are we missing?"

"My wife and Mr. Young's wife are back at the boardinghouse, seeing after the children," says Placide. "And, as I think we mentioned, the Greens are not in any condition to be interviewed."

"Yes, and as I think *I* mentioned, I'm extremely sorry to hear about their daughter. But I do need to speak to both of them, regardless."

Something about Placide's countenance—Jack can't quite put his finger on what it is—makes it obvious that he has no intention of delivering the Greens to Ritchie.

Ritchie must pick up on it, too, because the next thing he says, in a voice loud enough for everyone in the room to hear him, is: "Are we all clear on what will happen if the inquest committee finds the theater company guilty of either negligence or malice?"

A few men nod their heads, but there are enough raised eyebrows to warrant Ritchie spelling it out for them. "You will open yourselves up to both civil and criminal charges—with penalties that range from fines and jail time to death by hanging." He waits a moment, to let his words sink in. "Am I adequately expressing the severity of this situation?"

Jack looks around the room, studying the faces of the players. He would say that Ritchie has managed to capture everyone's attention quite thoroughly.

"Wonderful," says Ritchie as he claps his hands together. "So, here's how this will go. I will interview each of you, individually, in the taproom's snug." The snug is a small, semiprivate room that sits at the end of the bar. It has high walls and a little window through which the barkeep can pass drinks, and while most men love it because it gives them a place to conduct business away from prying eyes and ears, Jack hates it because it always feels—to him, at least—like the walls are closing in. "You'll wait here until you are called, and you will not leave the tavern until I say so. Are we clear on all of this?"

The men shift in their chairs. Only Caulfield is bold enough to give Ritchie a resounding "Yes, sir."

"Now, am I to assume that the mysterious boy Skelton referenced is the same boy who stands before me?"

Jack winces.

Ritchie does not take his eyes off him. "Is that a yes, Mr. Gibson?"

The air in the tavern's back room feels thick and stale, and when Jack tries to get out the word *yes*, his voice breaks into a thousand pieces. From across the room, Anderson glares at him.

"Good," says Ritchie. "In that case, we'll start with you."

❊ | GILBERT | ❊

*O*nce *Kemp and Price are gone,* Gilbert takes a deep breath and tries
to think fast.

He's got to get word to Della that Price knows—or at least suspects—
the truth. And together, they've got to get Cecily out of town as quickly as
they possibly can.

He thinks the stagecoach idea can still work. Price and Kemp will be
out looking for Cecily—no doubt about that—but as long as she's got a
good pass and a ticket to wave in the face of the conductor, there's no reason anyone will give her a second glance.

He casts his eyes around the shop. Nick and Ned are at their forges.
The apprentices are engaged. Ibrahim is bringing in coal, and Marcus is at
least pretending to distribute it.

A basket sits on top of Kemp's writing desk, and in it are a number
of dies for decorative work. Gilbert makes like he's going to pick out one
of the dies, but when he gets over to the desk, he swipes a couple pieces of
letter paper, the ink bottle, and a pen. Then he heads straight for the stairs,
which lead to the loft.

In the loft, he makes a beeline for his cot, where he finds the slit in the
mattress that he cut open and stitched back together upon his arrival at
Kemp's. He rips at the stitches until the hole is as big as his hand, then he
shoves his arm inside and feels around until he locates the tobacco pouch.
The weight of it brings him a sharp sense of relief.

He counts the money quickly, and after he's tucked it and the writing
supplies in his pants, he heads back down the stairs, out the back of the
shop, and around the side of the building to a shed, which is usually kept
unlocked. Inside, there is an unused workbench, where he spreads out his
supplies. He dips the nib of the pen in the bottle of ink, blots the pen on an
old rag, and quick as he can, writes himself a new pass.

The slave Gilbert Hunt has my permission to pass to and from the smithy of Cameron Kemp, so long as he remains in the city proper and does not cause a nuisance.

Gilbert doesn't have time to practice Kemp's signature, but he's seen it on enough invoices and receipts to make a decent attempt at it. As he shakes the paper dry—no pounce to hasten the process—he congratulates himself on the fact that this pass doesn't look much different from the one Kemp tore to pieces. Kemp, of course, would recognize it as a forgery, but none of the other patrollers will.

When the pass is dry, Gilbert folds it and puts it away in the same leather sleeve Kemp so recently emptied. Then he sets to work on a pass for Cecily. He gives her a new name and a slaver who lives far enough away it'll take anyone who stops her at least a week to confirm the document's authenticity. He also confirms she has permission to travel across state lines.

When Gilbert is finished, he puts this pass in the leather sleeve, alongside his own. His hands shake as he stows the ink bottle and the pen behind a bucket, then reaches behind his back to untie his apron.

The door to the shed opens, and he hears Marcus's voice behind him. "I was wondering where you got off to."

Gilbert jumps a mile. "Lord, you scared me."

"You writing yourself a new pass?"

"Can't say I am," says Gilbert, but Marcus is already eyeing the bottle of ink, which peeks out from behind the bucket. He reaches for it, holds it between two fingers, studying the sunlight as it bounces off the glass. "I can return this for you if you want."

Gilbert doesn't know what to say.

"The pen, too?" says Marcus, and Gilbert just nods as he watches him fish it out from the same hiding place.

Gilbert prays Marcus will leave, but he doesn't go anywhere.

"Why didn't you tell me about your niece?" he asks.

Gilbert realizes his mistake—he should have told Marcus about Cecily's death yesterday, as soon as he was done talking to Della. Now it looks like he was hiding the information from him, and he scrambles to explain. "Della gave me the news when she came by, but I didn't want to say anything until I'd told Sara." This is not a complete lie.

"So, that's where you were last night? At Sara's?"

Gilbert nods.

"And how'd she take it?"

Is Marcus playing with him? It's hard to tell. "I couldn't talk to her. She's still all wrapped up with her mistress, who's grieving mightily."

Marcus looks like he's chewing on every word. "So, I suppose it's Della you're going to see now?"

"She'll be needing me. Especially if Price is having a hard time swallowing the truth."

Marcus gives Gilbert a sympathetic nod, but it's tinged with something else. "No chance Price is right?" he asks. "And your niece really did run?"

"Not you, too?"

Marcus holds up his hands. "It ain't like that," he says.

"Seems to me, that's precisely what it's like."

Marcus lets out a low laugh, then steps out of the way of the door. "I'll cover for you. Not that anyone's paying much attention right now."

"Thank you," says Gilbert as he puts his apron down on the workbench and slides past him.

He's almost out the door when Marcus calls after him. "Last question."

Gilbert pauses, afraid to turn around.

"Does Kemp know you and Cecily are kin?"

Gilbert doesn't have to tell Marcus that if Kemp knew Cecily was Gilbert's niece, he'd be watching Gilbert a hell of a lot closer than he already is. "It's like what you say, about your smithing."

Marcus tilts his head, curious. "What's that?"

"He never asked."

❧ | SALLY | ❧

Sally has barely had time to get Maria back into bed, much less collect herself, when Mrs. Cowley knocks on the door.

"There's a man downstairs for you, Maria."

Maria looks confused. "What does he want?"

"He's here to take you home, love."

"Home?"

"He brought a buggy."

"Is it Harrison?"

"I think that's what he said, yes. Colored man about this high," Mrs. Cowley says, holding her hand a good six inches above the top of her own head.

Maria is in no way strong enough to travel, and Sally says so.

"That's what I told him, but he said he's under strict orders to bring her home."

"Orders from whom?" asks Maria, and then it dawns on Sally. This is Elliott's doing. He was livid when he discovered that she'd been listening in on the family's conversation, and he must have convinced his parents that Maria would be better off at home, out of Sally's earshot.

Maria's cheeks have gone pale, and her eyes dart between the two women. "Please, tell them I'm not ready. That I need more time."

Sally doesn't mince words. "Are you worried Elliott will hurt you?"

"No, I don't think so, I don't know," she stammers. "He's just so angry."

It strikes Sally as tragic that a girl who fought tooth and nail for her own survival, just two nights ago, should fear something as simple as being in the same house as her older brother.

"I won't be a bother," Maria promises.

"I've got no problem with you staying right where you are, but, unfortunately, it's not my decision to make," says Mrs. Cowley as she moves around to the other side of the bed. "Now, try to sit up, dear."

As soon as Maria is upright, her face goes white as a sheet.

"Get her other side?" says Mrs. Cowley, and Sally rushes to help.

Eventually, the two of them guide Maria down the stairs, where she collapses, exhausted, on the second to last step. Harrison, who has been waiting for her at the door, tells her how glad he is to see her, then asks if he can get her anything.

"I suppose they didn't send along a coat?" asks Sally irritably.

He shakes his head no. "But I do have a blanket in the buggy."

"I think I'm going to be sick," says Maria as she leans her head against the newel post.

Sally goes running upstairs for the same spittoon she delivered to Maria two nights prior, and by the time she returns with it, she has decided she will insist on accompanying Maria home.

"I'm going with you," she says after she's placed the spittoon in Maria's lap and located her own coat. To Harrison, she explains, "You'll be up in the driver's seat. And she can't travel alone in this condition."

"She's right," says Mrs. Cowley, and if Harrison were inclined to argue, he doesn't bother.

With Maria's blessing, the driver picks the girl up and carries her out the door and down the path to the road, where the Prices' carriage waits for her. Sally struggles into her coat, then hurries to catch up with them, and when Maria and her spittoon are tucked safely inside the carriage, she takes a deep breath and climbs in beside her.

🌸 | JACK | 🌸

Jack has hardly made it out of the snug before Placide pounces on him. "How did it go?"

If ever there was a question Jack doesn't want to answer. "Fine," he mumbles.

"Fine?" says Placide. "Fine? What did he say?"

"Ritchie?"

Placide flicks him in the ear. "Who else?"

Jack grasps for something—anything—to report about his interview. "He said he wants to talk to Twaits."

"That's not what I mean," says Placide as he steers Jack down the narrow hallway that leads toward the tavern's back room. "What's he asking? What does he want to know?"

It's not that Jack minds relaying their conversation to Placide—at this point, he has little choice in the matter—but he is concerned that Ritchie will come looking for him if Twaits does not materialize at the door of the snug in the next several seconds. "Mr. Placide, he really does want to talk to Twaits. Now."

"Fine," says Placide, then barks down the hall, "Twaits!"

When the actor emerges from the back room, Placide gestures in the direction of the taproom. "You're up next."

Twaits nods, then moves to slide past them.

"Wait, wait, wait," says Placide, grabbing Twaits by the shoulder. He turns to Jack. "Is there anything he needs to know?"

Jack tries to think. He's been forced to tell so many lies, in such quick succession, that he can barely tell up from down at this point. "Ritchie wanted to know who was coming and going out the stage door."

"And what did you tell him?"

"Uh, that I didn't know."

"You didn't even tell him about Caulfield?" says Placide.

"Do we have time for this?" asks Jack, who is terrified to admit to Placide that Ritchie spent the bulk of the interview asking questions that had nothing to do with the slave revolt. "He really is waiting."

Placide shoos Twaits off, then drags Jack into the front office, where he asks the tavern keeper's wife if she'll give them a few moments alone. "Don't take too long," she says as she hauls herself out into the hall.

"What did you tell Ritchie about all this Skelton business?" Placide asks when he's closed the door behind her.

Jack stalls for time. "You mean, about the article?"

"I assume he wanted to get to the bottom of it?"

Jack acknowledges that he did, but he stops short of telling him the truth, which is that Ritchie talked of little else. "He asked for an inventory of all the chandeliers, lamps, and candelabras the company owns."

"And did you give it to him?"

"What choice did I have?" asks Jack. "If I hadn't, it would have looked like I had something to hide."

"What else did he ask for?"

"He wanted a diagram of the chandelier's rigging."

"And am I to assume you gave him that, too?"

Jack nods.

"Jesus Christ," says Placide, who has begun pacing the small room like a caged animal. "Did you do anything at all to push the slave revolt story?"

"I—I did," Jack stutters. "I think."

Placide stops moving all of a sudden and stares Jack down. "I'm beginning to think you're the leak."

"The leak?"

"Someone told Skelton what happened."

"It wasn't me!" says Jack, fear rising in his throat. The last thing he needs is for Anderson or Placide to get it in their heads that he went to Skelton. "I don't even know Skelton."

Placide laughs. "You don't have to know him to tell him all our secrets."

"But I didn't," says Jack.

"Anderson told me what you said to him, on the way back from the capitol. About going to the authorities," Placide says.

Jack shuts his eyes. Of course he did. "I was just talking. I didn't actually do it."

"How do I know what you did or didn't do?"

"I didn't. I wouldn't."

"It's obvious you don't like what's happening here."

"Perhaps not," says Jack, "but I do like my own neck."

Placide lets out a low laugh. "You have a funny way of showing it."

"I'm telling you the truth. Honestly. I didn't go to Skelton."

"Well, someone who was backstage talked to him," says Placide. "That much is clear."

"What about Mr. Green?" Jack offers, but as soon as the words are out of his mouth, he regrets them.

Placide shakes his head, like he's got water in his ears and didn't hear Jack properly. "*John* Green?"

Jack nods.

"John would rather cut off his left testicle than see this company ruined."

It was stupid to bring him up, but Jack can't backtrack now. "Maybe, but he's also a grieving father, who feels personally responsible for his daughter's death."

"Partially responsible," says Placide sharply.

Jack ignores the insinuation. "You can see why he'd think he was doing right by Nancy."

Placide lowers himself onto a three-legged stool. "So, you're suggesting he went to Skelton to absolve himself?"

"It makes a certain amount of sense."

Placide sits there, stroking his beard, as the seconds tick by. Finally, he shakes his head. "If John were so bent on doing the right thing, why not let Skelton publish his name?"

It's a good question, and one Jack can't answer. "I don't know," he says. "Maybe he got scared."

Placide looks out the window. "I'll buy that. But that doesn't explain why he didn't give Skelton *your* name."

❧✱❦ | CECILY | ❧✱❦

I t is noon, and Cecily is back under the sailcloth, dreaming, when she hears the rolling call of a wild turkey.

She sits bolt upright in the canoe. The soft trill fills the air. "Damn it, Moses," she whispers under her breath as she hurries to the door of the boathouse and begins to drag the barricade of canoes she's built out of the way. When she gets the door open, the turkey lets out a long, loud yelp, and then he falls silent.

Somewhere, far off, there is a low rumbling noise Cecily doesn't like. She moves around the side of the boathouse, scanning the trees for signs of Moses. He promised her he'd go home, but now she knows she shouldn't have believed him. She looks up into the white oak, but he's not there. Of course, that doesn't mean he's not in one of the hundreds of other trees that dot the hillside. She studies the trees' bare branches, looking for anything that doesn't belong. A hawk's nest, a broken limb, a branch that hasn't yet dropped its leaves. Up on the ridgeline, she sees something move, but it is only a squirrel.

Cecily wants to shout for Moses, but something doesn't feel right. If he gave her his turkey call, then maybe he is trying to warn her of someone coming. She pulls his jacket tight around her frame and hurries back inside the boathouse, but she has no sooner closed the door behind her than she hears the sound of horses—at least two, but maybe three—cresting the ridge.

She lunges for the canoes and drags them back in front of the door. Then she climbs on top of them, throws herself against the door, and waits.

She assumes the party will make straight for the boathouse, but there is a shrill squeal from up on the ridge, and the horses come to an abrupt halt. One man yells something to another, but what they're saying, she can't tell.

Another squeal echoes down the hillside and across the water, and to Cecily's horror, she realizes that the noise is of Moses's making. Lord help him, but he must be trying to get the attention of the horsemen before they get around to discovering her.

From up on the ridge comes the sound of a scuffle, then the shouts of one of the men. "I got him!"

Without stopping to think, Cecily scrambles down off the canoes and works, as quickly as she can, to drag them back out of the way. When she gets the door open, she barrels down the path and up into the woods, toward the ridgeline.

As she hurtles through the trees, she focuses on the sound of the men's laughter, which grows softer as the party moves away from her. If Moses is crying out for help, she cannot hear him.

When Cecily arrives up on the ridge, she sees no sign of anyone.

"Moses!" she whispers at the trees, in case she got it wrong and he is still up in the branches, pretending to be a big fat turkey. "Come down!"

There is nothing.

Cecily gulps for air, feels the tears welling in her eyes and her chin beginning to shake.

All she can think to do is get word about Moses to her mama. But it's not a good time to be out. The winter sun is low and it lights up the woods, same way all those footlight lamps lit up the stage at the theater.

If Cecily runs into anyone, there will be no hiding, but she can't afford to wait another moment. She takes off running through the woods before she can convince herself that what she's doing is a very bad idea.

As Gilbert hurries away from the smithy, he looks behind him—once, twice, three times. Marcus isn't following him, but he takes a circuitous route anyway, skirting the lumber house and Market Hall before proceeding to Lynch's Coffee House, where the stagecoach book is kept.

His plan is to buy Cecily a seat, under her new name, then deliver the ticket and Cecily's pass to Della, along with the warning that Kemp and his men are on the lookout for Cecily and that it is most definitely time for her to go.

Della will panic—how could she not?—but this plan of theirs still feels like it could work. Provided the conductor accepts Cecily's papers, she'll be in Philadelphia by New Year's Day. From there, it'll be easier, and far less urgent, for her to decide what to do and where to go next.

The only thing that bothers Gilbert is that he hasn't discussed any of this with Sara. If he pays for this ticket and perhaps even gives Cecily a few coins for the journey, he'll be postponing Sara's purchase by months or even years.

He tells himself that Sara would make the same decision, if it were up to her. And that maybe none of this will matter if Phyllis Johnston comes through with her offer. She was so adamant that Gilbert deserved to be rewarded for his bravery. If the general accepts the terms of her proposal, which Gilbert assumes will be generous, Sara's future will be secure. In a matter of days, she could be looking for a job that pays a real wage—enough to replace whatever Gilbert has spent on Cecily's travel and then some.

At the coffeehouse, a few men sit at tables, sipping hot drinks and reading copies of the *Enquirer*, but the place is nowhere near as crowded as it usually is this time of day. What *is* crowded is the counter, where one old woman scurries to serve a long line of customers.

Gilbert gets in line and listens to the conversations around him. A man at the front of the queue has lost his wife and wants to send word to the woman's parents in Roanoke, as well as his own in Amherst. Another man lost his daughters and has got to find a way to tell his wife, who has been in London these last several months. One young woman needs her mother to send her mourning clothes from their country house. The stories swirl around him, and by the time Gilbert nears the front of the line, he feels nearly flattened by them.

He has retrieved the tobacco pouch from his pocket and is practicing what he will say about the stagecoach ticket when he notices a flyer tacked up on the wall.

RUN-AWAY

Two nights ago, from the theater, a tall, slim straight Negro wench, nam'd Cecily Patterson, about 19 years of age, of a yellowish complex-ion, has had the small pox, but is smooth faced, and talks good English, has the middle finger of her left hand crooked and cannot straighten it; was born in Richmond and belongs to Mr. Elliott Price Sr.; is sensible, cunning, and artful, and can wash, mend, and sew; Has on a gray dress, a blue shawl, and a pair of leather shoes; Last seen in the Negro gallery, Thursday the 26th of December.

Whoever will bring home the said wench to her master shall have 2 DOLLARS reward if taken in town, or 3 DOLLARS reward, if taken out of town, beside all reasonable charges.

All masters of vessels and others are forwarn'd not to entertain or carry her away as they will answer it at their peril.

ELLIOTT PRICE JR.

Gilbert tries not to be too obvious reading it, but the words are so close together that he has to squint to see them. Behind him, a white man lets out an exasperated sigh, which might have to do with the long wait, but might also have to do with the fact that he doesn't like seeing a Negro who can read.

Gilbert has barely gotten to the last line of the flyer when the man in front of him finishes up his transaction, and the woman behind the counter calls, "Next!"

"Go on, now, son," says the man behind Gilbert, and Gilbert bristles.

He can't buy Cecily a stagecoach ticket, not with this flyer all over town. *All masters of vessels and others are forwarn'd not to entertain or carry her away as they will answer it at their peril.* That doesn't just mean boat captains; it means stagecoach drivers, too.

And what's more is that Gilbert hadn't even considered Cecily's bad finger. All it's going to take is the conductor asking to see her hands, and she'll be sunk—doesn't matter how good her pass is.

Gilbert needs to get out of this line and out of this coffeehouse. He needs to go warn Della that their plan—as it stands—won't work. But the woman behind the counter is staring at him, and he doesn't want to draw attention to himself. He eyes a few glass jars on the counter, takes a half dime out of his pouch, and hands it to her. "A piece of rock candy, please."

Outside the coffeehouse, he shoves the candy into his pocket, sick that he's just spent money on something so frivolous. Then he turns toward the Price place.

Now that he's looking for it, he sees the flyer everywhere—tacked onto sign posts and horse hitches, pasted onto windows and building facades. When no one is looking, he rips one off a barber's pole, folds it, and shoves it into his pocket.

Elliott Price must have put up a hundred of these flyers, maybe more. Gilbert wants nothing more than to pull down every single one he sees, gather them up in his arms, and take them back to his forge, where he can use them for fuel. But the damage is already done.

Richmonders know that Cecily Patterson is not dead, or at least that Elliott Price does not believe her to be. The distinction hardly matters, but what does matter is that getting Cecily out of the city just got a great deal harder.

❧❋ | CECILY | ❋❧

W hen Cecily approaches the backside of her parents' cabin, she's shocked to find her uncle Gilbert is already there, hiding in the thick brush.

She creeps up behind him and gives him an awful start, but he doesn't dare say a thing. Instead, he just shakes his head at her, which is his way of asking what in the world she's doing up in the quarters in broad daylight.

"Moses," she whispers, but when she tries to say more, he puts a finger to his lips and gestures toward the street, where they can hear the braying of horses and the murmurs of the folks who live in the other cabins.

"Is it him?" she mouths, and he nods his head yes.

The men on horseback have brought Moses back to the Price property, which doesn't make any sense to Cecily until she hears Elliott's voice among them. "Look what we found upriver," he says, and a moment later, something heavy hits the ground with a thud.

Cecily drops to her knees, peers under the house and all the way out the other side, where her brother lies motionless in the street. She might have screamed, but Gilbert clamps his hand over her lips and whispers, "Make one sound, and you'll take us all down with you."

He's right. Of course he's right. If she is discovered now, it won't take Elliott long to realize she got help. And when he does, her mama, Moses, and maybe even Gilbert are going to be in for it.

Moses lies on his side, facing the cabin. He's banged up but not bleeding, and when he blinks once and then twice, Cecily convinces herself that he can see Gilbert and her, hiding in the house's long shadows.

Della flies down the steps of the cabin and out onto the street, but Elliott steps in front of her before she can reach her son's slumped form.

"Moses, baby, you all right?" she says, loud enough for the words to reach him where he lies.

"He's fine," barks Elliott. "Although I am trying to understand why we found him up in a tree on the Fulcher property."

"He don't have to be at the mill today," says Della, "on account of the fire. Overseer told everyone to stay home."

"That may be," says Elliott, like this is news to him. "But, in that case, why wasn't Moses at home?"

Della doesn't have a good answer for that, and Elliott knows it.

"Seems to me that, on a day like today, Moses shouldn't be doing anything other than grieving his sister's untimely demise."

"Who says he ain't grieving?" Della asks.

"He's got a funny way of showing it," says Elliott with a hollow laugh. "But then again, so do you."

Della's angry, Cecily can tell. But her anger won't get her anywhere with Elliott. "What do you know about grieving a child?"

"When Rosie lost Ben, you could hear her wailing all the way up at the main house."

"You want me to wail?" Della asks, her voice rising right alongside her rage. "Would that help?"

If Elliott answers her, Cecily can't hear what he says.

Della lets out a scream as loud as a screech owl's. "Is that better?" She does it again. "How about now?"

Elliott tells the men on horseback to get on, that he doesn't want them wasting all their good daylight. But Cecily knows it's got more to do with not wanting them to think he doesn't know how to manage his slaves. "I'll catch up once I'm through here," he says, after they've agreed on a meeting spot.

As soon as they're gone, Elliott disappears inside her parents' cabin, and Cecily and Gilbert shrink farther into the shadows of the house's crawl space.

"The girls," whispers Cecily, but Gilbert shakes his head, mouths, "Millie's got 'em."

They listen as Elliott turns the room above their heads upside down. She can hear him tear open her parents' mattress and overturn the trunk where they keep their quilts in the summer. Crockery ricochets off the thin walls, and when all the little animals Cecil's carved go skittering across the floodboards, Cecily holds her breath.

Della doesn't try to intervene. Instead, she takes the opportunity to go to Moses.

"Can you get up?" she asks in a voice that Cecily knows she is working hard to control. Slowly, Moses pulls himself onto his hands and knees, and Cecily feels weak with relief.

Her brother is standing on his own two feet by the time Elliott emerges from the cabin. "Care to explain this?" he asks the two of them, but Cecily can't see what he's holding.

"It's a shawl," says Della plainly.

"It's Cecily's shawl."

"All right. It's Cecily's shawl."

Cecily tries to picture the shawl he's talking about, and her breath catches in her throat when she realizes he means the blue one she wore to the theater. When Cecily got back to the cabin the night of the fire, she hung it on a peg near the door, and took Moses's coat instead.

Now she realizes her mistake. Elliott remembers it, must know she was wearing it when he last saw her, down in the cellar. "She wore it to the theater," he tells Della, as pleased with himself as if he's just won a game of ninepins.

Cecily's mama is quicker this time. "No, she didn't. She came back here and changed."

"You're lying," Elliott says, but there is a tiny fissure in his voice that Della must know she can exploit.

"She wanted to tell me about your plan to take her with you to your new place."

What Della is saying is true, it's just the timing that's off. Thankfully, Elliott doesn't know that.

"What'd she think you were going to do about it?"

Della knows better than to say anything. She just lets the two of them stew in an awkward silence.

"Well, regardless," Elliott says finally. "This should be all the patrol needs to track our girl down."

Della mutters something, but Cecily can't hear what. Apparently, Elliott didn't catch it either because he asks her to repeat herself.

"I said," says Della as clear as a bell, "she's not *your* girl."

Elliott laughs. "We got a set of papers that says different."

"You been all over her since she was a bitty thing. Your daddy won't tell it to you straight, but I will. That girl has the same blood you do, and what you done to her these last years is an abomination in the eyes of God."

Cecily squeezes her eyes shut. So, the rumor is true. All this time, the answer to the question she's been too afraid to ask had been right on the tip of her mama's tongue.

Gilbert gives her a pitying look, which she ignores. Then, because she cannot stand not knowing, she asks, "Does my papa know?"

He nods once, real slow, then whispers, "Always has."

Cecily is stunned, but she doesn't have time to think about what it all means because Elliott and Della are in each other's faces—Elliott telling Della he doesn't have to listen to her lies, and her screaming, "Yes, you do. And I ain't lying when I tell you that Cecily is with God, and that I am glad he saw fit to take her out of this wretched place."

Listening to her mama stand up to Elliott, after all these years of watching him take exactly what he pleased, fills Cecily with gratitude. But the feeling doesn't last because the next thing Cecily knows, Della is laid out in the middle of the street, blood pouring from her nose.

"Mama," Cecily moans, and starts to move out from behind the cabin, but Gilbert grabs her by the arm and pulls her back.

"She knows what she's doing," he whispers as they listen to Elliott haul her mother onto her feet.

"All of you, get up into the yard," Elliott shouts, loud enough to be heard by every slave in the quarters. "We're about to find out where Cecily is, once and for all."

T*he Prices' carriage is rolling down* H Street, when Sally notices a
sheaf of papers on the seat opposite Maria and her.

She flips through them, realizes they're runaway flyers, and shows them
to Maria. "Is your brother serious?"

"Reading makes me nauseous," Maria says, closing her eyes. "Tell me
what they say."

Sally begins to read aloud, and when she gets to the last line, she waits
for Maria to say something.

"He is completely serious."

Sally waves the papers in the air. "What is the matter with him? More
than fifty women died, including plenty of colored women. Why is it so
preposterous that Cecily should be among them?"

Maria sighs and leans her head on Sally's shoulder. "He's been infatuated with her my whole life."

"And she with him?"

"God no," says Maria quickly. "He's made her life miserable. Won't
leave her alone."

"Do you mean . . ." Sally can't say the words out loud, but she doesn't
need to.

Maria nods once, then looks out the window. They are passing the
canal, and there is a barge in the lock. "He's meant to be married next week.
Did you know that?"

"Married?" Sally is so startled she has to check to make sure her mouth
is not hanging open. No one in the family, including Elliott, has said one
word to her about an engagement.

"Though with all of the funerals, it hardly seems the proper time for a
wedding."

"Who is he marrying?" Sally asks when she recovers herself.

"Our cousin, Lavinia Price," says Maria. "She's a nitwit, and her father's in a great deal of debt. So, I think my parents are hoping my aunt and uncle will turn a blind eye to most everything he does."

"Poor Lavinia."

Maria shrugs, as if Lavinia's plight is the least of her problems.

Sally can barely comprehend everything Maria's telling her. If Elliott is infatuated with Cecily and engaged to Lavinia, then what was he doing asking her such personal questions on the ride back to Mrs. Cowley's? At the time, she had thought the behavior flirtatious, and now she's mortified she ever interpreted it as such.

It's like Maria can read her mind. "Elliott can be charming, when he wants to be. But more often than not, he's cruel."

That's an accurate description of the man Sally has come to know.

"I've spent my whole life living in fear of him—worried that I'll say or do something that will set him off. So, I can only imagine how bad it's been for Cecily."

The carriage slows and begins a steep climb up a private road.

"The other night I overheard him talking to my father," says Maria. "He said he wouldn't go through with the marriage if they didn't give him Cecily to take with him to the new place."

"Because Cecily, officially, belongs to your father? And not him?"

"That's right," says Maria.

"What did your father say?"

"His exact words were: 'How are you going to learn to love a woman faithfully if you're always dipping your wick where it doesn't belong?'"

Sally cringes. "Lovely."

"I know."

"What did Elliott say to that?"

Maria traces a small circle on the window, then turns it into a figure eight. "He laughed."

"So, your father didn't agree to the plan?"

Maria looks at Sally like she's thick in the head. "Oh, no, he did. He's as desperate to get rid of Elliott as any of us are."

"Does Cecily know? I mean, did she know? Before . . ."

Maria shakes her head vehemently. "I hadn't told her. I thought that if I could talk to my father first, when Elliott wasn't around, I could convince him to let me keep her instead."

"But you never did?"

Maria looks down at her lap. "I didn't have time."

"If she had known about Elliott's plan, would that have been enough reason for her to run?"

Maria sits up straight, and her tone takes on a sharp edge. "She didn't run."

"How can you be so sure?"

"She wouldn't have left me."

Maria sounds almost as delusional as her brother, but Sally lets it go. She is young, and in a family as loveless as hers, Sally thinks that perhaps it is all right for her to go another year or two believing that someone loved her best of all.

🌟 | **JACK** | 🌟

The day passes excruciatingly slowly for Jack and the rest of the members of Placide & Green. One actor after another disappears into the taproom, only to emerge looking shaken, or at the very least, subdued.

Placide dresses each of them down, and when he is satisfied with what they did or didn't say, he allows them to sit, relax, and order a tankard of ale, a plate of food, or both. "Eat up," he says, as if an extra serving of pudding might fortify them for the days ahead.

By the early afternoon, Ritchie has interviewed less than half the company, and the men are beginning to take bets on whether the interviews will extend into the following day.

"Were your ears burning, Gibson?" Anderson asks Jack as soon as he returns from his own trip to the taproom.

"Why?"

"Ritchie had a lot of questions about what you were up to with that chandelier."

Jack glances at Lydia, who gives him a sympathetic smile. "What did you tell him?"

Anderson seems confused by the question. "What do you think I told him?"

Jack just blinks. Honestly, at this point, he doesn't know.

"I stuck to the story," says Anderson, looking around the room. "As I hope you all have."

One person who seems to have had no trouble sticking to the story is Twaits. He sailed through his interview with Ritchie, and now he is back from his errand to the jail, too. Anderson asks how he managed, over at the birdcage, and he says there was nothing to it. "I just fingered a handful of men and said that I was sure I'd seen them near the stage door."

Jack squeezes his eyes shut and takes a deep breath. "You really went after specific men? What did the jailer do to them?"

Twaits shrugs. "I didn't stick around to find out."

"Jesus, Twaits," says Jack. "Do you have so little regard for human life?"

"Careful, Jack," says Anderson, and Jack feels the muscles in his neck tighten.

Young, Burke, and Perry are recruiting a fourth player for a game of whist, and Young asks if Twaits wants to be dealt in. He nods, takes a seat at the makeshift card table, and asks where Placide is.

"Across the street, I think," says Burke. "He went to see when the next Charleston-bound ship leaves Norfolk."

"Isn't he getting ahead of himself?" says West, who has installed himself on a window seat.

Perry plays a card. "Ritchie told me he expects to issue his report by Tuesday at the latest."

"We could speed this up if we just told Ritchie the whole thing was Jack's fault," says Burke.

Several men laugh, and Jack can feel his pulse quickening. "How many times do I have to tell you? I was following orders."

Anderson claps his hands, once and then twice. "Enough, everybody. And you," he says, looking Jack straight in the eye, "keep your voice down."

Twaits plays a card, then asks West how his own interview with Ritchie went.

West sighs. "Mostly, he just wanted to talk to me about selling the property."

"I assume you told him to go piss up a rope?" says Anderson.

West gives him an exaggerated eye roll. "I did not."

"What does he want the property for?" asks Twaits.

"He doesn't," West says. "The burial committee does."

"The burial committee?" says Twaits.

"Apparently, no one likes the idea of burying everyone at Henrico Parish Church."

Twaits screws up his face in confusion. "What's wrong with it?"

"Well, for one thing, it's a long way for all these mourners to walk in the cold," West says. "And for another, the folks at Beth Shalome aren't happy that the remains of so many Jewish citizens might come to rest in a cemetery that sits in the shadow of an Episcopal church."

"Did you hear about that one Jewish family? Every single person was killed," says Anderson.

"Everyone but the mother," Perry corrects him, and Jack thinks he might be sick.

"Can't they be buried in the Hebrew Cemetery?" asks Burke.

Anderson gives him an icy stare. "Are you volunteering to sift through the remains and figure out who's who?"

Jack cringes at the very idea, and when Twaits says, "Since when did anyone care what the Jews wanted?" he cringes again.

"Joseph Marx is on the monument committee. So, somebody cares, apparently."

"Well, I'm sorry," says Twaits, "but I fail to see how burying them in a burned-out theater is going to bring them closer to their God."

West explains, "I think the idea is that, eventually, the ruins will come down, and a monument to the dead will go up in their place."

Jack would hate to see West part with the property, but he likes the idea of building a monument that does not prioritize one man's god over another's.

"I see no advantage to selling," Anderson says.

West bristles. "Besides retaining a shred of my dignity?"

"Oh, I'm sorry. Is it not dignified to want to make a living doing the one thing we're good at?"

"I'm not suggesting we shouldn't attempt to make a living," says West. "Just that Richmond might not be the place to do so. At least for now."

"Do you know what I would suggest?" asks Anderson. "Not letting the worst actor in the company be the one who gets to decide where we do and don't perform."

The next thing Jack knows, West has lunged at Anderson, and the two are rolling around on the floor like they're a pair of wrestlers in the ring. All the men in the room are on their feet in a flash, and there are shouts from all sides, urging them to stop or maybe to keep going—it's hard for Jack to tell. West is bigger and stronger than Anderson, but Anderson is quick and knows how to move. They roll this way and that, grabbing at each other's hair and skin, their earlobes and their eyebrows—anything they can hold on to. At one point, they come so close to the hearth that Lydia screams for them to watch out or they will burn the tavern down, too.

All of a sudden there is a loud whistle, and Jack hears Ritchie's voice above the din. "What the hell is the meaning of this?" he yells as he moves into the middle of the fray, then motions for Twaits to help him pull the two men apart. The pair does not seem inclined to separate, and Jack worries that Ritchie will be clobbered in the process of convincing them otherwise. The headline will write itself: EDITOR ATTACKED TRYING TO INVESTIGATE THEATER FIRE. It is all the troupe needs.

Finally, West and Anderson are in separate corners of the room, and everyone takes a deep breath. West's mouth is a bloody mess, and when Ritchie releases Anderson, he sinks to the floor.

Ritchie casts his eyes about the room. "Would someone care to tell me what the hell this is about?"

No one says anything.

"Mr. West?"

West clears his throat, and for one blissful moment Jack feels certain he's about to tell Ritchie everything. But, after a long pause, all he says is "It was nothing."

Ritchie presses his fingers to the bridge of his nose. "I am astounded by how quickly this company manages to forget that we are here because a substantial percentage of the city is dead."

"We are extremely sympathetic," says Anderson quietly.

"Then act like it."

"What would you have us do?"

"My list is long, but why don't you start by finding Green."

❧ | GILBERT | ❧

Gilbert waits until Elliott and Della are halfway up the hill before he turns to Cecily. "You got to get out of here now," he whispers, "while everybody's looking the other way."

"But what about Mama?" Cecily says. "You heard what Elliott said."

"Your mama won't talk."

Cecily shakes her head, her eyes wide. "That's not what I'm worried about. He's gonna hurt her."

Gilbert sighs. "All the more reason for you not to be there."

His niece starts to cry. "This is all my fault. I got to undo it before I make everything worse."

Gilbert wants to laugh, but he reminds himself she's too young to realize how ridiculous she sounds. "You don't think you showing up in the yard, like Lazarus, is going to make things worse?"

She wipes her eyes with the palms of her hands, but the tears won't stop. "I'll tell him I acted alone. That she and Moses had nothing to do with it."

"No," Gilbert says firmly. "You show up in that yard, and you going to get your mother and brother sold south."

Cecily doesn't say anything, and for a minute he worries she's still considering it.

"You hearing me?"

Finally, she gives him a ferocious nod. "Then what do I do?"

He thinks for a second, but he's not coming up with much.

She starts to panic. "You got to tell me what to do."

"Go back to the boathouse."

"And then what?"

He doesn't have the heart to say anything about the flyers, nor to explain that the whole reason he was over here in the first place was to tell

Della that Cecily doesn't have a prayer of boarding a stagecoach without being recognized.

"I'm not sure. But we'll figure it out."

"Uncle Gilbert, I'm scared."

He's not in a good position to reassure her, not right now. "Just be careful making your way back. Steer clear of Kemp and that fellow he's with, Doug Gibson. I'll meet you there, soon as I'm ready to get you out of here."

"Tonight, you think?"

He leans down, kisses her once, lightly, on the forehead. "No idea," he says. "Now go."

When Cecily is gone, Gilbert makes his way around to the front of the cabin. A number of the men and women who live in the quarters have already begun to trudge up the hill to the yard, but Moses is still standing in the middle of the street, as if he has been waiting for Gilbert to emerge from behind the cabin.

"You all right?" Gilbert asks when he's close enough to wrap an arm around his nephew's narrow shoulders.

Moses nods.

Gilbert leans down so he's looking Moses directly in the eye. "You hear all that?"

"About Cecily?"

"And Master Price."

Moses nods again.

"It don't matter. None of it matters. Cecily's your sister, same as them babies are."

Moses looks relieved to have someone spell it out for him.

"Now your mama needs your help."

Moses is all ears.

"You need to run and find Master Price. Wherever he is, however far he got to."

"I don't have a pass."

"It's too late to worry about passes. Just don't get stopped."

"What do I tell Master Price?"

"Tell him Elliott fixing to whip your mama. That he's acting touched in the head, ever since he found out Cecily was dead."

Gilbert remembers the flyer in his pocket. He gives it to Moses. "Make sure Master Price sees this."

"What is it?" Moses asks.

"It's a flyer, offering a reward for your sister's return."

"What makes you think Master Price don't know about it?"

Gilbert shakes his head, points to Elliott's name at the bottom of the notice. "He didn't sign it."

Moses studies the page's neat type, and Gilbert regrets never taking the time to teach him his letters.

"Be sure Master Price knows Elliott's putting these up all over town, and that he's got the slave patrol out looking for her, too." Tracking a slave costs money. If Elliott Price Sr. cuts his son's purse strings, Cecily might have a fighting chance. "And remember, you got to make him believe Elliott's only got one oar in the water."

Moses rolls his eyes. "That ain't hard."

Gilbert can tell Moses is itching to get going, but Gilbert's got a couple more things to tell him, and he's not going to like hearing them. "I'm not going to be up there in the yard with your mama."

"What?"

"You on your own."

"But Uncle Gil—"

"There ain't a thing I can do for her. But what I can do is get Cecily out of here."

Moses's eyes meet his.

"We got to get her moved."

The boy doesn't disagree.

"If your mama makes it out of this all right, tell her I'm going to go give Samuel Jefferson and his carriage another try."

It's clear Moses is only half listening.

"Repeat what I just said back to me."

Moses doesn't take his eyes off the hill. "Tell Mama you're going to go see Samuel Jefferson."

Gilbert nods. "That's right."

Moses turns to go.

"One more thing, Mo."

His nephew stops, waits.

"You got to keep your mouth shut up there."

Moses looks at him like he's the one who's touched in the head now. "I know that."

"No, you don't," says Gilbert, who worries that Moses will crack in half if he sees what Elliott Price is fixing to do to his mama. "Your mama is going to keep Cecily's secret until her dying breath, if that's what it comes to."

Moses looks indignant. "I can, too."

❧ | SALLY | ❧

T*he carriage has barely rolled to* a stop in front of the Prices' home when Sally and Maria hear a sharp scream.

Sally doesn't bother waiting on the driver to open their door. Instead, she clambers out of the carriage, then tries her best to hurry Maria along.

They hear more shouting, and this time Sally can tell it's coming from the yard.

"Can you walk?" she asks Maria, and when the girl nods, Sally steers her—slowly—down a brick path and around the side of the house, where a small group of slaves has gathered.

In the center of the yard, a tall, thin Negro woman, who can't be much older than Sally, has been bound by the wrists and tied to a post. She kneels in the dirt, with her hands above her head, and from far away, it looks almost as if she's praying. Maybe she is.

Only a few feet away from her stands Elliott, lashing the ground with a long leather whip and screaming at the onlookers who have gathered at the perimeter of the yard. "Come closer! I want you all to see this."

"Elliott!" says Maria, who is gripping Sally's arm so hard, she's bound to leave a mark. "What are you doing?"

"What does it look like I'm doing?"

"Is this about Cecily?"

Elliott doesn't answer her, just shouts at the crowd. "Pay attention! Because if any of you know where Cecily's gone off to, and you keep it to yourself, you'll be the next one tied up to this post."

Sally sees the look of confusion on the people's faces. All they know is that Cecily is dead.

"Elliott," Maria says. She sounds calm, but Sally can tell she's shaking. "Della is not going to be able to tell you anything."

"Is Della her mother?" Sally asks Maria quietly.

"Yes."

Elliott circles the post. "You going to tell me where she is, Della?"

"I told you already," the woman says stoically, "she dead."

"And I told you, I need the truth."

"You won't hear it."

Elliott lays the whip across Della's back, and Sally winces.

"Maria," she says softly. "Should you get your parents?"

The girl nods, lets go of Sally's arm, and begins to back away. When she is several feet behind Sally, she turns unsteadily and teeters toward the house.

"Shall we try this again?" Elliott asks.

Della doesn't answer.

"Where is Cecily?"

No response.

The whip licks her back once more, but she does not cry out in pain. Instead, she lifts her head, looks at Elliott over her shoulder, and says, "This is how you treat a grieving mother?"

"I told you," he says. "You are *not* grieving."

Della struggles to speak. "Cecily went to the theater that night, same as Miss Maria."

Sally can't stand watching this. "Mr. Price," she says in as dignified a manner as she can manage, "I don't mean to intrude, but I have come to bring your sister home, at your request, and I wonder if you and your parents might have a few minutes to discuss her care going forward."

Elliott pulls his eyes away from the whipping post and stares Sally down. "I don't remember requesting you accompany her."

"I mean," Sally stumbles, "that she is here at your request."

Elliott laughs. "Spending two days putting cold compresses on my sister's head hardly qualifies you to meddle in our family's affairs."

Sally clears her throat. "I wouldn't presume—"

"Elliott?" comes the wavering voice of Mrs. Price from the porch. "What are you doing with Della out there in the yard?"

"Go back inside, Mother," he says as he winds the whip into a tight coil that sits in the palm of his hand. Then he leans in close and tells Della, "I wouldn't count on my mother offering you much in the way of protection."

Out of the corner of her eye, Sally sees Mr. Price coming around the other side of the house. He bellows his son's name. "Put down that whip!"

The boom of his voice startles Elliott, and he lowers the whip, but does not drop it.

Mr. Price is trailed by a tear-stricken boy, who has to be Della's son. "That woman is not your property," yells Mr. Price. "She is mine!"

"And don't we all know it," Elliott sneers.

If there is an insinuation in the statement, Mr. Price ignores it. He moves closer to his son before repeating himself. "I said to put down the whip."

There are murmurs among the people who are watching from the edge of the yard.

Elliott reminds Sally of a trapped animal. Ready to chew his own leg off if it'll set him free.

"Moses here tells me you think Cecily is alive," says Mr. Price.

"I don't think it, I know it."

"What proof have you got?"

"She saw her," Elliott says, pointing a finger at his sister.

Maria, who looks frighteningly pale, comes to stand beside her father. "I wasn't in my right mind when I said that."

"Sir," says Sally to Mr. Price, "it's true. She was experiencing severe delirium."

"I don't remember him asking you for your opinion," says Elliott, and Sally snaps her mouth shut.

"I'll take her opinion," says Mr. Price, "over the opinion of a man who refuses to accept his losses. No matter how painful they might be."

Elliott drops the whip in the dirt, and kicks it out of his way as he makes for the house. "This is a pile of horse crap," he shouts at his father. "But if you want to give up looking for a perfectly good slave, just because you got hoodwinked by her mother, then so be it."

"Leave her mother out of this."

"I'll just find her myself."

"Elliott," says Mr. Price, like he is speaking to a small child. "You will do nothing of the sort."

"You can't stop me."

"I forbid it."

Elliott stops and turns to look back at his father. "You forbid it?"

"This, this thing you've got with Cecily, it's an obsession," says Mr. Price. "I should have put a stop to it years ago. But it's gone on long enough."

"You, of all people, have no room to talk."

"Hear me, son. Cecily is dead. You are getting married in less than a week. And there is your sister's health to consider."

A smirk crosses Elliott's face. "Which sister is that again?"

Sally is so busy trying to decipher what he means that she misses Mr. Price close the distance between himself and his son. The next thing she knows, he is wrestling Elliott to the ground.

Maria screams, and Mrs. Price rushes from the porch. When she tries to pull the two men apart, Elliott elbows her in the chest and she is thrown backward.

No one else in the yard makes any effort to break the two men up. Instead, they watch as the Prices rut like a pair of bucks. Heads down, horns out. It isn't a fair fight—Elliott's got to outweigh his father by fifty pounds—but what Mr. Price lacks in bulk, he makes up for in pure, unfettered fury. The men pitch themselves against each other, again and again, and Sally can't help thinking about the carcasses of two whitetails that Andy found down near the banks of the Roanoke River. Their antlers had locked, and they'd died together, neither one of them able to so much as lift his head without the other.

Elliott shows no signs of tiring, but Sally can tell Mr. Price's stores have grown depleted. Soon, Elliott has him pinned. He lies there for a moment, staring directly into his father's eyes, while everyone else holds a collective breath. Sally assumes the skirmish has reached its natural conclusion, and that soon Elliott will help his father to his feet. So, when Elliott reels back his head and cracks his skull against his father's, she feels utterly unprepared for it.

Why does Sally continue to be surprised by the depravity of men? Perhaps because so much has been made of their civility? Her father prided himself on always being courteous in the courtroom. Her uncle, who sits on the bench of the General Court of Virginia, is considered by all to be a fair and honorable judge. Even her brothers—rabble-rousers, all of

them—diligently transcribed each of Francis Hawkins's *Rules of Civility &
Decent Behavior* into their copybooks when they were growing up. She
thinks of Hawkins's last rule, which was so often repeated in her childhood
home that she had once embroidered it onto a pillow: *Labor to keep alive in
your breast that little spark of celestial fire called conscience.*

These men have no consciences. Not Elliott, not Mr. Price, not Archie or Tom or any of the other men she encountered in the theater. They
pay lip service to the idea of civility, while doing whatever they want at all
times. Even Robert, whom she has missed so terribly these last three years,
was not a perfect man. She likes to believe that, were he in the theater, he'd
have stayed with her until the end, but how can she be sure, after everything
she's witnessed?

As Sally watches Elliott rise and stalk off across the yard, she wonders
if—in the time that has elapsed since Robert's death—she has remade him
into a man who never existed at all.

⚜ | GILBERT | ⚜

Gilbert *heads straight for Callum Murrow's* Carriage Shop, where he worked when he first came to Richmond, all those years ago. There's a small office in a house near the road, but the bulk of the work gets done in the barn at the rear of the property, and that's where he hopes he'll find Samuel Jefferson.

Most of the men who work for Mr. Murrow have cleared out, but Gilbert is relieved to find Samuel bent over a band saw, putting the curves in a spoke. He raises his hand, gives him a "Hey ho" from across the room, so as not to scare him.

Samuel looks up, peers into the dim light of the barn, and says, "Do my eyes deceive me or is that Gilbert Hunt?"

"Indeed," says Gilbert as he makes his way across the barn, sidestepping a crane-neck phaeton—nearly finished—and the skeleton of what will one day be a one-horse chaise. The two men clap each other on the back. "It's been too long."

"Sounds like you've had a busy time of it these last few days," says Samuel with a sly smile.

Gilbert goes stiff, trying to work out what he means, and Samuel lets out a long, soft chuckle and says, "Relax, I'm talking about your heroics on Thursday night."

Gilbert's shoulders loosen. "Right, that."

"I was at the green yesterday when all that cheering started. In all my life, I ain't never seen anything like it."

"I was as surprised as you were."

"That many white men, applauding a Negro. I told myself: Pay attention. You won't see this again."

"Why you working today?" Gilbert asks. "Ain't the shop meant to be shut down?"

"You know me," Samuel says with a shrug. "Never was very good at not working."

Gilbert glances around the barn. "Everybody else seems to have no problem with it."

"I won't see hide nor hair of them until after the funeral, I'm sure."

Gilbert picks up a mallet, feels the heft of it in his hand, and tries to call back the memory of working alongside Samuel. Gilbert had to attach the hoop to the wheel when it was red-hot, working as quick as he could, then it was Samuel's job to plunge the wheel into cold water. If their timing was perfect—which it almost always was—the result was a tight tire that didn't go anywhere. "You spoiled me for working alongside anybody else."

Samuel nods once, then says, "That's true. But something tells me you ain't here to talk about old times."

"No, sir," says Gilbert, trying to figure out the right way into the conversation.

Samuel cuts to the chase. "Is this about Della?"

Gilbert looks Samuel square in the eye, which tells Samuel all he needs to know.

"She came to see me yesterday. About Cecily."

"Who said anything about Cecily?"

Samuel throws the flats of his hands up in the air. "No one did. She just said she had a package she wanted me to take north. But I know her eldest is supposed to have died in the fire, and it doesn't take a genius to figure out what's what."

Gilbert's throat feels dry. "Della says you got a carriage that's just about ready to be delivered."

"A coach," says Samuel. "I'm only driving it as far as Alexandria, but I could get her to the depot in Washington, if that helps."

"When do you leave?"

"Tuesday."

"We need something sooner than that."

"I won't travel with anyone who ain't got free papers. And the man I use for them, he ain't in town till Monday night."

Gilbert brightens. "I can write her papers, if I got yours to work from."

Samuel gives him a crooked smile. "When did you learn to write?"

"My wife's mistress taught me," says Gilbert, and when the image of Louisa Mayo, sitting at that kitchen table with her primer, comes to his mind, he pushes it away.

"Free papers are not so simple to produce as a pass," says Samuel. "They're court documents. So, you got to forge the affidavit, but also the certification. Needs to look like it comes from two different hands. Three, really."

"I can do it. I know I can."

Samuel leans against his workbench. "What about the fee?"

"Della says you charging a hundred dollars."

"That's right."

"What are you doing with all that money?" Gilbert says, looking around the barn, like he expects Spanish dollars to start raining from the ceiling.

"You think my free papers are the only ones I ever bought?"

Gilbert has obviously struck a nerve.

"I got a family, same as you."

"I hear you," says Gilbert. "And I'm sorry if I caused offense. But Della and Cecil couldn't get their hands on that kind of money if they tried."

"People got ways."

"Not these people," Gilbert says sharply. "Della was dragged up to the whipping post this afternoon. And Cecil got thrown in the birdcage yesterday."

Samuel winces. "For the business with the slave revolt?"

"That's right."

"Two boys here in this shop got hauled down there yesterday evening. Don't know when they'll be released. Especially with Mr. Murrow out of town."

"It's all a bunch of lies," says Gilbert, thinking about the actors who came by the smithy looking for Kemp.

Samuel agrees, but that doesn't change anything. "I'm sorry," he says. "I'd like to help, but there ain't one Negro in this town who doesn't have a story every bit as sad as yours."

Gilbert knows when he's lost, and he prides himself on taking his licks like a man. But there's something about walking out of that barn, no closer to getting Cecily out of harm's way. He just can't do it.

He feels for the pouch in his pocket, tells himself that Mrs. Johnston's plan to buy Sara's freedom will work, and that all he's doing—by parting with this money—is putting off his own eventual purchase. "I'll pay for it," he tells Samuel. "But all I got is seventy-three dollars, and she has to be moved tonight."

Samuel eyes the money. "Why the rush?"

"It's complicated."

"Got anything to do with those flyers I'm seeing all over town?"

"Elliott Price is convinced she's alive."

Samuel smiles. "Sounds like he ain't wrong."

❋ | JACK | ❋

Jack has spent the better part of two hours looking for Mr. Green, when he finally discovers him in the taproom of The Swan.

He sits at the bar, in the same clothes he wore to the performance, but everything else about him—from the slump of his shoulders to the vacant expression on his face—looks so unfamiliar that Jack could easily have walked right past him.

Jack taps him on the shoulder, and Green nearly jumps off his stool. "Oh, it's you," he says before turning back to the tankard of ale in front of him.

"Sorry, yes."

Green lifts the tankard to his lips and takes a swig before setting it down on the bar with an unsteady thunk.

"May I join you?" Jack asks, and Green gestures to the empty stool beside him.

"We've been looking for you."

"I'm not hard to find. You've just got to look for the man with the hole in his heart."

The thing with these actors, Jack has learned, is that they can't turn it off. Even in his grief, Green is still grasping for a good line.

Jack doesn't think he can bring up Ritchie or the inquest right away. He's got to ease into it, or run the risk of losing Green altogether. "Is there any news about Nancy?" he asks.

Green shakes his head no.

"And Mrs. Green?"

"She's been back and forth between the capitol and the green a hundred times. Won't eat, won't sleep. Won't stop, she says, until she can identify Nancy's remains."

"Is that likely?" asks Jack, remembering what Anderson said about the Jews.

"Have you been over there?"

"To the site?" Jack's too embarrassed to tell him he hasn't been back since the first night, that he can't bring himself to stop and really take in what it is they've done.

"There's nothing to identify."

Jack closes his eyes.

"I told Frances we can hold a memorial service in Charleston. It won't be a proper burial, but it'll be better than whatever they're doing here."

"What does she say to that?"

Green gives a disbelieving laugh. "She says that if I think she's going back to Charleston with the man who killed her daughter, I'm a bigger fool than she thought."

Green's chin starts to shake, and the next thing Jack knows, he's got his head down on the bar and is sobbing uncontrollably.

Jack's seen Green cry plenty—when the role calls for it, any of the actors can summon tears—but he's never seen him like this. Tentatively, he extends a hand and pats Green's heaving back. "You're not a fool."

At that, Green's head lurches up, and he stares at Jack through bleary eyes. "Am I not?"

Jack doesn't know what to say. At the theater, Green has always come off as a man who knows what he wants and how to get it. He's a natural leader, who doesn't ask more of the troupe than he is prepared to give of himself. He expects the actors to show up on time, to be sober, and to come to rehearsals with their lines memorized. But he's not unreasonable. He understands that his actors are human beings, so he is quick to offer an advance or even, on occasion, a bonus, if the need is warranted. Earlier this month, when the actress Elizabeth Poe's end was near, it was Green who insisted on not just one benefit performance but two, so that there would be money for her burial but also for the support of her two small children.

Jack wishes he had a handkerchief to offer him. "I'm so sorry. For everything."

Green wipes his eyes with the palms of his hands. "It's not your fault."

"I could have refused to hoist the chandelier into the flyspace. I *should* have refused. It's just that I admired you, and I didn't want—"

Green cuts him off. "You need not say anymore."

There is something protective in Green's desire to stop Jack from flagellating himself, and it reminds Jack of the Skelton article. "Was it you? Who went to Skelton?"

"Skelton?"

"The article. In the *American Standard*. That spells out what happened with the chandelier."

"I don't know what you're talking about."

Jack wants to push Green on this, even though he's clearly in no condition to be pushed on anything. "You might not have known you were even talking to Skelton," says Jack. "Did you speak to anyone that night? About the fire and how it started?"

Green stares into his tankard. "How should I know? I wasn't in my right mind."

He has a point.

They sit there in silence for a few moments, each of them lost in his own memories.

"Mr. Green," Jack says finally, "I know this is the last thing you want to think about, but all the actors are being interviewed, over at the Washington Tavern, and Thomas Ritchie, who's heading up the inquest committee—well, he wants to talk to you."

Green shakes his head. "I can't talk to anyone," he says. "Not now. Not like this."

"Yes, that's what we told him," says Jack, "but he is quite insistent."

"Well, tell him to bugger off."

Jack swallows. "Mr. Placide has certainly tried that."

Green laughs, and for a brief moment, it is almost possible for Jack to forget that he is speaking to a grieving father.

"You should know that Mr. Placide is telling the committee, and anyone who will listen, that the fire was started by a mob of angry slaves."

Green rears back in his chair. "But that's not true."

"Right."

"So, why is he doing it?"

Jack struggles with what to say. "I think the general consensus is that if we admit to raising the chandelier into the flyspace—and to knowing that the chandelier was suspended from a broken pulley—we will hang."

"Did anyone even see any Negroes near the theater?"

"Just the ones inside, watching the performance, like everybody else."

Green is quiet for a moment, then he shakes his head in disbelief or disgust, Jack isn't sure which.

"Placide has instructed us all to testify to the fact that there was a band of Negroes near the stage entrance, brandishing torches."

"Earlier this afternoon, I saw three Negro men arrested," says Green. "Does that have anything to do with this?"

Jack recalls what Ritchie said this morning, about Negroes from across the city being rounded up and thrown into the birdcage. "Most likely, yes."

Green looks uneasy. "So, we're just going to let Richmond's colored folks take the blame for this?"

This is the opening Jack's been waiting for, and he takes it. "Maybe if you talked to Ritchie, you could tell him . . ."

"Tell him what?"

Jack hesitates. "The truth."

"You want me to turn on Placide?"

"Nothing as severe as that."

Green studies him closely.

"You don't even have to address the cover-up," says Jack. "For all Ritchie knows, Placide's right, and there really was some unrest that night."

"I'm confused."

"If you just tell him what you know—how I forgot to put out the chandelier and that you gave the order to raise it, without fully understanding what it would mean to do so—he's sure to be sympathetic. At the very least, he'll have no choice but to call off the arrests Kemp's men are making."

"What makes you think I'm not going to go tell Placide that you're over here, trying to convince me to turn on the troupe?"

Jack's breath catches in his throat. "I'm not. I mean, I thought, with Nancy . . ."

The smile slips off Green's face at the mention of his daughter's name.

"I'm sorry. I didn't mean to—"

"Relax, Gibson," says Green. "I'm not going to tattle on you. You're a good boy, even if you are a bit daft."

He drains his beer and pushes himself onto his feet.

"So, you'll talk to Ritchie?"

Green tosses a few shillings onto the bar. "I will, but you're not going to like what I say."

❈ | **SALLY** | ❈

After Elliott takes off, Sally and Maria and a few of the house servants help get Mr. and Mrs. Price inside. A woman named Rosie offers to take Mrs. Price upstairs, and Mr. Price's manservant guides Mr. Price into his study, where he collapses on the settee. Outside in the yard, a few of the slaves work to untie Della and see to her wounds.

Sally inspects the Prices' injuries. Mrs. Price has a bruised tailbone and maybe a broken rib—injuries she will be able to hide when it is time to be seen in public or receive visitors. Mr. Price's injuries are harder to cover up. He has a split lip that could probably use a few stitches, and his right eye is already starting to swell. It's horrifying to think that their own son is the cause of their suffering, but they seem resigned to it.

"I told you," says Maria to Sally as she walks her to the door. "He's cruel."

Sally makes Maria promise to take care of herself and to find an excuse to get out of the house if Elliott does not, indeed, follow through on his plan to wed. "You can come visit my mother and me at Hunting Tower, in Buckingham, this spring. I'll be there once Margaret has recovered."

"I will," says Maria as she hugs Sally goodbye. "Thank you for everything."

They are on the porch when they spy a woman in a canary-yellow dress getting out of a hired chaise. The woman has a mountain of red hair piled atop her head, and when she draws closer, Sally notices that her face is so heavily made-up she can have only one occupation.

"May we help you?" asks Maria.

"Yes," says the woman, who smells strongly of vanilla and cloves. "I came to see Elliott Price Junior."

"My brother is not at home," Maria says. "And I couldn't tell you when he'll be back."

Maria seems ready—and even eager—to send the woman away, but when Sally looks down at the woman's muff—a magnificent mink—she notices she is clutching a copy of Elliott's flyer in one hand.

"Do you have information about the runaway?" Sally asks.

"I do," says the woman. "My name is Miss Augustine Saunders."

Sally introduces herself, and Maria, somewhat begrudgingly, follows suit.

"Pleased to make your acquaintance," says Miss Saunders, "although I am sorry it is under these circumstances."

Maria nods.

Sally cannot think of a single set of circumstances in which a girl of Maria's breeding would be pleased to make Miss Saunders's acquaintance, but she keeps that to herself.

"What do you know?" asks Maria.

"I sat next to her in the gallery."

Maria gives Sally a quick glance. "Cecily?" she confirms.

Miss Saunders nods.

"How do you know it was her?" Maria asks.

"She introduced herself."

It takes Maria a moment to absorb this information, so it's Sally who says, "And do you believe she made it out?"

"I do," says Miss Saunders. "I was right behind her when we exited the gallery. Followed her all the way down the stairs and out onto the green."

"Did you?" says Sally, who can't quite believe what she's hearing. She's never put much stock in Elliott's theory that Cecily made it out of the theater alive, but perhaps she discounted it too quickly.

"Is it possible," says Maria, "that she went back inside?"

"I suppose anything's possible. But what would she have wanted to go back inside for?"

"*I* was inside," says Maria with such wild confidence that Sally feels embarrassed for her.

Augustine Saunders must, too, because she lets out a little snort, then gives Maria a pitying stare. "Were you the reason she was sitting in the gallery, sobbing her eyes out before the start of the show?"

Maria is at a loss for words.

"Because if you were, I doubt very much that she ran into a fiery inferno to save your behind."

Sally watches as it slowly dawns on Maria—just as it did on Elliott—that Cecily would never have willingly risked her own life to save her.

"Of course, you're right," Maria whispers. "I don't know what I was thinking."

Sally gives her hand a squeeze. It's a hard truth to acknowledge, but Maria is trying.

"Well, when I saw this," Miss Saunders says, folding the flyer in squares, "I thought I should offer up what little I know."

"Yes," says Maria slowly. "That was very good of you, and I will pass the information along to my brother as soon as he returns."

The woman gives Maria her card, and tells her to be in touch if she needs her to provide an official statement of any kind.

"I doubt that will be necessary," says Maria, and then she and Sally watch as Augustine Saunders climbs back into the chaise and disappears down the drive.

It's a lot to take in. That Elliott was right and that Cecily is likely alive and on the run. Maria would be within her rights to take this information to her father and demand that they begin to search for Cecily in earnest. But somehow, Sally doesn't think that's what she'll do.

"I wasn't very good to Cecily," Maria says as soon as the carriage is out of sight.

"The night of the fire?"

"And all the days and nights leading up to it."

Sally isn't entirely surprised.

"I knew what Elliott was doing. And I could have tried to stop it. Tried to help her."

"Well," says Sally, "keep this visit to yourself, and it sounds like you still can."

✲ | GILBERT | ✲

Gilbert *shows back up at the* kitchen house while Maddie's cleaning up from dinner.

"You seen Sara?"

Maddie nods her head in the direction of the loft. "She's up there, shutting her eyes for a few minutes. Elizabeth been running her ragged."

"I got to talk to her," he says apologetically. "It can't wait."

He's on the top rung of the ladder when Sara calls his name in that soft, sleepy voice of hers. "Gillie?"

"Hey, baby," he says, and crawls across the floor to her pallet, where she is curled up like a roly-poly. "You got a little room on that thing for me?"

She nods and scooches to one side, giving him enough space to crawl up behind her and wrap her in his arms. She smells like lavender and lye, and when his head is burrowed in her neck, he lets out a tired sigh. "This is all I wanted these last few days."

She knows it. Still half-asleep, she reaches for him and pats his face.

He allows himself to lie there for a few precious minutes before he lets the real world in. "Lecretia told me they got word Louisa didn't make it?"

She doesn't say anything, but her body starts to vibrate.

"I'm so sorry, Sara."

"I tell myself that, one of these days, she would have turned against me. Found her own ways to make life harder, same as Elizabeth does."

"Maybe," says Gilbert softly. "But you mothered that girl since she was a baby. You allowed to weep."

It's like getting his permission was all she needed, because she starts sobbing and doesn't stop. While she cries, he holds her tight and listens to Maddie banging around below. God bless Maddie for acting like she can't hear a thing.

Finally, Sara's body grows still in his arms, and he gets around to asking, "Did Phyllis Johnston come by today?"

"Big white lady?" she asks.

"That's the one."

"Came with her husband. Went straight into General Preston's study and didn't come out for at least a quarter of an hour."

"Was Elizabeth in there?"

"Lord, no. She ain't fit to hold her own soup spoon, much less receive company."

She rolls over onto her back so she can look at his face. "Why you want to know?"

"Mrs. Johnston came to see me yesterday. She's grateful for what I did over at the theater and is taking up a collection. Wants to buy my freedom."

"What?" says Sara, shooting straight up like a rocket. "Are you serious?"

"Don't get too excited for me just yet."

"Why?"

"There ain't no way Kemp's selling me right now."

"Did you tell her that?" Sara says, as if she can't quite believe it.

"Lay back down, will you?"

She does as he asks, and when she's in his arms again, he says, "What I told her was that, if she wanted to thank me, she could come over here and offer to purchase you."

"Me?"

"She'd buy you off the Prestons, then get you your free papers."

Sara looks at him like he's speaking French.

"I know I should have checked with you first. But there wasn't time. And if you get free, you can work, start saving. One of these days, when Kemp's cooled off or—better yet—is in the ground, you can buy my freedom."

"Oh, Gillie." Her voice sounds far away.

"I won't always be so expensive," he says. "I'll get older, I promise."

She rolls her eyes at him, which is really just an invitation for more.

"I'll get to the point where I won't even be able to swing a hammer." He glances in the direction of his pants. "Of course, by then I won't be able to swing much else, either."

She lets loose a low rumble of a laugh, which is what he's been after all along.

"It won't work."

"Why not?"

"Elizabeth ain't going to give me up, even with Louisa gone. *Especially* with Louisa gone."

"It's General Preston's decision. He who owns all of y'all now."

She gives him a look, like she's offended by what he's said, even though all he's doing is reciting the law.

"Mrs. Johnston says he's got big debts."

Sara's mouth drops open. "So, the silver that keeps disappearing is him?"

Gilbert nods.

"I knew it," she says, staring up at the ceiling.

"This can't wait," says Gilbert. "These white ladies are grateful, and they're ready to empty their reticules. But give them two months, and they'll forget all about this plan of theirs."

"It's just, Louisa—"

"Baby, Louisa's gone, and without her, you don't got a job to do."

She flinches.

"I'm sorry," he says, running a soft knuckle along the side of her face. He lays a series of small kisses on her eyelids, her cheekbones, her earlobes. When his mouth is close to her ear, he whispers, "There's something else I got to tell you."

❦ | JACK | ❦

Jack bangs on Professor Girardin's door, loudly and for several minutes, until Girardin's house servant, Ivy, finally answers it. In her arms she carries the Girardins' new baby, Mary Anne, who is squawking so loudly Jack has to shout to be heard over her. "Where's Professor Girardin?"

Ivy moves the baby to her shoulder and pats her back, which does nothing to quiet her. "He can't see you right now, Mister Jack."

Jack absolutely must talk to Girardin. His professor knows enough of the world, not to mention the theater company, that if Jack tells him everything, he will know what to do. "It's important," he pleads.

"It ain't a good time," Ivy says and begins to close the door on him, but Jack sticks his foot in the doorjamb and gives the door a little push.

"Where is everybody?" he asks.

"You are not hearing me," says Ivy. "No one can see you."

All of a sudden, Jack begins to panic. Could something have happened to Girardin? "He made it out of the theater, did he not? He's alive?"

"He made it out," Ivy says. "But alive might be putting too fine a point on it."

Just then, a deafening crash comes from the upstairs study, and Jack takes the opportunity to dart past Ivy and up the stairs to the second floor.

"Mister Jack! Get back down here. He don't want to see you right now, not even a tiny little bit."

Of course Professor Girardin will see him! He's never once sent him away.

The door to the study is closed, but sitting in front of it is the Girardins' four-year-old daughter, Adelaide, who stands when she sees Jack coming. "Hello, Addy," he says as calmly as he can, then tries the door handle. It's locked.

He taps on the door lightly.

"I said I didn't want to be disturbed," comes the familiar tenor of his beloved teacher's voice.

"Professor Girardin," he says, leaning his forehead against the thick door. "It's me."

"Jack?"

"Yes, sir."

"Go away."

The curt response surprises Jack. Should Girardin not be relieved to find that he, too, is alive?

Ivy has caught up to Jack, baby in tow, and she grabs him by the back of the shirt collar, then apologizes to Girardin through the door. "Sorry, sir. I told him not to come up."

"Get him out of here."

"Yes, sir," says Ivy, shooting Jack as sour a look as there ever was.

Jack had hoped that Girardin might be able to advise him as to what to do about Placide and Green and this whole business with the inquest, but now all he wants to do is set eyes on the man—make sure he is in one piece. "You were there. Are you all right?"

Through the door, Jack can hear a low chuckle that turns into something closer to a groan and then finally a wail.

"You need to go," hisses Ivy.

From behind the door, there is another loud crash, and this time Jack can make out the shattering of glass.

The noise has scared both girls. Mary Anne begins to scream once more, and when Jack looks down at Addy, she is standing in a puddle of piss as big as a hoop.

"What are we going to do with you, Miss Adelaide?" says Ivy as she takes the child's hand and leads her down the hall toward the nursery. When Ivy is about to round the corner, she turns her head and shoots Jack a look that says, *Get.*

Jack tries to think of what he can say that will convince Girardin to unlock the door. "I was backstage," he says tentatively, "where the fire started."

The words are no sooner out of his mouth than Jack hears the key turn in the lock. The door swings open, as if on its own accord, and the sight that greets Jack is like nothing he's ever seen before. Girardin's secretary is on its side in the middle of the room—its glass doors smashed, its desktop splintered, all the books and papers scattered from one end of the room to the other. There are other, smaller bookshelves that have been turned over, too, and the chair that Jack sometimes sits in when he visits lays in three distinct pieces.

It is only when Jack closes the door behind him that he finds Girardin sitting in the corner of the room with his head buried in his knees.

"Professor Girardin?"

Girardin lets out a long moan, and when he finally looks up, Jack takes a small step backward. His teacher's face is wet with tears.

"My precious boy."

Jack's heart fills with gratitude. That Girardin should see Jack so completely is a testament to the bond they share.

"My precious Lou."

Jack shakes his head involuntarily. "What's the matter with Lou?"

Girardin lets out such a loud sob that Jack starts to panic. Lou is six—too young to have attended the Hallerian Academy at the same time as Jack, but old enough to play stickball with him whenever he comes to borrow books from Girardin. He is a sweet boy with a gap-toothed smile, who thinks Jack walks on water.

Come to think of it, why wasn't he downstairs with Ivy when Jack arrived? Or even up here, with Addy? And what of his mother? Mrs. Girardin is rarely, if ever, separated from Mary Anne, who eats on such a regular schedule the professor had begun to call her his *petit cochon*.

A terrifying thought occurs to Jack, but he pushes it away and asks, "Where's Lou?"

Girardin's eyes are squeezed tight, and he shakes his head back and forth, like he can't bear to offer up the answer.

It doesn't make any sense. Lou is too young to have been at the performance. Except. Except. Except Placide & Green was staging his father's play. Jack can feel bile burning the back of his throat. He reaches for Girardin's arm, rephrases the question. "Was he at the theater?"

Girardin nods, and Jack lunges for the coal bin, where he vomits up everything in his stomach. For several long minutes, he hugs the rim of the bin, and when he can finally sit up, he keeps his eyes on the floor.

Jack can barely get the next question out, but he has to know the whole truth. "And Mrs. Girardin?"

Girardin's shoulders begin to heave, which tells Jack everything he needs to know.

"No," Jack sobs. "No, no, no, no, no."

It's not that Jack hasn't understood that the fire has had devastating consequences. He has. But until now, everything he's witnessed hasn't felt real. Somehow, Jack has managed to convince himself that the fire is just the biggest and most elaborate production Placide & Green has ever staged.

Jack doesn't know how many minutes pass, but eventually Girardin begins to speak. "I never intended to remain at the theater for the second piece."

Jack remembers him saying as much to him at rehearsals.

"But Mrs. Girardin's brother was with us, and when I announced that I was leaving, she said she wanted to stay."

"With Lou?"

Tears leak from Girardin's eyes. "He was asleep in her arms. I offered to carry him home and put him to bed, but she told me to leave him where he was. That she'd wake him for the pantomime."

Jack closes his eyes, whispers only, "Professor."

He waits for Girardin to ask him what he saw backstage, what he knows of the fire that killed his family, but the professor doesn't say another word for the rest of the evening. Eventually, he falls asleep in the same corner where Jack found him.

Jack came to Girardin's in search of advice, but now he sees that he doesn't need it. If he wants to do right by his professor and the scores of other families like Girardin's—not to mention the countless Negroes whose lives have been turned upside down by the theater troupe's lies—then there is only one thing to do.

How's Mama?" *Cecily asks before Gilbert's* through the door of the boathouse.

"I'm just coming from there."

"And?"

"She's all right," he says.

"What's that mean?"

"Your brother has her back down at the cabin, and he's tending to her."

"So, Elliott whipped her good?"

"He only got a couple of lashes in before Mr. Price showed up."

"He got him to stop?"

"That's what Moses says. Said the two of them men was fighting like a pair of pheasants."

Cecily would have liked to see that. "Any word on Papa?"

Gilbert shakes his head and hands her a large burlap sack. Inside is a dress and some other women's accessories.

"What's all this for?" Cecily asks.

"For when we get where we're going."

"And where are we going?"

"Callum Murrow's Carriage Shop. There's a freedman named Samuel Jefferson, works in the barn. He's going to give you a ride out of town, but he needs you to look like a lady doing it."

"No stagecoach?" she asks, surprised.

Gilbert shakes his head no.

"Why?" asks Cecily, who is secretly relieved to learn that she won't have to sit shoulder to shoulder with a dozen or more people who would just as soon turn her in as speak to her.

"Elliott Price has got runaway flyers up all over town."

She feels like she needs to sit down. "Flyers?"

Gilbert nods. "Most of the description don't mean much. A Negro wench, slim straight with a yellowish complexion, could be half the girls in the city, but he takes pains to describe your crooked finger, and I'm worried folks on the stagecoach—especially the conductor—will be looking for it."

"Oh," she says, a little taken aback. She runs her thumb along the bend in her finger. Somehow, it seems doubly unfair that Elliott should be able to both break the bone and then use the injury against her.

Gilbert reaches into his pocket and pulls out a slim leather sleeve. Inside are two pieces of paper, and he hands her one. "This is a pass, just to get you as far as the shop."

She turns the paper over in her hand.

"If you got another pass, linking you to the Prices, you'd best get rid of it now."

"I didn't take anything with me to the theater."

"Good," says Gilbert.

Cecily hates having to ask, but with something so important, there's no way around it. "What's it say?"

"It says your name is Ruth, that you're from King William County, and that you're owned by Mr. and Mrs. Curtis Fry, of Piping Tree."

"I don't know nothing about King William County."

He gives her a sly smile. "That's why I picked it. You got a good chance the patroller won't, either."

"I see," she says.

"The way that pass is written, right now, you got permission to move around freely. So, if anyone stops you, just tell them you in town with your mistress for the funeral, and that you out fetching her something to wear for tomorrow."

"Something to wear?"

He gestures toward the bag. "That'll explain you carrying a sack full of nice clothes."

"Right," she says.

"We're going to stay in the woods as long as we can. Follow First Street. Eventually, we'll pop out on I Street and act like we got no reason not to be there."

Cecily nods.

"When we're moving, keep your head down and your eyes on the ground. Don't make eye contact with anyone."

She nods again. "All right."

"I want you to walk ten or fifteen feet behind me. If I get stopped, for any reason, you just act like you don't know me, and keep going."

"And if I get stopped?"

He gives her a frown. "Sorry, Cecily. But you on your own at that point."

Of course she is. She feels silly for having asked, especially when he's done so much for her already.

"Is there anything else?"

She's got more questions—about a thousand of them—but he's pacing the room, and she gets the feeling he's ready to move.

Before they head out, he gives her a once-over. "When we get into town, take off that coat and carry it over your arm. Young woman like you wearing a man's coat makes you stand out."

She doesn't argue.

The walk through the woods feels like it takes longer than it did on any of Cecily's previous trips, but it's because Gilbert is so much more deliberate than she ever was. She follows behind him, as instructed, and every time he stops—to listen to the shrill cry of a chipmunk or the howl of a faraway coyote—so does she. After a time, they reach the edge of town, but they keep following the tree line, just like Gilbert said they would.

They are almost to E Street when they hear the baying of the dogs. At least three hounds, maybe more, coming from deep within the woods. Gilbert stops, then signals for her to catch up with him.

"Could be the patrol," he whispers. "Now that they got that shawl of yours, they might be using dogs."

The dogs are getting closer, their caterwauling more distinct.

"Not my first choice, but I think we got to walk straight through the city proper. Less chance Kemp will run his dogs through the center of town."

Cecily is so terrified she can barely acknowledge what he's just said. All she does is blink.

A steep gully runs between the woods and the street, and Gilbert helps Cecily down one side and up the other before separating from her once more. She remembers to remove Moses's coat.

Gilbert doesn't stay on First Street for long. Instead, he takes E and then weaves his way onto G, heading east. She knows he's trying to get them into the city's dense interior, where there are more sights, sounds, and smells to distract the dogs, but the first time she passes another person, walking in the opposite direction, she starts to think she might have been willing to risk any number of hounds if it meant staying out of view.

It's dark out, and that helps. But the streets in the city center are far from empty, and when she passes the Washington Tavern, she can hear the sounds of people arguing on the porch. *Just keep your eyes on the ground,* she tells herself over and over again as she walks past familiar street corners and storefronts.

At the Public Square they head north, which means the carriage shop can't be more than a few blocks away. Cecily shifts the sack of clothes in her arms. A boy runs past her, so close that she can smell the salt on his skin. She doesn't get a good look at him, but she wonders if he isn't the boy from the theater. What was it he'd asked her that night? *Is this real?* Such a simple question, and one that—two days later—Cecily's still not sure she's got an answer to.

She is so consumed with this boy that she fails to notice a man, up ahead, blocking Gilbert's path. Gilbert stops, but by the time she does, too, she's practically on top of them. Her impulse is to pull back, to wait for the hammering in her chest to subside or for Gilbert to start moving again, whichever comes first. But she remembers what her uncle told her—that the last thing she wants is to draw attention to herself.

So, she puts her head down and keeps on walking, without giving either man a second glance.

❧ | **SALLY** | ❧

How's the pain?" *Sally asks Margaret* when she goes to check on her before bed.

"I've been better," says Margaret with a tight grin, and Sally laughs because she hears something of her old friend in those three little words.

While Sally was at the Prices', Mrs. Cowley moved Margaret upstairs to Maria's old bed. The other bed in the room is empty now; the girl with the terrible burns took her last breath sometime in the middle of the afternoon. Mrs. Cowley saw that her body was carefully wrapped in a sheet and tucked under the stairs, where she waits to be picked up by the burial committee. John Gamble himself has promised that she will be included in the processional.

Sally hates to admit it, but it is a relief to be in this bedroom and not hear the poor girl struggling for breath. She cracks a window, just to try to get rid of the awful smell of burnt flesh, which hangs in the air, then she sits on the side of Margaret's bed. "Do you need anything? I can get you more laudanum. Or maybe some brandy?"

Margaret shakes her head. "I think I want to feel what it's like to be alive. We are alive, aren't we?"

Sally squeezes her hand. "It's a miracle."

"Don't credit the divine with this, Sally Campbell."

"The divine and I are not on speaking terms, at present."

"Very funny."

Sally grins. She would do absolutely anything to make Margaret laugh right now.

Margaret shifts in the bed so she is looking directly at Sally. "You didn't have to come back for me. In the theater."

A single tear slips down Sally's cheek. "Of course I did."

"Not everyone would have," says Margaret slowly, and Sally knows that they are not talking about everyone.

"Are we talking about Archie?"

Margaret nods.

Sally would like nothing more than to detail all of Archie's bad decisions. But she reminds herself it will do Margaret little good to know her husband is a cad. "He was frightened."

"We all were," says Margaret quietly.

Sally reaches for her sister-in-law's hand. It's true. Sally was terrified, and even now, thinking about what's next for Margaret, leaves her with a nearly paralyzing tightness in her chest.

Margaret looks around the room. "Where is Archie?" she asks.

Sally is embarrassed to tell her that he's gone home for the night, intent on sleeping in his own bed. So, she bends the truth. "He wanted to check on the children."

"How are they?"

"Concerned for you, of course," says Sally.

Her friend bites her lip. "This is too much for them to comprehend."

"They comprehend only that their mother is not with them, that she is being well looked after, and that she will return to them as soon as she possibly can."

Margaret reaches for Sally's arm, grabs hold of her sleeve. "Will I?"

"What?"

"Return to them?"

Sally is crying again—she doesn't know how to stop. "Of course you will," she says. "You don't think I went to all that trouble getting you out of the theater for nothing, do you?"

Margaret relaxes her grip, but the worry doesn't leave her eyes. "Archie told me that you were a proponent of amputating the leg."

The last thing Sally wants to do is cause Margaret to second-guess her course of treatment. "I had no right—"

"You had every right."

"Archie was committed to seeing you returned to your old self."

"My old self," says Margaret thoughtfully. "I don't think I'll ever return to my old self. Will you?"

"After this?"

"It feels impossible."

Sally doesn't disagree.

"That old self, she didn't know anything," says Margaret, and her voice has a hard edge to it that Sally doesn't recognize.

"That's not true," says Sally. "She knew a great deal."

"She knew how to make a mutton curry and burp a baby, but she didn't know a thing about prying open windows or shoving people out of them. She didn't know that the men she'd surrounded herself with were all cowards."

"None of us could have known."

"It's funny—I feel like we've been sold a false bill of goods."

"In what way?"

"Well, weren't we promised that if we married well, we would be taken care of? That our futures would be secure? Where is the security in a husband who would sooner climb over you than help you to your feet?"

"Are you speaking rhetorically?"

Margaret lowers her voice. "No, I am speaking quite specifically."

Sally can't believe what she's hearing. "Is that what happened? Archie climbed over you to get out?"

She nods her head. "I was in front of him. When the crowd surged, we both went down. It was impossible to get up, the people just kept coming. I thought we would die, right there, in each other's arms, except that the next thing I knew, Archie's hand was on my head, and his foot was on my shoulder."

"Oh, Margaret," Sally whispers.

"I was so naive. Even as he was pressing my head into the floor, I was thinking, 'This must be the only way. He's got to get himself to his feet, and then he'll pull me along with him.'"

"But he didn't do that?"

She shakes her head no.

"I knew you'd been separated," says Sally, "but I didn't realize how it had happened."

Sally tries to remember exactly what Archie said to her in the lobby, when she asked where Margaret was. She knows he didn't say anything about Margaret having been trampled. In fact, he made it seem as if it was likely she was ahead of them, on the stairs.

"We never had the type of marriage you and Robert did," says Margaret, fingering the hem of the quilt Mrs. Cowley has loaned her. "But Archie was a good husband, and I suppose I just assumed that I could count on him to take care of me."

"Of course," says Sally. "Who wouldn't have assumed it?"

"How do I look at him every day, from here on out? Knowing what he did?"

Sally can't stop thinking about her conversation with Thomas Ritchie. He would paint every man in that theater as a hero if he could. "Something tells me you are not the only woman in this city asking yourself that question."

Margaret snorts. "You're probably right."

From downstairs, Mrs. Cowley calls up and asks Sally if she'll check on Mr. Scott.

"You've become quite the Daughter of Charity," says Margaret. "I never would have guessed."

"I am full of surprises, it turns out," says Sally brightly. But then she turns serious. "You'll get through this, Margaret. I know you will."

"I am doubtful."

"I'm not saying it will be easy. But wasn't it you who just told me you wanted to put away the laudanum? To feel what it was like to be alive?"

"Did I?" asks Margaret, closing one eye. "That was a terrible idea."

"I don't think so," says Sally, with a smile. She plants a kiss in the middle of Margaret's forehead, which is mercifully cool. "In fact, I think it may be the best idea you've ever had."

❧ | **JACK** | ❧

J ack knocks on the door of the snug, and finds Ritchie inside, packing up his things.

"Are the interviews over?"

Ritchie lets slip an exhausted sigh. "Mr. Gibson, I think you know as well as I that they were over before they began."

Jack watches him slide his notebook into a satchel.

"I wondered if I might speak with you, sir?"

Ritchie motions for Jack to take a seat across from him. "Shall I close the door?"

Jack nods. When Ritchie returns to his seat, they sit there for several seconds, staring at each other.

"You were the one who wanted to speak with me," Ritchie reminds him as he moves to clean his spectacles.

"Yes," says Jack, but he's too afraid to go any further. "What I'm about to say, you can't tell the company you got it from me."

Ritchie returns the spectacles to his face without cleaning them. "Fine," he says.

"I'd like to retract the statement I gave you this morning."

Ritchie holds up a finger—as if to tell Jack to wait—then retrieves his notebook and a pencil from his satchel. When he has pressed the notebook open and wet the pencil with the tip of his tongue, he says, "Please continue."

Jack says the biggest, most important thing first—just in case he loses his nerve later. "It wasn't a slave revolt that started the fire."

"I've known that for some time."

"Was it the Skelton article that gave it away?"

Ritchie seems charmed by his question. "For a bunch of actors, none of your testimonies were particularly convincing."

"I'm not an actor," says Jack. "And at this rate, I'll never be one."

"Do you mind if we start at the beginning?" Ritchie asks.

Jack nods.

"You are, as I presumed, the boy Skelton references in his article?"

"I am."

"And am I to assume that Skelton got most of the details right?"

"Most of them, yes."

"So, it was you who raised the chandelier?"

Jack nods again.

"Did you know it was lit?"

"Yes."

"My understanding is that it's not common practice to raise a lit chandelier into the flyspace."

"That's right."

"So, why did you do it?"

"The short answer is because Green told me to, but the long answer is a little more complicated."

"I'd like to hear the long answer."

"We used the chandelier for interiors," Jack begins. "Ballrooms, great halls, that type of thing. It was in use for the final scene of *The Father*, as well as the first few scenes of the pantomime, which was fine until we got to the scene where everyone ends up in the forbidden forest."

Ritchie is writing down everything Jack says, and Jack pauses to make sure he doesn't need him to speak slower. "Go on," says Ritchie.

"Before the curtain raised, I should have lowered the chandelier to the floor, snuffed the candles, then raised the lamp into the flyspace."

"But that's not what you did?"

"I forgot."

"You forgot?"

"I got distracted." Even now, when he thinks about Mrs. Green and that bladder full of pig's blood, he loses his train of thought. "I feel awful about it. But I'm like that. There's always so much going on, and I never know where to look or what to do first."

Ritchie studies his notes. "So, the chandelier is just hanging there? Where it doesn't belong?"

"Right."

"And was there any danger in it remaining where it was?"

"None at all," says Jack. "It just looked ridiculous. Who wants to see a chandelier in the middle of a dark forest?"

"When did you realize you'd forgotten to deal with it?"

"When Green pointed it out, after Hopkins Robertson had made his entrance."

"Is that when he ordered you to raise it?"

Jack shakes his head no. "At first, he didn't care what I did with it. He just wanted it gone. But I explained that it had to stay where it was until the next set change."

"What did he say to that?"

"It's like he wasn't hearing me. He was completely focused on the fact that the chandelier was ruining this important scene."

"*Was* it an important scene?"

The question hardly bears considering. "Aren't they all important?"

Ritchie shrugs. "So, what did Green say when you told him to wait?"

"He didn't like it. Told me I worked for him and that I needed to do what he said."

"So, you raised it?"

"I argued with him for a little while," says Jack. "But what do I know? He and Placide have been doing this for decades, and I'm just some boy they hired for the season."

"What made you think it was such a bad idea?"

"At first, I was just thinking about the backdrops. They'll catch fire in a flash. But then I remembered the pulley."

"Pulley?" The way Ritchie says the word, like a question, makes it clear that this is the first time he's hearing about it.

"Up on the tie beam. It was loose or something. The chandelier would go up fine, but sometimes, on the way back down, the rope would pop off the wheel."

Ritchie peppers him with questions. Where, precisely, was the pulley installed? How long had it been broken? Whose job was it to fix it? Jack tells him everything he knows, and Ritchie writes it all down in his little book. "Did Green know?" he asks finally, when he has lifted his pencil from the page. "About the pulley?"

Jack nods slowly.

Ritchie leans forward. "And he ordered you to raise it anyway?"

"He wasn't thinking clearly."

"Surely, he knew that getting the chandelier down would prove difficult?"

"He must have," Jack agrees. "But with enough time, we could have come up with a plan."

"Why was there no time?"

Jack starts to tell Ritchie about how Twaits ordered Roy to bring the chandelier down, and the next thing he knows, a quarter of an hour has passed and Ritchie has filled a half-dozen sheets of notebook paper.

"What happens now?" asks Jack. He assumes he is headed straight for the birdcage, or maybe the gallows.

Ritchie doesn't say anything, just closes his notebook and slides it back into his satchel.

"I will accept my punishment—whatever it is."

"I need some time," says Ritchie. "A few hours, at least. I've got to talk to the committee, and figure out where we go from here."

"What do I do until then?"

"Go up to bed. Get some sleep. The most important thing to do is act like everything's normal."

Jack hates the idea of spending another night on that cot in Anderson's room, but what choice does he have?

"One last question," says Ritchie. "Who, precisely, witnessed you raise the chandelier?"

Jack thinks for a minute. "It was just me and Mr. Green and— Mrs. Green."

Ritchie's lip curls up at one corner. "She's who went to Skelton."

It's like Ritchie's just knocked the air out of him. "You know it for a fact?" he asks. "That it was her?"

"No," he admits, "but it's what makes the most sense."

"Because you think she wanted to hold the troupe accountable for Nancy's death?" says Jack slowly.

"Exactly."

"But what about Mr. Green? And me? She didn't out us, and she could have."

Ritchie rolls his shoulders, like it's been a very long day. "Mr. Green's easy to explain."

Jack waits with baited breath.

"She loves him," he says.

It's such a simple explanation, but maybe Ritchie's right. Maybe one mistake—even a mistake that killed their only child—doesn't erase every good feeling she's ever had for him. At least not entirely. "All right," says Jack, "but that doesn't explain not outing me."

"She knows you wouldn't have raised the chandelier if not for Green," says Ritchie.

Jack is indignant. "I might have."

"Are you hearing what I'm telling you?"

"I could have held my ground."

"Listen to me, Jack," says Ritchie. "Mrs. Green was letting you off the hook."

B y the time Gilbert slips into the barn, Cecily and Samuel are talking like they're old friends.

"You made it," says Cecily, who looks like she's about to fall over with relief when he greets them both. "I got so scared when that man stopped you."

"Just a customer, is all. He'd heard about Dr. McCaw."

"What happened to Dr. McCaw?" she asks.

"Nothing," he says quickly.

"Your uncle's being modest," Samuel says to Cecily. "He and the good doctor saved about a dozen women the night of the fire."

"Really?" she says, and the way she says it, Gilbert can tell she's genuinely awed.

"The God's honest truth," says Samuel. "But enough about him. Let's talk about you."

Samuel shows them a one-horse chaise that sits near the door of the barn. It's a two-seater, with an enclosed coupe and a boxed seat, up front, for the coachman. "This is the carriage I'm delivering to Alexandria. I don't know how much your uncle's told you, but I can get you as far as Washington. From there, provided these papers your uncle is writing are as good as he says they're going to be, you should be able to catch a stagecoach to Baltimore and eventually to Philadelphia."

Gilbert forgot he needs enough money to buy Cecily a stagecoach ticket for the second leg of her journey. "Samuel, I got to take the price of the stagecoach ticket out of the seventy-three dollars."

Cecily looks confused, and Samuel waves him off. "We'll work it out."

Gilbert is in no position to push, but he has a feeling that "working it out" means he'll be paying for that ticket one way or another.

"When do we leave?" Cecily asks.

"Funeral's tomorrow at ten," says Samuel. "I'm aiming to have this carriage leaving town a few minutes beforehand. We want everyone looking the other way."

"And you think it'll work?" Cecily asks, crossing her fingers on both hands.

Samuel shrugs. "I'll be honest. I liked the plan a little better when the funeral was going to be at Henrico Parish Church."

"Where's it going to be now?"

"There's talk they're moving it to the theater green."

"Oh," says Cecily, who's clearly taken aback by the idea.

"The green's only a few blocks from here," says Samuel, "but it shouldn't make too much of a difference. We'll take I Street to the turnpike, and avoid some of the crowds."

"You won't be taking anything anywhere," says Gilbert, "if I don't get to work on those papers."

"Agreed," says Samuel as he removes a document from a metal box on his workbench. He hands it to Gilbert.

Gilbert hasn't ever seen a set of free papers before, much less held them, and his hands tremble as he unfolds the document.

Let it be known that I, Callum Murrow, resident and citizen of the City of Richmond, do hereby manumit, emancipate, and forever set free from slavery the Negro man named Samuel, to be free and at his full and perfect liberty from and after the day of the date hereof. I remove my rights of property, possession, utility, and dominion, which I have possessed over this slave. Witness my hand and seal, this tenth day of April in the year of our Lord eighteen hundred and three.

Gilbert studies the document. Mr. Murrow's affidavit is certified by a justice of the peace, and beneath the certification is another attestation, this time by the magistrate, in the Court of Hustings, who recorded the deed.

"You think you can get the signatures to look that good?" Samuel asks.

Gilbert thinks of Louisa and how she had him sign his name over and over again in her copybook. "I know I can," he whispers.

"There's ink and paper over there," says Samuel, nodding his head in the direction of a small writing desk. "But you might want to bring it over to the workbench so you got the lamp."

For the next several hours, the three of them work in companionable silence. Samuel applies one last coat of lacquer to the coupe, Cecily hems the curtains that will hang inside it, and Gilbert writes and rewrites the manumission papers until they are perfect.

Cecily's papers look good—every bit as good as Samuel's, but there's something about seeing the two documents side by side that leaves Gilbert feeling hollowed out. For so long, all he's wanted—for himself and for Sara—is a set of free papers just like Samuel's. The real thing, bought and paid for with his own hard work. But now he realizes that all any of these documents are is words, and not even very mysterious words. Words like *free* and *rights* and *liberty*. How can it be that so few words, scratched on a piece of letter paper, are what's separating Sara and him from a life of freedom?

"Are you all right?" Cecily asks as she puts down her needle and thread and makes her way over to him.

She rests a hand on his shoulder, and he reaches up to pat it.

Maybe, if Mrs. Johnston comes through with Sara's papers, Gilbert will take a risk and write a set for himself. Take Sara somewhere far away from here—Pennsylvania or Ohio—and start over. If he sets up shop as a blacksmith, he might be too easy to find, but he is not too old to learn new tricks.

The last thing Gilbert does, before he says goodbye to Cecily, is read her free papers aloud to her, pausing so she can memorize all the pertinent facts.

"You must like that name, Ruth, if you're letting me keep it," she says.

He assumed she knew why he'd given it to her, but now he explains, "It was your grandmother's name."

She seems surprised. "Mama never said."

Gilbert nods.

"She used to go by Ruthie."

"Well, then," says Cecily as she wraps her arms around him, "I will do the same."

SUNDAY

❧❀ | ❀❧

DECEMBER 29, 1811

I*t's a little after midnight when* Gilbert makes his way down Locust Alley. The smithy should be shut up tight this time of night, so as soon as he sees warm lamp light pouring out of the window and onto the street, he knows something's wrong.

He slows, tiptoes to the window, peeks inside. There's no sign of Kemp, but Marcus is sitting alone at the table by the fireplace, and his face is banged up pretty good.

Gilbert lets himself in. "What happened to you?" he says when Marcus glances up at him. His right eye is swelling fast.

"I'll give you one guess."

"Kemp?"

He nods.

"Lord help us."

"He and Elliott Price and a few others came by here, looking for you."

Gilbert's stomach drops. "Why?"

Marcus gives him a look, like, *You really got to ask?*

Gilbert's got no choice other than to continue to act confused and to pray to God this has nothing to do with Cecily.

"Price remembered where he knew you from."

Gilbert swallows. "He did?"

"Mmmmhmmm," says Marcus. "Told Kemp you was Cecily's uncle. Which struck Kemp as mighty strange, considering you hadn't mentioned it, even with all the fuss about her going missing."

"I didn't see how it was any of his business."

"Well, he sure does think it's his business. Thinks this proves she's alive and you've been plotting how to get her out of town."

Gilbert forces out a laugh. "That ain't true."

Marcus's head goes crooked, trying to look at him out of his one good eye. "That's what I told him."

"And he didn't like it?"

Marcus nods. "Kemp thinks you and me is in cahoots."

"And you said we wasn't?"

"It don't matter what I say at this point. It only matters what he thinks."

"Marcus, I'm sorry you got pulled into all this."

"I don't even know what *this* is."

"It's nothing. Really."

"Don't feel like nothing."

Gilbert doesn't know what to say. Marcus has been a good friend, but he can't trust anybody with Cecily's secret.

"You should probably know," says Marcus as he stands to go, "that I told Kemp about the pass you wrote."

"You what?"

"I had to tell him something to get back on his good side, and that's the something I chose. Hope you can live with it, but if you can't, it really ain't my problem."

In the alley, Gilbert hears the clip-clop of horses' hooves.

Marcus nods his head in the direction of the door. "That's them, most likely, coming to see if you showed back up."

Gilbert is too stunned to speak.

Marcus taps the table with his knuckles. "Good night," he says, and makes for the stairs that lead to the loft.

Kemp is through the door within seconds, and the first thing he does is order Gilbert against the wall, where he pats him down, while Price and the other men snicker. When he finds the now-familiar leather sleeve, he waves it over his head and removes the pass. Then he reads it aloud: "The slave Gilbert Hunt has my permission to pass to and from the smithy of Cameron Kemp, so long as he remains in the city proper and does not cause a nuisance."

Gilbert winces.

"It's funny," says Kemp. "If I hadn't just ripped your pass up, I could almost be convinced I wrote this."

Even though Gilbert knows he's going to have hell to pay, a not-small part of him appreciates the compliment.

"Where'd you learn to write like this?" Kemp asks.

If Louisa were alive, he'd never consider giving her name to Kemp.

Now that she's dead, he's not sure it matters. But just in case it does, in case it could somehow come back around to hurt Sara, he says, "Pete Goode taught me."

"That bastard," Kemp says to the men who have assembled around him. "I should have known."

Elliott Price can barely contain himself. "Ask him about Cecily."

Kemp nods, then sets his gaze on Gilbert. "Is it possible that your pass ain't the only thing you wrote?"

"I don't follow," says Gilbert.

"Did you write a pass for Cecily Patterson?"

"My niece?"

"Don't act coy."

"She's dead, sir."

"Oh, don't give me that!" says Price, who is like a kettle, ready to boil. "You are lying!"

Kemp tries to quiet Price, then he turns back to Gilbert. "It does not look good that you failed to tell me something so important," he says.

"I did tell you."

Kemp screws up his face. "You said your niece died. But you didn't say who your niece was."

Gilbert is so tired of all the cat and mouse games they play. "Forgive me," he says, "but I did not think it mattered."

"Didn't think it mattered? Didn't think it mattered?" Price is shrieking now. "I want this man arrested! For forgery. For carrying false documents. For aiding and abetting a runaway. All of it."

"Whoa, whoa, whoa," Kemp says to Price. "We've got no proof he aided and abetted anyone."

But Price is out of control. He's grabbed a hammer and is waving it around like it's a bayonet. "If I don't see that man led away in chains," he says to Kemp, "I'm going to turn you in, too."

"Let's all calm down," says Kemp in the most soothing voice Gilbert's ever heard come out of his mouth.

Gilbert sees what's happening. It's all well and good for Kemp to go arresting other people's slaves, but when it's *his* slaves, that's another story.

Price is shaking he's so angry. "Let him off the hook, and just watch how fast I get that fancy title of yours ripped away from you."

"Hold on a minute," says Kemp, who must be busy contemplating how much he likes being able to tell people he is the first officer of the patrol. "No one said anything about letting anybody off the hook."

Price is at least partially appeased.

"Gibson, Stephens," Kemp says finally to the two other patrollers in the room. "Let's take him in."

The men advance on Gilbert. He sidesteps them, still trying to talk sense into Kemp. "I wrote a pass for myself, I'll admit it. But I swear to God, I don't know nothing about Cecily other than that she died in the theater."

They rush him then. "This will go easier if you don't fight back," one of them says in a snide voice, right before he pulls out a pistol and knocks Gilbert upside the head.

器 | CECILY | 器

I t's four o'clock in the morning, and Samuel and Cecily are putting the finishing touches on the chaise, when someone knocks softly on the door of the barn. Cecily ducks behind the carriage, just as she and Samuel had planned, but when she hears her mother's voice, she stands up and steps into the light.

"Mama," she says as she falls into Della's waiting arms.

Della winces. "Careful now."

Cecily releases her. "I'm so sorry," she says. "Did I hurt you?"

"I'll be all right."

Della's got a black eye Cecily can see, and God only knows what other injuries she can't. "I can't believe you're up and moving around."

Della pats her cheek. "Couldn't very well miss this."

"Gilbert told me what happened."

"Your brother has me fixed up good. Ran to Mrs. Cowley's for a salve."

Cecily takes her mother's hands in hers. "I'm so sorry, Mama. I'm so, so sorry."

"You don't have anything to be sorry for, baby."

"That's not true," Cecily says. "You said so yourself. I should never have come back to the quarters."

Della shakes her head in disagreement. "You did the right thing coming back. If you hadn't, your papa and me would have lived the rest of our days thinking you died in that fire. Moses too."

Cecily thinks of her sisters, who will know her only through stories. "One day, when they're older, will you tell the girls I made it out?"

Della squeezes her lips tight together. "When they's old enough to keep a secret, we surely will."

Cecily's eyes begin to water, and her mother pulls her close.

"We all going to be fine," Della whispers into her ear.

Samuel stops what he's doing long enough to ask Cecily if she wants to get dressed. "There's a little room in the back where we mix up paint," he says, pointing his head toward the far corner of the barn. "You can get changed in there."

Cecily retrieves a lamp and the sack Gilbert gave her. "Will you come with me, Mama?" she says. "Help me get ready?"

Della follows her into the room, which is lined with jars of linseed oil, hide glue, and pigments of every imaginable hue. In the center of the room is a table with a muller and slab.

While Cecily removes Moses's jacket and sweater and slips her dress over her head, her mother checks that the table is clean, then empties the sack onto it.

Inside is a dress and a jacket, a bonnet, a pair of satin slippers, a muff, and a valise. "Where'd Gilbert get all this?" Della asks in awe.

"It belonged to Louisa Mayo, Sara's charge."

"Ain't she going to notice it's missing?"

Cecily is surprised that, between all Gilbert's comings and goings, he hasn't told Della about Louisa. "She died, Mama."

"When?"

"In the theater."

"Lord almighty," Della says. "He never said a word."

The dress is made of a printed cotton—red with tiny black flower sprigs. It's got a square neckline, with long sleeves, and the whole thing is lined in a coarse linen, which Cecily hopes will keep her warm on the cold journey.

"It looks small," says Cecily, but as soon as Della slips the dress over her head and begins to work the buttons closed, they breathe out a sigh of relief; it's a near-perfect fit.

"How you going to explain a dress so fine?"

"Samuel says I should tell anyone who asks that my mother is a mantua maker, and that I'm going to Philadelphia to visit my sister, who's married to a minister."

"A minister sounds respectable."

"That's what he said."

While Cecily unlaces her muddy boots, Della examines the silk slippers, which are pale pink and trimmed in a light blue grosgrain ribbon. "These are just about the silliest shoes I ever saw," she says as she helps Cecily into them. They're a little too big, but Della finds some old rags and stuffs them in the toes.

"How do they fit now?"

"Better."

Della shakes her head. "You know you free when you wearing a shoe that foolish."

"Mama," Cecily says as she admires her feet, "I got something to ask you."

Della has reached for the bonnet and is adjusting the ribbon that runs across the brim. "What is it?"

"Is Uncle Gilbert paying for all this?"

Della clears her throat. "I don't know the exact particulars he worked out with Samuel, but it ain't free."

"He said something to Samuel about my stagecoach ticket from Washington to Philadelphia needing to come out of the seventy-three dollars he already paid," Cecily says, "and it got me worrying. Did Uncle Gilbert spend all that to get me in this carriage?"

Her mother doesn't say anything.

"Does Uncle Gilbert even *have* that much money?"

Della sighs. "He must."

"How?" asks Cecily. She doesn't know anyone who's got seven dollars, let alone seventy-something.

"Hiring himself out, back when he worked for Pete Goode. He's been saving a long time."

"What's he saving for?"

"What do you think, baby?" says Della. "Same thing we'd all save for, if we could."

"I can't go, then," Cecily stammers. "I can't take his money. Or let Samuel take his money."

"Shhh," says Della, glancing at the door. "Keep your voice down. If Samuel's agreed to take you, and Gilbert's paid for it, you going."

"How can I? When that money could go toward buying his freedom, or Sara's?"

Della rushes to reassure her. "Gilbert could have seven hundred dollars, and Kemp wouldn't sell, so there's no point even worrying about that. And your uncle was just telling me yesterday evening, when he came by to check on me, that there's a white lady in town, trying to buy Sara and give her her free papers."

"Really?"

"Sounds made-up," says Della, "but it's some sort of a thank-you for what Gilbert did the night of the fire."

Cecily loves the idea that there are people in town who want to do right by her uncle. "You telling me the truth?"

"I swear."

Cecily starts to relax a little.

"If you want to help your aunt and uncle, or any of us for that matter, then you get where you're going and you work hard and you find a way to take care of someone else, the way your uncle's taking care of you."

Cecily can do that, she can do anything so long as she's out from under Elliott Price.

"All right," she says. "That's what I'll do."

She reaches for the bonnet, but Della stops her. "We got to do something about that hair first."

Sally wakes sometime in the middle of the night, bleary-eyed and confused, to discover she has fallen asleep in Mr. Scott's room, her head resting against the foot of his mattress. She stands, startled, and when she does, the ladder-back chair she's been perched in tips backward and falls to the floor with a crash.

Sally winces, and Mr. Scott sits up, alarmed.

"I'm so sorry," she whispers in as soothing a voice as she can manage, "I didn't mean to wake you."

"You didn't."

It is the first coherent thing he's said since he told her, back in the box, that he wasn't much for plays, and she is so glad for it, she allows herself a real smile. "Well, maybe not. But lie back down anyway. Before you pop your sutures."

"Sutures," he repeats, like he is trying to summon the memory of a bad dream. He returns his head to his pillow.

"They're on your back."

He moves a hand to his face and touches the chalk. "And this?"

"It's a burn."

"A bad one?"

"I'm not a good judge, but I suspect your days of growing a beard may be behind you."

"Hmmm," he says as he absentmindedly strokes the hair on the good side of his face. "It's a good thing I was never very attractive."

"So, you *do* have a sense of humor," she says with a laugh. "I was worried."

"Have I been that bad?" he asks, and she just shakes her head and pours him a glass of water.

He drains the glass, then hands it to her and looks around the room. "Where am I?"

"Mary Cowley's. Do you know her?"

"I'm afraid not."

"She lives near the green and took in a number of injured people the night of the fire."

"I'm grateful."

"Do you remember getting here?"

Mr. Scott shakes his head apologetically.

"That's probably just as well," says Sally, but a tiny part of her regrets his lapse in memory. "What's the last thing you *do* remember?"

He closes his eyes, as if he has to think hard to come up with something. "I was in the box. Trying to calm the young woman with the big brooch, from Fredericksburg. What was her name?"

She was there with a pair of sisters, none of them older than twenty, but Sally can't remember her name. All she remembers is that Tom had been flirting with her, mercilessly, before the curtain rose.

"When she saw how crowded the hallway was, she panicked," says Mr. Scott. "I couldn't get her to move."

Sally cocks her head, as if a different angle will allow her to see the man in front of her more clearly. "So, you stayed?"

He nods, then tries to shift in the bed, but moving seems to be painful. "By the time I convinced her she wouldn't be trampled to death, I couldn't see six inches in front of me."

Even now, Sally can smell the smoke, can taste the hot tar in the back of her throat. She wonders if what he's saying is true, or if he is like every other man she knows—incapable of telling a story in which he is not the hero.

"Do you know what happened to her?" she asks.

He shakes his head. "We were in the corridor, that's the last thing I remember."

Sally would like to reassure him, to tell him that she remembers seeing the girl with the brooch—in one of the windows, or later, on the green. But she can do no such thing, so she changes the subject instead.

"I went to see Tom Marshall yesterday and asked him to get in touch with your sister."

"Ann?"

"I understand she's caring for your children?"

He frowns. "What did he tell her?"

"I don't know, but I assume he said that you'd been hurt and that she should come."

"Poor Ann."

"I'm sure she'll be happy to do it," says Sally, but now she worries they've done the wrong thing—summoning her to Richmond without his consent.

"She's done so much for us already."

"That reminds me," she says, reaching into her pocket for the *fausse montre*. "This fell out of your pocket the night of the fire."

She hands the false watch to him, and when he takes it from her, he immediately opens it to confirm that the miniature has survived. He lies there for several seconds, just staring at the woman's face.

"It's a portrait of my wife," he says finally.

"I had wondered," says Sally, "about the *FS*."

"The *F* is for Faith."

"She's lovely."

"It's a good likeness, but not perfect. She was even more beautiful in person."

"Tom said she died a few years ago."

"Yes," he says and snaps the case shut, as if he suddenly regrets bringing her up.

"My husband died three years ago," Sally offers. "I have no likeness of him, so I must trust my memory, which grows less reliable each year."

"I'm sorry."

"For my loss or my bad memory?" she says with a smile.

"Both, I suppose."

"I've been thinking about him a great deal these last several days. And in the theater, when I didn't know whether I would live or die."

"I thought of Faith then, too. It didn't seem so terrible, the idea of dying. Because I knew she'd managed to do it with such grace."

His words take the wind out of her. "Yes, exactly. Nothing ever feels quite so frightening again."

"I don't know," he says, meeting her eyes with a steady gaze. "The thing that frightens me now is the starting over."

JACK

It's still dark out when Jack is shaken awake.

"What?" he says, startled, as he tries to make out the shape of a man looming over him.

"Get up."

Anderson. Jack freezes in fear. Could word of his confession already have made its way back to Placide? Of course it could have. He was naive to believe otherwise.

"I didn't say anything," he whispers preemptively as Anderson rips the thin blanket from around his shoulders.

"I should hope not," Anderson says. "Seriously, get up. Placide wants us downstairs."

All Jack can think is that Ritchie has returned, with the rest of the committee, to make his arrests. "Did Placide say what this is about?" he asks as he rises from his makeshift pallet.

"I have my suspicions," says Anderson, but he is apparently unwilling to share them with Jack. "Come on."

In the tavern's back room, Jack can hear Placide issuing instructions. "File in, yes, all of you. There's plenty of room." He sounds so collegial, downright cooperative, even.

Jack arrives at the bottom of the stairs, and to his great surprise, Placide greets him warmly, with a clap on the shoulder and a *Just in time*. The greeting is so atypical that Jack immediately suspects something is wrong. Could this be a trap? Maybe word got back to Placide that Jack turned on him, and his plan is to wait until they have him entirely surrounded, then pounce? Jack eyes the door that leads to the taproom. He'll never make it out alive.

West, who is sporting a fat lip after yesterday's fight with Anderson, is seated at a table with Twaits and Caulfield and Lydia. He pulls out a chair and motions for Jack to sit.

"Where's Green?" Jack asks, but nobody's seen him since his interview with Ritchie.

Soon, Perry joins them. "What's this I'm hearing about the funeral moving locations?"

Jack looks at West, but West won't meet his eye.

"Roy says they're digging a big hole in the center of the pit as we speak," says Perry.

"You didn't sell, did you?" Twaits asks West, but he doesn't answer.

From the next table over comes Anderson's voice. "Maybe his dignity got the better of him."

"What does he mean by that?" Jack asks West, but before he can answer him, Ritchie arrives, accompanied by two men, and a pit forms in the bottom of Jack's stomach.

Jack had assumed Ritchie would bring the sheriff or some of his representatives to make the necessary arrests. But he recognizes the two men Ritchie has brought with him; they were at the capitol and are both members of the inquest committee. William Marshall and Samuel Somebody. Neither of them looks equipped to help Ritchie round up this many people. Jack cranes his neck to get a better look out the window. Perhaps there is a bevy of rougher, more able-bodied men waiting outside?

Placide claps his hands to get everyone's attention. "Quiet, please. Mr. Ritchie has something he wants to say to you all." He motions for Ritchie to take the floor.

Ritchie steps forward and shakes Placide's hand. "Thank you, Mr. Placide."

This is all so civil. Too civil. Jack has to be missing something.

"Thank you for joining us at this early hour. We are dealing with an extremely delicate situation that needs to be addressed before the funeral can get underway."

Jack isn't sure what the funeral should have to do with anything.

"It has become clear to us," says Ritchie, "that the fire was not started as the result of a slave revolt."

Here it comes. Jack would give anything not to be in this room right now.

"The real culprit was a faulty pulley and the bad judgment of several otherwise intelligent and capable men."

Ritchie pauses to let his words sink in, and the room begins to buzz. The players are clearly surprised to have had their version of events summarily dismissed, and Jack reminds himself that he, too, should act like he didn't know this news was coming.

"We have testimony outlining exactly how the fire began, and know for a fact that at least a half dozen of you were directly involved, to say nothing of the rest of you, who have lied through your teeth these last three days."

Jack looks at Lydia, wants to find a way to apologize to her for what is about to unfold, but her eyes are on her father.

"Who testified against us?" asks Anderson.

Jack is beginning to wish Anderson had just squeezed the life out of him, in that thicket, when he had the chance.

"It was Jack, wasn't it?" he says.

Ritchie is serene. "Mr. Gibson is not my source."

Jack is relieved to hear him say this, but Anderson won't let it go. "Well, then who was?"

"The same person who went to Skelton, of course," says Ritchie.

The room is quiet, until Twaits asks the obvious question. "And who was that?"

"You really don't know?" Ritchie looks almost amused. "I would have thought it was obvious."

A few of them try to guess.

"Green?" Twaits says doubtfully.

"Perry?" says Anderson, to which Perry shouts, "Hey!"

Ritchie is clearly enjoying himself. "Mr. Gibson, even you cannot figure it out?"

What is Ritchie doing? Now Jack has to pretend they haven't just talked about this very thing? "I, uh, I couldn't say."

Ritchie waits for the room to quiet, then he says, in a voice not much louder than a whisper, "You must promise there will be no retribution. The poor woman has been through enough."

"Woman?" some of the men repeat to themselves.

"My source is Mrs. Green."

The whole room takes a collective breath. "Christ," says Anderson, speaking for everyone.

"She was quite beside herself," says Ritchie. "It's only natural that she should want justice for her only child."

Some of the men shake their heads in sympathy. Others suck on their teeth. But it's clear, looking around the room, that Ritchie knows what he is doing. No one is going to go after Mrs. Green, not after what she's been through.

"So, now that we've put that sad business to bed," says Ritchie, "it's time to look toward the future."

Jack doesn't like where this is going.

"Mr. West has very generously agreed to sell the land the theater sits on to the city, which will allow us to bury the dead beneath the ruins." He waits a moment, to let this information sink in. "And, in exchange, we are prepared to cut you all a deal."

❧ | GILBERT | ❧

When *Gilbert comes to, his brother-in-law's* face is looming over him.

"Cecil?"

"That's me," he says, and Gilbert squeezes his eyes closed, then opens them again, to make sure he's not dreaming.

"You got a nasty bump on the head, but you gonna be all right."

Gilbert touches the top of his head, and sure enough, there is an ugly gash near his hairline.

Over Cecil's shoulder, he sees iron grating, and beyond that, the not-quite dawn. "Where am I?" he asks.

"The birdcage," says Cecil, and Gilbert pulls himself up on his elbows and looks around.

The birdcage is as strange a structure as any in the city; it sits at the northeast end of the market bridge and is shaped like an octagon, with a long parapet that runs around the perimeter. The brick building has iron gratings on three sides and a floor that rises up like an amphitheater so that everyone coming and going on E Street can see exactly who's been picked up overnight.

"Kemp and his men brought you in here a little while ago, which has got to be some kind of first."

"You mean, a first officer of the patrol arresting his own slave?"

"Exactly."

"It was Price who insisted on it," says Gilbert, and Cecil just shakes his head.

Cecil looks like he's aged a hundred years in the last few days. His shoulders are stooped, he's got bags under his eyes, and his lips are dry and cracked.

"Help me sit up," Gilbert says, and Cecil grips one of his hands and pulls.

When he is upright, Cecil sits down beside him. "You hear anything about Cecily?" he asks immediately. "Did she make it home from the theater?"

All Gilbert wants to do is tell his brother-in-law that Cecily's all right. But there must be a hundred men in the cage. Some of them are still asleep, some of them are trying to be, and some of them are wide awake and hungry for any morsel of information that might help them get out of here.

"Lean in," Gilbert says quietly.

Cecil's so sure he knows what's coming that he starts to choke on his words. "They couldn't find her, could they?"

"Closer."

When Gilbert is satisfied no one will hear what he has to say, he whispers, "For the benefit of everybody in here, I need you to act like I'm telling you she's dead. She ain't, but you act like she is. Understand?"

Cecil has to be confused, but he doesn't show it. He just nods real slow.

"I'm sorry," Gilbert says, this time in a voice loud enough for any eavesdropper to appreciate.

To anyone in the birdcage, it looks like Cecil's just gotten bad news. But the thing is, relief and sorrow don't look so different, at least in the beginning. When Cecil pulls his knees up to his chest, hides his face in his arms, and begins to weep, Gilbert can tell he's not putting on a show. His daughter is alive, and he is genuinely moved to learn of it.

They sit like that for a long time—Cecil softly crying into the sleeves of his coat, and Gilbert looking up at the pale moon, still visible in the violet sky. When his brother-in-law finally raises his head and dries his eyes, Gilbert gestures at the men around them. "This all because of the theater fire?" he asks.

Cecil nods.

Gilbert's never seen the jail so crowded.

"They just keep coming," says Cecil. "Every man more confused than the next as to why he's here."

"Anyone been released?"

Cecil shakes his head. "Slavers been down here all day, with affidavits and witnesses, arguing for the release of one fellow or another. That man over there," he says, tilting his head in the direction of an agitated young

man with a pockmarked face, "has a slaver and about twenty other witnesses saying he was serving at a dinner party on Thursday night, and it
don't matter."

"Master Price show up?"

"Him I haven't seen."

"Well, he's had his hands full with that eldest son of his," says Gilbert.

"Oh?"

"I'll let Della fill you in."

Cecil leans his head back and closes his eyes.

"So, what are they gonna do with everybody in here?" Gilbert asks.

"Damned if I know. There was talk, early on, about the gallows. But
now I'm not so sure."

"They won't do anything that drastic," says Gilbert. "Not when they
don't got any proof."

"Well, they got more proof than I'd like."

Gilbert raises an eyebrow in Cecil's direction.

"One of the actors came down here yesterday and started picking us
out. Must have pointed to about fifteen or twenty of us. A clerk wrote
down all our names."

"You saying he wrote down yours?"

"Mmmmhmmm."

"Like he's telling people he saw you?"

"Outside the theater. The night of the fire. Waving a torch around."

Gilbert shakes his head. "You wouldn't believe it if it wasn't true."

"Nope."

A thought occurs to Gilbert. "Was he a big man? The fellow who
picked you out?"

"That's right," says Cecil. "With eyebrows as thick as turds."

Gilbert should have known as much. "His name's Billy Twaits. Came
by Kemp's, trying to rile him up. That man is lying through his teeth."

"Well," says Cecil, "I hope somebody figures that out before they get
around to deciding what they want to do with the names on that list."

🏵 | CECILY | 🏵

Della finds a stool and motions for Cecily to sit, then she goes to ask Samuel if he's got a comb and some grease.

While she's gone, Cecily removes her headscarf and runs her fingers over her hair. She put it in a couple of thick twists last Sunday and hasn't touched it since.

To her relief, the bump on her forehead has gone down. When she presses on it, it's still sore, but in another few days, it will disappear completely.

Della returns with a wire brush and a jar of kerosene. "Best he's got," she says as she gets to work.

Cecily tries to savor the feeling of her mother's hands on her head, the care and love that goes into each brushstroke. She has been sitting, on a stool just like this one, for nineteen years, and it is impossible to believe that—if all goes well—this is the last time Della will ever perform this simple act of love.

"Mama," says Cecily, "what you said about Master Price and me. To Elliott, when you was in front of the cabin."

The brush in Della's hand stills. "You heard all that?"

"I came up from the boathouse, to tell you they had Moses."

"I see." She takes a deep breath, then says, "I'm sorry you had to find out like that."

Cecily doesn't mean to make her mother feel worse than she already does. "I think some part of me has known for a long time, but I was scared that if I said anything—that if Papa knew I knew—it might change something between us."

"Oh, baby," her mother whispers, "nothing could change the way he feels about you."

At some level, Cecily knows that's true. Yet she's still got to ask, "Gilbert told me Papa's always known. Is that right?"

Della lets out a note or two of amused laughter. "Why you think he named you Cecily?"

Cecily tilts her face up toward the ceiling, trying to get a good look at her mother. "I guess I thought you named me."

"No, ma'am," says Della, gently guiding Cecily's head back down into position. "You were his from the start, and he wanted you to have a name that said so."

Once Della has finished combing out Cecily's hair, she smooths it back into a neat bun, which she secures with a few of her own hairpins. "Now stand up and turn around," she says as she takes a few steps back to admire her handiwork.

Cecily does as she is told. "Do I look like a Ruthie Mills? On my way to Philadelphia to visit my sister?"

"Ruthie?" her mother whispers.

"It's the name Uncle Gilbert gave me—on my papers."

She smiles so big all Cecily sees is teeth. "Ruthie was our mama's name."

"That's what he said."

Della touches Cecily's cheek. "It was always hard for me to talk about her. I was so young when we was separated, and it hurt so bad."

"I'm sorry I'm adding to your hurt."

She shakes her head. "This is different. You choosing to go, not being sold out from under me. And you got something better for yourself in store."

"If I ever have a daughter," says Cecily, "she's gonna be tired of hearing about you."

Della's eyes have gone all glassy, and she blinks once and then twice to keep from crying. "I got to go soon."

Cecily doesn't know if she will be able to bear watching her mother leave. "Stay a few more minutes?"

"I can't," says Della with a sad smile. "It's getting light, and I got to go get ready for your funeral."

Just the sound of those words from her mother's lips sends a shiver up Cecily's spine. "Master Price said you could go?"

"He's letting anyone in the quarters go who wants to."

"Elliott must love that."

"No one's seen him since yesterday afternoon."

"You think he's still out there, looking for me?"

"Maybe," says Della. "But it won't do him much good soon."

Cecily assumes that some part of her will always be looking over her shoulder, expecting Elliott to jump out at her when she least expects it. With time and distance and a little bit of God's grace, she prays he'll forget her.

"Oh," says Cecily, remembering Moses's sweater and jacket. "Will you give these back to Mo? Thank him for loaning them to me, and tell him he don't make a terrible turkey."

Della takes the clothing and hugs it to her chest.

"I almost forgot," says Della. "I wanted to give you something." She reaches into her pocket and pulls out one of the little animals Cecil's always whittling. This one's the bluebird, carved from the river birch that grows in the woods behind her parents' cabin.

The bird is in flight, and Cecily runs her finger along the beak, the wings, the tail. "I love it," she says softly.

"Something to remember us by."

"I don't need anything to remember you by," says Cecily as she begins to sob. "You and Papa and Moses and the girls will always be with me, wherever I go."

❧ | JACK | ❧

T*he deal is remarkably straightforward. In* exchange for the land, which the burial committee dearly wants, the inquest committee is prepared to issue a report absolving the company of all wrongdoing.

Jack can scarcely concentrate on the words coming out of Ritchie's mouth. When he went to him last night with the real story, he thought he'd been doing the right thing, thought that his testimony would result in the troupe paying for what it had done. But now he sees that all he did was give Ritchie what he needed to blackmail West.

Ritchie places the papers in front of Placide, who has pulled up a chair beside Twaits. "Remember, it's a draft."

Placide's eyes are weak, so he hands the pages to Twaits, and it's he who reads the first few sentences aloud:

> We, the committee appointed by our fellow-citizens "to enquire into the causes of the melancholy catastrophe" which took place in this city, on Thursday night last—a catastrophe which has spread a gloom over a whole city, and filled every eye with tears—has given to this melancholy duty all the attention in our power. We feel it due to ourselves; it was due to the world, to collect all the lights which might serve to elucidate an event whose effects are so deeply written on our hearts. We have seen every person who was behind the scenes, that was best able to assist our enquiries, we have heard their statements, and after sifting them as accurately as possible, beg leave to submit the following report to our afflicted citizens.

"Christ, you're not the most succinct writer, are you?" says Twaits after he's taken a breath. "You should try to write for the stage. It'd break you of your run-on sentences."

"It might be worth remembering, Mr. Twaits," says Ritchie with a grimace, "that no one is off the hook quite yet. Until we have the deed to the land, it's still subject to change."

Twaits shuts his mouth and hands the report back to Placide. While Placide squints at it, Jack leans close and tries to read over his shoulder. He sees the words *chandelier* and *fatal* and *flawed*.

At one point, Placide looks up at Ritchie and says, "I thought you were going to make us look good."

"I'm a journalist, not a novelist," says Ritchie. "Every word in this report is true."

Placide tosses the papers into the middle of the table. "Well, if that's the case, then what, precisely, are we doing here?"

"Calm down," Ritchie says. "I think you will find that this report satisfies both our needs."

"Meaning?"

"I document all the facts—the existence of the chandelier, the order to raise it into the flyspace, and the subsequent order to bring it back down. But I have taken a page from Skelton's book and do not document who did what."

Jack can't believe what he's hearing, but Placide leans forward in his chair and says, "Go on."

"Well, take, for instance, Green's order to raise the chandelier," says Ritchie, gathering up the papers and shuffling through them until he finds the line he's looking for. "I say that the stagehand who raised the chandelier heard a voice, but that it reached him without his seeing the person."

"It was Green's voice," says Jack. He's already told Ritchie that.

"That may be, but did you *see* him?"

Is Ritchie really giving him a hard time, after everything he told him?

"Well, did you?" Ritchie asks again.

"Of course I saw him."

"At the exact moment he told you to raise the chandelier?"

Who's to say? "Maybe I was looking up at the chandelier, but I knew he was behind me."

"Ah, you see, I take this all into account," Ritchie says as he adjusts his spectacles and begins to read directly from the document. "'He does not pretend positively to recognize him.'"

"What does that even mean? I do not 'pretend positively to recognize him'? I don't have to pretend anything. I actually recognized him."

Placide scowls at Jack. "Mr. Gibson, you are not helping matters."

Jack is completely exasperated. It feels as if the lies will never end.

"What about Roy?" asks Placide.

"I make a point not to use his name. I just call him a carpenter. The same goes for Mr. Perry."

Anderson asks, "Is my name in there?"

"Yes," says Ritchie, but he rushes to reassure him. "I give you the credit for knowing the lamp had a problem and for attempting to inform the crew." Jack watches Anderson's chest grow as big as a barrel and thinks he might need to leave the room.

There is more shuffling of papers as the others demand to know their contributions to this alternate version of events.

Is it really this easy? West forfeits the land, the committee writes up this report, and they all go on their way? No fines, no jail time, no gallows, no nothing? At this point, Jack might even be invited to Charleston. Might get to play the role of Feste after all. He hates that there's a tiny part of him that thrills at the prospect.

"What about Mr. Gibson here?" says Anderson. "Surely, his name is all over that document?"

"Go to hell," says Jack.

Ritchie gives Jack a sympathetic smile. "I make reference to a stage-hand, but Mr. Gibson can rest assured that his name does not appear in the report."

Jack has to do something to squash the part of him that wants—no, needs—the acceptance of Anderson and the other actors. These men don't have consciences, and if he allows this charade to continue, he won't have one, either.

"My name should appear in the report," says Jack before he can stop himself. "All of our names should be there."

Everyone, including Lydia, looks at him like he's just committed treason.

"What?" says Jack, grabbing the report from Ritchie and waving it in the air. "Put my name on this thing. In big letters. I want it to read: JACK GIBSON STARTED THE FIRE."

"You didn't, though," says Ritchie.

"How do you know?" says Jack. "You only know what I told you."

Anderson is on him in a flash. "So, it *was* you who told!"

Jack hadn't intended to out himself, but what does he even care at this point? "We're responsible for the deaths of close to a hundred people."

Under the table, Placide slams his shoe down on Jack's foot, and Jack winces in pain. "I won't be silenced," he wheezes.

"You really went to the committee?" says Anderson. "After all of this?"

Jack glances at Lydia, whose eyes have turned to slits. "I was trying to do the right thing."

"The right thing would have been for you to never have been born."

"Stand down, Mr. Anderson," says Ritchie without so much as raising his voice. "There will be no retaliation."

"We would never," says Anderson indignantly. "This company is like a family."

West lets out a choked laugh. The deed to the property, which was once held by his actual family, sits in front of him.

"Well," says Ritchie, "I would advise the whole 'family' to leave town as soon as possible."

"I can get everyone on a boat leaving Norfolk by week's end," says Placide.

"I wouldn't dally getting to Norfolk, if I were you. Once word gets out that the fire can't be blamed on the city's Negro population, there are going to be a lot of disappointed people."

❀ | SALLY | ❀

An hour passes, and then two, and still Mr. Scott and Sally do not run out of things to say to each other. But the sun has risen, the streets are growing crowded, and soon the burial committee will arrive, ready to receive the girl under the stairs. Sally should go and offer to help Mrs. Cowley move her onto the porch.

"Do you need anything else?" Sally asks Mr. Scott as she stands to go. It's funny, but she doesn't want to leave.

"Will you return?" he asks, and without realizing quite what she's doing, she squeezes his hand.

"I will," she says. "Soon." It isn't an empty promise.

On her way downstairs, she stops to check on Margaret.

"Archie not here yet?" she says, feigning surprise when she notes he has not yet arrived. But Margaret is asleep and cannot appreciate the barb.

Sally regrets not closing the window last night. The room smells better—cleaner—but it's chilly. Thankfully, someone had come in during the night to put more coal on the fire and an extra quilt on the bed. She assumes that someone was Mrs. Cowley, and she is, as always, grateful for her kindness and good sense.

Sally closes the window, then shovels more coal into the grate. Finally, she turns her attention to Margaret, who sleeps deeply in the middle of the bed. Sally smooths the quilts, but it's not until she gets them pulled tight around Margaret's shoulders that she realizes her sister-in-law is shivering.

"Margaret," she says softly, "are you cold?"

Margaret doesn't respond.

"I left the window open last night, which was silly of me."

The talk is just nervous chatter. It's not until Sally touches her hand to Margaret's head that she realizes something is wrong. "Margaret?"

She rushes to the door, calls down the stairs to Mrs. Cowley. "There's something wrong with Margaret!"

She doesn't wait for a response, just returns to Margaret's bedside and rips off her quilts. Margaret shivers violently, but doesn't wake.

"Don't do this, Margaret," Sally pleads as she begins to unwrap the bandages around her leg. "Please don't do this."

Mrs. Cowley appears in the doorway. "What is it?" she asks.

"She's got a fever."

The old woman closes her eyes, like she's just been delivered a blow, then she joins Sally beside the bed.

When the leg is unwrapped, Mrs. Cowley touches the edges of the wound with the tips of her fingers. "Feel this?"

The skin is red and warm to the touch.

"It's infected?" says Sally.

Mrs. Cowley nods, then says, "I'll send Birdie for the surgeon."

"What good will he do now?"

"Not much."

Sally stands there for several long minutes, staring at her beloved friend. "God damn you, Archie," she says, more to herself than to Mrs. Cowley.

"Pardon?" says the old woman.

"He wanted her whole."

❊ | JACK | ❊

After the paperwork is taken care of, Ritchie remains at the tavern long enough to supervise the writing of an apology letter, which he intends to publish in the next edition of the *Enquirer*. "It is only fitting," he says as he presents Placide with paper and pen, but anyone with half a thought in his head knows that this letter has as much to do with selling copies of his newspaper as anything else.

Placide attempts to put a few sentences together, but nothing meets Ritchie's approval. Finally, Placide hands the pen to Anderson. "Why don't you try?"

Anderson demurs—for a moment, at least—then he takes the pen and scratches out an apology for the ages:

To the Citizens of Richmond:

In the sincerity of afflicted minds and deeply wounded hearts, permit us to express the anguish which we feel for the late dreadful calamity; of which we cannot but consider ourselves the innocent cause.

From a liberal and enlightened community we fear no reproaches; but we are conscious that many have too much cause to wish they had never known us. To their mercy we appeal for forgiveness—not for a crime committed, but for one which could not be prevented.

Our own loss cannot be estimated but by ourselves. 'Tis true (with one exception), we have not to lament the loss of life—but we have lost our friends, our patrons, our property, and in part, our homes. Nor is this all our loss. In this miserable calamity, we find a sentence of banishment from your hospitable city. No more do we expect to feel that glow of pleasure which pervades a grateful heart, while it receives favors liberally bestowed. Never again shall we behold that feminine human-ity which is eagerly displayed itself to soothe the victims of disease, and view with exultation the benevolent who fostered the fatherless, and shed comfort on the departing soul of a dying mother. Here then, we cease. The eloquence of grief is silence.

When it is done, Ritchie asks all of the company's lead actors to sign their names to it. Anderson does so, then hands the pen to Placide, who signs for himself and also Green because no one has seen him all morning. Young, Twaits, Burke—they all comply.

Only West refuses, which doesn't surprise Jack. "I think I've sacrificed enough for today."

No one argues with him.

After Ritchie has packed up his papers, the letter among them, he asks Jack if he would like to see him out. Jack nods, and follows him out of the back room and down the narrow hallway that leads to the taproom. At the door of the tavern, Ritchie turns to him. "You did the right thing, telling me the truth. Even if it doesn't feel like it."

"Nothing came of it."

"We needed the land—a burial on the site is what makes the most sense."

Jack gives Ritchie a nod of understanding, although the truth is that nothing makes much sense to him anymore.

"Will you stay here in Richmond?" Ritchie asks. "After the troupe goes back to Charleston?"

Jack hasn't given it much thought, but he doesn't see how he can possibly remain in this town. Everywhere he looks, for as long as he lives, he'll see reminders of what he has done. "I think I probably need to start over somewhere new."

Ritchie doesn't argue.

"It's strange, though. To think of going to a new city, whose streets my father has never walked."

"Your father was a good man."

Jack doesn't need Ritchie to tell him so, but he likes hearing it all the same.

"Something tells me you will be, too."

"You think so?"

"I do."

Jack flushes, then remembers that he wanted to ask Ritchie something. "What will happen to all the Negroes who were rounded up and jailed?"

"Your 'vile incendiaries'?"

Jack swallows.

"I suppose they'll have to be released," says Ritchie, as if he hasn't spent a moment thinking about them. "Can't very well keep them locked up if we've got a confession from Placide and Green."

"Will they be released soon?"

"Eventually."

Ritchie places his hat on his head and tips it in Jack's direction. "If we meet again, may it be under better circumstances."

Jack prays to God there are better circumstances waiting for him.

He watches Ritchie go, then returns to the back room, where Placide is shouting orders at anyone within earshot. Placide has hired two private coaches that will carry the company to Norfolk. If they move quickly, he tells everyone, no one will know the players have left town until long after they're gone.

It has been decided that Placide and Twaits will remain behind, for a week or two at most, to close up the company's accounts. Green will also stay in Richmond for the foreseeable future, although it is not clear how useful he will be to the company. He wants to convince Frances to return to Charleston with him, which seems unlikely given the circumstances.

Placide sends the women and children back to the boardinghouse to pack. "The coach will pick you up from Mrs. Barrett's," he instructs. "Have the trunks ready."

When Lydia makes to follow her mother out of the tavern's back room, without so much as a backward glance at Jack, he reaches for her hand and whispers, "May I speak with you?"

She removes her hand from his and shoves it underneath her cape and out of reach. "There's nothing to say."

"Are you angry with me?"

Her mother tells her she will meet her outside, and Lydia promises that she'll be only a moment. The room clears.

"Should I have told you?" Jack asks.

"That you were planning to turn us all in?"

He nods.

"I'm not your keeper."

"No, but I thought we were—"

"We were what, Jack?"

Jack wishes there were a word for the person you think about when you're drifting off to sleep. The person whom you believe might see you as you really are. In the end, all Jack can say is "Friends."

Lydia softens. "I don't blame you for what you did," she says finally.

"But you wouldn't have done it."

She shakes her head no. "I know Anderson was being facetious when he called the company a family, but from my perspective, it's true."

"Lydia—"

"If you hurt the company, you hurt my father, my mother, and—ultimately—me."

"But what about all those other families? In the audience? Aren't they hurting, too?"

"It's terrible what happened," Lydia agrees. "And, if I could change it, I would. But I fail to see how sending my parents to prison, or worse, will make those families whole."

Now that she's stated her position so clearly, Jack feels stupid for ever believing she might have sided with him. "Your father is lucky to have you," he says softly.

"And I him."

Before Jack can say another word, she bends down and places a whisper of a kiss on his cheek. Then she is gone.

Jack rubs his cheek as he takes the stairs to the tavern's guest rooms. Anderson's room is empty, the door ajar, and when Jack spies the actor's leather valise at the foot of his bed, he decides to take it. It's the least the scab can do for him.

In the room he shared with Robertson and Burke, Jack packs his comb, his sleeping cap, and his extra shirt. Then he reaches under the bed, where he's hidden a stack of maybe a dozen scripts. He runs his finger over the spines. *The Castle Spectre*, *Adelgitha*, *The Curfew*. All are favorites of his that he couldn't bear to return to the trunk, backstage, where Placide stored the company's extra scripts. Of course, now, no one will ever know that these copies weren't destroyed with the rest of the trunk's contents.

Jack can't take them all with him, not when he doesn't know where he's going or how long it will take him to get there. But he pulls the stack out from under the bed and finds the one script he wants. It's a copy of *The Father*, which will always remind Jack of what could have been. He slips it into the valise and leaves the rest of the scripts in the middle of the floor, where one of the other actors is sure to find them.

Downstairs, Jack runs into Placide, who doesn't greet him so much as ask him to leave. "You're still here?"

"I'm on my way out."

"West was looking for you."

"Oh?"

"He's outside, I think. Watching the procession."

Jack nods, tries to think of something he can say to Placide in parting. *It was a pleasure? I'm sorry things didn't turn out better?* Anything he comes up with will sound utterly daft. Anderson acted like it was an honor to get to wipe Placide's arse, and maybe under different circumstances, Jack would have felt the same way. But after everything that's happened, Jack has come to believe that men like Placide shouldn't be treated like they can do no wrong. In fact, that might be the worst thing for them.

器 | GILBERT | 器

Gilbert *watches through the bars of* the birdcage as the street below him begins to bustle with people, all of them on their way to the theater ruins. By midmorning, the streets are so crowded, people are having a hard time getting their carts and buggies down E Street.

It hurts Gilbert to think about missing the funeral, losing the chance to say goodbye to Louisa. But he reminds himself that colored folk will be at the back of the procession, so he's probably just about as close to the funeral, here in the birdcage, as he was ever likely to get.

Out of nowhere, Sara appears on the street below. She is wearing her best dress and has pulled her hair into a tight knot at the back of her head. She looks beautiful, but he can tell she's worried, just seeing the pinched look on her face.

Sara speaks with one of the guards and is allowed to climb the stairs to the catwalk that circles the cage. Gilbert watches her approach and is struck by how lucky he is to call her his wife. "You found me," he says when she's close enough to hear him without his having to shout.

"When that boy you sent said you had paid him in rock candy, I was sure he had the wrong man."

Gilbert grins. "It's the only thing I had on me."

She reaches through the bars and touches the top of his head, feeling the spot where the skin is split open. It hurts, but he lets the pads of her fingers press on the swollen skin.

"Everything go all right with the delivery?" she asks.

"As far as I know," he says.

She looks relieved. "So, why you in here?"

"Kemp caught me with a fake pass. And Price is throwing a fit, thinking I got something to do with Cecily's disappearance."

She shakes her head in disbelief.

"It'll sort itself out," he says. "Kemp's still head of the patrol, and every day I don't work, he's losing money."

"What about the rest of them?" she says, tilting her head in Cecil's direction. He gives Sara a wave.

"It's all this business with the theater fire."

"Hey, Cecil," she calls, then asks Gilbert what their brother-in-law knows.

"I told him as much as I could get away with."

Sara nods, speaks to Cecil directly. "I'll try to pay a visit to Della later. Check in on her."

Cecil gives her a nod of thanks.

She looks past him, at the dozens upon dozens of men perched in the birdcage like canaries. "I'm hearing folks say it was the actors who set the fire."

He turns and gives Cecil a knowing glance. "Doesn't that sound about right?"

Cecil just shakes his head.

When Gilbert returns his attention to Sara, she's got tears streaming down her face. "What's wrong?" he asks as he wraps his hands around hers.

"The Prestons won't sell."

He closes his eyes. Tries to take in what she's saying. "Won't sell right now? Or ever?"

"General Preston called me into the parlor this morning and told me about Phyllis Johnston's proposal. Said it was a very generous offer, but that I have to understand Elizabeth needs me now more than ever."

"Because of Louisa?"

"No, Gillie," says Sara.

"Why, then?"

Her face crumbles, and she can barely get out the words. "She's having a baby."

What Sara's saying to him doesn't make sense. "Missus Elizabeth is having a baby?"

Sara nods.

"Ain't she too old?"

"She's forty-four."

Gilbert wants to sit down, but there's nowhere to sit without leaving Sara's side. "A baby," he whispers.

"They've known for a few weeks, but haven't told anybody yet."

Gilbert tries to think fast. "Did the general already tell Mrs. Johnston no? Because it don't have to be you that raises that baby. They can take the money from all those white ladies and buy a wet nurse. Someone who's raised her own children and knows how it's done."

He's said the wrong thing, knows it as soon as the words are out of his mouth.

"I spent seventeen years raising Louisa," she says slowly. "Just because I never had a baby of my own don't mean I don't know how it's done."

"That's not what I meant," Gilbert soothes.

"The general told me that Elizabeth can't imagine this baby being brought up by anyone other than me. She wants me to help him know his brother and sister."

Gilbert counts up the years in his head. By the time this baby of Elizabeth's is grown, Sara will be forty-eight years old. Too old to start a family on their own terms.

Gilbert can feel the tears welling up in his eyes. "Is there no end to what they'll ask for?"

Sara just shakes her head and releases a choked sob.

He feels like a fool for leading her on, for making her believe that they ever had any control over their own lives. What was it he had said, just a few nights ago, when he pulled her onto his lap in the kitchen house? *It ain't always going to be like this.* She hadn't believed him then, he could tell, but something had shifted in her these last few days. Maybe it was losing Louisa or maybe it was hearing about Mrs. Johnston's offer. Maybe it was just knowing how Cecily had seized her chance at a different kind of life when it was presented to her. Whatever the reason, Sara had begun to believe Gilbert, had begun to believe that they were on the cusp of something better.

"We can still have a good life," he promises. "You at the Prestons' and me at Kemp's. It ain't that far, between our two places. And it'll get warmer soon. We'll be back in the garden, where the jasmine smell so good."

"Oh, Gillie," she whispers, and he knows her heart is breaking.

"I'll keep trying, Sara. You know I will. And there will be other opportunities. By and by."

She gives him that old, familiar disbelieving look of hers, and he feels a little steadier. Gilbert can live with disbelieving, because even now—after everything that's happened—he thinks his dreams might be big enough for them both.

❦ | JACK | ❦

Jack finds West on the tavern's front porch, watching the mourners file past. "Placide said you were looking for me?"

"Yes," he says, reaching into the pocket of his coat for a letter. "I realize you won't be coming with us to Charleston, so I wanted to give you this."

Jack turns the letter over in his hand. It's addressed to *To Whom It May Concern*. "What is this?"

"It's a letter of introduction."

"From Placide?"

"No," says West with a short laugh. "It's from me."

Jack wrinkles his forehead.

"My name won't get you far at Drury Lane," says West. "But it might get you a bit part at John Street. When you get there, ask for Eddie."

"I don't deserve this."

West nods, more to himself than to Jack. "I understand how you might feel that way. But what happened at the theater was a terrible tragedy—not evidence that you don't belong on the stage."

"You really think so?"

"I do. If you love the feeling you get when you're in a theater and the lights go out, and you're willing to work very hard, then you'll figure the rest out."

"I don't know what to say," says Jack.

"There's a little sterling in there, too. Enough to get you up to New York."

"Thank you."

"You may not have heard," says West, "but I've recently come into a little money."

"I did," Jack says, playing along, but then he gets serious. "I'm sorry you had to sell the property."

West waves off his sympathies and tips his hat in the direction of the funeral procession. "If I ever needed a good reminder that it doesn't matter, this is it."

A group of clergy, in their vestments, walks past.

"It's hard to believe that this is how it ends," says Jack as they watch the street.

"This isn't an ending," says West. "It's just an intermission."

"You think theater will ever return to Richmond?"

West shoves his hands in his pockets. "'Time heals all wounds.' Isn't that what they say?"

"It's difficult to imagine."

"Yes, but thankfully, that's what we actors are good at," he says, and he gives Jack's arm a light squeeze.

In the distance, the bells toll. "I thought I might join the procession," says Jack. "Pay my respects to the dead."

"That's a nice idea."

"Do you want to join me?"

"The stagecoach will be here soon," says West, "so I think this is as far as I go."

Jack tucks West's letter into the valise, then gives the case an affectionate pat.

"Goodbye," he says as the two shake hands.

Jack is halfway down the tavern's porch steps when West calls after him, "Is that Anderson's bag?"

Jack turns. "It might be," he says with a sly grin.

West laughs. "He won't hear a word about it from me."

❦ | SALLY | ❦

Sally stands on Mrs. Cowley's front porch, looking for any sign of Birdie or Dr. Foushee. It's half past nine, and Birdie's been gone for almost two hours.

It's no surprise. The city is overflowing with people and the streets are packed with funeral goers. Sally puts the girl's chances of locating Dr. Foushee, not to mention convincing him to pay a house call during the funeral, at less than nothing. Still, she watches the road.

Upstairs, Mrs. Cowley is giving Margaret a sponge bath. They have tried a willow bark tincture and a yarrow root tea, too. The most any of these treatments can do is fight the fever—not the infection—which means that all they're really doing is making Margaret more comfortable.

Archie has not shown back up at Mrs. Cowley's, and Sally can't say she's surprised. The city is grieving, but it's also chock-full of out-of-towners, and if she knows Archie—and she thinks she does—he is shaking hands and offering condolences like calling cards. When he eventually comes to check on his wife, Sally will have a hard time looking at him, much less explaining the turn Margaret's condition has taken.

Sally can watch the funeral procession snake its way around the perimeter of the green. It is just as it was described in the *Enquirer*. First the city's clergymen, then the immediate families of the deceased. Dignitaries—members of the Common Council, the Court of Hustings, the legislature, and half a dozen other entities—are next, and behind them are regular citizens on foot and, finally, on horseback.

Among the city's clergymen, she recognizes Reverend Blair and Reverend Buchanan from Sunday services at the capitol; they are accompanied by a rabbi, a priest, and several other men of God whose robes Sally doesn't recognize.

When the families of the deceased pass by, she spots the governor's wife right away. The young woman wears a stunned expression on her face and is trailed by at least a half-dozen children, including the boy who sat between her and her husband at the theater. He looks a good deal older than he did three days ago.

Sally also catches sight of the actress she spoke with at the capitol. Was her name Nancy? No, that was her daughter. The woman has shed her bloody nun's habit, which is an improvement. Instead, she wears a long cloak, in funereal black, with a bonnet to match. Sally is intrigued by the fact that she proceeds unaccompanied; she'd have thought the members of the theater company would have come out in droves to mourn the loss of one of their own.

Sally does a double take when she looks out into the crowd and sees William Wirt walking—head down—amid the mourners. To her knowledge, no one in his family has died.

Eventually, the procession stops in front of Mrs. Cowley's house and a man approaches the porch. "We're here for the girl you've got waiting for us."

Sally clears her throat and says, "This way." Then she leads him and another man through the front door and down the hall, until they are all staring at the dead girl, wrapped in a sheet, under the stairs.

"Have you discovered who she is?" Sally asks as the men stoop to pick her up.

"We haven't," says the man. "There are so many missing girls. And only a few of their bodies have been identified."

"Should we try though?" Sally asks as she follows them back down the hall. "Surely, her parents are somewhere in the procession."

"Mrs. Cowley said the face wasn't recognizable."

"No," Sally agrees. "But a mother knows her own child."

"It won't work," the man says. "It's too complicated to arrange, and to what end?"

Sally begins to argue, then stops herself. Maybe he's right. Who would want to know that her child suffered for two long days, surrounded by strangers? Perhaps it's better for all these mothers to think that their daughters died instantly, that they didn't suffer?

"Do you have anyone else for us?" the man asks as they arrive back on the porch.

Sally thinks of Margaret upstairs. "No one," she says firmly.

She watches the men carry the girl down the steps and into the throng of people moving toward the theater's ruins. The girl gets smaller and smaller, but as Sally watches her disappear into the crowd, something in her snaps.

Without stopping to think about what she is doing, she dashes down the steps and into the procession, cutting and weaving her way through the mourners, until she catches sight of the girl once more. She follows her all the way to the theater site, where the procession comes to a halt.

In the center of what was once the pit, a wide hole yawns open, and the men lay the girl down beside a few other bodies, a pair of oversized mahogany coffins, and an assortment of urns. Reverend Buchanan, who is leading the service, urges the mourners to come as close as they can, and those who can hear him do as they're told. "We brought nothing into this world, and it is certain we can carry nothing out. The Lord gave, and the Lord hath taken away; blessed be the name of the Lord." He begins to read Psalm 39, but Sally doesn't hear the words. All she can do is stare at the small white bundle laying on the edge of the abyss and wonder at a Lord who would give the women in the theater neither the capacity to protect themselves nor the ability to articulate the barbarousness of their experiences. This poor girl's story—and that of so many others—will be buried with her.

After Reverend Buchanan has given his homily, the pallbearers use an ugly system of ropes to lower the boxes and urns into the oversized grave. Sally has a hard time watching the scene unfold, but she forces herself to remain where she is and to confirm that the girl has gone in the ground. When the body has disappeared into the gaping hole, Sally bows her head and says a private prayer. Then she immediately turns to go.

"Excuse me," she says quietly as she slips through the crowd and retraces the same path she took three days' prior—across the green—to Mrs. Cowley's.

In Margaret's room, the old woman keeps vigil.

"How is she?" Sally asks.

"No better, no worse."

Sally offers to sit with her, and Mrs. Cowley stands to go.

"Have you some paper and a pen?" Sally asks as her hostess prepares to take her leave.

"Of course."

And because Sally feels she owes her some explanation, she says, "I was thinking I might write my own account of the fire. While the details are still fresh in my mind."

"For the *Enquirer*?" Mrs. Cowley asks, doubtful.

Sally sighs. "There is no chance Mr. Ritchie will publish it."

"I would have been surprised."

"No, it will have to be enough to write it for myself. And for Margaret. For Margaret's children. And perhaps, if I am very lucky, my own."

糸Ⅰ CECILY Ⅰ糸

"A*re you about ready to go?*" Samuel asks Cecily after he has hitched the chaise to a horse.

Cecily looks around the barn, to be sure she has left no trace of herself behind. The free papers are on her person, and the remnants of her old life—her dress, her socks, her boots—are packed away inside Louisa Mayo's valise. In her pocket, she carries the bird her papa carved, hopeful that it will bring her luck. "I'm ready as I'll ever be," she tells Samuel as she rubs the bird's wings with the tip of her crooked finger.

Samuel walks around to the side of the chaise's coupe and opens the door, like he's a footman and she's some fine lady who's used to being helped into and out of carriages. He takes her bag, then offers her his hand so she can climb up into the seat. It's trickier than the ladies make it look—managing her skirt and the tiny little footstep at the same time, all while wearing such ridiculous shoes. When she is seated, he hands her the bag and she clutches it to her chest.

"I was going to tell you to keep the curtains drawn, but I think that, in the middle of the day, that might draw more attention to you. So, just sit low in your seat, and keep your bonnet down."

"I can do that."

"Of course, if we're stopped, I want you to sit up straight and tall, and act like you got every right in the world to be there."

Cecily smiles. "I can do that, too."

Samuel closes the carriage door and gives it a pat. Then he climbs up into the driver's seat. Cecily hears the short clicking noise he makes to get the horse to go, and the next thing she knows, the carriage is moving.

It's bumpy as Samuel steers them out of the yard and onto Twelfth Street, but once they are going in the right direction, the ride gets a little smoother, and Cecily has to remind herself not to look up, not to watch as the pieces of her life go trundling by.

They have barely gone a city block when their progress slows. Cecily begins to hear Samuel shout warnings like "On your right" and "Coming through." A few times, he has to pull the horse way back because someone has darted in front of their path. Once, when he does this, Cecily tumbles out of her seat.

Soon, Samuel brings the carriage to a near stop. "Road closed," a man announces, "on account of the procession."

Cecily hears Samuel ask him about a detour.

"Head east on I Street, then circle the theater and come out at the Baptist meetinghouse. You should be able to cross there."

If Samuel's nervous about changing up the route, Cecily can't tell. He talks to the horse in a calm and easy tone, and it has the effect of comforting her, too.

At H Street, where Samuel was expecting to cross, the crowd of funeral-goers is so big the horse can scarcely move. The chaise sits in the same spot for what feels like a quarter of an hour before Samuel recruits two men to clear them a path across the intersection.

They make their way, haltingly, across H Street, and when they do, Cecily glances out the window, in the direction of the green. She sees hundreds of heads bowed in prayer. Is this it? she wonders. Her own funeral? Never did she imagine anything so grand.

The carriage lurches forward—one block, then two. They are making their way around the Public Square now, but it is slow going, and Cecily is so nervous, she can't concentrate on anything but the creak of the wheels underneath her. She closes her eyes, tries to take a few good breaths, and that's when she hears a familiar voice, on the street, screaming something about a runaway slave.

Her eyes pop open, and her back straightens.

"Missing since Thursday night!" Elliott shouts. His voice sounds frantic, as if he's possessed.

Cecily shrinks into the carriage seat, trying to make her body as small as possible.

The carriage slows. From up in the driver's seat, she hears Samuel yell, "Watch out, sir," but Elliott, apparently, is paying him no mind.

"Take this," he says to someone. "Yes, here's one for you, too."

The carriage comes to a complete stop, and Cecily's pulse is pounding so hard, she can hear the thumping in her ears. Samuel says politely, "Sir, may I ask you to move?"

Elliott does not move. Instead, he shouts, "Have you seen a colored girl? Nineteen years old? About this high?"

"I have not," says Samuel, his voice as cool as creek water.

Cecily keeps her eyes on her lap, prays the brim of her bonnet is wide enough to hide every last feature on her face.

"Have *you*?" Elliott demands, and it takes Cecily a minute to realize he's not talking to Samuel anymore. He's moved on to someone else.

Samuel clicks his tongue and the horse starts to go.

As they move out, Elliott lets loose a mighty howl that rattles the carriage's windowpanes.

Please God, Cecily prays, may that be the last sound she ever hears him utter.

When the chaise is well past him, Cecily casts a quick glance out the window behind her. There Elliott is, in the middle of G Street, thrusting flyers in the faces of anyone who will be persuaded to take one. He looks like a raving lunatic—with his unshaven face, matted hair, and blood-stained shirt—but there is something Cecily appreciates about his disheveled appearance. She likes the fact that the Elliott Price the world now sees looks every bit as ugly as the man she's always known. The mourners give him a wide berth.

The horse picks up speed, and the voices of passersby fall away. At Brook Road, the carriage heads north, toward the turnpike, which will carry Cecily all the way to Washington.

She removes her bonnet and smooths her hair. The chaise is flying now, and she looks out the window as the last vestiges of the city that contains everyone she loves, and every experience she's ever had, disappear. Soon, Richmond will be a memory—just as surely as that theater up on the hill.

Cecily is so busy counting up her losses that she nearly misses him. A boy, brown as the James River after a week of rain, standing under a large white oak. He squints at the carriage, like he's looking for something, and when she realizes it's her he's looking for, she raises the pink palm of her hand to the glass. He doesn't wave—he is too smart for that. All he does is nod his head. Less a goodbye than an *I'll be seeing you.*

Author's Note

When the Richmond Theater burned to the ground on December 26, 1811, it became the greatest calamity, in terms of sudden loss of life, that the relatively young United States had ever experienced. The fire was reported in Virginia, naturally, but also in New York, Boston, and even as far away as London.

Up and down the Eastern Seaboard, people wrote frantic letters back and forth, attended memorial services, and read everything they could get their hands on about the fire. Printers in Philadelphia, New York, and London published commemorative books that put much of the reportage and the official committee findings in one place.

These documents were extremely useful to me as I imagined what the fire and ensuing recovery efforts might have looked like. However, I would not have been able to write this novel without Meredith Henne Baker's meticulously researched history of the fire, *The Richmond Theater Fire: Early America's First Great Disaster*, published by the Louisiana State University Press. For anyone who wants to know more about the fire or even just this period in American history, I cannot recommend Baker's book highly enough. She does such a remarkable job presenting so many different people's experiences that one of my biggest challenges as a novelist became deciding which true stories I might be able to weave into my fictional narrative.

I ultimately chose to center my story on the lives of four people who experienced the fire firsthand and were, in one way or another, forever changed by it. The characters of Gilbert, Jack, Sally, and Cecily are all based on real people who lived and breathed, although we know considerably more about some of them than others.

Gilbert Hunt really was an enslaved Black man who worked as a blacksmith in Richmond. The basics of his backstory—being born to an enslaved woman who worked at a tavern in Piping Tree, Virginia, coming to Richmond at the age of fifteen with the tavernkeeper's youngest daughter to work for the carriage maker she married, and being bought and sold several times as a blacksmith—are accurate.

Hunt was at the Mayo-Preston house, visiting his wife, when word of the fire broke, and according to his account of the events of the evening, he immediately took off running in the direction of the theater. He had a special attachment to Elizabeth Mayo Preston's daughter, Louisa, because she had taught him to read, and it would appear he was quite shaken by her death. The story about him begging Sy Gilliat for a mattress—a request that was flatly refused and never forgiven—is also true. At the theater, Hunt stumbled upon Dr. James McCaw, perched in an upstairs window, and the two worked together to save nearly a dozen white women from the flames. The last person Hunt saved was McCaw himself, who suffered injuries identical to the ones I've described in the novel.

Word of Hunt's heroics spread, but because he was Black, his story was not documented in any of the official reports about the blaze and its aftermath. Twelve years later, as a member of the city's volunteer fire brigade, he again demonstrated his bravery when a fire broke out at the Virginia State Penitentiary and he saved the lives of several hundred men by cutting an opening in one of the prison's walls.

There may very well have been talk in 1811 and 1823 about buying Hunt's freedom, to thank him for his selfless actions, but I found no evidence of it. In 1829, Hunt purchased his own freedom for eight hundred dollars, and the following year he set sail for Liberia on the *Harriet*. The trip was likely funded by the American Society for Colonizing the Free People of Color of the United States. It's unclear whether Hunt intended to settle in Liberia permanently, but after several months in the country, which he described as "as beautiful as any I had ever seen," he returned to the United States and eventually to Richmond. By then, Virginia law dictated that newly freed slaves had one year to remove themselves from the commonwealth, but—perhaps because of his contributions during the fire—Hunt received special dispensation to stay. He continued to work as a blacksmith, became a deacon at the newly established First African Baptist Church, and was a founding member of the Union Burial Ground Society. Hunt died in 1863, at about the age of eighty-three.

One of the reasons we know so much about Hunt, as compared to other enslaved people of the day, is that a group of Richmonders came together in 1859 to fundraise for his retirement. The idea was to produce a pamphlet documenting the highlights of Hunt's life and his contributions to the community, then sell copies of the pamphlet for fifty cents each. A white writer named Thomas Ward White, writing under the pseudonym Philip Barrett, was engaged to interview him and write down his story. "We shall make him, to a great extent, his own historian," White claims in the first chapter of the thirty-four-page pamphlet. The document, *Gilbert Hunt: The City Blacksmith*, is a remarkable sometimes-first-person account of a life that spanned slavery and freedom, but it is important to remember, when reading original sources such as this one, that in 1859, the South was desperately looking for ways to justify the continuation of slavery; producing and disseminating Hunt's biography may have had less to do with funding his retirement than with reinforcing the narrative of the kindhearted master and the devoted slave. For instance, White claims Hunt told him that he always loved his master. Maybe that's true, but I have taken the liberty of assuming that life for Hunt was not as rosy as Barrett would have us believe. In Cameron Kemp, I endeavored to create a man that any of us would wish to be rid of.

The historical record does not give us much information on Hunt's first wife, whom I have named Sara. She is referenced in *Gilbert Hunt: The City Blacksmith* as working for Elizabeth Mayo Preston, but in census records, all evidence of her falls away. In the 1830 census, Hunt is listed as residing with a woman, whom historians assume to be a second wife.

After Louisa's death, Elizabeth Mayo Preston did go on to have one more child—a son—with her second husband, General John Preston. I have no way to know if that late-in-life pregnancy, at the age of forty-four, had any bearing on the Hunts' future happiness, but it's unlikely it helped matters any. General Preston served as treasurer of the commonwealth from 1810 until 1819, but when an audit brought to light the fact that his books were eighty-seven thousand dollars in arrears, he and his family moved back to his homeplace in Montgomery County, Virginia, in some disgrace. My theory is that General Preston took all the people he owned—including those he'd acquired through his marriage to Elizabeth Mayo—with him. Montgomery County is almost two hundred miles from Richmond, so a distance that great would have amounted to a permanent separation for the Hunts.

The boy, whom I have named Jack Gibson, is an elusive figure in much of the source material about the theater fire. In both newspaper articles and the inquest report, a young stagehand is referenced, but for some reason—perhaps his own protection—he is never named. Child-labor laws did not exist in 1811, so it would not have been unusual for a boy of fourteen—or younger—to work for a theater company such as Placide & Green and to find himself handling open flames and all manner of pyrotechnics. As a mother of teenagers, it was not hard for me to imagine how such a scenario might quickly have gotten out of hand.

John Green and his wife, Frances, did lose their daughter, Nancy, in the fire. She was the only member of the theater company to perish, and the circumstances of her death, as I presented them, are largely true. Because the show was oversold and she was not performing that night, her father ordered her to remain back at the boardinghouse, where they rented rooms. She disobeyed, went to the performance with friends, and suffered the same fate as so many of the audience members.

Did Green give the order to raise the chandelier that ultimately killed his daughter and seventy-one other people? We'll never know. But, in the inquest report and news coverage, it's clear to me that someone is being protected. The inquest committee made a point of stating, in its official report, that it did not believe a manager ordered the young stagehand to raise the chandelier, but we also know that Frances Green refused to return to Charleston with her husband and, in fact, lived out the rest of her days in Richmond, alone. In the two centuries since the fire, she has been portrayed in poetry, prose, and even plays as a grieving but also slightly unhinged mother, who wandered the city for days in her bloody nun's habit. A more practical—and less damning—explanation is that she understood the full extent of her husband's role in her daughter's death and couldn't bear to live with him.

Initially, Placide & Green really did try to blame the fire on a slave revolt. We know this because a peculiar letter, dated December 27 and signed by members of the company, appears in the *Enquirer* in early January, insinuating as much. Was it Placide who decided to blame Richmond's enslaved community for starting the fire? Again, we'll likely never know, but it wasn't hard for me to imagine that, while Green was in the throes of his own private grief, Placide might have taken matters into his own hands.

I like to think that whatever Placide did that week backfired on him, because after getting the troupe back to Charleston, he left the company in the hands of his wife, Charlotte, and went to work for the Olympus Theater, with Billy Twaits, in New York. He died sometime that same year, of unknown causes.

In the novel, I make several allusions to Elizabeth Poe, a beloved actress and member of Placide & Green who died of pneumonia, just weeks before the fire took place. Poe had two young children—an infant daughter and a three-year-old son—who had already appeared onstage in some of the company's productions. After their mother's death, the children were adopted by local Richmond families. You must forgive me the gratuitous references; Poe's young son grew up to become the poet Edgar Allan Poe.

Family legend places Patrick Henry's daughter, Sally Henry Campbell, in the theater the night of the fire. Sally was a thirty-one-year-old widow whose husband, Robert Campbell, had recently died. Robert was a tobacco merchant who worked alongside his brother Archibald, and they were indeed the brothers of the famed Scottish poet Thomas Campbell. Interestingly, in 1798, Robert made arrangements for Thomas to come to the United States and tutor Patrick Henry's younger children. The brothers wrote back and forth, trying to nail down the details, but Thomas's immigration to the US never happened. His book *The Pleasures of Hope* was published in 1799 and launched his career as one of the most formidable poets of his generation.

As a childless widow with few responsibilities and no real home to speak of, Sally would have spent a great deal of time on the road, visiting family and friends. I do not know who she was visiting in Richmond in December of 1811, nor can I find evidence that Archibald and his wife, Margaret, were living in Richmond at that time. We know the pair married in New York in 1804 and that Archibald died in Richmond in 1830, but the years in between are largely unaccounted for. I hoped that Sally's relationship with Archie and Margaret would provide a lens through which Sally could examine what the men inside the theater had done—or not done—for the women they loved.

I think it's a good guess, given Sally's social status, that she was in the boxes and not the pit on the night of the fire. The story, passed down in her family, was that she was saved from the flames by Alexander Scott, a newly elected delegate from Fauquier County, but as you have no doubt noted, I chose to invert the story. I have always been interested in how the stories we tell shift over time, and it occurred to me that the story of a woman's heroism, in that era, might very well have been recast as a story that reinforced gender norms and this elusive idea of male chivalry.

Whatever happened between Sally and Alexander on the night of the fire eventually led to their marriage, a year and a half later. Sally moved to Fauquier County to live with her new husband at Clermont, and they had three children, which I would guess came as a welcome surprise to Sally after the years of infertility she experienced as Robert's wife.

While Sally may have gotten the children she desired, her marriage to Alexander was short-lived. He died in 1819, when Sally was pregnant with their third child. Because his sons from his first marriage inherited Clermont, Sally was forced to return to Seven Islands, just across the river from her family's home at Red Hill. At Seven Islands, Sally raised their children, took care of her mother, and lived out the rest of her days. She died in 1856, at the age of seventy-six.

In 1811, Richmond had no hospital, so anyone who escaped the theater with burns or wounds of any kind would have been treated in a private home—theirs or someone else's. I owe local historian Jeff Cartwright a huge thanks for bringing to my attention the story of Mary Cowley, who was called a "ministering angel" during "times that tried men's souls." When Mary Cowley died in 1847, at the age of ninety-five, her obituary credited her with nursing more than three thousand people, and specifically addressed her service in the aftermath of the fire: "At the burning of the Richmond Theatre her name became memorable for the great number of extraordinary cures which she performed on those who were burned." Cures aside, what fascinated me about Mary Cowley was that her obituary specifically referred to her as being a descendent of the "aborigines of this country." This may, of course, mean she was Native American, but there is also a distinct possibility that she was of African descent and used an Indigenous identity—not uncommon at the time—to move through the world with greater freedom than her Black counterparts. Had she self-identified as "colored" or "mulatto," her obituary would never have been allowed to be published, and her story—like the stories of so many other African Americans of this era—would have been lost to time.

Out of the seventy-two people who died in the fire, at least six were Black or multiracial. In the newspapers, which printed information about the dead, these victims' names were listed separately from their white counterparts, and historians have long been flummoxed by two of them in particular. A person named Philadelphia appears on the list of the dead, but is indicated as "missing"; and a "woman of colour" named Nancy Patterson also appears on the list, but with the notation "supposed to have perished." It is that phrase "supposed to have" that captured my attention and inspired the story of Cecily Patterson.

Because the theater's gallery had its own entrance for free and enslaved Black people, and because those in the gallery recounted an orderly evacuation down a short flight of stairs, there has long been speculation that some enslaved Black theatergoers—perhaps Philadelphia and Nancy among them—may have made the split-second decision to use the fire as cover and make a run for freedom.

With Cecily, I followed that idea to its logical conclusion, imagining a world of such violent contradictions that even a devastating fire could mean radically different things to different people. For many, the Richmond Theater fire spelled the end of everything that mattered, but I like to think that, for one brave woman, maybe it didn't.

Acknowledgments

This book was my pandemic baby, written in snatches between supervising virtual school, homeschooling a second-grader, and making bulk runs to Costco, so it feels particularly bittersweet to be turning the page.

To Chad Luibl, my agent extraordinaire. I feel incredibly lucky to get to work alongside someone who understands me and my work so completely. For the late-night texts and the books that show up at my front door, but mostly for being such a tireless advocate, thank you. To everyone at Janklow & Nesbit, including Roma Panganiban, who always comes through with such stellar advice, I'm sincerely grateful.

Where to begin when it comes to Carina Guiterman? This book is better—in every possible way—because you're my editor. I don't know how you keep it all in your head, but you do. You are funny and wise and when I'm reading your edits, I laugh far more often than I cry, which is a good thing, I think! To Lashanda Anakwah, thanks for being Carina's wingman, and mine.

To Maggie Gladstone, Alyssa diPierro, Danielle Prielipp, and the publicity and marketing teams at Simon & Schuster, thank you for beating the drum. To everyone in sales, but especially to Wendy Sheanin, who will always have a special place in my heart because we were wiping down airplane seats with Clorox wipes in early March of 2020 with absolutely no appreciation for what was to come, thank you for hitting it out of the park once again. To Jackie Seow and her team, who deserve so much love for designing such a stunning cover, thank you. And to the copy editors, page designers, and production specialists who turned an unwieldy Word document into this gorgeous book, you have my eternal devotion.

When it came to researching this Richmond story, I enjoyed an embarrassment of riches. I mentioned Meredith Henne Baker, who wrote a nonfiction account of the Richmond Theater fire, in my author's note, but I did not mention the fact that, when I reached out to Meredith to tell her what I was working on and to suggest we meet for coffee, she showed up with all her old research materials in a reusable grocery bag. Her generosity is unmatched.

Thank you to the librarians and archivists at the Library of Virginia and the Virginia Museum of History & Culture. Both institutions have extensive collections of materials relating to the fire, and they remained committed to making them available to researchers even at the height of the pandemic.

Special thanks go to Katherine McDonald, with Historic Richmond, for giving me a behind-the-scenes tour of Monumental Church. For anyone who hasn't visited the church, built as a monument to those who perished in the fire, I cannot recommend it highly enough.

Thanks to local historian Jeff Cartwright, who saved me so much time by providing several meticulously crafted spreadsheets that documented who owned what property in Richmond in 1811. As I mentioned in the author's note, Jeff also gets the credit for leading me to Mary Cowley.

Big props to Chris Oliver, Bev Perdue Jennings Associate Curator of American Art at the Virginia Museum of Fine Arts. It's not every day I need an early Americanist, but when I do, it's nice to know I have such a knowledgeable one on speed dial!

To Matt Cricchio and April Sopkin, who workshopped early pages of this novel on my patio in the fall of 2020. We sat six feet apart, and as the months grew colder, we added more layers of clothing and eventually an outdoor heater. Their reads were great, but to be able to talk about writing during a period of time in which we could do little besides doomscroll—that was the real gift.

Meredith Henne Baker, Tom De Haven, Savannah Frierson, Sara Moyle, Ruthie Peevey, and Eve Shade have all read early versions of the novel, and I am so appreciative of their careful reads and thoughtful feedback.

I am also thankful for the support I received from the Eastern Frontier Educational Foundation, The Hambidge Center for Creative Arts & Sciences, The Rensing Center, Porches Writing Retreat, and CultureWorks. Special thanks go to Margot Douaihy, Cynthia Grier Lotze, and Willie Johnson, who spent a beautiful summer afternoon walking the perimeter of Norton Island with me, brainstorming exactly how a fourteen-year-old kid might have set the theater on fire. A very special shout-out to Tamsen

Wolff, associate professor of English at Princeton University, whom I met at Norton Island and later enlisted to help me with some early American theatrical references. I must also give thanks to Thomas Manganaro, Kevin Pelletier, Anthony Russell, and Louis Schwartz—all faculty at the University of Richmond—who gallantly came to my aid with answers to last-minute questions about early nineteenth-century theater productions.

Because I was writing this book during a period in which many residency programs were closed, I will be forever grateful to the family and friends who filled the void and gave me the time, space, and sustenance I needed to finish this project. Thank you to Mary North and Mindy and Baldwin North for the magical cottage they loaned me on the Lost Planet; to Kristen Green for two pandemic writing retreats that required extensive quarantining to make happen but were worth every precious minute; and to my mother, Sara Moyle, who allowed me to camp out at her house, fed me a steady stream of sandwiches, and otherwise ignored me. That's hard to do! A giant shout-out to Claire Gibson, Lauren Francis-Sharma, and Blair Hurley, who assembled in Sparta, Tennessee, for a writing retreat that was as restorative as it was productive, and who have continued to serve as a support system for me in the months since. And to Nicole and John Velez, Tamsen and Tony Kingry, and Kara and Charlie Kuhn for feeding me during the dark days of December when I was so deep in the manuscript, I barely got out of my pajamas, much less left my house.

To my children—Gabriel, Clementine, and Florence. There is no debating that writing this book had taken my attention away from you. For all the times I disappeared upstairs to the office and you refrained from rolling your eyes, thank you. My wish for you three is that you find something you love doing so much the work never feels like a chore.

And finally, to my husband, Kevin, who has been by my side through it all, but never more so than during the pandemic. Thank you for believing in this dream. Then, now, and always. I love you.

About the Author

RACHEL BEANLAND is the author of *Florence Adler Swims Forever*, which won the National Jewish Book Award for Debut Fiction. She is a graduate of the University of South Carolina and earned her MFA in creative writing from Virginia Commonwealth University. She lives with her family in Richmond, Virginia.